Feather

Laurie Lyons

RING OF FIRE PUBLISHING

ISBN-13: 978-0615695969
ISBN-10: 0615695965

Feather

Published by
Ring of Fire Publishing
Seattle, Washington, U.S.A.

This is a work of fiction. Any similarity with real persons or events is purely coincidental. Persons, events, and locations are either the product of the author's imagination, or used fictitiously.

Cover image by Marius Muresan. Used with permission.
Cover design by Stephen Penner.

Acknowledgements

I would like to thank my publisher, Ring of Fire Publishing and the amazing team that put this book together. I need to thank all my delightful friends who have always loved and believed in me. I will always be grateful for my high school English teacher Mrs. Graham who looked me in the eye and told me I was an excellent writer. I wish to thank my supportive family, particularly my brother Robb who has taught me that failure is only possible if you quit.

We are all given Angels in this life. I was blessed with three. Thank you to my children Ethan and Julia for reminding me every day of why I was born. Most of all thank you to my husband Trevor for without you, nothing for me is possible.

I encourage you to figure out who the Angels are in your life and set about the business of making them happy. For, like the characters in my book, I believe that is the purpose of life.

True Love,
Laurie Lyons

Prologue

Date: June 20 - 5 Years from Now

She fell. Tripped really. Her foot slipped and although she might have been able to save herself, if she had the inclination, she didn't. So technically, it was an accident and that was how it had to be. By her estimation, there were twenty five solid concrete steps on this staircase. As her body charged forward, her left shoe fell off and twisted lightly in the air behind her. A flash image came to her mind of the day she bought that shoe; it was during a better time - a much better time. But now the shoe was off and she had tripped and because the stairs were made of concrete and numbered twenty five - the fall would kill her. For that simple fact she discharged the better time - the shoe shopping time and she rejoiced. She felt joy in her own death, deep, full, unabashed joy. She was finally being let out of her own personal Hell and her soul grasped at salvation with everything it had left.

Seconds before her head hit the twelfth step, she twisted her body, looked up at the sky, smiled and whispered, "Thank you, thank you, thank God it's over."

Today was the summer solstice; she thought that was a nice touch.

Chapter One
Fallen

"The drops of rain make a hole in the stone,
not by violence, but by oft falling."
~ Lucretius

Date: Unimportant

He was dreaming, or so he thought - it was almost impossible to tell the difference between dreaming and awake when the light was close like this. It didn't really matter anyway — he had stopped caring about trivialities a long time ago. There were others about, someone told him to look for her. They told him he could see her. He was grateful for that. "You will have to forget," Peter told him, "this will not be simple. You will forget that you were grateful." He nodded his understanding and looked toward his destination. "Try not to forget that we are watching, that you are loved." He nodded again, eager to go. "And try your very best to stay away from them." From who? He asked, already leaving. He couldn't make it out at first but then Gabriel answered for them, Gabriel always spoke for everyone,

"From the Demons, Brother. Try to stay away from the Demons."

Date: March 20 This Year – The Spring Equinox

Lucy sat in the auditorium with a civil smile on her face, feigning interest. The theatre was so full that there were several people standing at the back. Despite Lucy's boredom, the air in the theatre was electric because the audience was captivated by Dr. Hannon's lecture. Students and faculty alike were taking notes and whispering comments to each other. Lucy was decidedly *less* than captivated. She sat in a state of awkward boredom and waited. Maybe she would have been excited too; if this wasn't the hundredth time she had seen this lecture. After all, Dr. Hannon was an excellent speaker; charming and informed and his topic was certainly one that Lucy knew a great deal about. Much to Lucy's dismay, Dr. Hannon had jovially called this lecture, "The Lucy Presentation." The audience was spellbound and absorbed with Lucy Bower the bright-eyed red headed eighteen year old University student from Kansas who was currently bored out of her mind. Lucy kept the courteous look on her face and watched Dr. Peter Hannon at the lectern.

"Lucy's eidetic or photographic memory manifested itself just before the age of two," he explained to the lecture participants. "She could read by the age of three and it was at that point that the infallibility of her memory was realized. Lucy's memory is connected to visual stimulus only. What she sees or reads can be recalled with perfect clarity at any point in the future and there has been no limit to the amount of information she can remember at one time. Lucy can absorb hundreds of facts in a remarkably short time and recall them with perfect precision. It's the most extraordinary photographic memory ever recorded." He talked a bit longer about neural pathways and cerebral activity patterns. Lucy continued to smile respectfully and wait. "Now ladies and gentlemen, I would like you to see what Lucy can do."

Lucy sat up straighter – now it was her turn. She felt a slight twinge of reticence as the audience hummed like a beehive waiting for her. It was clear that this is why most had come. Although she had done this a hundred times, she still felt nervous. After all it wasn't like her 'talent' was common. Most people had never seen anything like Lucy before. She took a deep breath and stood.

"Lucy," Dr. Hannon smiled at her. Lucy smiled back, her green eyes sparkling, eager to please, "could you memorize the people in the first three rows of the audience please?" Lucy nodded sharply and got to work. She walked to the edge of the stage and began pacing it slowly from one end to the other. She looked at each person in turn.

"Now you will notice," Dr. Hannon filled the silence so Lucy had some time, "that we have asked you all to wear name tags. As I mentioned, Lucy's memory cues are visual. She requires a visual reminder of your name. If you told her your name while she was looking at you, she would remember that too. Lucy remembers every conversation she has ever had face to face. This makes it difficult to disagree with her." The audience laughed.

"Lucy's memory is actually very average with auditory cues, if Lucy hears a song, she won't remember the tune more accurately than you or I would. However, if she heard the song and read the lyrics at the same time she would remember it forever. But I doubt we will get Lucy to sing for us today."

"You don't want that. Trust me," Lucy piped in. The audience laughed again. Lucy nodded lightly at Dr. Hannon indicating she was ready.

"Would the first row please come up on stage?" Dr. Hannon called. They quickly obeyed as they were eager to be a part of the action. Lucy walked to her usual spot at the corner of the stage and turned her back to the line of people.

"Lucy, please list the order of the people in the first row from left to right."

"Sam, James, Margaret, Jason, Kevin, Tammy, Ken, Steven…" and so on. She listed them quickly and the audience gasped a little.

"Lucy, could you please tell me what Ken is wearing?" Dr. Hannon prompted.

"Blue pinstriped shirt, brown belt, blue kakis, brown shoes, black socks, silver watch, gold ring, third finger left hand." There was a large audible gasp from the auditorium and Lucy smiled. There was then laughter from the viewers as it was clear Ken had raised his pant legs to show off the color of his socks. Lucy continued with the rest of the row. For the second and third rows Lucy just had to list their names and she did so without pause. Dr. Hannon then had her recite the periodic table, the Presidents of the United States and the Kings and Queens of England in order with years. The English portion was new and for the benefit of a visiting doctor who just so happened to be from Oxford. Finally, and in true performer form, Dr. Hannon produced a phone book from under the lectern. He had Lucy read a page at random and recite the names and phone numbers.

The audience was astounded and gave a rousing round of applause when the performance was complete. Lucy smiled, pleased that she had done well. Really, where else is all that information useful but on a University campus? Dr. Hannon smiled warmly at her as she took her seat again. He then fielded a litany of questions most fairly scientific and a little dry. One student raised his hand. Dr. Hannon called on him.

"I've read several of your publications on Miss. Bowers

memory and you have mentioned a few times that the subject does not enter a REM sleep cycle. Could you elaborate?"

"Yes and no," Dr. Hannon replied into the microphone, "it's true that Lucy does not dream." There was a clear sound of interest from the spectators. "But really I can't elaborate on it. Lucy has had several sleep test sessions. Her brain does not enter REM sleep and she does not experience what we call dreaming. In fact, there is no evidence that her mind does anything at all while sleeping. Her patterns reduce to remarkably low levels to the point where they are almost unreadable. This seems to have no effect on her though. Lucy sleeps well and wakes up refreshed. Well, when she gets enough sleep. However, since she has entered college this is proving difficult." He winked at Lucy and she smiled and gave a half shrug back. The auditorium laughed again. "What I believe is that Lucy's mind is such a powerful machine that when she hits the 'off' switch it rests completely. There has never been any explanation found but it has never affected Lucy's life or memory."

Dr. Hannon answered a few more questions but they had gone over the time limit and the audience was getting restless. He thanked everyone for coming and added that he would stick around for any extra questions. The audience began to stand, don their coats and make their way to the exit. Dr. Hannon turned off the microphone and walked over to Lucy, "Nice work as always, thank you Lucy."

"No problem at all," she answered grinning. She gestured over his shoulder, "The British guy is waiting to talk shop with you." Dr. Hannon glanced over his shoulder at a stern looking man standing on the stage in a blue suit.

"Ah yes," he smiled, the corners of his eyes crinkling, "my work is never done." He glanced at his watch, "Brian is going to kill me if I am late. We were supposed to go to a movie tonight." He patted Lucy's arm. "Thank you again my dear. Do you need me to find you someone to walk you back to the dorm?"

"No I'll be fine, thanks Doc." Lucy reached behind her chair and picked up her coat and bag, "I'll drop by next week for lunch kay?"

"Sounds good. Head out the stage door so you don't get stuck in the crowd," he winked, "They look like a rowdy bunch tonight!"

"Positively terrifying," Lucy called over her shoulder with a grin and headed back stage. Dr. Hannon waved as he turned and walked toward the British Scientist.

There was only one source of light back stage, a bright red exit sign. She headed towards it, stepping carefully over bundles of wires. She pushed on the door's bar and found herself outside. The sun had gone down during the lecture but the University campus was well lit. The lamp posts sparkled in the moonless night, illuminating the pathway. Lucy only had a short walk to her dorm and she turned left down the path along the almost empty quad.

Mulbridge University was set around the quad. It was a huge tree lined grassy square filled with pathways crisscrossing through it and most of the University's early twentieth century stone buildings fronted onto the quad. Newer additions to the school were set back slightly. Compared with other Universities in Illinois, Mulbridge was small - registering an average of 8000 students on any given year.

Lucy passed by a glass window and saw an image of herself reflected back. She didn't look too fatigued considering it was almost nine o'clock and she had been going full throttle all day. Her bright thick auburn hair waved back from her pale face and rosy cheeks. The small amount of makeup she had applied to her full lips and vibrant green eyes that morning was still vaguely present. She wore a moss green hoodie and white v-neck shirt that unexpectedly did not have a coffee stain on it.

As she walked, Lucy mused about what she had to do when she got home. *Finish a textbook, start a paper, maybe call mom?* She saw her dorm building up ahead and picked up her pace in anticipation of being home. *Check and make sure uniform is clean for work tomorrow, call Anastasia, pack school bag for tomorrow....*

WHAM!!

Lucy was suddenly sitting on the sidewalk. She had hit something while walking and had fallen. She looked around bewildered and looked up to see what, well, who, she had run into. What she saw made her mouth fall open in shock. He was tall, taller than average even considering Lucy was sitting down. He looked like a student, perhaps a freshman like Lucy or sophomore maybe, but not a senior. He wore a pair of dark blue jeans and a white collared shirt; hardly the rumpled attire of the average University guy. His clothes looked like they had just been pulled out of a dry cleaning bag and put on with care.

He had a smooth angled face with a strong jaw and high cheekbones and his skin was perfectly smooth. His hair was so black that it was almost blue and it was cut fairly short but it was thick and wavy giving the impression that if he allowed it to grow it would turn into ringlets. He had a high forehead, a strong brow and the most stunningly beautiful grey eyes Lucy had ever seen. They were perfectly round with black lashes framing brilliant almost silver irises. Lucy had just smashed into the most handsome man in the world. She was so busy staring at him that she didn't realize that he was talking to her.

"What?" she said sounding far more irritated than she was. She realized she was still sitting on the ground.

"I am so sorry," he answered with his voice full of concern and then cleared his throat. His voice was strong and yet tender. He reached out to help Lucy up. She ignored everything she had ever read about stranger danger and reached willingly for his hand. Electricity ran from the strange man's hand like a live wire and Lucy almost twitched with the jolt of the connection. His hand was warm and soft but she could feel strength behind it. He gently pulled her to standing and she found herself within inches of him. He smelled like sunshine, salt water and honey all at once. She had to stop herself from closing her eyes, leaning into him and breathing deeply. Lucy was mesmerized. She shook her head to clear it. *What a sap you are Lucy.* She thought to herself.

He looked at Lucy and reacted like he was seeing her for the first time. His eyes widened in surprise and he pulled his head back a half an inch. "Oh, it's you," he said as though he knew her.

"Um, yeah it's me," Lucy said awkwardly. She knew for a fact that she had never met him before. Even someone without a photographic memory would never forget meeting someone like this but if he thought he knew her that was just fine. It would be wonderful to know him. Lucy stepped back half a step when she realized that she was gawking at her new friend. A half a step was all that she could manage. Then he smiled at her.

That was the clincher.

His teeth were straight, even and bright white, his lips were full and pink and his entire face lit up. It was like the smile was created for her and her alone, that he had never smiled at anyone like this before and never would again. It made Lucy want to throw her arms around him and never let go. Lucy shook her head again to clear it, *Get it together Lucy, seriously you need to start to function here or the guy is going to think you are nuts.*

He cleared his throat and asked, "What are you doing here?" He was still smiling. Lucy looked away from him to answer hoping that would help her form a coherent sentence. She couldn't let him go on thinking that he knew her - it would be awkward at their wedding one day. She took a deep breath.

"We don't know each other," she said not without disappointment, "I go to school here."

"Oh," he said with curiosity, "we haven't met?"

"No, but we can now." Lucy replied brightly, "What are you doing here?" *Please say you came to watch the lecture* she pleaded silently.

"I don't really belong here," he said slowly looking warily around them as if to figure out where 'here' was.

"You don't go to this school?" she asked.

He gave a half laugh. "No, no I don't," he said carefully. Lucy tried not to make her disappointment show too much.

"I don't think the administration cares if students from other schools come visit the campus." She chewed her bottom lip, for some reason it was suddenly extremely important that he stay.

He turned his head to look at her. "No, I mean I don't belong…well…" He seemed to be struggling to explain. He glanced around them again nervously as if he was expecting someone to yell, "Hey you stop!" at any moment.

"Are you meeting someone?" Lucy asked. *Please say no.*

"Yes… no… I mean no," he cleared his throat again and looked around them. He began looking about with more study in his face. He took in the area around him, the buildings, the park benches and the lights from the far off intersection. He even tapped his toe on the concrete as if to confirm its existence. *What is this guy on?* It was as if he was seeing everything for the first time. Lucy stood watching him, fascinated.

He took a deep breath – smelling the air - and reached out tentatively for a leaf on a branch that was close. He stroked it lightly with his finger tracing the edges and the veins of the leaf. He cocked his head and smiled at it like it was a newborn baby or a fine piece of jewelry. Lucy watched, completely enthralled with his behavior. He brought his hand under the leaf and stroked it again with his thumb and then slowly lowered his hand to let it fall and rest on its stem.

He looked around as if absolutely spellbound with everything. Lucy kept watching the leaf and for a moment after he let it go it sat motionless on the stem. He turned slightly to get a better look at a light post and Lucy could have sworn that she saw the leaf lift itself ever so slightly and slowly until it was almost parallel with the ground. It seemed, unbelievably, to be reaching for him. Lucy blinked twice and the leaf twitched slightly and fell slowly down to sit motionless again. She watched it in silence for a moment longer.

"*Cornus alternifolia,*" she muttered.

"Pardon me?" he was staring at her now with the same level of fascination.

"Oh," she glared at her feet. Sometimes Lucy's brain decided to work all by itself. This spontaneity usually resulted in a deeply humiliating situation. Lucy's stomach clenched with the realization that this was going to be one of those times. "It's the name of the tree, commonly known as the Pagoda Dogwood," she spouted, *shut up you idiot, stop talking*, "best in moist, acid to neutral soils; growth rate initially slow," *stop please please please stop*, "it thrives in rich woods; wooded slopes and bluffs." Finally her brain listened to her pleading and was silent. There was a long painful pause.

He cleared his throat. "Do you...like trees?"

"No, I um… well they are great and all," she paused, and glanced up at his expectant face, "I ….I…. have a photographic memory," she finally stuttered out.

His grey eyes widened in disbelief his jaw fell open, "No," he almost whispered and shook his head slightly from side to side, "it's not possible."

"I assure you it is totally possible and not a big deal," she snapped at him – ready for a fight. "It's just a talent like any other talent. Some people can run really fast or play football, this is my gift." He seemed unaware of the fact that she was offended by his comments and stepped closer to her. He was again within inches of her. She breathed in and forgot that she was irritated.

"Who gave you this ability?" he almost demanded.

Lucy was taken aback, "Well I was born with it."

He immediately relaxed and cleared this throat, "Of course you were. That makes sense." He nodded almost to himself and then turned his attention again to Lucy, "How does it work?" he asked.

"Well…" she began.

"Would you mind?" he asked, "if we sit down? I am…" he paused as though finding the word, "tired, yes tired."

"Oh ya sure," Lucy had to admit that standing in the middle of the sidewalk was getting a little awkward. She motioned to the closest park bench.

"No," he said carefully clearing his throat again, "inside, please I am…" he paused and cleared his throat again, "cold". Lucy thought it was actually nice outside because the wind had died down for once. She knew she should probably just tell him to mind his own business but for some reason she couldn't. It wasn't just because he was gorgeous, although that helped. This guy was intriguing to say the least and despite the definite freak level, there was something more there. Lucy could feel it.

She was like the leaf in that she was drawn to this total stranger. Lucy felt the strongest need to hold his hand, to hug him and to run her hands through his thick black hair. She sighed lightly at the thought, and coming out of her reverie, realized with horror that she was reaching towards him. He was looking at her hand and then back at her face with interest. Lucy dropped her hand, shoved them both into her pockets, took a deep breath and started walking towards the dorm. He followed.

"I'm Lucy," she said risking a glance at him sideways.

"Lucy," he said back to her.

"Ya, Lucy. What's your name?" she asked climbing the steps.

"Who me?" He looked surprised.

Lucy laughed. "Of course you, what, you think I have imaginary friends or something?" He paused and looked directly into her eyes. Lucy froze as their eyes met for the first time. His were a deep grey and Lucy had never seen that eye color before. His eyes were so clear that she could see right through them. Ignoring all rules of polite, safe distance, she went up on her tiptoes to get a better look. They seemed to go on forever, into this vast world of crystalline light and color. Lucy became more enraptured by the second.

"My name is Nathaniel," he whispered because she was so close to him now. She could feel his warm breath on her cheeks.

Lucy mumbled something that sounded like, "Nice to meet you," and she forced her heels back down to the concrete. She stared at the ground and made a promise to herself to not look him in the eyes anymore – it could become addictive. As he opened the door for her, he glanced around the quad again and up at the sky as if making sure nothing was watching them. Lucy headed into the building forgetting that she had papers to write, phone calls to make and a bed to sleep in. She forgot about everything except being where she was. As they walked into the foyer he cleared his throat again.

"Do you have a cold?" Lucy asked.

"No. Why?" Nathaniel sounded surprised.

"Well you keep clearing your throat," she explained. "I thought you might be getting sick."

"I haven't used my voice in a while that's all," he said distractedly as he looked all around him with the same sense of study. Lucy wondered what that meant. She hoped he wasn't a convict or something but had to be honest that it didn't really matter to her. Lucy just needed to know more about him.

They entered the small hole in the wall that passed for a coffee shop in the girl's dorm. There were only two other tables occupied; one by a mousy girl who was studying alone and the other by two giggly girls who were clearly making plans or reliving plans. Neither table looked up as they came in and Lucy was a little disappointed. She wanted to see if anyone else had the same reaction to her new friend as she had. She threw her bag down at a table near the window. Nathaniel obediently sat down.

"Coffee?" she said glancing in his direction being sure not to make eye contact.

"Um sure?" he said it like a question. Lucy walked over to the counter, poured two coffees, and grabbed a handful of cream and sugars and two stir sticks. She put them on the counter by the register and fished through her pockets for some change.

"Two coffees?" the pimply-faced clerk asked.

"Yup," replied Lucy with a distinct, *'isn't that obvious?'* tone to her voice. He shrugged, probably assuming that Lucy was just cranky with midterms and handed her back her change. Lucy turned back to the table to see that Nathaniel had opened her book bag, pulled out her copy of Hamlet and had it flat open in front of him reading. Lucy was usually a private person so it was surprising that it didn't bother her that he had rifled through her bag.

From this distance, he was still gorgeous. He sat casually in the chair, like he had been sitting there for hours rather than thirty seconds. His shoulders were broad and defined, she watched as he shifted his arms to flip the page and wondered if he would even notice at this point if she never came back to the table. He looked up as though in answer to her question. He scanned the room quickly and found her standing twenty feet away staring at him. Nathaniel smiled and something like relief passed his face. He would notice if she had left. Lucy felt butterflies fill her stomach and bat up against her lungs. She swallowed hard and walked towards him.

Lucy put the coffees down and slid into the seat across from him. Nathaniel was still smiling at her. She was torn, she wanted him to stop so she could focus but the thought of that smile going away was painful to think of. He took the coffee she offered him and left the copy of Hamlet forgotten open sitting between them on the table.

"Thank you," he said, "this is more comfortable."

"No problem," Lucy replied adding cream and sugar to her coffee and taking an experimental sip.

"So you were saying?" he prompted. He propped both elbows up on the table tucking his hands under his arms and cocked his head to the side, ready to listen.

"Oh," Lucy snapped back in again, "my memory."

"Yes," he encouraged, "your memory." Lucy took a deep breath.

"Well, it appears I was born with it. My parents said they started to figure that something was different about me when I was two and could tell them exactly what my grandmother was wearing when she came to visit two months before. By the time I was reading the whole thing took off." She took another breath and checked for a reaction. Nathaniel seemed enthralled, eager and ready for more. Lucy continued. "They realized that everything I saw, that everything I read was stuck in my head forever, there seemed to be no limit to my memory, I could recall things I had just seen as clearly as I could recall something I had seen years before. They brought me to doctors and scientists and psychologists, testing me over and over. They made sure I didn't have a brain tumor, autism or epilepsy. The scientists tried to quantify everything in my head. I had sleep tests, awake tests, tests with images, numbers, letters, words I didn't know, places I had never seen and I was infallible every time."

"Infallible," Nathaniel almost whispered.

"Yup," Lucy tapped her temple, "it gets in here and it cannot leave, even if I want it to." She continued, "When I was twelve we met Doctor Hannon who has been watching over me ever since. He's awesome. He has written hundreds of journals and articles about me. He knows more about my brain than anyone. He's a good scientist and I like that he prefers to see me as a person and not a subject. It has been determined that my photographic memory is possibly the most accurate and effective in the world."

"He sounds like he cares about you." Nathaniel said with a smile.

"The feeling is mutual," Lucy replied. She relayed the "show" they just put on in the auditorium. "I am also fairly certain that I got my full scholarship because of him. My marks were pretty good but this school was the only school to offer me such a lavish deal." Nathaniel glanced around with his eyebrows raised. Lucy laughed in response. "I know, this place doesn't look so lavish but room, board and books all included for four years with an option for a masters or even a doctorate down the road is pretty lavish."

Nathaniel whistled. "That is excessive, you must be very smart."

Lucy shrugged, "Ya, I do ok. But the school really wanted the Doc to do his research here and I think they might have thrown my deal in as a part of the package. He is one of the foremost specialists on the internal workings of the human mind in North America. Since he started working with me, he has published some amazing work on the nature of the human memory system. Me studying here makes his life a lot easier. My mom is also thrilled to have me here with him."

"A chaperone." Nathaniel smirked.

Lucy smiled, "It's kind of pathetic but I don't really need one." Nathaniel raised his eyebrows and she laughed out loud, "Sad but true. I mean, I could call him if I ever needed bail money or to bury a body or something but I haven't really needed to."

"So you aren't a criminal," Nathaniel nodded with a smile, "pretty boring Lucy."

"You wanna hear boring?" She sat forward and spoke softly with a heavy note of conspiracy in her voice, "I had this master plan in high school that I was going to read every reference manual I could and go on Jeopardy to win enough money so I would never have to work a day in my life."

"That didn't work out?" he whispered back with mock surprise. He was almost laughing now, "I can't imagine why it wouldn't work. It seems like a flawless plan."

"No," Lucy rolled her eyes dramatically, "apparently they do research on all the applicants and once they figured out who I was they said that I wasn't allowed to go on the show."

"They research the applicants?" Nathaniel was laughing now. "Why, I never would have thought! They ruined everything!

Now you have to work for a living!"

Lucy laughed too, "My master plan for world domination was thwarted." They both laughed. He was tall, dark, handsome and funny? This was almost too much for Lucy to take in.

"So what's the master plan now?" he asked.

"Well, school, job and grow up," Lucy shrugged, "pretty simple."

"What did you mean when you said you remembered things that you don't want to?" he asked.

"Well," Lucy shrugged again, "I remember every crappy book I have ever read and every ghastly movie I have ever seen."

"That's all?" he prompted.

Lucy chewed her lip and stared at the copy of Hamlet on the table, "I can recite every nasty note written to me by caddy girls in junior high." She rolled her eyes, "The rumours got pretty bad for a while. They claimed I was a robot, an alien, that I took drugs to improve my memory, lots of dumb stuff. I remember every word, everything."

"That must be awful," Nathaniel said with real sympathy in his voice. He reached over and laid his hand on hers. His skin was soft and smooth and very warm. Lucy's hand almost melted under the pressure as if her bones were liquefying under his influence. Warmth radiated up her arm to her elbow and she felt that whole side of her body relax to the point that if the table were not there it would have hung limp at her side like a noodle.

"I see your aren't cold anymore," she managed to say quietly.

"No," he half smiled, "I am better in here. This is..." he paused and searched for the word, "wonderful." Lucy couldn't help but to agree. She half nodded. This was wonderful. This Nathaniel guy was something else. There was another silence but it wasn't awkward. It was as if Lucy and Nathaniel had known each other for years. She felt a need to be near him but not really a need to impress him. Lucy looked up and saw that Nathaniel was smiling at her again. That personal wonderful smile and she felt the heat from her arm spread to her chest where it sped up her heart rate. She smiled back. Lucy wasn't sure why this guy was sitting here listening to her life story but at this point while staring into his stunning kind face she really didn't care. She however, wanted to know his life story and quickly decided to change the subject to fulfill that goal. She opened her mouth to ask about him.

"So what is your major now that you are here?" he asked again with unwavering interest. Lucy paused, irritated that she had been thwarted in her efforts.

"Double major in history and English," she answered quickly. She was determined to move on. "Are you in school?" she asked and much to Lucy's annoyance, Nathaniel completely ignored the second half of her answer.

"What are you going to do with a double degree in History and English?" Lucy paused again debating whether to ignore his question but when she looked at him his face was so sincere and earnest that she couldn't ignore him.

"I don't really know but it has to have something to do with books."

"Why?" he asked intrigued.

"Because I love books." Maybe if Lucy kept her answers short enough he might move on and talk about himself. No such luck.

"Like Hamlet?" He said gesturing to the copy still sitting open in front of them. Lucy grinned. Nathaniel had figured her out already.

"Yes, like Hamlet, any Shakespeare, novels, history books, reference manuals, encyclopedias, atlases, dictionaries, you name it.

If it's on paper and bound together, I adore it."

Nathaniel gave a half-cocked smile and raised one eyebrow. "You ADORE the dictionary?" Lucy giggled. He started to laugh too and while laughing said, "Please don't tell me you have read the entire dictionary?" Lucy threw her head back and laughed full out realizing how bizarre that sounded.

"Jeopardy remember?" she pleaded with him.

Nathaniel put his head down and chuckled as he barely uttered, "Right right. Sorry I forgot - world domination through a brilliant vocabulary." Lucy howled with laughter.

They laughed easily together for a moment longer. When she composed herself, Lucy sniffed and absentmindedly glanced at her watch. It was past eleven. She looked around her and saw that the clerk had pulled the flexible cage around the counter and left. At some point the mousy girl and the giggly girls had left as well. How long ago was that? She and Nathaniel had been sitting here talking for almost two hours. *Time flies when you are having fun.* She thought to herself. "No doubt," she muttered. She realized that both of them hadn't been talking. Only Lucy had been talking. She knew no more about Nathaniel then when they walked in here. In fact, she knew nothing about him; not where he was from, his last name, if and where he went to school, nothing. It made Lucy uncomfortable to be in the dark about things. Her controlling side began to grumble. She took a deep breath and started with, "enough about me..." but again he cut her off.

"I'm very sorry but I have to go," he said sounding sorry indeed, "it's late and I have somewhere I have to be."

Lucy's heart sunk. "Oh sure," She replied with fake confidence, "I'm sure your girlfriend is waiting for you. I have things to do myself."

"A Girlfriend?" he answered looking confused. Lucy looked

at him doubtfully.

"No?" she asked.

"No," he said clearly, "do you have a boyfriend?"

Lucy found it promising that he cared.

"No," she said and he looked relieved; another good sign.

He started to stand and released her hand to take the empty coffee cups to the garbage. Lucy fought the urge to reach out and grab him again. Her hand felt cold and papery like it had been asleep for a while. When he turned to deposit the cups in the garbage she shook her hand trying to get the blood flowing. She stood and tucked her copy of Hamlet back in her bag and slung the bag over her shoulder. They walked side by side back to the foyer and Lucy could feel electricity passing from his shoulder to hers. She could NOT be imaging this.

The foyer was a wide-open tiled space. The building itself was much older but renovations in the late 60s resulted in an avocado and orange décor that was painful at times to look at. There was a huge set of locked double doors on the one side that led to the cafeteria. All the dorms used the same cafeteria and were connected in a star pattern around it. There was a small convenience store that was connected to the cafeteria for any emergency items the students needed. Each dorm had a small coffee shop like the one Lucy and Nathaniel just left. Lucy walked to the bottom of the huge staircase that went up to the girl's dorm rooms. Each girl in the four-floored building had her own room but shared a bathroom on each level. Nathaniel had his hands in his jeans' pocket.

He motioned to the stairs with his elbow, "Is this where you live?"

"Yup!" Lucy smiled. "On the fourth floor, it's pretty fancy hey?" she added sarcastically. He laughed. "Where do you live?" she asked boldly expecting another rebuff. Instead he paused and thought for a moment.

Then Nathaniel smiled to himself, looked her in the eye and said with all sincerity, "I promise to show you one day." Any other time, any other guy and that would sound creepy and a little strange. At that moment however, in that space, it felt like a real promise. Lucy would get her answers but not today and suddenly she felt like he was worth the wait. She just nodded her head- she didn't want to speak, she couldn't think of a thing to say.

Nathaniel reached out and with a slightly curved hand, ran the back of his fingers down Lucy's cheek. Her face warmed instantly with his touch. A tingle spread from his fingers to her skin and up to her hairline. Lucy felt a shiver go down the back of her neck to her shoulders and arms and goose bumps erupted on her skin. It was such a wonderful feeling that she had to will herself to not lean into his hand and rub against him like a cat. Nathaniel let his had drop but the feeling still lingered for a moment.

"Goodnight Lucy," he whispered.

"Goodnight," she managed to utter while still reeling from his touch. He turned and walked to the door. When his hand touched the handle, Lucy snapped out of her reverie.

"Where are you going now?" she almost yelled in desperation.

Nathaniel stopped, turned back towards her and smiled. "That Lucy, I don't know", he said and walked out the door. Lucy stood alone in the foyer struggling with her urge to run after him. The foyer felt cold and vacant with Nathaniel gone. She turned finally to walk up the stairs to her room, tripping a couple of times because she kept glancing back at the door to see if Nathaniel would come back.

Chapter Two
Crazy

"If we weren't all crazy, we'd just go insane.
~ Jimmy Buffett

Lucy's alarm exploded into her head promptly at eight the next morning. She was never one to linger in the morning and was usually eager to start a new day. Today however she turned off the alarm and didn't get out of bed - instead, she stretched and settled back on her pillow. Sighing, Lucy looked around her room. It was the standard issue single dorm room - a twelve by ten square space. Lucy lay in her futon bed that doubled as a couch during the day. There were two end tables that were constantly littered with coffee cups, her phone and keys. Along the opposite wall were two bookshelves filled to the brim with books except for one shelf that held a small TV. In between the shelves was her desk and computer. The far wall from the door had a large window that opened but was covered in a grate to prevent any college pranks or final exam depression jumps. In one corner was an impossibly small closet and beside the door was another petite bookshelf that held bags for every occasion. Lucy was a bit of a bag hoarder and had a bag for the shower, a bag for makeup, a bag for school, a bag for work and a bag for going out.

While lying sleepily in her bed, Lucy's thoughts immediately went to Nathaniel. Her photographic memory allowed her to recall his face in detail – devoid of any opinions and thoughts that confuse most people's memories. She stared at an image of him in her head. She studied every line and curve of his features until she came to the ultimate conclusion that his face was perfect. There wasn't one flaw to it at all. She wondered if she would see him today. Would she "bump" into him again? Mulbridge was not the biggest University in Illinois but the chances of running into Nathaniel again was slim to none - especially since he didn't even go to the school.

What if she didn't run into him though? What if she never saw him again? Something close to panic invaded her thoughts. What would she do? Lucy had to admit that this was a strong reaction to have towards a basic stranger. He was so amazing though that Lucy had a hard time getting him out of her head. Her thoughts were interrupted when she glanced at the clock and realized that now she was late.

Lucy leapt out of bed, grabbed her makeup bag off her shelf and ran out the door and down the hall to the communal bathroom. When Lucy opened the door she was assaulted with steam, smells of hair products and loud female chatter. She smiled. This was the way she started her day. Having missed the morning rush, there were only two girls in the process of getting ready. One of the four showers was running full force with billows of steam pouring above the stall. The other girl was at the sinks, her hefty makeup bag propped on the tiny shelf below the mirror.

"Hey Lucy!" yelled the one at the sink. She was petite with

iridescent blond hair, big eyes, and a bright smile. She was applying mascara with a heavy hand. Her name was Paige Marston but she usually introduced herself as, 'The Trouble from Tennessee'. Paige loved the fact that she had the exact same measurements as Marilyn Monroe and worked every inch of it.

"Hey Paige," Lucy replied smiling. There was another yell from the shower.

"Morning Lucy!" Lucy recognized the soft soothing voice of Suzanne Upton. Originally from Maine, Suzanne was tall and so thin she looked as though she would blow away at any moment. In fact, everything about her was thin; her legs, her neck, her hair and her lips. Her voice was especially thin as Suzanne was painfully shy but little by little as the year had passed she had opened up to her dorm mates.

"Hey! Suzie Q!" Lucy yelled back over the shower sounds. She grabbed a spot beside Paige at the communal mirror, "What's the story ladies?"

"Paige has decided that the boys are having a party tomorrow night." Suzanne's voice floated smoothly from the shower. Lucy pulled her soap out of her bag and started washing her face.

"You decided?" Lucy glanced at Paige while throwing water on her face. Paige grinned mischievously. Lucy dried her face and pulled out her toothbrush and manically began brushing her teeth.

"She's decided that Nick will today decide to have a party tomorrow night," Suzanne explained, as her long neck stretched over the top of the stall. Paige and Nick had been dating since September and were deeply in love.

"It's been too long since we had one" Paige explained while shamelessly adjusting her cleavage. "I simply have to plant the idea."

"Inception!" Lucy yelled with her mouth full of water in the sink.

"Do you think that Simon will be there?" Suzanne asked with her innocent eyes wide. Suzanne had an immense crush on Simon MacFarlane but was so shy she could barely do anything about it. She had been dropping vague hints since September but so far she hadn't gotten anywhere with the equally introverted Simon.

"Yes sweetie," Paige said lightly, "Since Nick and Simon are best friends and roommates, I think we will see Simon at the party."

"It would certainly be awkward if he wasn't invited," Lucy grinned and then whispered to Paige, "Can you talk to Nick to talk to Simon. Make this," she motioned he head towards Suzanne's shower, "happen? She's dying inside." Paige grinned back and nodded.

"Nick isn't a problem," Paige said loudly while glancing meaningfully at her rear end in the mirror, "it's the pit bull I can't figure out." The girls knew whom she meant. Markus was Nick's resident advisor and the senior took his job far too seriously. Dorm rules stated that; no more than five students may be in a room at one time, students of the opposite sex were prohibited past ten o'clock at night and loud music was not allowed at any time day or night. However, most RA's were lenient, remembering what it was like when they were freshmen. The girl's RA Vanessa was a ghost that simply yelled from behind her door. Lucy didn't even know what Vanessa majored in. Her lack of attention suited the girls well. All eight on the floor had adjusted reasonably well to college life - none were failing, pregnant or anorexic and that made Vanessa's life easy.

Markus however enjoyed patrolling the hallways at all hours monitoring his jurisdiction. He carried his cricket bat on his shoulder and would knock on doors and yell things like, "Ladies it's ten o'clock time to get your beauty sleep!" or, "That music is too loud; I don't want to write a report now!" It was unfortunate because the girls liked hanging out at the boy's dorm. The boys shared two to an apartment and because of that had living rooms, small kitchenettes and more room.

"Can your drug him Suzanne?" Paige asked almost too seriously. Lucy giggled.

"Sorry, freshman nursing student here," Suzanne said as she got out of the shower and wrapped a towel around herself, "No narcotics until I am a senior."

"Well, we can't wait that long now can we?" Paige stamped her bare foot in protest. Lucy had finished her teeth, brushed her hair and was finishing up her makeup with some mascara.

"Markus signed up for the charity row-a-thon tomorrow," Lucy piped in.

"How long does a row-a-thon go?" Paige asked.

"24 hours," Lucy replied. "It starts at four and goes all night and the next day in the gym."

"How did you manage to find that out?" Suzanne asked.

"I read it on the notice board outside the student's union office last month."

"Girl?" Paige grinned at her down the length of the mirror, "You and that memory of yours are a life saver. What would we do without you?"

"Everyone needs a Lucy," Lucy replied grinning, "I have to go, I'm late." She started throwing stuff back into her bag.

"Can you come tomorrow night?" Paige asked, "You don't have plans or anything do you?" Lucy paused. Did she have plans? Tonight? Tomorrow night? She pictured Nathaniel's face again. She shook her head to clear it. This was getting ridiculous.

"I'll be there!" she said heading for the door.

"Don't you have poetry at nine?" Suzanne asked while applying lip balm – her only choice of adornment. "Poetry" came out as "O - e - ty"

"Yes," Lucy rolled her eyes while pulling open the door, "on the other side of campus. I am so late."

She took off through the door and heard Paige yell, "Have a nice run!"

"Thanks!" Lucy yelled halfway to her room.

Once in her dorm room, Lucy threw on her jeans and a t-shirt and took a quick look at herself in the full length mirror on the backside of the door. Her jeans were tighter than her mother would like but in Lucy's opinion, they were just right. On Lucy's feet were the best shoes ever invented, converse sneakers. Lucy loved her strappy sandals and pretty clothes as much as the next girl but for day to day it was jeans, hoodies and converse. Lucy was pretty, or so she had been told but she had never been the high maintenance girl with fake nails and dyed hair. She felt it took far too much work. Her own red curls appeared wild at times but really, so was Lucy so it suited her.

Nodding at her refection, Lucy grabbed a hoodie and her book bag from the floor and blasted back into the hallway and down the stairs two at a time. There was no time for the cafeteria so Lucy headed to the café she and Nathaniel had sat in the night before. She glanced around the packed tables thinking he might be there. *Do you honestly think that he sat here all night waiting for you?* She chided herself. She didn't look at her watch, she knew she didn't have time to make this stop but there was always time for coffee.

Lucy grabbed a donut and a large coffee. While waiting in line she mixed in her cream and sugars and ate half her donut. When she got to the front of the line she recognized the same greasy clerk from the night before. She half smiled and held up the coffee and half donut for him to see. She tossed the five-dollar bill down that she had been pinching between two fingers.

"Only one coffee today eh?" the clerk asked while handing her the change. Lucy put down her coffee to shove the change in her pocket.

"Um ya," she replied confused. Before she could say anything else he had moved on to the next girl in line. Lucy shrugged and headed to the door. As she stepped out into the bright quad, she was immediately in a crowd of students. There seemed to be something interesting among the trees in front of the dorm. Lucy thought back to the Pagoda Dogwood leaf from last night and was immediately interested too.

"What's going on?" she asked a male student who was much taller than she.

"The flowers," the student answered in a slightly vague tone. He seemed completely hypnotized by the situation. Since she seemed to be getting no more information this way, Lucy pushed her way to the front and immediately, she knew why the guy had seemed hypnotized. Around each tree in the quad were vines of thousands of colorful flowers. Instead of the strong deep brown trunks, the quad was alight in a rainbow of blooms. There had not been flowers there the day before, or ever for that matter. It was both mystifying and deeply beautiful. Nearby, members of the gardening crew stood shaking their heads dumbfounded.

"Grew up overnight I tell ya," one was saying to another, "in all my years I never seen anything like it."

To think that this had anything to do with Nathaniel was beyond foolish but Lucy could not help but wonder if the two things were related. Shaking her head to dismiss such silliness, Lucy looked at her watch as she moved back through the crowd and cursed out loud. She only had four minutes to make it to poetry. She shoved the rest of her donut in her mouth, took a long swig of her coffee so it wouldn't spill through the lid holes and took off at a dead run.

Lucy made it to poetry just in time to hear Dr. Lewis call, "All right people lets settle down now." She was out of breath but celebrated the fact that hadn't split one drop of coffee. She took a spot in the back and pulled out her poetry anthology, a notepad and a pen. The book was just for show but the notepad was a necessity. Dr. Lewis had a habit of not using the board to write things down. This irritated Lucy because then she actually had to watch him while he said it or listen and write it down in order for her photographic memory to capture it. At 9 a.m. this was a challenge. The class was an average fifty students; big enough so most students could remain anonymous but small enough for the keen students to shine. Lucy preferred to stay anonymous. There were no marks for class participation and Lucy really only cared about the marks.

Although Lucy was proud of her gift, she knew it often made other people feel dumb. She didn't like that. She also didn't like the awkward and incessant questions that came with it. One guy in her last semester had asked her in all seriousness if she could see the future. Lucy had replied that she in fact could see the future and he was going to be a moron for the rest of his life. Nope, she was fine with being anonymous, especially first thing in the morning.

Dr. Lewis was starting a new poem; "Ulysses" by Tennyson. Lucy flipped open her book to the appropriate page but didn't look at it. She watched as the other students began scanning the page with fervor. The good thing about poetry especially for English majors was the low reading requirements. Students didn't have to stay up all night reading a novel that was up for discussion the next day. Poems were generally short and could be perused quickly at the beginning of class. "Ulysses" was a longer poem, coming in at a mean seventy lines but most students had gotten the gist by the time Lewis cleared his throat to begin. Lucy opened her mind to her personal library, found the appropriate volume, flipped through it and immediately had the entire verse splayed out in her head. She also opened up any reference materials she had read about the poem in case Lewis decided to branch out. She picked up her pen and took notes dutifully for fifty minutes.

As Dr. Lewis dismissed them, Lucy looked at the clock and her heart sank. It was 10 a.m. which meant her science option and she despised science. Science was the one field that highlighted Lucy's weaknesses. Lucy didn't like highlighting her weaknesses. She had never excelled at the sciences, she never cared that a neuron was there, if she couldn't see it, what's the point in talking about it? It never made any sense to her. However, the University insisted upon yearly science options for English and History majors and despite Dr Hannon's good connections and chocolates delivered to the registrar, Lucy was still stuck with Chemistry 101.

It was the option that all the Fine Arts students took because it was purportedly the easiest – coined "scopes for dopes" by the Freshman Class. Lucy wholeheartedly disagreed. She could memorize what happened in each experiment but the problem was that each experiment ended slightly differently. Even if they used the same materials, in the same quantities, it still had a somewhat different result. How could Lucy use her memory when there was no predictor of behavior?

It was so infuriating and her lab partner Janielle just made it worse. Janielle was not your typical science geek. For one, she was beautiful – with layered shoulder length hair professionally died every two weeks, fake nails, fake boobs, a great figure and a tan that could only be bought. Not only did she spell her name with a superfluous vowel (the "I") she claimed her parents had chosen that spelling. No parent consciously intends for her child to spend her life saying, "My name is Janielle, with an I" and have the rest of the world ask, "where?" In addition to her stupid name choice, Janielle had a mean streak to her and her favorite pastime was making Lucy look stupid. It was one thing to be smart, but it was another to be a self-righteous snit about it.

There was more than one instance where Janielle would puff out her fake chest pout her lips and gasp, "oh Luceeee, what HAVE you done?" and Lucy would have to restrain herself from punching Janielle in the throat. Janielle was completely useless at all other subjects and especially at the challenges of life and yet, could predict the outcome of an experiment with unfailing accuracy. Lucy dreaded these ninety minute-long torture labs and as she stepped out into the quad she silently pleaded for a miracle.

And as if someone had heard her, he appeared. There was Nathaniel, sitting on the grass of the quad, leaning against a tree. He still looked completely perfect in the light of day. The sun caught the dark colors in his hair and it glinted in the sunshine. Lucy hesitated for a moment, would he remember her? Would he want to talk to her? Then he glanced over in her direction and grinned and waved to her. It was the smile that Lucy had seen the night before and those butterflies came back with a vengeance. Without any further hesitation, she bounded over and grinned down at him.

"I've been looking for you…" Nathaniel said, as he stood up beaming. Lucy again forgot all other obligations, fell into step beside him and they walked toward the park behind the campus.

"Been looking for me?" Lucy wondered, "why?"

"Well, I need to test a theory," Nathaniel replied. He glanced up at the sky and squinted into the sun. He strolled with an easy gait, one that made others feel at ease.

"And what theory is that?" Lucy said as she walked.

He was silent for a moment, "I'll let you know when it comes true ok?"

Lucy laughed. They had reached a park bench tucked into the shade of a maple tree and Lucy plopped down. Nathaniel sat slowly next to her. She looked out at the park. It was a dazzling bright day and a few students were lounging about and enjoying the early spring. Lucy kept her eyes forward; she made a conscious effort to not look at Nathaniel because she found him so distracting.

"So have you been thinking about me all morning?" he asked in a slightly teasing tone.

Lucy snorted, "Hardly!" she exclaimed. "Frankly pal, I don't even remember your name."

"I thought you had a photographic memory?" He countered.

She laughed again, "I do but only for the important things," she giggled.

"Nice," Nathaniel said sarcastically, "very nice."

Lucy laughed again. "Sorry buddy, I have got a lot on my mind." She shrugged, "some things just don't make the cut."

Now it was Nathaniel's turn to laugh, "I will keep that in mind." There was a pause, "it's too bad though," he commented while leaning back in the bench and gazing up at the sun.

"Why?" She challenged smiling.

"Because I thought about you all morning," Lucy started to laugh but then took a sideways look at him. He was staring right at her - a shiver ran down her neck.

"You should," she stumbled on her words, "you should, keep yourself busy."

"Oh I am plenty busy," he replied and smiled at her.

"Cryptic much?" She challenged.

He shrugged, "Not really, to be honest, I don't really remember. You see, I have a terrible memory."

Lucy shook her head, "Stop it,"

"No!" he exclaimed, "really, can't remember what I had for breakfast! I'm horrible."

"Well then how did you remember me?" Lucy shot back.

"That's why I kept you on my mind all day," he tapped his temple, "steel trap now."

She laughed. There was silence again.

"You look pretty today," he said quietly. Lucy suddenly wished she had showered. She reached up and touched her hair, the red ringlets had splayed into a wild mess, half of which she had twisted up with a pen. She rolled her eyes. "Thanks," she said as she pulled out the pen and shoved it in her bag.

"I suspect though that you look pretty on most days," he said leaning forward to catch her eye. Lucy turned her head to look back out at the park.

"Thanks," she tapped her toe. She was not used to this type of conversation. "You are wearing the same thing that you wore last night." She blurted then cringed.

He looked down at himself. "You are correct," he nodded, "your memory really is something."

"I'm sorry," she said with a sigh, "I say stupid stuff sometimes."

"It's not a stupid thing and I AM wearing the same clothes two days in a row," he laughed, "no one is perfect."

"No, I guess not," she shook her head. "It's just my memory is great most of the time. I mean, it helps me but sometimes, when it matters most, it sucks."

"When it matters most," he smiled lightly.

She rolled her eyes again, "I just meant,"

"You thought about me all morning," he leaned into her.

"No!" she lied, "I was busy,"

"Doing what?" he challenged.

And so Lucy ran through the last 2 hours of her life in painstaking detail. The classes, the girls in the dorm, everything.

"A party," Nathaniel smiled, "that sounds fun."

Lucy nodded, "Yeah, they tend to be." She fell silent and realized that yet again she had just talked incessantly.

"Yup," Nathaniel said with a smile, "sounds really fun."

Then it dawned on Lucy, "Oh my God," she said, "what an idiot I am."

"Don't say that," he replied quickly.

"No, I mean," she shook her head at her own dimness. "Would you like to come to the party?"

"Why yes, what a great idea, I would love to come to the party."

"Cool," Silence. Where Lucy sat, slightly uncomfortable, Nathaniel could not be more at ease.

"Tell me about your parents. Where do they live?" He asked.

"They are divorced." Lucy replied plainly, "because of me." She added looking out at the park.

"No! That can't be!" He sounded so genuinely offended on her behalf that Lucy laughed a little.

"I assure you it's true. I read the divorce papers." Nathaniel still shook his head in disbelief. Lucy rifled through her mind and pulled that file from its shelf in her head and quoted directly, "The Plaintiff (that's my father) claims irreconcilable differences with the Defendant (that's my mother) over the care and handling of their daughter's unique abilities. The Plaintiff in good conscience can no longer be party to decisions made on his daughter's behalf and furthermore refuses to contribute anymore to her detriment." Nathaniel stared at her stunned. "I know," Lucy said calmly, "it seems unkind but my Dad had his reasons for leaving my Mom. I assume from the papers that he didn't like me being tested anymore or a part of conferences or lectures. I like it though." Nathaniel started to say something but Lucy continued, "My father loved me very much. He and my Mom stayed good friends and he came to all my school stuff and Christmas and everything. He didn't abandon my Mom or me. He just stopped having anything to do with my photographic memory. He would never talk about it again. He was a good man and a wonderful father."

"Was?" Nathaniel asked training his eyes on her.

Lucy sighed. "My father died in a car accident last year. A drunk driver killed him."

Nathaniel's face fell and he sighed too. "That's so sad. I'm sorry."

"It is sad," Lucy almost whispered, "my Mom and I were devastated," she took a deep breath to steady herself. "But life goes on. I wanted to postpone University for one more year to stay with Mom in Kansas but she wouldn't hear of it. She said my father would be furious if he knew that because of him I had missed out. She's probably right but I felt bad leaving her." There was another little pause and Lucy sighed, "Let's change the subject."

"So what class are you skipping right now?" he obeyed.

"I normally don't skip," Lucy said quickly.

"Noted,"

"But it's chem and I hate it."

"Chemistry is wonderful," Nathaniel said shocked.

"Now there is your first fault," Lucy grinned, "no normal person actually likes chemistry."

"Really?" he was intrigued.

"Truth. As a matter of fact, the possibility that you live with your mother, dress up like cartoon characters and have dead bodies in your basement just went up to 85 percent."

"That can't be good," he smiled.

"It does not look good for you," Lucy chided.

"What should I do?"

Lucy shrugged, "The damage is done."

He nodded soberly, "Would it help to say that I like biology more?"

"No, definitely not,"

"Oops," he replied. They smiled at each other. "Did I mention how pretty you look today?"

"Yes," Lucy smiled, "sure did."

"Really?" he nodded, "just wanted to make sure." He paused. Lucy let her eyes meet his.

"Hey!" she exclaimed, "your eyes changed color."

"Sorry?" he asked with a slight tilt to his head.

"Last night, your eyes were grey, today, they look blue-ish." Lucy shook her head, "I've never seen that before."

Nathaniel sighed seriously, "You know what this means don't you?"

"What?" Lucy was intrigued.

"That you thought about me all morning,"

"HA!" Lucy exploded in laugher and slapped him playfully on the arm.

Lucy looked at her watch. It was almost 1130. She was amazed again at how quickly time passed when she was with this guy.

"This is becoming a pattern," Lucy said as she tucked a stray red curl behind her ear.

"What," Nathaniel asked, again leaning into her and

studying her face, "running into each other and talking for hours?"

"Yup," she said smiling, "if I didn't know better, I would say that you were stalking me."

"Busted," Nathaniel grinned.

Just as Lucy was going to come up with a witty reply, a dark shadow crossed over them. Lucy shaded her eyes and looked up to see Janielle standing over them like a centurion, hands on her wide hips and mad as a hornets nest. Lucy dropped her head. She was above all things, a good student, and she had let another good, albeit bitchy, student down today.

"Hey Janielle," Lucy mumbled. She started to explain that she had just run into her new friend Nathaniel and if Janielle would just take a good look at him, she would completely understand why Lucy skipped.

"I don't want to hear your bullshit Lucy," Janielle snapped, "I just worked my ass off so that you could get my mark. Today was the midterm." Lucy gasped, of course it was! How had she forgotten something so important? The feeling was both terrifying and exhilarating.

"I was just...." Lucy started to motion to Nathaniel but again, Janielle cut her off.

"Look, I don't share my marks with people that I LIKE let alone...well... you. Just because I got stuck with you as a lab partner does not mean I have to put up with a bunch of crap. I thought you were supposed to be smart with some sort of super brain. But you can't tell time! You owe me," she spouted, "just so you know. I have never been so pissed at someone. You are an idiot." And she stalked off. Lucy looked after her and vowed to make it better, somehow.

"Sorry about that," Lucy said to Nathaniel, "she never liked me."

"I get the impression that the feeling is mutual," Nathaniel replied.

Lucy smiled, "This is true," and squinted her eyes at him. "She spells her name with an extra "I". I find that annoying."

"Totally logical," Nathaniel nodded and grinned at her.

Lucy rolled her eyes, "Not JUST that, she's, well, she's..." she struggled.

"She looks to be a very unhappy person." Nathaniel offered and Lucy had to agree. "Which I am as well because I really must go."

"Sure," she replied, trying to sound casual, and counter the desperation her heart suddenly felt. "I have to get to class anyway. I'll see you later." She started to get up but Nathaniel reached out and grabbed her hand. Gently, steadily, with the utmost of care, he lifted her hand to his mouth, turned it over and touched his lips to the inside of her wrist. Lucy gasped, shivers flew up her arm and her knees buckled, forcing her to sit back down on the bench. He placed her hand back on her lap. Lucy sat frozen, afraid that if she moved the magic would break.

"Where will you be tonight?" He whispered.

"Munzie's on Elm Street." Lucy whispered back.

Wordlessly, Nathaniel stood up and started to saunter away but turned and started to walk backward, "You proved my theory by the way," he called back. Lucy startled out of her trance, she looked up and raised her eye brows in question. "I'll tell you tonight!" He smirked when she rolled her eyes in frustration, turned back around and walked away. Lucy sighed.

At noon, she had her intermediate Shakespeare class. Lucy sat down in the middle of the desks and pulled her class materials out despite having a small case of the shakes after her last encounter with Nathaniel. She pulled out her copy of Hamlet, notepad and pen; this time all three were for show. Dr. Black wrote almost everything important down on the white board allowing Lucy to sit and absorb without thinking, well, she could think, think about Nathaniel. Dr. Black began the lecture where they left off on Wednesday; Act 4 Scene 5 Line 185. It was the part where Ophelia has gone mad with her love for Hamlet and her father's untimely death. Lucy once again found the book in her head and let it fall open to the scene.

> *"And will a not come again?*
> *And will a not come again?*
> *No, no he is dead*
> *Go to thy deathbed*
> *He never will come again"*

Lucy opened her copy of Hamlet to the appropriate scene and froze. There, tucked in the crease of the book was a leaf, a *pagoda dogwood* leaf to be exact. It was fresh and bright green like some natural bookmark. Nathaniel must have put it there. Was it the same leaf? Was it the leaf that seemed to reach and quiver for his attention? Lucy had never picked up her bag off the ground. She had never left it alone - Nathaniel had no way to get to it. She knew she hadn't seen anything in his hands. There weren't even any pagoda dogwood trees in the park behind the campus. Lucy shook her head.

She twirled the leaf between her fingers. Lucy was uncomfortable with so many questions without answers. Her mission in life had always been the facts, the truth and the whole story. She never went half way. Lucy made a promise to herself that if and when she saw Nathaniel again, she would not get distracted and would get his story. She was shaken up during the lecture and was grateful that Dr. Black hadn't called on her. After he dismissed them, Lucy packed her bag, placing the leaf carefully back into her book and headed for the Student's Union Building.

As she cut through the quad, Lucy saw the dogwood tree that she and Nathaniel were standing beside last night. She was tempted to go and examine it. Could she find the same leaf? She could see it clearly in her memory. It was dark though and here in the light of the day the tree would look different. Lucy wasn't sure if she could confirm if it was the same leaf. She deeply hoped that he would come to Munzies tonight because Lucy was determined to get answers from him. With a new sense of purpose, Lucy walked into the student's union building for lunch.

The food court was crowded. Lucy joined the shortest line up of the eight or so vendors lining the walls. She bought a sub and a can of coke and turned to scan the huge room. She quickly found the group she was looking for. Paige and Suzanne were sitting with three others in the middle of the rows of tables. Two were boys. Nick, Paige's stocky black haired boyfriend, Simon, Nick's roommate and Suzanne's soon to be boyfriend who was tall and lean with a shock of red hair. The last person at the table was Anastasia. They saw her at the same moment she saw them and they all hollered and waved. Lucy grinned. She had found a place where she belonged and it felt great.

Lucy remembered the first painful week of school when she didn't even bother looking around the food court because she knew she had no friends. It was excruciatingly awkward. Finally in the second week, she was sitting alone in the dorm cafeteria at dinner, pretending to read when she heard a loud, clear voice say, "Hey are you a loser like me?" Lucy had looked up to see a beautiful girl with long silky black hair, big blue eyes and a body that made boys drool and girls sick. Her name was Anastasia and she and Lucy had been best friends from that moment on. Anastasia lived in the same girl's dorm but on the second floor. They had made friends with the girls on the fourth floor because Anastasia had determined that the second floor girls were tools. Paige and her cleavage had been responsible for bringing in the boys.

They had formed their own gang. The group spent most of their non-class time together. Most of them worked at Munzie's and they ate lunch and sometimes dinner together. They hung out together almost every weekend. These were Lucy's people. Lucy slid onto a stool across from Anastasia and dropped her bag on the floor at her feet.

"Did you make it on time this morning?" Suzanne asked from the other end of the table.

Lucy nodded, "I ran like the wind baby." Suzanne gave her the thumbs up.

"Nice work with the pit-bull covert information Lucy," Nick said before he shoved almost an entire hamburger into his mouth. The girls had clearly filled him in on the row-a-thon.

"No problem," Lucy replied while unwrapping her sub, "I am here to serve your party needs."

Nick was still chewing his half a cow so Simon responded, "Our party needs," he motioned to himself, "are your party needs." He motioned to Lucy like he was bestowing a gift on her.

Everyone moved on further discuss the plans for the party and the new addition of flowers through the quad. Suzanne was lecturing on the dangers of global warming and Lucy took the opportunity to sneak in a private conversation with Anastasia. She leaned slightly over the table. Anastasia instinctively leaned forward as well, sensing that Lucy had something to discuss. She looked expectantly at Lucy, waiting.

"Do I have a story for you," Lucy began. She knew she could tell Anastasia everything about Nathaniel. She could tell her about the leaf, the warm tingles, everything. She decided to start at the beginning, "So after the conference last night..." Lucy began.

But Anastasia cut her off in an effort to move the story along, "You mean after you sat in the coffee shop by yourself like the loser that you are..." Anastasia was smiling at the joke.

Lucy didn't smile.

"What?" she asked while losing her train of thought. Anastasia took the last fry out of the paper cup in front of her and dipped it into her ketchup.

"I thought you've already read Hamlet," she said casually while popping the fry in her mouth.

"I have," Lucy said slowly.

"So," Anastasia swallowed, "Why were you sitting all by your little lonesome last night reading it?"

All by her lonesome?

Lucy searched her memory. Had Nathaniel left the table? Had he gone to the bathroom? No, she was positive that at no point was she sitting at that table alone. She brought up the image of the café. She confirmed that there were no pillars or obstructions that would make anyone see her but not Nathaniel. If Anastasia had been at the door, or in the café, or even just walking by, she would have had a clear view of their table. Her heart started to race. She began to sweat and pant slightly. Lucy reached over and grabbed Anastasia's arm.

"Stasia," she said desperately, "this is very important. Tell me precisely what you saw last night. Please tell me every little detail."

Concern pressed into Anastasia's features. "Lucy you look like someone just punched you in the face! Are you ok?"

Lucy shook her head, "I'm fine. I just need you to tell me with as much detail as you can what you saw last night," she said firmly.

"Well," Anastasia sighed, "I don't have your talents but I'll try my best," Lucy forced a small smile. "I was coming home late from rehearsal, I was dead tired. I came in the foyer..."

"Time?" Lucy prodded with a hint of rudeness.

Anastasia ignored the tone. "Um...let me think. Rehearsal was supposed to run until nine but it went until nine thirty but we stood around talking for a while. So it must have been ten or shortly after." Lucy was sure that she and Nathaniel were both sitting at that table at ten.

"Kay..." Lucy nodded with encouragement. Anastasia took a deep breath and looked at the ceiling to better remember.

"I saw you in the café, sitting by the window, there were two other tables, that creepy girl from the third floor and two annoying chicks."

"Good." Lucy encouraged, "What was I doing?"

"You had two cups of coffee in front of you and that beat up copy of Hamlet open on the table in front of you." Anastasia paused and looked at Lucy's face. She determined that more information was needed so she pressed on, "You were like talking to yourself and gesturing with your hands."

"To myself," Lucy muttered to no one. A roar started in her ears. Anastasia must have gotten the wrong impression from Lucy's reaction. She thought Lucy was offended.

"Listen babe, I would have said hi but I was bagged and you looked busy. I just figured I would leave you to it and hit the sack. I would not have been good company. Trust me."

"You're sure that I was alone at the table, that there wasn't anyone else with me?" Lucy was starting to go numb.

"No..." Anastasia was trying to get the right answer here, "were you supposed to be meeting someone? I thought that you were just reciting Shakespeare like how you test yourself sometimes." A look of shock crossed her face, "Oh no! I wasn't supposed to meet you was I?" she pulled out her iphone and started flipping through it with panic, "I am so crazy with the recital coming up that I am forgetting everything. I am so sorry babe. And you got me a coffee and everything and you waited all alone and had to read a book you have memorized to pass the time and then I'm so tired and full of myself that I don't even say hello and let you know I'm alive and I totally ditch. I swear, I am the worst friend on the face of the planet; seriously you can kick my ass for this. I deserve it, I can't believe I did that!" Lucy reached over again and stopped Anastasia's hand from ripping apart her phone. She had worked herself up into such a state that Lucy was sure it would not survive the frantic page poking.

"You didn't ditch me," Lucy said sounding calmer then she felt.

Anastasia froze, "I didn't?"

Lucy shook her head somewhat reassured that her friend cared so much about standing her up, "No babe, we weren't supposed to hang out last night."

Anastasia leaned back and blew out a huge gust of air, "Oh thank God, but," she looked back at Lucy confused, "who were you meeting?"

"No one," Lucy said. The roar in her ears got louder and she felt beads of sweat on her upper lip. What was going on here? Had she imagined an entire human being? A person that walked, talked, laughed, opened doors and drank coffee? She had invented a man who could touch her and damn near make her dissolve? Why would she do such a thing? People who had episodes like this were usually having a nervous breakdown or crazy. Was she crazy? She couldn't be.

Then a new horror occurred to her. What if something was

wrong with her brain? It could be an aneurism or a neurotoxin; both of which could cause hallucinations. What if her brain had finally reached its performance limits and in the process of shutting down it was starting to malfunction? Like what Dr. Hannon always said – that Lucy's brain was a well oiled machine that she ran at a max all the time. What if her brain had just run out of gas? Terror instantaneously consumed her. Lucy choked back a sob and looked up to see the entire table was staring at her with concern.

Anastasia reached back over the table and slowly put her hand on Lucy's arm, "Are you ok Lucy? You look like you need an Atavan or something."

Lucy quickly shook her head to compose herself and forced a small scoff, "Sorry guys, I'm fine. I just realized that....." She began to rise from the table.

"That what?" Suzanne asked still concerned.

"I have to find my lab partner," Lucy stuttered.

"That cow who spells her name with the superfluous "I"?" Suzanne challenged, "why?"

"I screwed something up," Lucy grabbed her bag, "I have to find her."

"I'll come with you," Nick said as he started to stand, "I have to head over to sciences anyway."

"No!" Lucy almost yelled and Nicks face froze in shock, "I'll go and find her, thanks." She turned and almost ran out of the building. She sprinted to the sciences building, her mind a blur. By the time she got there, Lucy was in a full blown panic. She found Janielle in the cafeteria beside the biology lab; she was talking with bright animation to a group of wide eyed science nerds who were hanging on her every word. Lucy stormed up, grabbed Janielle's chair and spun her around.

"Janielle!" she yelled into her shocked face, "Who was I with in the park?"

Janielle froze, mid-sentence and slowly adjusted her facial expression to deep contempt as she glared at Lucy, "I was in the middle of something." She growled.

"Yeah, whatever," Lucy said and pushed herself closer to the busty blond. "Listen, I was sitting with someone in the park when you came up, did you recognize him?"

Janielle laughed out loud and the ice and happiness of it made Lucy's heart stop. "You think you were with someone?" Janielle challenged, "Really? Is that what you think?"

"Yes," Lucy almost whispered. Her hands began to shake as she pushed the chair away and slowly stood.

"Then you are not only a moron, you are a delusional moron." Janielle spouted back. She turned to the table, "she totally slacks all term, bails on the midterm and then I find her sitting on a bench talking to herself about being stalked." She looped her finger in the air beside her head. "Psych consult please!" she sang and the table erupted in laughter. Lucy stumbled back from them, knocked over a garbage can, found her feet and sprinted.

Lucy didn't think about Nathaniel as she pounded across the campus. She didn't look around the quad for him. She did not want to see him anymore. Lucy was frantic to NOT see Nathaniel again. She carefully ran through her memory looking for gaps or lost information but it all seemed intact. She ran through the events of last night, and this morning, watching them like a movie in her head, trying to find evidence that Nathaniel wasn't imaginary.

She thought of the coffee guy being surprised that she had bought two coffees. Of course he was surprised. She was alone. He couldn't see Nathaniel either. There was so much loss for her to cope with. She might be losing her memory and she was losing Nathaniel. He had somehow implanted himself in her life and yet now, there was no way she would see him again because he was a figment of her imagination. She tried not to panic but it seemed like the right thing to do.

Lucy slowed her pace as she opened the glass doors to the psychology building. She ran toward salvation, safety. Janielle was right, she needed a psych consult, she needed Dr. Hannon. Was he even in his office? Lucy loaded up the schedule he had shown her at the beginning of the semester in her mind. She saw the calendar clearly, Monday, Wednesday, Friday 11:30-1:30 Office Hours. She nodded to herself. At least something in her head was still working.

As she climbed the thin dark staircase a thought occurred to her. Lucy was not the only one who would be devastated with this news. If Lucy lost her mind and or her memory, Dr. Hannon would lose his research topic. He had built almost his entire career around Lucy and her unique memory; all other topics and subjects had been dropped the moment he met her. Every publication, all the meetings, the studies, the experiments, the thousands of dollars in government grants and University budgets would all be wasted now.

Dr. Hannon would become a laughing stock.

Lucy quickly decided that she didn't have to tell Dr. Hannon everything to get some answers from him. She didn't have to tell him about Nathaniel in order to solve this mystery. It was, after all just one episode and it might never happen again. Lucy took a deep breath and was a bit calmer when she reached the second floor and walked the short hallway to Dr. Hannon's office. For now, she would keep the details a secret. Hopefully, it would never become necessary to tell him the whole truth. She sucked in a deep breath, wrung her hands together and knocked on the door.

"Come in!" Dr. Hannon called from inside. Lucy opened the door and poked her head in. Dr. Hannon's office was not huge but it was certainly larger than any other office at the University. Dr. Hannon looked up from his enormous mahogany desk and his face lit up, "Lucy!" His sparkling eyes could barely be seen over the stacks and stacks of paper on his desk. Dr. Hannon was exceedingly disorganized. The only person who kept him on time and prepared was Gail, his administrator. She somehow managed to make sense of those massive piles so papers got graded on time, letters sent and memos acknowledged. Lucy assumed that Gail had taken a long weekend because Dr. Hannon's paper mountains were bigger than ever.

"It's so nice to see you!" he extolled while coming around the side of the desk to put his hands on Lucy's shoulders. He gave her a light squeeze and smiled showing how genuinely happy he was to see her and let go. This small act broke Lucy's heart even more. Hiding the truth from Dr. Hannon was going to be harder than she thought.

"Coffee?" he asked. He didn't pause for a reply but instead headed over to the small coffee station he had set up in the corner and poured two cups. He mixed in cream and sugar and returned, talking the whole time; "I have received twenty emails today from doctors and students who were at the conference last night. They have been requesting more information. They just can't get enough of you Lucy. Sorry the coffee is from this morning, Gail took a long weekend."

Lucy took the cup, sat at one end of the couch and dropped her school bag on the floor. Dr. Hannon sat at the other end of the couch and crossed one leg over the other. He waited, knowing Lucy had come here to say something.

"Doc, when was my last MRI?" Lucy spoke quietly while staring at her coffee cup. She couldn't see if there was any reaction on his face.

"You would remember better than I would Lucy, I think it was January of last year. Does that sound right to you?" Lucy nodded. "Why?" Lucy decided not to answer that.

"And everything was normal right? I mean...normal for me," Lucy's voice was monotone and soft. She was worried if she displayed any emotion at all she may crack and start to bawl.

"Yes Lucy, normal for you," he paused, "is there something wrong?"

"What if there was?" Lucy probed in the same robotic voice. Dr. Hannon's voice was not so robotic- it was full of concern.

"Then we would look into it and fix it. Lucy, what's going on?"

"But what if you couldn't fix it? What if I couldn't be fixed? What would you do Doctor? What would you do for work?" she finished quietly.

"Lucy look at me," he said firmly. Lucy shook her head. She could feel him leaning over trying to get into her line of sight. He sighed and continued, "If I could not have you as a subject, I could do many other things. I admit that none of them would be as fascinating as you are but I would survive. Please do not forget that I consider myself a fairly smart man." Lucy could feel him smile at the joke but she didn't look up. "Lucy look, if you want out of the program, you leave, that's all. I wouldn't be angry with you. I would completely understand. My research takes up a great deal of your time, time that as a young freshman you might prefer to spend with your friends or," he hesitated, "dare I say, a boyfriend?"

Oh God! Don't cry. Don't cry.

Lucy managed to shake her head but could not open her mouth for fear of releasing the floodgates of her misery. "Oh," Dr. Hannon sat back, "Well, whatever it is, you can tell me. I won't be upset. I promise." There was a long silence. Dr. Hannon seemed to be contemplating something.

"Lucy," he asked carefully, "did you see something strange?"

At this Lucy's head snapped up and she stared at him her mouth agape. "Like what?" she almost yelled.

He startled in shock at her sudden reaction and responded quickly sensing her urgency, "Spots of light, or spots of dark? Images tracing themselves across your vision?"

Lucy relaxed and put her head back down, "No. Nothing like that." *Just imaginary dream men,* she thought.

"Any problems with your depth perception? Are you bumping into things?"

Hot guys in the quad? "No."

There was another long pause as Dr. Hannon contemplated his next line of questions.

When he spoke again, his voice was soft, "Lucy, have you had any new memories pop up?" Lucy looked at him again, this time with total confusion in her eyes,

"What do you mean new memories?"

"From your childhood maybe? From before anyone knew about your gift?"

"From before I was two?" Lucy asked completely confounded.

"Yes," he answered calmly, "anything like that?"

Lucy shook her head, "No, why?"

Dr. Hannon seemed to relax a little, "Well, despite my many years of study, the brain is still a mystery. We don't know why it does some of the things it does and sometimes it can play tricks on us."

"It can?"

"Yes," Dr. Hannon laughed a little, "even a brain as perfect as yours can show you strange things or store images for a long time without you knowing. Your brain isn't physiologically all that different from everyone else's. People remember new things all the time. What we think is a random thought is actually a memory of something we have read or seen but just forgot about. Your brain is usually far more accurate, being able to see a memory exactly how it happened. Most people do not remember anything from before the age of two. You might be different. I would not be surprised at all if your mind came up with images from infancy."

He didn't seem worried about this at all, "In addition to that Lucy, you are exhausted. College takes a toll on a student. You have been pushing it very hard the last few months and maybe you just need a break. Even the most powerful jet engine needs an oil change every once in a while. Our minds need vacations too. Yours especially with all its extra talents might just need a reprieve. Why don't you take the weekend and try to rest your mind a little? I won't tell you not to study or go to the library because that would be impossible for you but maybe go easy on your poor head for a few days. You will be amazed at how much better you feel." Lucy nodded. That wasn't a bad idea after all. Maybe she was just tired. "Go be a normal, vapid eighteen year old for a couple days. Doctors orders," he added with a grin, "Now would you like to tell me what is really bothering you?" Lucy took a deep, shaky breath and a gulp of her coffee. It tasted like metal but she didn't mind.

"Not today," she said with conviction. Dr. Hannon began to protest, "But I'll make you a deal, if anything changes, I promise to let you know." Lucy felt much better. Her mind was tired and it was playing tricks on her. This made complete sense. She would rest her mind this weekend; it wouldn't be hard with work tonight and the party tomorrow night. She really had little studying to do. She had to cut her brain a break. She was just human after all.

"That's a deal," Dr. Hannon said starting to rise. Lucy stood too and glanced at her watch, 12:45. She had just enough time to make it to Ancient History.

"Thanks Doc," she said sincerely and picked up her bag.

"I didn't do anything."

"You did actually." Lucy started to walk to the door.

"Well, then I am glad to be of service." Lucy laughed. Dr. Hannon started to return to his desk but stopped, "Oh and Lucy, tell that boyfriend of yours to be nice to you."

"I told you Doc, I don't have a boy…" Lucy started but he cut her off.

"I may be an old graying professor who lives with a very handsome man, but I," he tapped his temple, "am a remarkably astute chap. I have seen my share of lovesick freshman girls and I am telling you my dear, he isn't worth it if he makes you sad."

"But Doc…"

"I am a genius young lady," he waved his hand dismissing her and sat back behind his desk, "now go or you will be late. I have no interest in hearing from Professor Johnson about you being disrespectfully tardy."

Lucy rolled her eyes, sighed and walked out the door. Lovesick? Lucy thought that was a little strong of a term. She had a crush, that's all- a crush on a figment of her imagination. She had daydreamed, that's all. She had daydreamed because her mind was tired. She had spent the past 16 years overloading her brain with piles and piles of information and now it was fatigued. She sighed as she pulled open the door of the psychology building and headed out into the sunshine.

Anastasia was leaning against the closest bike rack, her arms crossed. "Nice try loser."

Lucy smiled, "Piss off and mind your own business."

"You ARE my business," she spouted and pushed herself to

standing as she sauntered over. "You might have fooled the rest of them but I know you better." She walked over to Lucy, opened her arms and wrapped her in a tight hug.

"I'm fine," Lucy sighed into Anastasia's thick hair. They pulled apart. "I just talked to Dr. Hannon. I'm just tired. I'm going to take the weekend off and then everything should be fine. If I am not ok, I will come back and deal with it ok?"

"Tired hey?" Anastasia challenged, "You don't say! Up all night, reading a bunch of stupid books the size of my ass, spending days on end in the library? I can't imagine why you are tired!"

Lucy giggled, "I get it ok?"

"You better because I really don't want to have to beat the crap out of you," Anastasia shot her a tough look.

"Yeah yeah yeah," Lucy rolled her eyes, "like you could."

Anastasia hugged her again, "Ok, keep me posted. I gotta get to rehearsal. I will see you later for work right?"

"You bet," Lucy smiled, "and by the way, thanks for caring, really, I appreciate it."

Anastasia started to walk away and waved at her over her shoulder, "That's m'job loser!" she called and headed off towards the theatre. Lucy smiled after her for a minute before turning towards her own class.

He doesn't exist. She thought to herself over and over. It became a mantra and with each step she deepened her resolve, bringing her closer to control and sanity.

He doesn't exist, he doesn't exist.

Then she imagined Nathaniel's face again and her confidence began to falter. He had felt so real, so solid and so wonderful that it was inconceivable to her that she could have invented him. She remembered how funny he was and how interested he was in her. Lucy had always been too independent to need a boyfriend. The boys she dated in high school were agreeable enough but no one had really caught her attention, not like Nathaniel had caught her attention anyway. Since starting college, the thought of a steady boyfriend had never even crossed her mind; she had been too busy with friends and school.

Why was she so attached to someone she had met for a few hours and literally knew nothing about?

Because you made him up, she thought to herself. Of course! Nathaniel was the perfect guy because he was a figment of HER imagination. His perfection proved that he was fictitious! Lucy had made up the ideal person for herself. Just like Dr. Hannon had said, she was tired and maybe she did need a boyfriend, a real one. She would give her mind a rest, get a nice real boyfriend and everything would be just fine. Lucy laughed at herself. The past eighteen hours had been nothing but a bad dream and now it was over. If she could, she would have forgotten about the whole thing. Lucy took a deep breath resolving to start this incredibly long day over again and pulled open the door to her Ancient History lecture.

Chapter Three
Questions

"Sometimes the questions are complicated
and the answers are simple"
~Dr. Seuss

Ancient history had been deeply boring as usual but Lucy stuck it out and almost sprinted back to her dorm. The horrors of the day were now tucked back away in her memory and she had no intentions of bringing them up again. She was finished with her classes for the day, it was Friday, she had the weekend in front of her and it was going to be a weekend she was taking off. Lucy got back to her room and saw that her harried departure this morning had made a disaster of the space. She set to work, picking up clothes, making her bed back into a couch and straightening her meager amount of belongings. Because her room was roughly the size of a shoebox, it only took twenty minutes to make it look pristine. It was 2:30 and Lucy had plenty of time to get ready for work. She stripped down, pulled on her housecoat, seized her makeup bag, shower bag and towel and headed to the bathroom.

The bathroom was empty when she got in and Lucy rejoiced that she would get the good shower stall. The middle shower stall was also known as the 'money shower'. It had the best water pressure and it didn't react in anyway to toilet flushes or sinks being turned on. One was guaranteed to get a long hot satisfying shower if you were blessed enough to get the 'money shower'. Lucy preferred baths but she hadn't had a good long soaking bath in months. There were only stand up showers in the dorms and she hadn't been home since Christmas. The 'money shower' was the best alternative. Lucy let the hot water roll over her for a moment allowing it to wash away her worries and the stresses of the day. She renewed her conviction that the last several hours were nothing more than a bump in the road. It was an episode brought on by a tired photographic memory and a freshman college life. She reached for her shampoo and heard the bathroom door open.

"Who's in here?" Paige demanded heading to the toilets on the far wall.

"Me!" Lucy called back lathering up her hair. Paige recognized her voice and stopped to lean against a sink.

"Oh hey Lucy, you ok?" she asked, "You looked pretty weird at lunch."

"Oh yeah!" Lucy called back trying to sound light, "I'm fine." Lucy hadn't yet thought of a story to explain her bizarre behavior at the lunch table and frantically began to concoct one in her head. Before she could think of one, she heard the door slam open again.

"IT'S FRIDAY!!!" Suzanne and Anastasia yelled together barreling into the bathroom.

"Hell yeah!" Lucy yelled from the showers.

"Amen! I am considering wearing a tube top as a skirt tonight." Paige replied.

"You are a whore," Anastasia said laughing.

"I need to make some extra cash," Paige giggled and headed into a bathroom stall.

"Do you think that would work?" Suzanne asked wide eyed.

"I think she was kidding," Anastasia smiled but paused. "But with Paige, you never know."

"HA!" Paige yelled from the stalls.

The girls all worked on Fridays and were enthusiastic about it. Munzies was a casual grill but had the best food and service in town. When tourists came or parents and kids came shopping for schools, the town hotel staff always recommended Munzies for dinner over the several other stuffy, expensive restaurants in town. It was the best place to eat and the best place to work. The environment was fun; everyone made money and had a blast doing it.

Lucy finished her shower and headed for the sink while tying up her bathrobe. "Can Nick drive?" she asked Paige.

"Yup," Paige was applying blush; "he and Simon will be waiting for us downstairs at 3:30." Everyone started at four on Fridays to catch the early school rush before the townspeople got off work. Nick usually drove everyone and although it was a tight squeeze in his Civic, it was better than taking the bus. The girls all finished getting ready and darted back to their rooms to change into their uniforms; black v-neck tops and black skirts. Lucy was almost at her door when Suzanne stopped her.

"Hey Lucy," she whispered softly, "You ok?"

"Yes I'm fine, I just..." Lucy was lost for words. She still hadn't thought of a story yet.

"You just had a freak out," Suzanne finished for her nodding in comprehension.

Lucy relaxed and smiled. "Yeah, just a freak out. I'm fine now. Go get changed." Suzanne kissed Lucy on the cheek and ran down the hall to her room. Lucy rushed into her own room and pulled on her uniform. She pulled her workbag off the shelf and double-checked its contents; apron, float, pens, notepad, computer card, gum and a nametag. Lucy involuntarily scowled at the nametag. The nametag was the only part of the job that everyone hated but their jack ass of a manager Shawn made them wear them. Lucy thought they were tacky and unnecessary. Servers often switched tags throughout the night so Lucy became Nick or Suzanne until Shawn caught them and made them switch back. Lucy added her keys and her wallet to the bag and threw it over her shoulder.

Lucy looked at herself in the full-length mirror hanging on the back of her door. She had to admit that she looked pretty cute. She had a nice figure and the skirt hugged her hips and her legs weren't too long but shapely. Her neck was long and lean and her face was very pretty.

"Not bad," she said to herself approvingly, "for a girl who went crazy for a little bit today, not bad at all."

"Move bitches!" Paige yelled from the hallway. Lucy grabbed her bag and walked out the door while pulling on her coat. Suzanne and Paige were walking slightly ahead of her and they didn't slow their steps for Paige to reach out and bang on the RA Vanessa's door, "Suzanne, Lucy and Paige are going to work!" Paige yelled.

"Ok!" came a muffled, flighty voice from within, "Have fun!"

"Do you think she would have said the same thing if you had told her we were going out to buy some crack?" Lucy asked comically as they descended the stairs. The girls laughed.

"Probably!" Paige said as they met up with Anastasia on the second floor and hurried out the door. Nick was waiting in his car and Simon stood beside with the passenger door open and the seat flipped forward to admit them.

"Looking good ladies!" Simon complimented as they started to pile into the back seat.

"As per usual," Nick replied training his eye on Paige as she leaned over to kiss him before plopping down half on the seat and half on Suzanne. Once the backseat was sufficiently full of women, Simon pushed his seat back into place, slid in and closed the door.

"Hit it buddy," Simon commanded. Nick's foot responded and the car lurched forward. "I love Fridays!" Simon added as Nick turned out of the University to the main road to town. Simon hit play on the ancient CD player and Hedley blared from the speakers at a deafening level. Lucy grinned. Tonight was going to be a great night- she could feel it.

They had gotten to work in one piece which was a miracle considering that Nick drove like a maniac. By four, they were all standing in the restaurant's pass-through with the five other servers who were working that night. Simon was on the kitchen side of the pass-through, standing beside the head chef Ben, his kitchen uniform gleaming white and his carrot top hair confined beneath his chefs hat. He was the assistant night chef and loved it; his shy demeanor preferring the intensity and camaraderie of the kitchen to dealing with customers. Shawn, the night manager called them all to order and ran through the usual Friday night pre-shift and pep talk. His pep talks were on the best of days annoying, and on the worst of days, like this day, he was downright offensive.

"Ladies, keep your lipstick fresh and if your skirt slides up a little, there is no need to panic, think of the regulars." Anastasia made a vomiting motion behind his back.

"But what if MY skirt slides up a little?" Nick challenged, "Can I call the labour board then?" Shawn ignored him and kept yammering. Lucy tuned him out.

By the time he was finished, the foyer was full and the hostesses were starting to seat, "Let's do this people." Shawn yelled as everyone scattered to greet the first tables.

It was a busy Friday night. Lucy had great tables and the kitchen was on the ball. Food was coming out fast and perfect, people were happy and as a result, tipping well. "Hey Lucy," Ben called from the line. Lucy looked up from the coffee she was pouring. "Who is better looking? Me or Simon?"

"Ben," Simon laughed while plating a steak and poking it gently to confirm its doneness, "When I went out with your Mom last night she said I was way better looking than you." This earned him a cuff upside the head but judging from the gales of laughter from the staff within earshot, Lucy figured it was worth it.

"I think whoever sells me my dessert bill for table 21 is the best looking," Lucy said indicating her apple crumble waiting to be run. Ben was faster, he grabbed the ticket and flung it across the hot plate to Lucy's waiting hand. "Ben wins!" Lucy grabbed the dessert in one hand and punched the ticket with the other; "he is so hot I might just start taking off my clothes right now."

"Awwww Lucy!" Simon moaned. Lucy laughed. Shawn came into the pass-through.

"Ben, table 62 has an allergy to onions. She wants the Alfredo, is that ok?" Ben stared at the ceiling thinking of the recipe when he thought of a better idea.

"Lucy?" Ben looked at her and when Shawn rolled his eyes he replied, "shortcut!"

"Um," Lucy thought for a second. She flipped through the recipes in her mind; "Onion powder in the sauce but there isn't any in the rose sauce if she wants to swap that in."

"HA!" Ben yelled, "She thinks I'm hot and she makes me look

smart!" Lucy laughed and went to run out her dessert and coffee. Her memory wasn't failing her - it was just fine. She ran the coffee and dessert to table 21 and headed to a computer station to print their bill. Suddenly, Anastasia was at her elbow.

"I hate the new girl," she hissed in Lucy's ear.

"There's a new girl?" Lucy asked. She had been so busy all night that she hadn't even looked at any other section to see if there were trainees.

Anastasia stomped her foot in irritation. "The one with the greasy hair who looks like she is going to hang herself at any moment!" Lucy looked up and did see the gangly girl following Nick around training with him. Anastasia was usually dramatic but Lucy had to admit that she was right about this one; the girl did look very depressed. "She just ran a salmon to my table and asked them 'who ordered the fish thing?'" Anastasia raged, "Honestly, is she trying to make me lose money?"

"What's her name?" Lucy asked.

"What's who's name?"

"The new girl." said Lucy starting to laugh.

"Her name is 'new girl'," Anastasia raged, "and by tomorrow she will be known as, 'the new girl that never came back to work because Stasia made her cry!'"

"You are going to Hell Stasia," Lucy was laughing.

"And you my friend will be there with me," Anastasia grinned, "If you will excuse me, I have a young life to ruin." She headed off on her mission, weaving around servers and customers towards Nick and his poor shadow of a trainee. Lucy pulled her bill from the printer while still watching Anastasia. She laughed to herself as she pulled out a pen from her apron to sign her bill when she froze, pen suspended in mid air.

Nathaniel sat at one of the tables by the pass through,

smiling at her. He wore jeans and a tight black t-shirt. He looked amazing. His face was as beautiful as it had been 12 hours before. His eyes glistened with the smile on his handsome face. Lucy had two very mixed feelings; she was horrified and yet elated to see him. She could not stop her heart from fluttering and her palms from sweating at the thrill of seeing him again. She could not stop herself from wishing that she could run to him and hug him tightly. With that, though, came a mental horror. She was having a hallucination, for the third time in twenty four hours.

A busser named Kim was walking past and Lucy stopped her. "Hey Kim, can you do me a favor?" Lucy asked lightly.

"Sure," Kim said shrugging.

"Bring this bill to the guy sitting at 43 please." Lucy handed Kim the billfold and waited. Kim took it, nodded and started to walk towards table 43. She stopped.

"Hey Lucy, are you new? Did you forget your table numbers?" Kim asked jovially.

"Why?" Lucy asked swallowing hard.

"There isn't anyone sitting at 43. It's empty. Where do you want this to go?"

"Ha," Lucy said trying to sound normal. "Just kidding, thanks Kim, don't worry about it." Kim shrugged and walked away.

The blood began to pulse in Lucy's ears so hard it drowned out the pumping music. Her throat went dry, her hands began to shake and tears began to blur her vision. She blinked them back trying to will her self back to sanity. *He's not real. He's not real. He doesn't exist. He doesn't exist. Breathe. Breathe.* Lucy realized that she had been holding her breath and released a huge lungful of air.

Nathaniel's facial expression changed to concern and he walked over to her. "Lucy?" he said with worry. He was standing beside her but Lucy didn't look at him, she stared straight ahead.

"Lucy, are you alright?"

"You aren't real," she managed to mutter between clenched teeth, "You aren't real." He nodded as if this confirmed something for him.

"I assure you Lucy that I am very real," he reached out as if to prove this to her but she flinched away.

"Go away, get out of my head," she turned on her heel and walked quickly back to her section. She billed table 21, cleared plates from 22 and collected a visa card from 23. Lucy didn't even look at any of her tables while doing this. *Keep it together. He doesn't exist.* Lucy went to the computer in the pass-through to run through the Visa card.

"Lucy," he was behind her this time, leaning over her shoulder. She could feel his breath on her neck and an involuntary shudder coursed down her spine.

"Not real, not here, ignore it," she whispered to herself.

"I am telling you Lucy," he said with confidence, "I am completely real." She felt him put his hands on her shoulders and ran his thumbs up the back of her neck. Heat radiated from him and Lucy felt her muscles relax in response. It took everything she had not to lean back into him, close her eyes and become enveloped in his tenderness. Lucy instead stiffened and rolled her shoulders violently, shaking him off.

"Lucy?" Shawn called her from the opposite end of the pass-through. *Please ask about the dude man-handling me. Please.* "You're cut, finish your tables and get off my clock," Shawn didn't wait for a response but walked away to cut more staff in preparation for the end of the rush. It was usually at this point that Lucy would offer to take over for another server to be able to stay longer. For once, she could not wait to get out of the building.

"Lucy," Nathaniel said softly. She ignored him and turned

abruptly to the restaurant. She billed her last table and cleared the last of their plates. She managed to smile and wish them a good night. Lucy only had a few side duties to do and then she could leave. She could leave and mourn the loss of her sanity and her life, as she knew it. This might be the last night she worked. This might have been her last day of school. It was all over now. She had to hold it together for a little while longer. No one could see her lose it. She would go home, call Doctor Hannon and he would take her to the hospital and make sure that she was well taken care of. She walked to the computer in the corner to settle her checks and print off her cash out report. Nathaniel appeared beside her seconds later.

"Please leave me alone," she said begging in a whisper.

"Look," he said, "I am real and I can prove it to you. Watch." He walked calmly over to the doorway to the pass-through. It was by far the busiest, most crowded spot in the restaurant. There was a constant flow of servers, bussers, hostesses and managers coming and going with plates and trays full of food. To stop and stand there was something akin to a death wish. If you didn't actually get knocked down, you would certainly receive a tongue lashing from someone who had to go around you. Nathaniel stopped, turned, crossed his arms and stared directly at Lucy to prove his point. Lucy assumed that everyone would just walk right through him but that didn't happen.

It was obvious that no one could see Nathaniel. He was certainly a guy that would get noticed. It was clear though that they knew something was there. Lucy watched as staff members moved around Nathaniel, without even realizing that they were doing it. It looked like someone had thrown a rock in a river and forced the water to change its path. Lucy watched in amazement as Shawn, his hands piled with dirty plates, did a graceful pirouette in an effort to avoid Nathaniel. No one around Shawn seemed to notice this bizarre behavior.

Nathaniel looked at Lucy expectantly and then held up one finger. *There's more? Lucy thought.* He walked a few feet over to where Anastasia was setting up a coffee tray. She set out two cups and reached over to fill a bowl with creamers. She then bent down to retrieve a new sugar caddy from the shelf below the counter. When she wasn't looking, Nathaniel picked up the coffee pot, filled the cups and set the pot back down. Anastasia rose, and reached for the pot. She paused as she realized that the cups were already full, glanced around and seeing no one in the vicinity, shrugged and carried her tray away. Nathaniel put both hands out, faced them palms upward as though he had just performed a magic trick. He walked back to Lucy, "See? I am real." A million questions flooded her mind but Lucy held them at bay.

She took a deep breath and muttered, "Fine, you are real. For right now though I am at work and will get fired if they see me talking to myself like a crazy person. Please wait outside for me." Nathaniel grinned, thrilled with this. Lucy watched as he walked back out through the front doors, customers and staff walked around him without even knowing he was there.

Lucy was on the brink of hysteria while doing her side duties. She stocked the straws and teas and took out the garbage while barely holding herself together. The fact that Nathaniel was a solid object did not change anything. Lucy was the only one who could see him. She ignored the ridiculous emotional voice in her head that was rejoicing that he was real and he had come to find her. She instead focused on the serious, solid voice that was urging her not to get too involved but figure this out and make him go away. The two voices seemed to be having a war in her head and the stress of it was going to crack Lucy in half. She finally finished her duties and managed to balance her cash out. She grabbed her belongings from the staff room, didn't say goodbye to anyone and bolted out the back door.

Lucy headed for the bus stop. She didn't look around for him and within seconds she could hear his footfalls as he reached her and fell into step at her side. "Lucy I..." he started. Lucy did not break her step or look at him,

"I have no interest in looking like a mental case even if I am going crazy. Do not talk to me until we are alone."

"You aren't going crazy," he said with conviction.

"Stop!" she almost yelled at him.

"Sorry," he muttered. He tucked his hands in his jeans pockets and dropped his head like a scolded puppy. Why did he have to be so cute? They sat at the bus stop side by side. Lucy stared into the night thinking of all the questions she would ask him and making a massive effort not to look at him. Nathaniel sat at her side, his elbows resting on his knees. He didn't seem uncomfortable or awkward. In fact, Lucy had never met anyone who seemed more comfortable in his own skin. She could feel him beside her and when a breeze blew by she could smell him – that wonderful sea salt, honey smell.

The bus pulled up and Lucy almost clawed the doors open in an effort to get some distance between she and Nathaniel. The bus was mostly empty. Lucy headed to the back and Nathaniel followed. Lucy sat in the last row in the corner by the window. Nathaniel moved as if to sit beside her but Lucy pointed covertly to her left. A look of amusement crossed his face but he obeyed – walked three feet over and sat down. The bus lurched forward and Lucy looked out the window. A few moments later, the bus stopped to admit another passenger. The man who got on was disheveled and filthy. His hair was matted and stuck up at all angles and his clothing was ripped and dirty. The man was talking to himself.

Actually, he was arguing with him self, "You're wrong! That is how it happened. You have it all wrong!" he stated as he showed his bus pass and walked down the aisle, "I did not do that! That was you!" He took a seat a few rows ahead of Lucy, "How could you pin that on me? Not me, not me, not me!" Lucy saw the bus driver roll his eyes in the rear view mirror before pulling out. Lucy raised her eyebrows and looked at Nathaniel.

He got the point immediately and laughed out loud, "No Lucy," he said shaking his head, "That guy is actually crazy." Lucy snorted in response and looked back out the window. They rode the rest of the short drive in silence back to the University. Lucy got off at her stop and walked quickly back to her dorm. Nathaniel walked at an easy gait beside her. She entered the building and took the stairs two at a time, rushed down the hall not pausing beside Vanessa's door to knock and yell, "Lucy's home for the night!"

"Ok babe!" came the muffled voice from inside.

"With an invisible man," Lucy mumbled to herself. She got to her door, fished her keys out of her bag and unlocked it. Lucy took a step in her room and felt Nathaniel behind her. She turned to him, "I need to change, wait out here." She sounded calmer then she felt. She closed the door on him. As she pulled off her uniform and pulled on a pair of sweats and a tank top she wondered what would happen if she didn't open the door. Would he stand out there all night? If he did stand there all night was it because he wanted to or because he was on a mission to drive her mad? There were so many questions and so much she needed to know. While she pulled her mass of red curls into a pony-tail, Lucy thought of her list of questions for Nathaniel. She had a game plan firmly in place before she opened the door.

Nathaniel was still there with a small smile on his gorgeous face but he was holding two coffees and a paper bag. "Hungry?" he asked as if this was a study date. Lucy realized that she was starving. Today she had only eaten a donut and two bites of a sandwich at lunch. That seemed like days ago. She recognized the cups from the café downstairs; he must have run down while she was changing. That was sweet of him. She sternly reminded herself that sweet or not, he was not real.

"Did you steal that stuff?"

Nathaniel looked shocked and insulted. "Of course not."

"Then how did you pay for it?" Lucy demanded.

"I left money in the register," he explained calmly, "with a tip."

"Oh," Lucy said feeling like a jerk.

"Can I come in?" he asked holding up the food like a peace offering. She didn't answer but moved aside. He walked in and looked around. "Nice," he said with the same tone that implied this was a social call.

"Look," Lucy demanded, "I'm going to need some answers here." To her dismay, Nathaniel shook his head.

"First we eat," he said with authority, "I am hungry and so are you. I don't want you to be hungry."

"Fine," she pouted. This was not going well. She thumped down on the couch to show her displeasure. Nathaniel set the coffees down on her side table and pulled two turkey sandwiches, two bags of chips and two bottles of water from the bag and set them all in between them on the couch.

"I cooked all day," he joked. Lucy stopped herself from laughing. He looked amused at her for a moment but said nothing. They ate in silence. Lucy was on pins and needles but Nathaniel still looked completely content and comfortable. Lucy finished her late dinner and balled up the wrappings and tossed them in the bag.

"So..." he said conversationally, "how was the rest of your

day?" Lucy stiffened, rage coursed through her. How dare he make light of this whole thing?

"It was horrible!" she shot at him, her voice full of venom.

"Oh," he said surprised. Tears started to prick at her eyes again but she stopped them reminding herself that crying would only make things worse. She rounded on him.

"I woke up this morning in a really good mood because I had met this awesome guy last night but I soon discovered that I had made him up in my head so I went and scared the crap out of my friends and my mentor. Then I decided that I wasn't crazy, I was just tired so I go to work and discover that the guy isn't imaginary, he's just invisible to everyone but me so I am not fully crazy, but there is something definitely wrong with me. There is something so wrong with me that even if I am not crazy I will be by the time I wake up in the morning so yeah pal, I had a pretty crappy day!" She was out of breath from her tirade and sat breathing heavily, waiting for a reaction.

"So…" he asked starting to smile, "I'm the guy right?"

"ARGH!" Lucy growled and threw herself against the back of the couch in frustration.

"Lucy, Lucy," he leaned over to her, she shied back, "I was just kidding, calm down it's going to be ok." She glared at him sourly. He reached back and picked up her coffee. While handing it to her he said, "I've eaten, you've eaten, let's get to the bottom of this together ok?" She took a sip of her coffee and began to calm down which angered her again because she was listening to him. She curbed her anger and took a deep breath.

"Ok, I need some answers," she said calmly.

"All right," he replied professionally.

"From you."

"Got it," he leaned back and crossed one ankle over his knee.

"I promise to answer what I can."

"Good." Lucy nodded. She was in control now. This is what she wanted, an interrogation, information, facts and knowledge. This was what she could do - she could get answers. She decided to start at the basics.

"Are you alive?"

"Yes," he answered while checking his pulse.

"Please don't joke," she said sternly.

"Sorry," he replied soberly.

"Are you a ghost?"

"No."

"Are you sure?"

"Yes." So there went her 'I see dead people' theory. Time to move on.

"What is your name?"

"Nathaniel."

"What is your last name?"

"Last name?" he looked up at the ceiling thinking, "I don't know."

"You don't know or don't have one?" Lucy prodded.

"I don't know and I don't know if I have one."

"How old are you?"

He glanced down at himself, "Nineteen?"

"You're guessing," she said irritated.

"Yes," he said with conviction. Lucy sighed. It appeared that her invisible man also had amnesia. The irony of the two of them together in the same room did not escape her.

"Where did you come from?"

"I don't know for sure."

"How did you get here?" Nathaniel lit up pleased that he knew the answer to this one.

"I fell."

"You fell?" she stared at him.

"I fell." he repeated.

"You fell from where?"

"Well from higher up obviously." He cocked his head, "That's how I fell."

"Ok," Lucy began to build a theory, "so you fell, hit your head, became invisible and have amnesia."

"Good theory," he said quickly while nodding, his dark hair glinting in the light "let's go with that and talk about you."

"No," Lucy was stern, "I am not even remotely close to done."

"Ok," he said sitting back on the couch, "Go."

She paused and rethought. "What happened before you fell?"

"I had a dream," A smile touched the edges of his lips.

"A dream?" Lucy asked dubiously, "What was the dream about?"

"You," his face broke out in a full grin.

"Me?" Lucy was stunned, "What was I doing?"

"We were in a park, we were laughing and you were taking pictures."

"Oh," Lucy thought that sounded nice, "I was taking pictures?"

"Yes, of me, the scenery, everything," he replied. "That's why I was so surprised about your photographic memory."

"I see," Lucy said. At least the dream made some sense, "So how soon after the dream did you fall?"

"Right away."

Lucy had no more questions about the dream, or none that would be appropriate to ask. "Am I the only one who can see you?"

"It appears that way, yes."

"Why me?"

"I don't know."

"Did you know yesterday that I was the only one who could see you?"

"No, I didn't," he shook his head to confirm.

"When did you figure that out?"

"Today," he replied. "I had some awkward moments."

"That was the theory you were trying to prove," she said as the pieces fell into place together. "Why didn't you tell me?"

"You still would have freaked out and most likely not believed me." She agreed with that.

"Do you have a wallet?"

"No."

"Jewelry?"

"No," he said checking his wrists to be sure.

"Scars, identifying marks, tattoos?"

"No, no and no."

"Were you looking for something last night?" she asked, "You seemed to be looking around."

"Maybe," he shrugged.

"Looking for what?"

"I don't know."

"What did you mean last night when you said you hadn't used your voice in a while."

"That's how it felt."

"Why hadn't you used your voice?"

"I don't know," he shrugged again. Lucy changed her line of questioning again. She was getting desperate for any information at all.

"Why don't people run into you if they can't see you?"

Nathaniel took a moment to think.

"I believe they sense something is there and the subconscious mind reacts for them."

"Why didn't Anastasia become more concerned when the coffees filled themselves? She's not a dumb girl, why didn't she even question it? Why didn't anyone see a coffee pot floating in the air?"

"Well," he said thoughtfully, "I discovered today that anything I am holding becomes invisible too so that's why no one saw a floating coffee pot. Anastasia didn't question the coffee because the human mind assumes that which is most logical. Anastasia assumed she had filled the cups herself and just forgot about it."

"Does that work for me too?" Lucy questioned. "If you touched me, would I become invisible too?"

"Nope," he shook his head, his jet black hair glinting in the light, "I tested that today too. While your 'friend' Janielle was talking to you, I touched your arm. You didn't disappear."

This was not getting better and Lucy was getting more frustrated as each second passed. "Can I see you because of my photographic memory? Does this have anything to do with my particular brain?"

"I don't know," he said. Lucy was getting frustrated.

"Do you have a mother?"

"Everyone has a mother," he replied with certainty.

"Who is she?"

"I don't know." Nathaniel shrugged.

"Father?" Lucy probed.

"No idea."

"Friends, cousins, a boss?"

"Sorry, I've got nothing."

"What is your purpose here?"

At this, Nathaniel showed his first signs of frustration. "That," he said tersely, "is what I am trying to find out." He paused. "Look Lucy, we can do this all night if you want. I just really enjoy your company either way." He smiled at her but stopped when he got a look of coldness in return. "But the answer is generally going to be that 'I don't know. I have almost no idea of what is going on. I am frustrated too but at the same time there is no reason to act on it. I can only assume that the answers will come when I am ready for them. I just have to have faith." Lucy looked at him stunned. Such a zen-like approach was totally out of her realm of capabilities. She decided to ignore his point all together.

"What do you do?"

"I don't know."

"Do you have anything to do with the flowers in the quad? I also found a leaf in my Shakespeare Anthology."

"I don't know."

She moved on again, "Where did you get the money to pay for the food?"

"I don't know."

"Did you steal it?" she asked this casually, trying to get him to admit to something.

"I am no thief," he replied quickly and sternly.

"How do you know you aren't a thief?"

"That much I do know," he sounded like he was sure about that answer. She was out of questions and had no more information then when she started. She tightened her jaw. This wasn't fair. It wasn't fair that Nathaniel should literally fall into her life, cause chaos and have no answers for it. She began firing questions at a rapid rate, barely waiting for the answer. She purposefully repeated some questions in an effort to catch him in a lie.

"How old are you?"

"I don't know."

"Where were you born?"

"I don't know."

"What is your mother's maiden name?"

"I don't know."

"What do you do for a living?"

"I don't know."

"Is someone looking for you?"

"I don't know."

"Why are you here?"

"I don't know."

"How do you get back from where you came from?"

"I don't know."

"Why me?"

"I don't know."

Lucy finally, after a long day of holding it together, cracked. Her mask of composure began to break. Her anger, frustration and pain spilled out of the crack in a wave.

"STOP SAYING THAT!" she yelled.

"Saying what?" his eyes widened in shock.

"THAT!"

"What?" he said, desperately as if he would do anything to please her.

"Stop saying 'I don't know'!"

"But Lucy," Nathaniel said pleadingly, "I don't know and I wish I did. I know this is very…"

"I HATE THOSE WORDS!" she yelled at him. Lucy's walls were made of concrete and although it made her room very susceptible to temperature changes, it also allowed her to scream her head off and her floor mates could not hear her.

"You hate the words, 'I don't know'?" he was speaking softly like how you would talk to an angry caged animal. Right now that was exactly what Lucy felt like. "Why?"

"Because I've never said them!" she stood up and started to pace, "I know everything!" she raged. "I know more than anyone at this University or in this town. I know all the answers, I always have. Always. What I need to know, I learn and then I have it. Forever. I know the periodic table, the migrating patterns of the monarch butterfly, the complete works of Shakespeare and how a refrigerator works! I know the name of every star in the solar system, I know the name of every country in the world and its capitol and its gross national product, I know all the presidents and how a carburetor operates, I know the complete history of Ghingas Khan and Ghandi and Mozart. I know the rules of polo and how to make wine! I know everything!" her voice began to break and a sob forced its way to the surface, "EVERYTHING! But I don't know this!" she slammed her foot on the ground, "and I don't know you!" she pointed violently at him, he did not flinch, "I don't know what's going on and I need the answers and I can't.... I can't..." she sobbed again, an ugly guttural sob, "I can't get them...and...I feel like I am breaking..." she couldn't finish. Lucy was exhausted from her tirade and she staggered back to the couch and fell on it. She put her head in her hands and let the cry come.

The cry had been waiting all day to arrive and it was violent and relentless when she allowed it to flow through her. It shook Lucy to the core and she thought her chest might break open with the force of it. She sobbed and wailed into her hands. Suddenly, Nathaniel was kneeling in front of her. He wrapped his arms over her shoulders and tucked her head into his neck. The warmth enveloped Lucy and despite her better judgement, she leaned into him and cried. He held her, strong and supporting, willing to wait forever for the bawling to cease. She allowed herself to get swept away with him for a moment - permitting herself to need him so much that it hurt.

But the bottom line here was that Nathaniel was the reason for her crying. This could not go on. She could not allow it. With every bit of strength she could muster, Lucy pushed against his chest as hard as she could, "NO!" she growled at him. Nathaniel leaned back on his heels looking uneasy but not upset.

"Lucy," he said softly with so much caring that she almost faltered.

"No!" she increased her resolve, "No, you don't get to do this! I want my life back. Do you hear me? I want my brain, my emotions and my life back in my own control. I want you to get out of here and leave me alone!" she snarled at him, "Get out!" Nathaniel immediately stood up and stepped back from her.

"If that is what you want Lucy," he said with sadness in his voice, "then you will never see me again."

"Go away," she said with more conviction then she felt. Nathaniel moved to the door. He opened it but paused and looked back at her. She jutted her jaw out defiantly and looked him directly in the eye. "I said GO!" she yelled.

"If you ever need me," he said.

"I won't," she shot back, her voice was full of disgust.

"But if you do," he sounded so hurt that Lucy wanted to die, "you just have to call me." He walked out the door without waiting for a response and closed it quietly behind him.

"Hate to break it to you pal," Lucy yelled at the now closed door, "but you don't have a phone!"

Nathaniel was gone and the emptiness in the room was overwhelming. It felt as if the lights had dimmed and the heat had shut down. Lucy fought the urge to run after him and tell him she didn't care that he was invisible or imaginary or anything at all. She just wanted him to hold her again, hold her forever and never let go. She couldn't do that though, it had to be wrong. He was gone forever, Lucy would never see Nathaniel again and despite the fact that she had know him only a little more than twenty four hours, the impact of that was devastating. He was gone and a new wave of pain hit Lucy's chest. She fell over on her couch and cried. What had she done?

Chapter Four
Answers

"The reason I talk to myself is that I'm the only one
whose answers I accept."
~George Carlin

Lucy woke up the next morning. She was lying on her couch and wearing the same thing she had been wearing last night. She sat up and crumpled tissues fell off her like snow. Lucy rubbed her arms. She had pulled a thin blanket over herself at some point in the night but it was no replacement for her cozy comforter. It was early, just past dawn and Lucy wrapped the blanket around her and waddled over to the door to check the thermostat. She turned it up knowing full well the effects would not be felt for several hours. Lucy stood for a moment and took stock of herself. Surprisingly, she felt ok. She had to come to terms with the fact that there were no answers and no amount of crying would change that. She didn't acknowledge the twinge of pain she felt thinking of Nathaniel walking out the door. Her life was back in control and that was what mattered. Lucy resolved not to think about him, she wouldn't even think his name. If she didn't think about him then this pain would pass, eventually.

Lucy took a deep breath. *Keep busy. Don't think about it.* She resolved to herself. The first order of business was a much-needed shower and (her stomach growled in protest) some food. She picked out a clean set of clothes, grabbed her shower bag and headed to the bathroom. It was far too early for any of the other girls to be awake on a Saturday so Lucy had the bathroom to herself. She took her time showering, drying her hair and applying a little makeup. Looking at herself in the mirror, Lucy noted that she looked and felt much better. Her stomach growled again, "ok, ok," she muttered.

The cafeteria was fairly empty. Lucy loaded her plate with eggs, bacon and toast. She grabbed a coffee and an orange juice, took a seat and tucked in. While eating her monstrous meal she considered what to do with her day. *Keep busy. Keep busy. Don't think about him.* There was laundry to do and she could go to the library. There was also the party at the boy's dorm that night which should offer plenty of distraction. She finished her breakfast, deposited her plate on the rack and headed back to her room. She collected up her dirty laundry and walked back down the stairs and one floor down to the basement laundry room.

The laundry room was the same décor as the rest of the dorm. There were rows of Harvest gold colored washers and dryers and the counter tops were covered in peeling Formica. The floors were layered in an avocado green peel and stick tile but it was clean and the room brightly lit. Lucy loaded two washers and sat down to wait. The two armchairs, couch and TV were obviously donations and also from the seventies. Lucy leaned over and turned on the TV which was a huge wooden box that you had to physically turn a dial. She watched the news half hoping to hear about a missing young man who might have amnesia. No such luck. The weather man came on with his bright smile and wacky tie.

"Ok folks, it appears as though we have all moved to Florida!" He bellowed as he stood in front of a map of Illinois. "Here's the thing, and I have never seen anything like this before. The town of Mulbridge and surrounding area continue to have unexpected, unseasonably warm temperatures. This time last year, we were having a snow storm and today, the mayor has authorized the water park to be opened! It is a great time to live in Mulbridge everyone! And look at this," the satellite imagery changed slightly, "we SHOULD be a part of this massive precipitation front that is currently overtaking Chicago, but nope, it is slipping north and avoiding us all together. So get out there and enjoy it Mulbridge because I have NO idea how long it is going to last!"

"The weather man doesn't know how long the weather is going to last," Lucy mused moodily while shaking her head. The flowers in the quad popped into her head. Could Nathaniel really have anything to do with all this? *Could it hurt to do a little research on him?* Her inner voice gently prodded. Lucy felt like a drug addict. She needed to keep herself busy and stop thinking about him.

Lucy was folding her laundry a little while later as her mind wandered over and over the same thoughts. *Stop thinking about him.* She urged herself. Suddenly, the fluorescent lights above her began to flicker. Lucy winced at them.

"This place is falling apart," she murmured as two of the lights went out altogether. Then all the others started to flicker and Lucy stopped what she was doing. Was there some sort of power surge? Was there a problem with one of the circuits? Then Lucy could hear a light squeaking sound from off in the corner of the room, from behind the washing machines by the door. The room was half dark and the other half was flashing on and off. The noise got louder and multiplied. Lucy went up on her tip toes to peek over the row of machines and squealed in fear at what she saw. It was rats. They were streaming in a line from between two washing machines. There were at least ten of them and more were coming. Lucy scrambled on top of the washing machines and screamed again as they came closer. They weren't ordinary rats either. They were huge, some the size of cats with large red eyes. Terror gripped her when she realized that they surrounded the machine she was crouched upon. They weren't just passing through, they seemed to be after her. The rodents clambered at the washing machine, trying to climb up, their claws leaving huge gouges in the harvest gold paint. Lucy looked toward the door.

"Help!" she screamed. "Somebody help!" The rats seemed to respond to her yelling and became even more intent to get to her. They scrambled over each other; their small squeaks had become full screeches. They began climbing on top of one another and were creating ladders of rat bodies for others to climb up higher. Soon they would reach the top of the washing machine. Lucy started jumping from one machine to the other, making her way toward the door but this was where most of the rats were and the door opened inward. The sea of huge rodent bodies would block the door from opening even if she could lean over and reach the handle which she couldn't.

Lucy was trapped.

Her mind worked quickly thinking of option after option for escape. She scanned the room again, trying to think of a way out. The flow of rats had stopped and now they were either climbing on top of each other or running in a track around the washers trying to find a way to get to her. Lucy's eye caught a sight of red off in the far corner. It was the fire alarm. But how to get to it? It was over where the couch and TV were and there would be no way to reach it from the safety of the washing machines. But she could reach them from the TV.

Silently thanking the solidity and heartiness of 1970 electronics, Lucy ran to the end of the row of washers and made the easy jump to the top of the large oak TV. She crouched there for a minute to make sure that it would indeed hold her weight. When the rats realized where she was, they abandoned their previous ladder technique at the washers and started a similar process at the base of the TV. The TV was lower though and Lucy had to kick at a rat as she leaned over and pulled the red handle. It screamed in protest and fell back, only to get back up and try again. The bell exploded into the air and muted the squealing rats. Lucy jumped back to the washing machine and crouched waiting, hoping, praying that someone would come.

The rats did not like the raging clanging of the fire bell and started to migrate back to their point of entry. More than half of them were gone but the other half were still clawing fervently at the washing machine when the door flew open and a maintenance man burst into the room with a fire extinguisher in his hand.

"Fire?" he yelled over the bell looking at Lucy.

She shook her head, pointed at the ground and yelled, "Rats!"

The maintenance man looked down at the ground and hollered at the swarms of rats at his feet. Using the only weapon he had, he blasted the fire extinguisher at the hoard and they quickly began to disperse, crawling back over each other to go out the way they came. Finally, the last one ran its now white tail out between the two machines. The repair man, whose nametag on his sweat-stained uniform said, "Cliff" looked up at Lucy in shock. His hair was thin and greying but his shocked eyes were a bright blue.

"What the hell was that? I've never seen so many rats!" he

yelled while pulling out a walkie talkie and yelling into it. "All good Jim, call off the alarm." The bell immediately stopped.

"You should have been here three minutes earlier, there were twice as much!" Lucy exclaimed as he helped her down off the machine.

"Are you hurt?" he asked as he examined the runnels of chipped paint on the side of the washing machines.

"No, fine really," Lucy said being somewhat surprised herself to find that she was unhurt and relatively not upset.

"It must be the warm weather." Cliff said, "They must be having trouble finding dens because it's been so dry. But really so strange though." He looked around and shook his head, "What room are you in so I can put it in the report?" He pulled out a piece of paper and a pencil, licked the pencil and looked at her expectantly.

"4B Lucy Bower," she replied while walking back and retrieving her basket of clothes. "And you can tell them that there were at least fifty of those things in here. They gotta get someone in."

"Yeah," Cliff said as he tucked away the paper and ran a weary hand across the back of his neck, "just do me a favor and don't spread this around. The last thing I need is massive panic in the girl's dorms."

"I can do that," Lucy agreed as she moved to the door, "as long as you promise to take care of it. That was seriously creepy. It felt like they were after me."

Cliff laughed, "Stupid animals, they were probably trying to get to the water in the machines."

Lucy shuddered lightly as she looked at the floor, immediately the image of all those rats popped into her head. She shook it off.

"You sure you're ok?" Cliff asked. He leaned towards her in that nice Uncle way. He was concerned and Lucy didn't need him to be.

"I am fine." she smiled at him in a reassuring way and headed out the door.

She brought her laundry up to her room, put it away, cleaned her room and sat down on her futon. She thought about what Cliff said about the weather. This was the third time that someone had talked about odd occurrences due to the climate. The third occurrence since she 'bumped' into the invisible Nathaniel that doesn't know who he is. Lucy sat back and tapped her finger over her lips as she thought. It just didn't add up and Lucy could not accept something that didn't add up. With determination, she stood quickly and took a sharp breath. Lucy would go to the one place that was full of answers. Grabbing her bag, Lucy decided to go to the library.

The library foyer was dark, especially compared to the blinding morning sun outside. Lucy paused to allow her eyes to adjust. Then she glanced around and took it all in. Despite the strangeness of her mission, Lucy still felt a thrill when she walked in the library even though she had been there a million times. The term 'kid in a candy store' applied. Lucy loved the library and the information it held. She loved books.

The library was the oldest building on campus and by far the best cared for. Restorations had been done every decade to ensure the building's historic integrity. The efforts showed. Lucy looked around at the dark mahogany walls, shelves and tables and marveled at the grandeur of it all. To her left was the massive curved circulation desk. The entire wall behind the desk was covered in hundreds of pigeonholes that were once used for storing circulation cards. Now, however, they were mostly empty because the library had become computerized several years ago. In front of Lucy were five huge tables surrounded by twenty spindle chairs. To her right were the books. About fifty shelves in three rows were jam packed with books. Behind the shelves, on the far right wall was a door that led to an attached computer lab. The lab had been added in an effort to modernize the University. It was tucked away to still maintain the library's historical vibe. On the left wall beside the circulation desk was a pair of mahogany French doors that led to the stairway to the second floor. The second floor held shelves and study carols ran the outside walls to allow for private study sessions. Lucy took a deep breath- this was exactly where she should be.

"Hi Lucy!" came an energetic voice from behind the desk. Lucy smiled at Ruth, the head librarian. Ruth was the happiest person Lucy had ever met. She was a round woman with black curly hair, rosy cheeks and a smile that would melt an iceberg.

"Pretty dead in here," Lucy observed noticing that she was the only student in the room.

"Well," Ruth replied grinning, "it is Saturday dear. No one comes in on Saturdays when it's not finals, no one except for you that is." She winked kindly.

"I just have to do some research," Lucy said.

"You know where everything is doll. Let me know if you need anything." Ruth turned and went back to her paperwork.

Lucy headed for the computer lab. She sat at the first computer in the row and wiggled the mouse so it came to life. She typed in her ID number and password to log in. Lucy rarely used the Internet. She preferred to rely on books and her own knowledge for research. She was sure she was the last person in North America to prefer to use snail mail. Well, other than...him. She mailed handwritten letters to her mother who was much annoyed with this. Even Lucy's mom Sandra was far more computer savvy than her daughter and used her computer for everything from shopping to socializing with friends. "Ten minutes," Lucy promised herself as she wiggled in her chair, "that's all you get pal. I have a life to lead."

She began with the state missing person's website. She searched through every picture of every person that had gone missing in the last week and then extended her search to a month and a year before. She looked through every face and every profile but found nothing. She looked through newspaper articles in the area concerning accidents involving falls at construction zones or skydiving accidents – nothing. Lucy had gone well past her ten-minute limit but she was so wrapped up in it that she didn't notice or care. She looked through the crime stoppers website and the FBI's most wanted list feeling slightly relieved that he wasn't a serial killer. She looked up alien abductions but nothing fit the bill. She even searched for things like "invisibility" but found nothing but a website for a girdle that hid panty lines.

Lucy sat back and stretched. She glanced at her watch; it was two in the afternoon. Ten minutes had turned into three hours and she had no more information then when she started. She had tried her best and it appeared that he was to remain a mystery forever. Lucy felt her usual twinge of discomfort at mysteries but she pushed herself to move on. She had done everything she could and she had to let it go.

This whole situation was taking way too much time and effort on her part. She decided there was no connection between the warm weather and the invisible man. Lucy still thought that he could certainly still be a figment of her imagination or some kind of manifestation of an exhausted brain. The rats? Well the rats were the by-product of poor building maintenance and warm weather. She sucked in a deep breath and stretched. Enough was enough.

She logged off the computer and stood up. When she got back into the main building, Ruth was shelving in the far corner. It was clear no one else had thought to ruin their Saturday with a trip to the library. Since she was here, she might as well get something accomplished. Lucy had systematically been reading every book in the library and therefore committing them to memory. It was sadly, one of her favorite things to do. Currently, she was starting a new book, "Prisioners of War" by Alex Cartman and so she started at the A's and worked her way down the long aisle. *Read it, read it, read it* she thought as she passed all the A's and the B's. It was a childish routine but one that helped her to refocus. This reaffirmed the solid hold that Lucy had on the facts and reality of her life. The figment of her imagination or whatever Nathaniel the invisible man was would never be back and Lucy could get back to her well-ordered and controlled life. She retrieved the book and sat down at one of the tables. She opened it up and began to read.

A few moments later, Lucy was irritated to catch her mind wandering once again to Nathaniel. She had read the same paragraph three times. She shifted in her seat, took a sharp breath and forced herself to refocus. She started to read again but the nagging voice in her head was relentless. *There is one more thing you can try.* Lucy rolled her eyes at her own stubbornness. She could not let this go.

If Lucy concentrated very hard, she could use her brain like a search engine. If she didn't know what book to reference she had, in the past, allowed her brain to flip through the massive amount of information in her mind and find the answer while drawing from several sources at once. It was difficult and it usually gave her a headache but this was Lucy's last bit of hope. It was a long shot considering she had been thinking about this problem for two days now and nothing had popped up but maybe it was worth a try. She wondered also if it was the mystery itself that was bothering her or was it something more? How did he have such a strong hold on her? Maybe if she exhausted every effort, it would be easier to let this whole thing go.

The trick was that Lucy had to come up with the right question for this system to work. She weighed the options; there was no reason to ask something about Nathaniel's identity because she had never met him before. There had been no evidence in the newspapers that he even lived close so there was no point asking something specific about his origins. Finally, she settled on the only things that he had been certain about last night. He had fallen and his name was Nathaniel. It wasn't much but it was all she had to go on. With a big sigh, she laid her book down, rested her head on her forearms on the table, closed her eyes and thought, "Why did Nathaniel fall?" She released the question into her mind's extensive library. She squeezed her eyelids tight as she willed the question out until it took on a life of its own; tumbling and twisting through the recesses of her brain.

The words meticulously went through every bit of information. Images and pages flashed in her head at breakneck speed, the applicable words lighting up in response. Lucy had to view the results and dismiss them fast enough to take the next set of information. She could feel her head starting to ache in protest. She ignored it and continued. She saw every fall she had ever witnessed, she flipped through every book that had the words "why did" pushing novels, newspapers and magazines to the side the instant they appeared. The pain in her head increased and began to pulse through her temples. She had been at this for several minutes now, longer than she had ever had to before. The answer usually came quickly but her question had been so vague it was taking much longer. Lucy's brain became frantic; cross referencing now and pulling sentence after sentence to the forefront over and over. Lucy knew she should give up but she just couldn't bring herself to give up on this – on him. Lucy grunted in pain and effort as she pushed her mind faster, forcing it to find the answer. Finally, it pulled out several works and pushed the words out to her. Lucy stopped her mind and her mouth fell open in shock.

"FALLEN ANGEL,

ANGELS NATHANIEL, GABRIEL, MICHAEL,

LUCIFER FALLEN ANGEL"

Lucy's eyes snapped open and she sat panting in shock for a moment before she jumped from her chair and sprinted across the library to Ruth.

"Ruth! Ruth!" she yelled running up to her and grabbing on to the book cart to keep from falling over. "I need every book you have on Angels. The real ones, not hokey wear a pin on your lapel Angels but REAL Angels, the guys in Heaven with wings."

"Holy moly hon," Ruth's eyes were wide, "Are you ok?"

"I'm fine, I just need the books can you help me?"

"Sweetheart," Ruth replied lovingly, "You ears are bleeding. I'll get the books and some tissue." She slid past Lucy to the circulation desk.

Lucy reached up and touched her fingers to her ear. She saw with a form of detached shock that indeed, her ears were bleeding.

"Worth it," she muttered.

Chapter Five
Options

*"A peacefulness follows any decision,
even the wrong one."*
~Rita Mae Brown

Lucy spent the rest of the afternoon pouring through books on Angels, divinity and the holy order of things. She had never considered herself a religious person. Her parents had never taken her to church but they taught her the difference between right and wrong. They had taught her that there was a God and a Heaven but now that Lucy had to face it head on she wasn't sure what it all meant. She searched and searched and although Nathaniel's name was that of an archangel, not much else fit. There were no other reports of Angels being sent to Earth other than in the role of guardian or to pass on the word of God. The Immaculate Conception, the birth of Jesus and the burning bush were all events that were paired with the appearance of an Angel.

Angels came down to Earth to do things, to warn or prepare

humans for an upcoming happening. Why would he be sent here with no idea of his purpose to wander about invisible? Lucy also couldn't understand what she had to do with this. The people who had historically seen Angels were divine people. Lucy felt she was a good person but certainly not a holy person. She figured that it must be a strange fluke that she could see him. It must have something to do with her photographic memory not with whatever his celestial purpose on Earth was.

There was no mention of nature responding to Angels in any of the material. Lucy could not find a reason for the leaf's bizarre behavior the other night or the unseasonable weather. In Lucy's own reasoning though, she thought it would make sense for nature to be drawn to an Angel walking the Earth. God made nature. If Nathaniel was an Angel, it made sense that nature would respond to him. The rat incident didn't fit but Lucy considered Cliff's explanation and figured that it was possible the warm weather was throwing them off. Lucy also had a problem with how Nathaniel looked. He didn't look like the Angels in the books. His face and body were Heavenly but wasn't he supposed to have wings? Or be blond and blue eyed? The jet black hair and the crystal grey eyes did not fit with ones 'angelic' ideas. The images of Angels Lucy saw had wings, halos, robes and at times, a staff or a trumpet. The jeans and t-shirt were a little off the mark for angelic apparel. Lucy sighed. What was she supposed to do now?

Should she ask him about this? Was it healthy to have an invisible Angel in her life? Was it responsible to call him back into her life when she had been struggling so hard today to get him out? What about the feelings she had for him? Can you have feelings for someone like him or was it blasphemy or something? Would Lucy just be torturing herself by spending time with him? Lucy wondered if she needed more time to think about it and as if on cue, she heard the doors of the library fling open.

"Hey loser! Are you in here?" Anastasia yelled at the top of her lungs ignoring the furious shushing she got from Ruth. Lucy remembered the party and decided that would be a perfect way to distract her and give her more time to think. She jumped up, grabbed her bag and the bloody tissues and hurried over to the circulation desk.

"Ruth leave the books, I'll come back tomorrow to reshelf them," she said dropping the tissues in the wastebasket.

Ruth dragged her face away from her stare down with Anastasia to smile at Lucy, "Don't worry about it dear, I don't close for another hour so I have plenty of time. Unless you would like me to leave them out for you?"

"No thanks," Lucy shook her head and moved to the door, "I'm all done. Thank you for your help Ruth." Anastasia had not moved from the threshold of the door. As far as Lucy knew, this was as close to the library as Anastasia had ever gotten. It was as if the dance major feared she would turn to stone if she entered. Anastasia pushed the door back open with her backside and stood there allowing Lucy to pass through.

"Have a good night Ruby!" Anastasia yelled into the library.

"Ruth," Lucy whispered the correction.

"Whatever," Anastasia replied rolling her eyes and letting the door slam. "It's embarrassing that you are my friend." Anastasia challenged as they walked down the stairs. "I find you in the library? Really? You know it's Saturday right? AND you were supposed to be resting this weekend." Lucy just shrugged. She certainly couldn't tell Anastasia about what she was actually doing in the library. She also decided to omit the rat story, Cliff was right; he would have mass panic on his hands.

Lucy and Anastasia hurried back to the dorms and, after

picking out the perfect outfits, met in the bathroom. Lucy was surprised to find it empty. "Are we late? Where are the rest of the girls?" she asked while opening her makeup bag.

"At the party already, Paige went to go help Nick set up and Suzanne went too. Paula, Michelle and the others are there too." Anastasia replied while plugging in her straightening iron.

"You mean Suzanne went to see Simon," Lucy said rolling her eyes.

"Probably, I honestly don't know what they see in those guys."

"Really? I like Nick and Simon," Lucy said with a little pout in her voice while attempting to smooth her hair.

"Oh I do too!" Anastasia exclaimed. "They're good guys and fun to hang out with and all but they're not all that mature you know?" Lucy pictured a conversation she had witnessed between the three men about how if you filled a bathtub with ice at a party, it wouldn't melt because the ice would keep the other ice cold.

"I guess you're right," Lucy conceded. "But that's college boys for you."

"There has to be at least one guy on this campus who is more than just a college boy," Anastasia said hopefully. Lucy thought of Nathaniel and her heart warmed a little. Would she ever see him again? Was he an Angel? How do you call someone who doesn't have a phone?

She sighed, "That guy is out there Anastasia, you just have to figure out a way to find him."

"Totally," Anastasia agreed while smoothing her hair.

"I'm sorry we're late," Lucy started on her makeup, "I lost track of time at the library."

"I was running late too. I was at the studio and lost track of time myself. You can still come to the recital tomorrow night right?"

"I wouldn't miss it for anything babe," Lucy confirmed. "Are you nervous?"

"A little," Anastasia said carefully, "but I'm mostly excited." She paused, "It's like I can't wait to show off you know? It's an awesome piece and I'm really good for the part. I guess I am looking forward to everyone appreciating it and me." She paused again, "That sounds shallow and vain doesn't it?"

"Not at all," Lucy thought of her own talent and the pride she felt when she got to show it off, "you are a beautiful dancer and you have worked very hard to get where you are. I think it's normal for you to be proud of yourself. I know I am."

"Thanks babe." Anastasia grinned at her in the mirror.

"Now, who is going to be at this party?" Lucy prompted. Anastasia was, as Lucy had suspected, a perfect distraction from her worries. They chatted easily about gossip and rumors floating around. When they were sufficiently preened and prepared, Anastasia threw her arm over Lucy's shoulder and they regarded themselves in the mirror,

"We are too hot for words," Lucy noted.

"I second that," Anastasia agreed, "Let's stay friends forever ok?"

"Ok," Lucy pulled her into a tight hug, "I love you babe."

"Love you too," Anastasia looked at her watch, "let's make tracks, we are crossing the line from 'fashionably late' to 'the jerks that couldn't show up on time.'"

Nick and Simon's room was on the second floor of the boy's dorm. As they climbed the stairs they could already hear the party a floor above.

"How many people did Paige invite?" Lucy asked with shock.

"It sounds like she invited the entire residence population,"

Anastasia replied quickening her step, "This is going to be good. Maybe we will meet our mystery men tonight!"

Mine isn't here, Lucy thought ruefully. She vowed to herself that she would take this time to relax and be with her friends. She still wasn't sure what to do with her new found theories or even how to get a hold of Nathaniel to tell him. She quickened her step and looked forward to a fun night.

The party had spilled out into the hallway and the girls made their way through the gauntlet of bodies greeting people along the way to Nick's room. There were more people packed into the small dorm apartment than Lucy thought possible. The tiny kitchenette was packed, people were standing or leaning all over the modest living room and more students moved in and out of the two bedrooms. Glancing around, Lucy recognized ninety percent of the partygoers so when Anastasia threw her hands in the air and yelled, "We're here!" there was a roar from the crowd.

The girls spent the first few minutes hugging everyone before taking a seat on the coffee table in the middle of the room. There were hundreds of conversations all going on at once but Nick immediately pulled in Lucy's attention. He was sitting in the corner of the couch with Paige tucked contentedly under his arm. He was talking to a guy Lucy had never met before. The guy had shaggy bleach blond long hair and board shorts on.

"There she is!" Nick exclaimed, "Lucy, Lucy, Lucy I need your help."

"I've got your back," Lucy replied accepting a soda from Simon.

"My friend John here and I are having an argument, my computer sucks and I need you to settle some things for us."

"Got it," Lucy twisted herself so she was facing them. She smiled at John who did not smile back. He didn't seem convinced that Lucy could help at all.

"Who won the 1975 World Series?" Nick asked.

"The Cincinnati Reds," Lucy answered quickly.

"YES! YES!" Nick yelled, "I am my own hero!" Paige grinned beside him.

"Are you a fan of baseball?" John asked sharply as though it was Lucy's fault that he was wrong.

"Not at all," Lucy replied, "I don't think I have ever sat through a game." John's face fell in disappointment and confusion.

"She's the one I was telling you about," Nick explained.

"The camera girl?" John asked to clarify. This was not a term Lucy liked and her friends were well aware of her aversion.

"The camera girl?" Paige and Anastasia said in unison rounding on Nick.

Nick raised his hands defensively "Those are his words, not mine."

The two of them then turned on John, "Her name is Lucy," Anastasia clarified sharply. Paige nodded as if to say 'what she said'. John ignored them, his eyes narrowed and he regarded Lucy suspiciously.

"So you can memorize some baseball stats, big deal, I know tons of guys who can do that."

"Think what you want pal," Lucy said casually, "I don't really care. But I have a photographic memory and the biggest downside is that I won't ever be able to forget those atrocious shorts you are wearing."

"Oh!" the room roared at the jab but John ignored them and Lucy's insult. He leaned forward and flipped his hair back. Lucy sighed. She had been here before. He was going to ask her some random question that he didn't even know the answer to and try to embarrass her. It was not going to work.

"What team did the Red's win against?" he yelled over the crowd. His voice was tight and combative. Everyone felt the air of tension and went silent.

Nick tried to diffuse the situation. "Dude, take my word for it…"

John didn't even look at him and Lucy answered, "The Boston Red Sox."

"How many games did the series go to?" he fired at Lucy.

"Seven," Lucy replied almost before he was done the question.

"Who was the MVP?"

"Pete Rose." There was a pause while John thought of another question, Lucy took advantage of his delay and continued. "The first pitch of the series was from William Simon to Carlton Fisk at Fenway Park. The sixth game of the series was the most memorable. It was a twelve-inning game at Fenway Park. Bernie Carbo hit a game tying home run in the eighth, Dwight Evans made an eleventh inning catch that stopped Joe Morgan from getting a go-ahead home run. The biggest moment of game six was the walk off home run by Carlton Fisk in the bottom of the twelfth that gave the Sox a seven to six win to push the series to a seventh game. The Cincinnati Reds have won the World Series five times, 1919, 1940, 1975, 1976 and 1990. Do you want the details of each series or do you believe me now?"

"Do you only know sports stats or?" John's tone had changed from animosity to reserved appreciation.

"No," Lucy replied smiling kindly at him, "anything I read or see is stuck in my head."

"Do 'Green Eggs and Ham,'" Simon said nudging her.

"No!" Nick chimed in, "'The Grinch!'"

"It's not Christmas," Anastasia chided Nick.

Lucy looked at John. "Your choice," she said pointing at him.

He smiled at the peace offering and said, "'The Cat in the Hat' please."

Lucy smiled again and nodded. Simon turned down the music and

Lucy began, "The sun did not shine. It was too wet to play. So we sat in the house all that cold, cold, wet day...." By the time she was finished reciting almost everyone was listening and Lucy received a round of applause.

John smiled at her, "Impressive."

Lucy smiled and nodded back. People started yelling more requests.

"The periodic table."

"Do Shakespeare."

"Catcher in the Rye." But Lucy had had enough and she elbowed Anastasia lightly.

Anastasia knew the signal. "People, we are here to party – I vote we dance! Crank it Simon!" she announced to the room. Simon didn't have to be told twice, he reached for the dial and turned the music up to deafening levels. Anastasia jumped up and pulled Lucy and Paige with her. Lucy danced for several songs, laughing and joking with everyone around her. It felt good to relax. She reflected that nothing had to change unless she chose it to. Good music, great friends and laughter surrounded her. Lucy had options.

Lucy didn't have to find Nathaniel again; her life was good, great in fact. If she figured out a way to call him it would be bringing problems and heartache into her life. Why would she do that? Now that she was almost sure of what he was, why did she need to call him? Lucy's life didn't have to change; her reality could stay the same. He would go on and haunt some other unsuspecting girl – a girl that needed an Angel in her life. Lucy didn't need saving, she was perfectly happy. Lucy had options.

She excused herself from the group and made her way down the hall to the bathroom. There were no women's bathrooms in the men's dorms and the girls never wanted to go down to the public bathrooms on the main floor. The rule during parties was the boys avoided the urinals and only used the stalls allowing both sexes to share the bathroom. Lucy walked in without a worry. A few girls were at the mirrors preening themselves and Lucy chatted with them while she washed her hands. She said goodbye to them and opened the bathroom door. A guy she didn't know stood in the hallway, leaning against the opposite wall.

"If you are waiting for the bathroom to be empty, you'll wait all night. Just use a stall, the girls don't care," she explained politely to him while starting to walk past.

"Actually," he said, his voice deep but smooth as silk, "I was waiting for you." Lucy looked at him. He was tall and built with light blond hair that was slicked back on his high forehead. He had bright, clear blue eyes under dark lashes. His jawline was strong and his cheekbones high. He was handsome, very handsome in fact. Lucy was reminded of a GQ ad she once saw. He smiled at her a charming, disarming smile. Then something occurred to Lucy. This was the second stunningly gorgeous man she had met in the past forty-eight hours. The coincidence was unnerving. What if this guy was invisible too? What if she was a magnet for Angels lost on Earth – some kind of homing beacon for the divinely confused? The three girls came out of the bathroom and Lucy's fears dissipated. They stopped and stared at the guy before starting to giggle and skipped down the hall.

"Have fun Lucy!" one of the girls yelled back over her shoulder. So this guy wasn't invisible. That was good.

"I'm Roman," he said reaching out his hand. Lucy took it, he was strong but she was a little disappointed that's all she felt. Here was a totally gorgeous guy at a party who wasn't invisible. Why couldn't she get tingles from him?

"I'm Lucy," she said, "Roman huh, is that your real name or...?"

"Yes, it's a little embarrassing," he looked down sheepishly and grinned. "My mom is a huge fan of 'Days of Our Lives' and there's a character on there..."

"Roman Brady," Lucy grinned.

"Uh huh," he scratched the back of his head, "Like I said, embarrassing."

"Not at all," Lucy replied earnestly, "I think it suits you." Why couldn't she get the butterflies from this smile? He was cute, sweet and not a lost soul.

"You think so? Thanks," he paused, "that was pretty cool in there with the Dr. Seuss stuff."

"Party tricks," Lucy shrugged. "What's your major?"

"Third year engineering."

Lucy winced. "That's tough stuff."

"You could say that. It gets to you sometimes. Some people more than others."

"Like how?" Lucy had to admit that she was pretending to be interested. She wanted to like this guy. Why couldn't she like him more?

"Well, this girl in my fluid dynamics class had a breakdown yesterday."

"What happened?" This was an interesting story, why didn't she care?

"She stood up on her chair and twisted her body into the shape of a sigma," he said smiling.

Lucy pictured the sigma symbol; Σ. "I would imagine that would be difficult."

Roman laughed. "Oh it was, we wouldn't have known what she was doing if she hadn't kept saying 'look I'm a sigma' over and over again until they dragged her away."

"That's horrible," Lucy said laughing, "funny, but horrible."

"Uh huh, after they took her away the prof just kept on teaching like nothing had happened."

Lucy laughed again. "That's insane."

"That's engineering for you," he stopped laughing and looked at her, his eyes were a light bright blue, they sparkled, "you have a wonderful laugh."

Lucy felt uncomfortable and she had to ask her self why. Here was a really nice, really funny, really good-looking guy giving her a compliment. Why did it feel so wrong? Why couldn't she see this as an option?

She changed the subject, "So why aren't you crazy?"

"I give myself Saturday nights off," he shrugged. "So far it has worked."

"Good idea," Lucy had nothing more to say to him and was about to excuse herself but he jumped in.

"I have no plans for next Saturday."

"Oh?" Lucy's discomfort increased.

"Yeah," he continued. "If you are free maybe we can do something?" He gave her a hopeful look. Roman seemed great; he had no baggage, no secret life and no mysteries about him. Why wasn't Lucy jumping at the chance to go out with him? Why wasn't she taking this option? Would she always wonder what would have happened if she had found Nathaniel again? Would she wake up every day and ask 'what if?'

For the first time in twenty-four hours, Lucy allowed herself to bring Nathaniel's face to mind. Her memory allowed her to see him perfectly, not clouded by emotions or wishes. What she saw still stunned her. His face was perfection and infinitely more beautiful than Roman's or anyone in the world for that matter. He smiled at her in her mind's eye. It was the smile that felt like it was hers and hers alone. It was warm, caring and full of genuine joy. She heard his voice, so full of disappointment and pain that she wanted to cry all over again, 'If you ever need me again, you just have to call me.' Lucy realized that if she was the only person who could see him he was literally alone now. She had tossed him out screaming like a banshee. He had no one - no one but her.

She was out of options.

Roman cleared his throat awkwardly. Lucy had forgotten all about him, "Oh, yeah. Sorry, I can't go out with you. I am going to be busy on Saturday." She started to move down the hall.

"Oh," Roman rallied. "Well maybe some other time." Lucy thought about that option but it didn't sound good to her either.

"No," she said not making an effort to spare his feelings. "I'm going to be busy for a while." Lucy ran down the stairs, she had to get home…now.

Lucy would never get him out of her head. She would never get him out of her heart. She didn't care anymore that no one could see him but her, all she cared about was that she see him and soon. Lucy had never needed a guy in her life and she had spent the past two days convincing herself of that. She should have been convincing herself that people could need each other. With out her he was alone and without him Lucy was a mess. She could go to as many parties and meet as many guys as she wanted to but none of it would cover him up or make him go away. Lucy realized with a shock that she needed him desperately, not to save her or complete her but because she didn't think she could have it any other way. Lucy was out of options and knew deep down she had only ever had one.

Lucy got back to her room, turned on the lights and began to pace. "How do you call an Angel?" she asked out loud. She searched her brain for any clue he had given her. "The leaf!" she cried and leapt for her school bag. She rifled through it until she found her copy of Hamlet and turned the book upside down. Nothing. She flipped the pages, nothing. She knew she had put the leaf back in there, where did it go? She pulled everything out of her bag, nothing.

Then panic struck her. What if the leaf had been a part of his...magic...she thought for lack of a better word. What if the leaf disappeared when he did? What if she was too late? What if he was gone for good? The panic increased. No, no she wasn't done yet. After she had finally accepted how integral he was to her, he was gone? That wasn't fair. Lucy scrambled for other ideas. She looked through the programmed numbers in her phone thinking he might have left something in there, nothing. She tore her room apart, throwing cushions and clothes out of her way looking for a note, another leaf or anything he might have left behind, nothing. She was desperate now. Why was this so hard? How could it be so easy to be around him and yet it was so difficult to reach him?

Then she thought that that might be the key. He was so genuine, so earnest that this shouldn't be difficult. She was thinking too hard. He had told her to 'just call him'. Could it be that easy? Could he hear her? It was worth a shot. She stood in the middle of the room, took a deep breath and in a normal voice as if he were in the hall she called his name,

"Nathaniel." It was the first time Lucy had said his name out loud and she was surprised by how familiar it felt. His name rolled off her tongue like she had said it a thousand times. There was silence. Lucy listened to her blood pumping through her head, the tick of her clock and her short uneven breathing. Nothing.

Her phone let out a piercing, shocking ring. Lucy jumped. She didn't look at the caller id as she slowly leaned over picked it up, opened it and put it gently to her ear, "Hello?" she said in almost a whisper.

"Hey loser it's me," Anastasia bellowed through the earpiece. Lucy let out a gust of air. *There goes that idea.*

"Hey Stasia, you ok?"

"Yes, thanks for saying good bye asshole. Anyway, sorry to wake you but you know that guy Roman? Jane said she saw you guys talking in the hall."

"Yeah, what about him?" Lucy tucked the phone against her shoulder and started pulling books from her shelf and flipping through them thinking he might have left something in another volume.

"Well listen, he's gorgeous and so cool and I was wondering how into him you are?" Lucy smiled. At least Roman was moving on quickly and she had to agree, he was cool.

"I am not into him at all."

"Really?" Anastasia sounded thrilled.

"Nope, give it your all."

"Oh I intend to sweetheart, go back to bed. Love you bye." The phone went dead and Lucy closed it and put it back on the table. She didn't know what to do next. She thought she should try calling him again. That had felt like the right answer and maybe he didn't hear her the first time. Maybe she had to be clearer.

She took another deep breath and called a little louder this time, "Nathaniel, can you come? I need you." There was a knock at the door. Lucy rolled her eyes. What now? She moved quickly to the door and whipped it open. Nathaniel stood there, leaning against her doorframe smiling the most dazzling smile Lucy had ever seen.

"You only ever have to call me once Lucy," he said. "I will always come."

Chapter Six
Truths

*"Reason is the natural order of truth; but imagination
is the organ of meaning."*
~CS Lewis

Lucy was so relieved and surprised to see Nathaniel that she threw herself forward and wrapped her arms around his neck. He responded immediately by holding her tightly to him. She tucked her face into his neck and breathed deeply, taking him all in. Finally she pulled back and they grinned at each other.

"Come in," Lucy said. She reluctantly let him go and lead him inside. Nathaniel walked in and he didn't seem to notice the state of Lucy's room. Her frantic search had left the room looking like she had just been robbed. He sat down on the couch and Lucy sat across from him. She had been so obsessed with getting him here she hadn't thought of what she would say when he arrived. There was a moment of silence.

"Are you an Angel?" Lucy came right out with it. It felt better to say it out loud.

"Yes, I am," he replied not sounding shocked at all by the question.

"Why didn't you tell me last night?"

"I was going to, but you kicked me out before I could. Plus I don't think you would have believed me."

"You could have still tried to tell me!" she exclaimed thinking that would have made her day so much easier.

"You told me to answer your questions," he said with half a smile. "You didn't ask."

"From now on," Lucy put on her best scolding voice, "you are to offer up any and all information."

"Got it," he saluted her. There was a pause as Lucy waited expectantly, "Oh! Right now?"

"Of course right now!" Lucy said laughing. She waited but Nathaniel seemed unsure of where to start, "So you're an Angel," Lucy prompted.

"Yes."

"So you are a dead person whose soul ascended to Heaven?"

"When you put it that way…."

"Well, were you ever alive and visible and everything?"

"I think so," he replied thoughtfully, "because things seem familiar, but I don't remember ever being mortal."

"So you are Nathaniel, the Arch Angel right?" Lucy asked hoping she put that the right way. She didn't want to insult him.

"No Lucy, there is more than one Nathaniel in Heaven. That's a different guy," he explained. "I am a lower Angel, the longer you are up there, the more responsibilities you are given."

Lucy nodded understanding, "I read about different levels of Angelic Order and…"

Nathaniel was shaking his head. "We don't have levels with names and graduations to the next level and stuff, when you are ready to take on more responsibility, you do."

"How long have you been in Heaven?"

He shook his head again. "I have no idea, time means very little up there. A second can seem like a hundred years and a hundred years can feel like a second. Time is an Earthly concept."

"What were your responsibilities?" Lucy asked completely out of curiosity. What kind of job does one have in Heaven?

"Nothing really, I helped guide people in," he shrugged.

"Like a divine tour guide? The welcome wagon?"

Nathaniel laughed. "I guess, but most people don't need much help, once you get there it's all pretty clear. No brochures or maps are required."

"So there is a Heaven." Lucy thought she would make this point very clear for her own understanding.

"Oh yes," Nathaniel replied with confidence.

"And that is where we go when we die?"

"Not everyone and not everyone right away."

"So there is also a Hell then," Lucy said coming to her own conclusion.

"Yes," Nathaniel nodded, "not that I've been there but there is an awareness that there is another place."

"Why don't you know?" Lucy asked confused. Were these people divine or what?

"Lucy," he said with a little laugh, "it's not like we are invited down for meetings or anything. There is no contact between the two Guilds."

"So do you have to believe in God to go to Heaven?"

"I don't know what people believe in before they get there, I only know that they believe when they get there."

"So there is a God," Lucy again stated this as fact.

"Oh yes," he said with conviction.

"What's he like?"

Nathaniel shrugged a little like he was lost for words, "It's not like God is sitting behind a desk and you check in or anything or even that he is a he or that God's name is God... it's just easier to call God that. People call God a lot of different names and they are all correct."

"What does he look like?" Lucy asked again needing specifics.

Again, Nathaniel struggled for words, "I don't really know. God is just there, you kind of feel God more than see God."

"This is not as concrete as I was hoping for," Lucy muttered sourly.

Nathaniel looked frustrated too, "It's hard to explain, I'm sorry."

"Ok, so what is Heaven like?" she emphasized the word 'like' hoping for adjectives.

He thought for a minute before answering. "There are moments in our lives that are so wonderful, so joyous, so breathtaking that we can't find words for it. It is as if the human language is insufficient to describe it. Those moments are a gift from God. God gives you these pieces of Heaven so you know what to look forward to. That's what Heaven is like. There are no words to describe it." He looked at her eagerly, hoping that this would explain everything. Unfortunately, Lucy could not think of one time in her life that she could not describe with precise detail. She had never been at a loss for words. She nodded understanding to him anyway because it was obvious he was giving it his best shot and she didn't want to harass him about it.

"Ok," she said moving on. "Then who are the Guardian Angels that watch over people?"

"Exactly that," he replied simply, "they are Angels in Heaven that watch over people."

"So when people say that something good happened to them it was because of their Guardian Angel?"

"Not really, Angels won't make you win the lottery or get a promotion or make you thinner, that's not the way it works."

"How does it work?" Lucy was enthralled.

"They help in ways that they can," Lucy shook her head, not comprehending.

"Ok," Nathaniel shifted on the couch thinking of an example. "So there is a mother of five having trouble making ends meet. She's a receptionist at a huge company. Christmas is coming; she has no money to buy gifts for her kids or a turkey or anything. She's panicked. The Vice President of the company walks past her everyday and has never looked at her twice in the two years she has worked there, he just picks up his mail and walks away."

"So an Angel makes the guy give her money right?" Lucy cut in pleased she was getting the concept.

"No, not at all," Nathaniel corrected. Lucy almost pouted at getting the answer wrong. Nathaniel leaned forward as if delivering a punch line. "An Angel makes the Vice President look at the receptionist."

There was a pause.

"What?" Lucy cried. "What good would that do?"

Nathaniel smiled, "Every person has free will, the ability to make all their own decisions. Even if an Angel could, they would not take away your free will. Your ability to choose your own course is the greatest gift God gave you. The Angel would only cause the VP to look at the receptionist because that is all he is allowed to do. The VP would pause and really see the receptionist for the first time. He would notice her out of fashion clothes, her worried face, the pictures of five children on her desk and he would know that Christmas was approaching."

"Then what does the Angel do?" Lucy asked.

"Nothing."

"Nothing?" Lucy was once again totally confused.

"Nothing," Nathaniel said calmly, "the Angel sits back and waits, hoping the man will make the right decision. Hoping he will realize that he has no children and more money than he could ever spend in a lifetime; hoping that he will go to human resources, get the receptionist's information, spend a day shopping and sneak over to her house and leave boxes full of toys, food and a little extra money for rent. The woman would never know who helped her but she would always claim that an Angel helped her."

"And if he doesn't help?" Lucy countered, "If he just shrugs and thinks 'not my problem' and goes on with his day?"

Nathaniel shrugged lightly. "Then the Angel moves on, trying to help someone else."

"But what if no one helps her?" Lucy debated.

"Someone always helps," Nathaniel said smiling.

"Why?"

"Because people are inherently good." He said smiling. "And remember that kindness is contagious. People who have good done to them do good unto others. It multiplies upon itself."

"But what happens to the guy who didn't help her?"

"Nothing," Nathaniel said simply.

"Nothing? He doesn't get into a car accident or lose all his money in a stock market crash?" Lucy asked shocked.

"Nope," Nathaniel smiled again, totally in love with this concept, "that's free will. He can decide to do whatever he wants to. Maybe he will think about it later and wonder if he should have done something. Maybe he will help the next time he has the opportunity, maybe he won't but you will never be punished for exercising your free will."

"So," Lucy spoke slowly trying to put it all together, "Angels help people become Angels for other people?"

"Yes!" Nathaniel exploded. "Exactly! And it's not just for strangers. Humans are supposed to be Angels for those we love the most. Mother's are Angels for their children, husbands are Angels for their wives and so on."

"That's nice," Lucy said smiling, "I like that."

"I like it too, but I'm not a Guardian."

"How do you know?" Lucy asked. "Maybe that's your new job?"

"Guardians don't wander around on Earth, they don't need to. They can do their work from up there," he pointed at the ceiling. "In fact, I don't know of any Angel that is walking around. I am one of a kind."

"Then why are you here?"

"I have no idea. I know they sent me but I don't know why."

Lucy nodded but paused, thinking. She needed to ask a very delicate question. Something had been nagging at her since she did her memory search in the library. She debated asking because at this point it didn't matter to her at all. If they were trying to figure this out though, it was something that needed to be discussed. He hadn't picked up on the clue when she mentioned Hell so Lucy would have to come right out with it.

"Don't fallen Angels become...um..." she stumbled on her words and looked down at her hands, embarrassed.

"Lucy I am not a Demon," he said simply.

She looked up and he was reaching out his hand, she gave hers willingly. She felt his warm pressure seep through her skin. She looked into his eyes and there was no need for clarification, he was sure. He had no doubts. They stared at each other for a long time. Lucy was lost again in his deep eyes – they looked steel grey again today, her mind went blank and she only thought of him. He tightened his grip on her hand and the warmth surged further up her arm. *A kiss would be nice right now,* Lucy thought to herself. How would it feel to kiss him? Lucy imagined his full warm lips on hers. If her hand had such a strong reaction to him what would her lips do?

She had to focus. She looked away and stood up, it was difficult for her to think with him so close. "Ok," she said taking a deep breath and starting to pace, "What about the leaf? How did you do that?" Nathaniel leaned back on the couch.

"I didn't," he said.

Lucy stopped and stared at him. "Then who?"

"The leaf," he said quietly realizing that this concept was alien to her.

"So the leaf got itself into my book. Why?" she asked. Nathaniel was right not to tell her until today. She would not have believed him.

"Nature seems to have an affinity for me," he explained.

This was what Lucy had thought of in the library. "Because nature is made by God and it recognizes your connection to him?" Nathaniel nodded. "The weather seems to have exploded as well, would you have anything to do with that?"

"I'm not sure about that," he replied, "I might. Which isn't a good thing."

"Why?" Lucy asked.

"Well," Nathaniel seemed to be choosing his words carefully. "I am fairly sure that while I am here, I should keep a low profile and the weather really isn't helping."

"While you are here..." Lucy muttered but didn't quite register the comment. She moved on to other questions.

"But how are you getting other stuff like clean clothes and money?"

"That's the interesting part," he said but Lucy thought all of this was interesting. "All I have to do is think of something I need and suddenly I have it."

"Give me an example," Lucy furrowed her brow deep in thought.

"Well," he said. "When I was in the café, I chose what we needed and thought, 'I need money to pay for this.' I reached into my pocket and there was almost the exact right amount of money in there. I left it in the till for the clerk and came back up here."

"Have you tried wishing for other things?"

Nathaniel laughed, "Yes, but it doesn't work. I tried thinking that I needed a hundred dollars but since I really didn't need it, it didn't work. That's how I know that Heaven has not abandoned me here. I am getting help when I need it."

Then Lucy came up with a brilliant idea. "Have you tried thinking that you need to be visible?" she asked excitedly. Nathaniel's face was full of disappointment; Lucy knew her answer, "No go huh?"

"No go," he said shaking his head.

Lucy kept thinking. "What if this is some kind of accident. What if you literally fell through the heavenly cracks?"

"Lucy," Nathaniel smiled warmly at her. "Where I come from there are no accidents."

"But you were looking around like someone was coming after you," Lucy prodded excited she was getting explanations.

"I was," he replied sitting forward and propping his elbows on his knees, "I thought someone would come and give me instructions. Just because I have never heard of an Angel on Earth doesn't mean it could never happen. I was waiting for guidance."

"But you looked scared."

"I was a little," he admitted without pride. "I was very disorientated, I didn't understand what was going on and that was a little unnerving."

"And then?" Lucy prompted.

"And then you were there, the one from my dream, with a camera for a memory and I felt...." he paused.

"What?"

"Drawn to you," he finished lifting his head to look at her.

"Oh," Lucy whispered. It was all she could manage.

"So I figured I should stick with you, that this all must have something to do with you."

"Is that how you could hear me when I called?" she asked.

"Yes."

"How did you get to my room so fast?" she imagined a huge set of wings and dismissed it.

"I heard your voice, thought about you needing me and suddenly I was outside your door," he snapped his fingers, "like that."

"Huh," Lucy looked at him and he gave her is very special 'for Lucy only' smile. Butterflies filled her stomach. Nathaniel was so gorgeous it almost hurt to look at him. He was kind, smart, funny and easy to be with; basically, he was the perfect match for Lucy. She grinned at him; her perfect guy was sitting on her couch. She didn't care that no one could see him but her, she was just happy to have him. This, however, could not last indefinitely could it? Her stomach tightened at the thought and she began to pace.

"You appeared so quickly," she said almost to herself, "what if you disappear just as quickly?" Nathaniel started to answer but Lucy cut him off. "What if it was a mistake? What will they do when they figure it out? How are we going to find out your purpose here?

If we do find out your mission and you accomplish it, won't they just take you back again? What if I'm supposed to do something? What if I fail?" His comment of 'while I am here,' came back to her and she realized that Nathaniel thought this was a temporary situation as well. She was pacing furiously now, making turns every five steps because her room was so painfully small.

"Am I supposed to find the answers for you? What if I can't? What if they take you back? What would I do then?" She was breathing heavily now, the weight of her thoughts sinking in. Lucy was so wrapped up in her own worries that she almost forgot that Nathaniel was there. "What am I supposed to do? Think Lucy! Think! You have to figure out this problem because if you don't they are going to take him back again. There are no other options, he must stay and you must make that happen. Now that you started to fall in love with him, you can't let them take him back!" Lucy stopped in her tracks. She was standing a foot away from her door with her back to Nathaniel. She realized that she was not alone and she had just said something very personal and very inappropriate. Embarrassment swept through her. Slowly, painfully she turned around to face him.

Nathaniel was standing, staring at her with shock on his face. *This is horrible*, Lucy thought to herself. She could almost feel the rejection in the air. She waited for him to cock his head to one side and explain to her with pity that he didn't feel that way about her. *Why did you have to open your big mouth?* She reproached herself.

"What did you say?" he finally asked, his face blank and unreadable.

"You heard me," she said defensively. "And you can go ahead and tell all your Angel friends about the little human girl who fell for you and you can all have a really good laugh over it. I don't care." There was no reaction in his face and Lucy stood there waiting. *Just get it over with,* she pleaded with him in her head.

"Lucy," he finally said. "My Angel friends would be very jealous of me."

"Really?" she fired at him. "Why?"

"Because," he said as a small smile touched the edges of his lips, "they don't get to do this."

He crossed the tiny room in two strides and grabbed Lucy's face in his hands. Forcefully, he pushed himself into her and they both slammed back into the door. He looked into her eyes and smiled before he lowered his face to hers and kissed her.

It took Lucy a second to figure out what was happening. A moment ago she was expecting him to tell her he wasn't interested at all and now he was kissing her- and it wasn't just any kiss. Her lips were ablaze with his warmth and her knees felt weak. Heat radiated through her face and electricity tingled down her spine. She was grateful she was leaning against the door or else she thought she might fall down. Lucy threw her arms around his neck and locked her fingers never wanting to let go. She kissed him back. Nathaniel ran his hands through her hair and trembles coursed down her neck and spine and her entire brain emptied of knowledge. For the first time in her life, Lucy could only think of one thing. Nathaniel filled her thoughts completely. Every bit of her wanted, no, craved him. She could only breathe and clutch onto him hoping and praying that this moment would last forever.

Chapter Seven
Bliss

"Now a soft kiss - Aye, by that kiss
I vow an endless bliss."
~John Keats

Hours later, Lucy saw the sun begin to rise. She lay with her head on Nathaniel's chest listening to his heart beating. They were fully dressed. The past few hours had gone by quickly. They had spent them talking, laughing and kissing. Lucy could not get enough of kissing Nathaniel; every time he touched his lips to hers she felt a new surge of feelings for him, every kiss was like a first kiss. Lucy, of course, had done most of the talking. She told him all about her life, her friends and her hometown. She told him everything she could. She felt like she needed to share everything with him in case he disappeared into thin air.

Nathaniel had said little, both because he had so little to share and because he was so interested in her. He spent most of the time laughing at her stories or asking questions for clarification. Nathaniel seemed as eager to hear about Lucy's life, as she was to share it. She had asked him more questions about Heaven and his divine past but made little headway. For once Lucy was content with the lack of information - having him with her was enough. Lucy was in love with an invisible Angel who had no idea who he was and she was totally content with that.

The sun moved another inch and struck Lucy's eyes. She squinted and groaned turning her face into Nathaniel's chest. He peeked down at her and laughed. "You are so beautiful Lucy," he said.

"Oh yeah?" she rolled her eyes. "I can just imagine what I look like after no sleep."

Nathaniel laughed again. "You look stunning."

"I'll take your word for it."

Nathaniel reached up and played with the red curls in her hair. Lucy felt tremors run through her. She considered sitting up and kissing him again but then something occurred to her. She did sit up but stared straight ahead.

"It's Sunday," she said factually.

"Ok, it's Sunday," he repeated.

"We have to go to church!" she exclaimed.

Nathaniel threw his head back and laughed. Lucy shifted so she was looking at him indignantly, "I'm serious! Shouldn't we go and pay homage or light a candle or something?" He was laughing so hard he wrapped his arms around his stomach. His laugh was so infectious to her that she started to laugh too. She hit his leg playfully. "Really, I mean it, shouldn't we go?"

Nathaniel's laugh slowed to chuckles and he wiped his eyes. "Lucy," he said trying to compose himself, "when was the last time you walked into a church?"

Lucy thought about it. "Two years, and three months ago," she replied accurately.

"And did you go there to pray?" he asked smiling.

"It was for my cousin's wedding," she said realizing where he was going with this. Nathaniel started to laugh again. Lucy mocked a pout. "Really, it wasn't that bad, I thought it was," she paused, "pretty."

"Oh well," he waved his arms in the air. "Pretty. That's a reason to pick a religion out of a hat, because it was pretty."

"Why are you laughing?" Lucy asked with her voice full of petulance.

Nathaniel sobered and sat up putting his hands on Lucy's cheeks, "Because God is laughing right now Lucy."

"Why? Why would he laugh at me?"

"Because it's ridiculous that you want to go to a church for the first time in your life when you, God and I all know that you have no desire to go."

"But doesn't God like it when people go to church?" she asked.

"Of course," he explained lovingly. "But only if they want to go. He likes people who don't go just as much." Lucy looked confused so he went on. "If you feel that church, or any place of worship for that matter, is a good place for you to go, then you should go. If you feel good being there, then you should go but if it just feels like a pretty building, then God doesn't want you to go. He doesn't want you to suffer through anything on his behalf. He wants you to be happy." He let go of her face and held her hands. "And I can not tell you how much it means to me that you would go somewhere you don't want to just for my sake."

Lucy smiled, "But if you have to go…"

Nathaniel laughed a little again cutting her off, "Lucy, those people are trying to get where I've already been. God doesn't need my devotion, he knows he has it." Lucy dropped her head. "What is it?" he asked concerned.

"Well, I..." she struggled for words that didn't sound silly or cheesy. "I wanted to say thank you," she said keeping her eyes downcast.

"For what?" he asked sounding confused.

"For you," Lucy replied in a voice so small she was surprised he heard her. Nathaniel put his hand under her chin and lifted her face gently up to meet his gaze.

His face was full of love and appreciation, "You are the most wonderful creature alive Lucy," he smiled at her. "And I have a much easier way than going to church." He let go of her face, took her hands again, looked up at the ceiling and said, "Thank you for helping me find Lucy." He looked back at her and shrugged. "There you go, easy as that."

"Really?" Lucy said incredulously. "That's it? No kneeling or bowing or speaking Latin?"

Nathaniel nodded once. "That's it. If you want to speak in tongues, you are more than welcome but God doesn't really care."

"And someone," she paused. "Is listening?"

"God is always listening, especially to thank yous."

Lucy took a deep breath, closed her eyes for good measure and spoke the first time in her life to someone she wasn't sure existed until last night, "Thank you for sending me Nathaniel." she said out loud, *and I'm sorry but you can't have him back* she added silently hoping God could hear that too because it was the most important part. She opened her eyes and looked at Nathaniel. He nodded sharply.

"Good, now we must move on to more pressing matters."

"Like what?" she asked.

"I have to go to the bathroom."

"You have to go to the bathroom?" Lucy said surprised.

"Yup, I eat, sleep and go to the bathroom. I am a miracle."

Lucy laughed, "No, I just thought that…"

Nathaniel saw where she was going and interrupted her, "I am human Lucy. I even bleed."

"You do?"

"Yup, I poked my finger yesterday to test it."

"Well, don't do anymore tests," Lucy warned him. "I only know first aid in theory, I have never practiced."

"Done." He stood up and stretched and started to head for the door.

"But there isn't a men's washroom on this floor," she countered. Lucy couldn't have Nathaniel walking through the bathroom with her friends in various stages of undress all around him.

"I'm going downstairs," he reassured her. "But," he grinned, "it would be far more convenient if I could just…"

"No way pal," Lucy laughed. "Dream on."

He put his hands up defensively, "I'm joking!" He walked back to her and kissed her on the temple, Lucy closed her eyes in response. "I'll be right back." He whispered in her hair and left the room.

Lucy leaned back on the bed and stretched. She could not believe how much her life had changed in a mere forty-eight hours and had changed for the better. Lucy knew she had never been this blissful. She knew that from now on, her life would be divided into two sections; before Nathaniel and after him. She hoped the after lasted longer than the before had. She didn't want to think about him being taken from her. Lucy vowed to take each moment she was given with Nathaniel and cherish it. She never did anything half way, she fell in love with him completely and she would do everything she could to keep him. He was now a reality to her existence and there was no way back. Since she now knew bliss, she had no intentions of letting it go. She smiled and stood up.

Lucy's room was a mess. Her searching the night before had left the place in a shambles. Lucy started to clean up. While putting her jacket in the closet, she caught a glimpse of herself in the mirror. Lucy stopped to stare. She was never one to look good in the morning, especially after a night where she hadn't slept a wink. She realized with amazement that Nathaniel was right - she looked beautiful this morning. Her makeup had worn off at some point in the night and she stood plain faced in the mirror. Her cheeks were rosy and her green eyes were bright and shining. Lucy was glowing. *Happiness looks good on you,* she thought and smiled at her reflection. Lucy went back to cleaning and within a few minutes had her room back to rights. The door opened and Nathaniel slipped in carrying two huge plates filled with bacon, eggs, sausage and toast.

"Hungry?" he asked grinning at her.

"Starving," Lucy grinned and plopped down on the couch taking a plate from Nathaniel as he sat beside her.

"There was nowhere to put money so I'm assuming this is free?" he asked taking a bite of bacon. Lucy nodded while taking a mouthful of scrambled eggs.

"Three squares included in the scholarship. I rarely eat breakfast or lunch there so they owe me a few." They ate in silence for a bit, both of them too hungry to talk.

"So," Nathaniel said after scraping his plate clean. "What's your plan for the day?"

"Well," Lucy thought. She would have liked to stay holed up with him all day in her room but she did have some things to get done. "I have studying to do, I need to go visit Dr. Hannon because I freaked him out the other day and I should go reassure him that he still has a job. And Anastasia's dance recital is at seven tonight."

He raised his eyebrows. "That's a busy day." Lucy nodded and put her unfinished plate down, "done?" he asked. Lucy nodded and smiled as he picked up the plate and without asking finished it for her. *Well he certainly has the appetite of a normal college boy,* she thought.

"Do you want to come with me?" she asked hopefully.

"I don't think I would make a good study partner for you." he replied and traced a line along her cheek with his finger leaving a trail of warmth running down her face, Lucy half closed her eyes in response.

Point taken.

"You could come see Dr. Hannon with me," she suggested but Nathaniel shook his head.

"No, that's your private time with him, I would get in the way. But," he added, "I would love to come to the recital with you if I'm invited."

"Of course you are!" Lucy lit up. "Oh I can't wait until you see Anastasia dance, she's wonderful. She's only a first year and the final number always goes to a senior but she auditioned and blew them away. She got the part and has been working on it non-stop for weeks. I haven't even seen the entire piece but it's going to be fantastic!"

"Then it's a date," he replied. "I'll come by at 6:30 to pick you up, I assume it's on campus?"

Lucy nodded and asked, "But what are you going to do until then?"

"I have a few things to do."

"Like what?" What would be on an invisible Angel's agenda for the day? Before he could answer, Lucy jumped as a huge slam echoed through the room. She turned to see Anastasia standing at the door having just thrown it shut. She was still in her pajamas.

"This must be Anastasia," Nathaniel mused. Lucy grinned sideways at him and gave a small nod. It felt so strange that Anastasia could not see Nathaniel. Lucy had to stop herself from introducing them. She knew they would adore each other as much as she adored each of them. She immediately felt a twinge of sadness that she could not share this new part of her life with Stasia. Nothing in her life had ever felt real until she told her best friend and now she had to keep secret the best thing that had ever happened to her. Lucy sighed at the unfairness of it all, but she would take what she was given and be grateful for it, even with limits.

"GIRL! I have to talk to you!" Stasia stormed in the room and looked at Lucy, "You look great today! Are those the same clothes from last night? Babe, that's a cute shirt, don't sleep in it. You ate breakfast already? Two plates? Oh man, you have to bring down your dishes more often. Look I know you have a ton of crap to do but I have to tell you about that guy at the party! He's awesome! I mean awesome!"

She kept going and Nathaniel stood up from the couch, walked directly in front of her and leaned over to Lucy's ear, "That is my cue to go," he said smiling. Lucy smiled too.

Anastasia took Lucy's smile as a response to something she had said, "I know! It's great right?" Anastasia took the spot on the vacant couch not realizing why she hadn't sat there before, "Oooo, you must have slept in this spot, it's super warm."

"I'll see you tonight," Nathaniel spoke quietly in Lucy's ear; she struggled to not turn her head to look at him one more time. He leaned closer and kissed her neck just below her ear. Lucy took a sharp breath.

"Totally!" Anastasia yelled assuming that Lucy was listening to her, "I know!"

Nathaniel chuckled softly in Lucy's ear. "Totally," he whispered breathing softly on her neck. He stood back up and moved to the door, "if you need me before then, just call and I'll come." Lucy glanced over but he was already gone, she hadn't heard the door and wondered if he had just wished himself somewhere else.

As it turned out, Lucy and Anastasia had both had amazing nights. Roman seemed as perfect to Anastasia as Nathaniel did to Lucy. Roman was not only smart, funny and handsome he was also richer than Midas having been born to some old family further east. He was also very cultured and knew almost as much as Anastasia did about art, music and dance. Anastasia was thrilled. Lucy found it ironic that they had both found their dream guys on the same night - ironic but perfect. It was a wonderful twist of fate that they should both be this happy at the same time even it Stasia didn't know about it.

They continued their conversation in the shower with the two of them yelling over the stalls. Lucy was off to see Dr. Hannon and Stasia had to get to dress rehearsal. They hugged and Lucy reassured her that she would be at the recital.

"Is your new guy coming?" Lucy asked.

Anastasia shook her head. "He has something he can't get out of and it's good he's not coming. I would be nervous with him there."

"Well, I won't see you before so," Lucy hugged her again, "I love you and you are going to be great."

"Thanks babe, love you too," Anastasia ran down the stairs, "Thanks for listening!" she hollered back over her shoulder.

"Any time!" Lucy said to the empty stairwell. She headed back to her room and grabbed her coat and bag. She looked around for her keys and eventually spotted them on the bookshelf. Lucy reached out to grab them but stopped. Sitting beside her keys was a flower. Not just any flower but a Compact Amazon Lily. It was the size of Lucy's palm and bright white. It was one of the most rare flowers on the planet. Lucy picked it up gently and cradled it in her hands. She smelled the incredible scent. Where did Nathaniel get such a thing? It was one of a kind and unseen by the majority of the world – just like him. She grinned and put the blossom softly back on the shelf.

Beaming, Lucy crossed campus to the psychology building. She thought of how different her mood was this time compared to the last time she made this walk. She knew now that her memory wasn't crashing and it didn't even need a break. Lucy wasn't going crazy, she was happy. She bounced into the building and took the steps two at a time. Lucy knew Dr. Hannon would be in his office because it was Sunday. On Sunday's Brian did his client calls and Dr. Hannon always came into the office to get out of the house and get some work done. Lucy made her way down the hall and knocked on his door.

"Well this can only be my Lucy," came Dr. Hannon's voice from inside. Lucy pushed open the door and popped her head in.

"Am I bugging you?" Dr. Hannon was in his usual Sunday spot. He sat casually on the couch with a pile of student's papers at his feet and an AM radio playing a basketball game.

"Not at all! Come in!" He waved at her and started to get up but he looked so comfortable that Lucy said,

"Stay there, I can get my own coffee." Today the coffee was freshly made and Lucy poured a cup for herself and a new one for the doctor. She sat down on the couch beside him and tucked her feet beneath her.

"Well," he turned to look at her, "I have to say that you look much better than you did on Friday."

"I am better," Lucy said smiling. "I'm sorry I scared you I just had a little freak-out."

"I admit that I was a little concerned," he took a sip of his coffee. "But I am amazed that something like that hasn't happened before."

"Why?" Lucy asked perplexed.

"Lucy, since I have known you, you have always been fine."

"Isn't fine good?" Lucy countered.

"It's good but it's not great," Lucy shook her head in confusion. Dr. Hannon explained, "People are supposed to crack under pressure. That's how we know what our limits are. We push ourselves mentally and physically too far, find our breaking point and realize our boundaries. We constantly push past each breaking point fighting harder and harder to handle more and more. The human mind is in a constant state of striving to improve and in doing so sometimes pushes itself too far." He took another sip of coffee. Lucy didn't interrupt; she knew more was to come. "You Lucy, have constantly pushed yourself to the extreme mentally and yet you have always been fine. I have always been a little shocked that you never cracked, never needed a break and never seemed to have a limit. Friday was a bit of a relief for me because I was glad that your mind finally found a limit. That's why it needed a break, even a brain as commanding as yours has its boundaries and I was glad to see it."

Lucy thought about that for a minute. She considered how she felt that afternoon and the term 'cracked' certainly applied. The thought of losing her memory and sanity was the original factor because it would change her life indefinitely. Friday night though was a different story, she had spent the entire night crying because she had sent Nathaniel away and demanded that he never return.

Thinking back on it, the Nathaniel breakdown seemed far more powerful to Lucy. She had been in love with him from the start.

"I felt guilty too," Dr. Hannon cut into her thoughts.

"Guilty? Why?"

"Because I was the one pushing you. I have scheduled all your tests and conferences and the studies. I was the one forcing your brain to fire on all cylinders and since you never complained I figured it was ok. But I am the doctor Lucy and I shouldn't have pushed you so far. I should have pulled back on the reins years ago or even lightened your load when you started your undergraduate studies. It was irresponsible of me and I apologize." Lucy felt awful that she couldn't share the real reason for her breakdown the other day. Dr. Hannon thought it was his fault and Lucy felt terrible.

"Doc, I did all that stuff because I wanted to and I will keep doing it because I enjoy your work almost as much as you do. I have always known that you have my best interests in mind. If I feel too pressured I promise to let you know."

"Are you sure you are up to more work Lucy? Because if you want to..."

Lucy broke in, "I even gave my mind a break last night and can't you tell how much better I am today?" She assumed that the blank thoughts she experienced while making out with Nathaniel last night would constitute a break. Who has time for facts when you are kissing a gorgeous Angel?

"Well that's good," he said visibly relieved but Lucy still felt the need to reassure him.

"To be honest, my little breakdown had nothing to do with my memory it was...something else."

"HA!" he slapped his hand on his leg. "I am a genius! What did I tell you? It was a boy right?"

"Yes," Lucy laughed at his enthusiasm. "A boy." The word

boy seemed a weak description of her Nathaniel but it would have to do.

"And he is?" Dr. Hannon leaned forward expectantly.

"No longer a problem," Lucy avoided lying. She also avoided mentioning the rat incident to Dr. Hannon. Lucy did not think that he would be able to restrain himself from calling her mother.

"That's my girl!" he slapped his leg again and Lucy grinned. "Now don't give me the gory details, college love dramas bore me to tears." *This one wouldn't,* Lucy thought. He stood up and walked over to his desk and lifted a piece of paper, "I did receive an interesting letter from a prominent psychotherapist in Poland. He would like to meet you and run some tests." He scanned the letter, "Inducing lucid dreams, watching your REM cycle (or lack thereof) and of course seeing your memory work in person. Nothing we haven't covered before. Are you up for it?"

"I am not eating eighty pounds of polish sausage and then taking a nap," Lucy said with a smirk.

Dr. Hannon pretended to write that down, "No polish sausage...got it." He looked at her and raised his eyebrows in warning, "Now Lucy if you aren't up for this."

"I promise to tell you," Lucy finished for him.

They talked for a few more minutes about schedules and logistics. Dr. Hannon would have no problem getting the University to sponsor the conference but the funding applications would take some time. The conference would have to take place during the summer semester because Lucy would be at the University for the summer. A double major meant double the classes plus Lucy was considering a masters – she had no intentions of being at school until she was thirty. Summer classes would be necessary for a few years at least. They settled on mid-June and Lucy glanced at Dr.

Hannon's jotted notes so she would remember. She gave him a hug, thanked him and left him to his marking.

Lucy headed back to her dorm and grabbed lunch on the way to her room. She sat at her desk and flipped on the computer. While it was sluggishly warming up, she wondered what Nathaniel was up to today. She imagined his face in her mind and closed her eyes with remembrance. She reached over and took the lily off her shelf. She placed it in front of her keyboard under the monitor where she could see and smell it while she worked. It was better that she had a reminder of him. It would have to do until she got to see him again.

Lucy studied for a few hours finishing papers, editing others and reading textbooks and novels. She noticed the sun going down, she glanced at her watch to see that it was 6:00 p.m. and she only had a half an hour to get ready. She poured over her closet looking for just the right thing to wear and sighed when she realized her wardrobe consisted mainly of jeans, hoodies and a few cute shirts to wear to parties. Digging in the back, she found a mid-length skirt that she paired with a pink v-neck satin blouse. She looked at herself in the mirror and thought she looked cute but something was missing. She walked over to the bookshelf, gently picked up the lily and using a bobby pin, delicately secured it in her auburn hair just above her ear. She applied a little makeup, some perfume, pulled on her heeled sandals and looked at the clock, 6:25. She sat down to wait. Picking up the remote from the table, she turned on the tiny TV tucked in her bookshelf, scanned the channels and found a rerun of 'Who wants to be a millionaire.'

"Who's autobiography is titled 'A Long Walk to Freedom?" Regis Philbin asked dramatically.

"Nelson Mandela," Lucy answered before he was done with the question, "final answer." She waited while the contestant made their choice, the right one and the music and lights on the stage pulsed with the excitement of it all. After the contestant decided to keep going, Lucy looked at her watch again, it was 6:30. Nathaniel should have been there. She refused to worry about him disappearing on her. He said he would be here and he would. Lucy trusted him. 6:32. Lucy tapped her toe impatiently.

"What king was married to Elenor of Aquitaine?"

"Henry II – The Duke of Normandy," came Nathaniel's voice from the door. Relief flooded through Lucy and she jumped up and ran into his waiting arms. She grabbed him tightly around his neck and he lifted her easily off the ground.

"Oh you came back!" she said.

"I told you I would," Nathaniel said softly and lowered her smoothly to her feet. He held her out at arms length and looked her up and down, "You look beautiful. I didn't think that flower could be outshone but you have proven me wrong,"

Lucy blushed slightly, "Thank you." She took a moment to look Nathaniel over as well. He was wearing black pants and a green collared shirt. As usual, his face was flawless and she didn't think she had ever seen such a gorgeous man in all her life. "You look great," she observed.

"Thanks," he said looking down at his clothes, "I thought I should step it up a notch from jeans."

"But you could wear sweats and no one would know."

"You would know," he said as if that was enough reason. He looked at his watch, "We have to go," he said authoritatively. Nathaniel took her hand and he led her out the door. It was a short walk to the auditorium but no one was around so they could talk.

"The watch is new," Lucy observed.

"Yup," he replied while stretching out his arm to admire it. The watch had a silver face and a brown leather strap. It was exactly the type of watch Lucy would have bought for him. "I needed it to be on time tonight."

"But you were late," Lucy said with a laugh in her voice.

"Sorry about that, I had something I had to take care of."

"What?"

"You'll see."

They were in the lobby now so Lucy let go of his hand and stopped talking. They made their way up the stairs to the theatre. When Lucy walked in her heart sank. All the good seats were taken. The only seats left were the back row and the balcony. Lucy had wanted to sit closer so she could see Anastasia better. They should have left earlier and Lucy was very disappointed. Nathaniel pointed to the second row. Lucy couldn't even see it they were so far away.

"It will be full," she muttered under her breath but Nathaniel was already walking in front of her down the steps. She sighed and followed. He stopped at the second row and when Lucy caught up to him he said,

"Would you look at that? What luck." In the middle of the row were two vacant seats with a reserved sign on them.

"Did you do that?" Lucy asked not moving her lips.

"I knew you would want a good seat," he said motioning for her to move into the row. Lucy started to make her way past all the irritated people already in their seats. She looked back over her shoulder to see how Nathaniel was doing but he wasn't there. Lucy looked forward again to see him sitting in one of the seats like he had been there all day.

"Could you teach me that trick?" Lucy asked quietly when she reached him.

"Sorry, it's secret Angel stuff," he said smirking as she sat down. Lucy opened her program and pretended to be reading it while she talked.

"So this is why you were late?"

"This and that," he said pointing under her seat. Lucy looked and saw a huge bunch of gorgeous white roses tied together with a long piece of thick grass. "I thought I would get her flowers if it's ok with you and if of course you give them to her for me." Lucy couldn't believe it. Could he get any better?

"You are very thoughtful, thank you," she said, her voice choking up with emotion.

"Anything for you," he leaned over and kissed her fingers holding the program.

The lights dimmed and the audience went silent. The head of the Fine Arts Department walked out on stage. She introduced herself, thanked everyone for coming and recognized the teachers and choreographers sitting in the audience.

"Are you nervous?" Nathaniel asked in Lucy's ear. She felt his breath on her neck and she shuddered.

"Very. This is a big night for her."

Nathaniel reached over and squeezed her hand, "You're a good friend."

"She's a good friend to me," Lucy muttered getting much better at not moving her lips. The department head left the stage and immediately, the curtain opened. The first number was a group jazz piece. Anastasia was one of many and Lucy had to casually point her out to Nathaniel amongst the fifty other identical costumes. Other numbers followed, hip hop, more jazz, ballet and two more smaller group numbers. Finally the last piece finished and Lucy took a deep breath.

"Is this it?" Nathaniel asked and Lucy only nodded in response. Anastasia was dancing a contemporary piece. It was the story of a man trying to leave his girlfriend and her desperation to keep him. Anastasia had to display all the emotions that one would go through; pain, hate, love, panic while dancing the choreography perfectly.

The curtains opened to Anastasia curled upon a simple wooden chair wearing nothing but a white t-shirt and panties, her hair loose and wild. The song choice was 'Halleluiah' by Rufus Wainwright and as the piano started to play, Anastasia lifted her head. The audience gasped at the anguish in her face as her male counterpart Frances entered from stage right. He wore only a white pair of shorts. Anastasia had described Frances as 'strong as an ox but as boring as the day is long'. It was good that he was strong because the first thing he did was pick up Anastasia's chair with her in it straight over his head and tip her out of it. She spilled out on the floor landing in a crouch and Frances threw the chair aside.

They danced in unison for several counts, each muscle moving in harmony. Anastasia threw herself at Frances and wrapped her arms and legs around his torso, he spun, arms out, not holding on to her until she again fell to the floor, this time in a heap on her side. The dance continued with Stasia clinging and grasping at Frances as he continuously pushed and clawed her away. Both dancers showed the pain of losing each other and not being able to stay together. At one point, Anastasia took a running leap at him only for Frances to bend almost completely backward, allowing her to run over his torso and land on the ground above his head. She literally walked all over him.

The dance was captivatingly powerful and Lucy felt tears well up in her eyes while feeling the characters pain. The dance ended with Anastasia and Frances twisted together on the floor. When the music ended, Frances got up slowly and left Anastasia alone in the fetal position in the spotlight. There was a moment of silence as the curtain closed. Then the entire audience exploded, everyone jumped to their feet clapping and yelling. Lucy stood too, cheering and crying in joy at Anastasia's success. The house lights came up and everyone stopped clapping and reached for their coats to head to the lobby. Lucy flopped back down in her seat and Nathaniel sat back down beside her.

"That was amazing," he said but Lucy held up one hand to silence him.

"Shhh," she whispered, "listen." They heard a chorus of voices around them. Lucy listened carefully,

"What's that girls name? She's extraordinary," one person said.

"That girl at the end was fantastic," said another. Lucy grinned and looked at Nathaniel.

"I wanted to hear everyone talking about how great she is so I can tell her all about it later. I am so proud of her."

"Interesting song choice," Nathaniel said with a half smile.

"Was there a secret chord that David played and it pleased the Lord?" Lucy asked.

Nathaniel laughed, "I'll ask him the next time I see him." He smiled at her. "Thank you for inviting me. I loved it."

"I wouldn't want to be here without you," Lucy replied realizing how true that was. "Let's go see her."

They walked into the now packed lobby and they discovered in this situation it was better if Nathaniel walked ahead of Lucy. People involuntarily moved out of his way and this created a bubble of space around them. Lucy glided through the crowded room with ease. Nathaniel preferred this method as well over following Lucy around as if he were an invisible shadow. He moved through the crowd with confidence protectively checking on Lucy every few steps. He stopped when he heard a voice call Lucy's name. They turned to see Paige and Nick making their way through the crowd towards them.

"Wasn't that awesome?" Paige beamed.

"The other stuff was boring," Nick offered and Paige rolled her eyes. "But Anastasia was wicked." Simon and Suzanne appeared beside them with the same sentiments. Lucy felt like she was being rude not including Nathaniel in the conversation and ignoring him. A well-dressed couple appeared beside them. It was Anastasia's parents, James and Carol Rooke. Anastasia was the carbon copy of her mother so naturally, her mother looked like a movie star. She had dark brown hair styled in a French twist, deep blue eyes and a gorgeous youthful smile. Her father had silver close-cropped hair and a goatee to match. James Rooke was a partner in a law firm in Chicago. Carol Rooke was board of director for numerous charities.

Anastasia had said that the only argument she had ever had with her parents was over her decision to attend Mulbridge. They could not understand why Stasia had wanted to go to this small University when she could attend NYU or even Harvard. Anastasia had felt that she needed to branch out on her own and Mulbridge was the only school that the Rooke's had never contributed financially to. The pair looked like they dripped money but like Anastasia, they did not act like it. They joined the group easily and greeted everyone.

"Which one of you taught that girl to dance?" Simon asked. The couple laughed as they both pointed to Carol.

"I have two left feet," James Rooke explained. "Her mother was in charge of the dancing."

"Not like we had a choice," Carol piped in. "One of her first words was 'dance'". James Rooke took his wife's hand in his own and lifted it smoothly to his face and kissed it. Mrs. Rooke smiled at him lovingly. It was a sweet moment and the friends all smiled. Lucy felt Nathaniel bend over slightly and kiss the top of her head.

Suddenly, Mr. Rooke's eyes snapped up and he glared at a spot just above Lucy's head. His face went pale and he gasped in shock. Lucy felt Nathaniel stiffen behind her and he didn't move his lips from her head, he held his breath. The group all turned to see what he was staring at but it was obvious from their blank stares that they saw nothing.

Lucy was the first to speak, "Mr. Rooke, are you alright?" He didn't respond but just kept staring and squinting his eyes in confusion. Lucy's heart started to race. Could Mr. Rooke see Nathaniel?

Carol looked at him her face full of concern, "James, honey what's the matter?" She kept looking over Lucy's head too and back to Mr. Rooke in an effort to see what he was seeing. His wife's voice seemed to have an effect because Mr. Rooke snapped out of his trance immediately. He composed his face and even managed a small laugh. Lucy felt Nathaniel relax too and start to breathe again. He slowly straightened up.

"Sorry darling, I just thought I saw something," he said shaking his head to dismiss the topic.

"What did you see Mr. Rooke?" Lucy asked quickly.

He laughed and shook his head, "Nothing Lucy, I'm just getting old that's all." He smiled warmly at her but still cast a wary glance over her head as if expecting something frightening to appear. He began to turn away but Lucy reached forward and touched his arm stopping him.

"Did you see something or did you see someone?" Her friends all stared at her. Lucy knew she was being rude but she didn't care.

"I didn't see anything at all Lucy," Mr. Rooke said firmly. She began to press further but Nathaniel grabbed her upper arms tightly.

"Let it go," he said quickly in her ear. Lucy didn't think she could let it go. Mr. Rooke had seen Nathaniel; she knew it and Nathaniel knew it. She went to ask again by taking a deep breath and starting to lean forward again but Nathaniel squeezed her arms, his heat binding her. "Let it go," he almost growled in her ear. "Trust me," he added. The intensity of his voice got through to her and she stopped. Lucy's anger flared; she did not like being handled or told what to do.

The theatre doors opened and the cast came spilling down the stairs to the applause of their friends and family. Anastasia and Frances had the great honor of being last and the pair paused at the top of the stairs to take a bow. Nathaniel finally loosed his grip on Lucy so she could tuck the flowers under her arm and clap. Anastasia had changed into a stunning purple top and a pair of black cigarette pants. She looked gorgeous as she raced down the stairs to her proud parents. Anastasia hugged everyone in the group leaving Lucy for last. They stood for a minute looking at each other.

"You did it loser," Lucy said quietly. Tears welled up in Stasia's eyes.

"I did?" she whispered back.

"You were flawless," Lucy said. Anastasia leapt forward and threw her arms around Lucy and hugged her tightly. They broke apart and laughed through their tears. Lucy remembered the roses, they were a little squished from the hug but still beautiful. She handed them to Stasia.

"Oh wow!" Anastasia said while burying her face in the blooms. "They are so gorgeous! Thank you! Where did you get them?"

"I...um...I've got a guy," was all Lucy could think to say. Anastasia turned back to the circle of friends around her.

"Thanks for coming guys. Mom, Dad, really, it's awesome."

"Of course honey," her father said. Lucy saw him again glance over her head anxiously, "I'm just happy you decided to put on some pants."

Everyone chuckled but Anastasia rolled her eyes, "It's a costume Dad!"

"A costume my dear, has sequins and ruffles. What you wore tonight in front of five hundred people, was underwear." Anastasia laughed.

Assuming that they had put in enough time and not wanting to intrude, Nick, Paige, Simon and Suzanne said their goodbyes and left. Lucy chatted a bit more with Anastasia whispering the extra comments she heard in the audience much to Stasia's glee.

"Hey listen, Mom and Dad are taking me out for a late celebration dinner. Do you want to come?"

"Say no," Nathaniel ordered from behind her. Lucy jumped a little. She realized that Nathaniel hadn't even moved a muscle in fifteen minutes. He was frozen and barely breathing. Lucy again felt her anger rise. He was telling her what to do and for no good reason. Wouldn't it be a good thing if Mr. Rooke could see Nathaniel? "Please," he added in a softer tone and Lucy couldn't refuse him.

"Sorry, I can't," she did not miss a look of relief cross Mr. Rooke's face before he changed it into one of disappointment. Anastasia started to protest but Lucy shook her head, "I have class in the morning, unlike some people I know."

"Ok babe," Anastasia hugged her again. "Do not wake me in the morning." Lucy laughed. All dance classes were cancelled on the Monday following recitals. Lucy said her goodbyes to the Rooke's and made her way to the doors. Nathaniel moved slowly behind her. He was treading cautiously like a stalking lion while keeping his eyes trained on Mr. Rooke. Lucy picked up her pace when they left the building and headed straight for the dorm. Nathaniel caught up with her easily and walked casually at her side. Lucy planned in her head the litany of questions she would fire at him the moment they were alone. She would also make it clear that she was not one to follow blind orders. The incident with Mr. Rooke was yet another thing that Nathaniel had chosen not to share with Lucy.

She had shared her entire life with him and yet he seemed to be keeping everything a secret. They reached her dorm and Lucy, in a full tantrum now, sprinted up the stairs. Behind her she heard Nathaniel chuckle and follow. Lucy stalked to her room after knocking on Vanessa's door for her nightly check in. She opened the door, stormed in the room and left the door open for him behind her. Lucy stormed to the other side of the room, threw off her coat and turned, hands on her hips, glaring at Nathaniel. He smoothly entered the room, took off his coat and sat on the couch. Lucy took a sharp breath to begin her tirade but he cut her off,

"Has James Rooke ever had a major accident?" he asked calmly. Lucy stopped short; he had once again caught her off guard. She didn't answer. "It would have been fairly recently, within the last year. A long stay in the hospital perhaps? An illness?" Lucy glared at him. He sighed, "Lucy, do you trust me? I mean really trust me? Do you know that I wouldn't ever lie to you or lead you astray? Do you understand that I am unable to do that, especially to you? Because if you do trust me then answer my questions."

Lucy knew in her heart that Nathaniel would never deceive her. He was right of course. She was always questioning and always suspicious. That wasn't fair to someone who had never hurt her and plainly didn't have any intentions of doing so. The fight went out of her. She thought of the song choice from Anastasia's dance,

Maybe I've been here before

I know this room I've walked this floor
I used to live alone before I knew you
I've seen your flag on the marble arch
Love is not a victory march

Lucy realized that she didn't have to be right with Nathaniel all the time. She didn't have to fight for every square inch of leverage. She didn't have to win, this wasn't a victory march and it wasn't about getting answers. Lucy didn't want a broken Hallelujah and she didn't want to walk this floor alone anymore. She wanted Nathaniel and in order to have him, she had to trust him.

Lucy walked over to him, took his face in her hands and kissed him softly on the lips, "I love you," she said staring into his beautiful eyes. "I don't know how I fell in love with you, I don't know why I fell in love with you, but I know I do. I will love you forever. I give up, I give in, I trust you completely and I will never doubt you." She walked over to her shelf, picked up her pajama's and walked over to the door. She didn't look back at him, "If you feel the same way about me then find yourself some pajamas, you are sleeping over." Lucy opened the door and left for the bathroom.

When she got back she opened the door and smiled. Nathaniel had set up the bed and was sitting in a pair of blue pajama pants and a tank top on one side of the bed. He was stretched out reading a magazine. He looked totally at home. Lucy crawled in beside him and tucked herself under his arm. Nathaniel kissed the top of her head.

"Anastasia's father had a massive heart attack last summer," she said. "Stasia almost had to delay school because he was taking so long to recover in the hospital. Please explain to me what happened." Lucy didn't need Nathaniel to respond to her comments a few moments ago. His actions spoke for themselves.

"Sometimes," he said while playing with her hair. "When people have almost died, they can see things they shouldn't or couldn't before the incident."

"Like what?"

"Well, sometimes they have a heightened sense of hearing or smell or sight. Often, they attribute these changes to a renewed love of life but really it is because that for a second, their soul touched Heaven and the soul always retains something from that. It is usually short lived, lasting a maximum of a year or so. Mr. Rooke obviously saw something."

"Do you think he saw you clearly?"

"I doubt it, he most likely saw a light or an outline or a glimmer of me."

"Why did you stop moving? Why didn't you want him to see you?"

"Lucy," Nathaniel chuckled a little. "The man would have another heart attack if he witnessed a man materializing in thin air." Lucy realized that other people did not want to see Angels; it meant that they were dead. Lucy of course was the exception to this rule. "I am sure you would have told me it you recently..." he added.

"No," Lucy replied. "No near death experiences for me."

"I didn't think it could be that easy." Lucy smiled and yawned in response. "You are exhausted, close your eyes," he said. She obeyed and immediately felt herself sinking into sleep, "Sweet dreams my Lucy."

"Don't count on it," she murmured into his chest.

"Hmm?" it sounded like Nathaniel was falling asleep too.

"I don't dream."

"Really?"

"Nope," she said shifting against him to get closer to his

warmth.

"Interesting," he muttered and she could feel his body relaxing into sleep. The lights went out by themselves.

"Did you do that?" Lucy asked.

"Yes," he kissed her head again, "I'll do anything for you Lucy." She allowed the darkness to take her and Lucy slept deeply and soundly, safe in Nathaniel's arms.

Chapter Eight
Demons

"Something wicked this way comes."
~William Shakespeare

Time passed quickly for Lucy and Nathaniel and they slipped into an easy routine. They would wake up and Lucy would go to classes and Nathaniel would go out. Lucy asked him several times where he went but she received increasingly vague answers and finally gave up. They would meet up for dinner or later in the evening if Lucy had other plans. There were a few more parties that Lucy had to go solo to because they were far too crowded for Nathaniel to attend. Anastasia's new guy Roman was at them all. He and Lucy got along well and Lucy was pleased there were no hard feelings.

Her feelings towards Nathaniel intensified every day. She was surprised to find herself craving his presence so badly that it physically hurt some days. Every morning that Lucy woke up she looked to the ceiling and whispered.

"Thank you for Nathaniel. I am very sorry that you can

never have him back. He is mine forever."

Nathaniel was more extraordinary than Lucy had originally thought. He was physically far stronger than a normal man, one day picking up the back wheel of a car to experiment at Lucy's insistence. He could run like the wind and jump about fifteen feet in the air from standing. Nathaniel knew a great deal of history as well. He knew small details that couldn't be in any book. He told Lucy that Queen Elizabeth I had a pear shaped birthmark on her left forearm. He didn't know if he had this information from meeting her in person or if he obtained it from meeting her in Heaven. He was well versed in science and biology, knowing facts and figures about Earth or the human body that even Lucy was unaware of. Nathaniel could also find things. He could find almost anything like Lucy's keys or a book in the library without consulting the catalogue. He could tell Lucy where anyone was at a specific moment in time like Anastasia or Dr. Hannon and of course he could find Lucy at the drop of a hat if she called him.

It was a bright morning in early May when everything changed. Lucy was supposed to meet Dr. Hannon for a quick discussion about the upcoming conference and would be late due to a group meeting. She called his office from her dorm room in the morning.

Lucy frowned at the phone.

"What's wrong?" Nathaniel asked.

"He's not answering," Lucy said, "that's odd."

"Maybe he's with a student," Nathaniel offered.

Lucy shook her head and reviewed her memory, "Nope, never once have I called this man and he didn't answer his phone." She tried to dismiss the strong tightness that had started to settle in her stomach. "You know, I am just going to run by his office on my way to class. I am sure it's nothing but he might need me or something."

"Do you want me to come with you?" he asked.

"Naw," Lucy answered, "I'm sure it's fine."

Nathaniel kissed her lightly on the forehead as she shrugged on her coat and headed out the door. Lucy cut through the quad and increased her speed slightly as she approached the psychology building. Something wasn't right, something wasn't right at all. That tightness in her stomach increased and by the time she reached the stairs she was sprinting. She thought that maybe she should have Nathaniel come with her but for what reason? She felt like something bad had happened but she had no way of knowing if she was right or if she was just panicking for no reason.

Out of breath and sweating, Lucy ran down the hall of the psychology second floor and burst into Dr. Hannon's office. At first, all appeared fine and she laughed at her own dramatics. Dr. Hannon's office was exactly as it had been the last time Lucy was here. She scanned the room, referencing her memories to any anomalies in the space and nothing was obviously wrong. Taking one step into the room gave her more of a view and what she saw made her scream in terror.

Dr. Hannon lay on his side, behind his desk. Although, Lucy would not have known it was him if he had not worn that same sweater in September when he and his partner Brian took Lucy out to dinner. His face was a mashed and bloody mess. His eyes were engorged and bleeding from the corners. His cheeks were double the size and ripped to shreds, the skin hanging in lumps off his face. Much of the damage had happened to the back of his head. Blood matted in clumps through his hair and large hills were beginning to form on his skull. His lips were swollen to be a thick line and a steady stream of blood and saliva was streaming into a pool below his head.

Lucy ran to him and fell on her knees at his side. Her hands fluttered in the air, terrified to touch his broken frame. Relief flooded through her as Dr. Hannon moaned. He was alive.

"It's ok Doc," Lucy tried to sound calm. "It's going to be ok. I'm here now."

"No no no," he mumbled, it sounded like he was underwater. "No Lucy no."

"Shh shh shh," Lucy consoled, tears popped to her eyes, "I am going to call an ambulance and everything is going to be ok."

"No Lucy, Go" it sounded like 'Oh-see Ohh -ho." Lucy shook her head. Go? Go where? He mumbled something else that Lucy couldn't understand. He was so agitated though that it must be important. Maybe he had something that he wanted Lucy to pass on to Brian or something special he wanted to say to her.

"What doc?" Lucy said softly while leaning in closer. "What are you trying to tell me?"

He surprised her by reaching up quickly and grabbing a handful of her red curls in his bloody fingers. He pulled and Lucy fell forward until her face was an inch from his. His eyes opened a millimeter and breathing deeply, he yelled as clearly as he could, "IT'S STILL HERE!"

Fear clutched deep into her heart. Someone had done this to Dr. Hannon and they were still in the room. Even worse, Lucy felt that Dr. Hannon, even in this state, would not use the word IT if he didn't feel that was the right word. Something, that wasn't human, was in the room with them and it was capable of great destruction. Having used all the energy that he possibly could, Dr. Hannon released Lucy's hair and fell back onto his oriental rug. Lucy mind worked in overdrive. She would have to leave Dr. Hannon here in order to save both of them. This could possibly risk his life further for the animal to finish what it started. It was a risk she would have to take. She would have to run for the door and hope she made it; the chances were slim that she would. She tensed her legs in anticipation of bolting for the door but it was for nothing.

It wasn't a hand that pressed into the back of her neck, it felt too large, too powerful and Dr. Hannon was right, it wasn't human. Lucy was immobilized with terror- her neck and shoulders tensed and the muscles went rigid. At first there was no sound save the wet aspirations of Dr. Hannon's now unconscious form and Lucy's own dry, short pants of breath. A growling started from the creature behind her and Lucy swallowed the bile that rose in her throat. It wasn't the growl of an animal, or even a man, it was the rumble of a monster. Lucy closed her eyes as she could feel its breath push against her hair, sending tendrils of curls fluttering against her cheek.

She realized with terror that it was sniffing her.

The growling increased in tone and volume - it didn't like what it smelt and Lucy could feel the pressure on her neck tighten further. Claws now dug into her flesh and she whimpered in agony. She kept her eyes shut tight as the pressure twisted her neck, forcing her to turn her head. She was now facing whatever had her but still did not have the capability to open her eyes. The hot breath hovered over a spot on her forehead and the growling deepened to a snarl. Tears pours out the corners of Lucy's closed eyes as she prepared herself to be torn to pieces. But nothing happened. The creature seemed to be waiting for something. Something that wasn't happening. It stopped snarling. Lucy didn't know if this was a good or a bad thing.

Suddenly, it threw Lucy to the ground beside Dr. Hannon. She kept her eyes closed as she heard it spring back. Whatever it was, it was agile and it was enormous. Then, it was gone. It didn't go out the door, or the window. The monster had simply vanished.

"Why didn't you call me?" Nathaniel almost yelled as he paced at the end of Lucy's hospital bed. He had been there for fifteen minutes and had asked that question ten times. Lucy had waited a long time before getting up off the rug to reach for Dr. Hannon's phone. She, to her own horror, laid there crying for more than half an hour. Everything was a blur after she called 911 and it had felt like moments between then and now when it had in fact been hours. The claw gouges on her neck had needed ten stiches and other than whiplash, Lucy was otherwise in good shape. She chose not to answer the question again but countered with her own repetitive query,

"Can you go check on him please?"

Nathaniel shook his head. "I just did and they are still reconstructing his face. There weren't any internal injuries or they would have started there." Nathaniel was able to sneak into Dr. Hannon's operating room and give Lucy far more updates than anyone else could.

"But how do you know that?" Lucy challenged for the tenth time herself, "how do you know it's all facial injuries. He could need a new spleen or something. "

"I think they would have started with that." he explained calmly.

Lucy shook her head, and lay back on the pillows, completely exhausted. She had told the police everything she knew. They were thrilled that the girl with the photographic memory had been inches away from the assailant. They were equally unhappy that she had not opened her eyes an inch. They had no theories as to who had done this and despite Lucy's explanations and pleadings; they did not believe her that the perpetrator was most certainly NOT human. There had been no evidence of an animal in or out of the office and certainly no witnesses of a creature of the size and strength that Lucy described running amok through the campus on a bright sunny morning.

They were silent for a while. Only the empty ticking of the clock cut through the quiet. Nathaniel wandered over and looked out the window into the night.

"What was it?" Lucy pondered almost more to herself.

"I think it was a Demon," he whispered back.

Lucy sat up. "A Demon?" she asked. "There is such a thing on Earth? Aren't they all in Hell?"

Nathaniel turned to her, "There is such a thing on Earth ." He walked over and sat on the edge of her bed. He reached out and took her hand. "Lucy," he explained, "the world runs on a very specific and delicate balance of right and wrong. I have explained to you how Angels work in this world. Our understanding is that there is something on the other end of that. An opposing force if you will."

"And it's Demons?" Lucy asked.

"I remember hearing about them, vaguely really, when I was in Heaven. They are what make up the other Guild." He shrugged and looked back out the window. "I don't even know what they are really."

"What do you mean, 'you don't know what they are,'" Lucy bristled. "How is it possible that and ANGEL could not know what a DEMON looks like?"

"They can take different forms," Nathaniel squinted as he looked out the window, as if he was trying to remember something.

"What different forms?" Lucy prodded. "What kind of forms? Like an animal? It certainly seemed that this thing was an animal."

Nathaniel only shook his head.

"What?" Lucy demanded. She sat up in bed and shook his

arm. "Hello, Earth to Angel boy – some help here. Why would a Demon attack Dr. Hannon? Me?"

He snapped his head around to look at her, "Lucy," he said shortly, "I don't think you understand how it is. We don't, ever, talk about Demons, we don't actually talk about humans all that much, let's be honest here, we don't really talk all that much up in Heaven. The last thing we discuss is the guys in the place that we didn't go to. Everyone thinks that people in Heaven are so obsessed with the nether world. Let me make it very clear to you that such a thing is very trivial to us...very. So I have no idea what a Demon looks like or what their motivation is for anything at all!"

"Well then we are in a great deal of trouble," Lucy shot back.

Nathaniel replied in the same short tone. "I know that!" His voice softened immediately. "Trust me Lucy, I am as frustrated as you are here. I would love to know WHAT attacked you today so I could go and take care of it. But I don't so let's just wait."

"I love being bait... Dr. Hannon too," Lucy challenged, "I am sure he LOVES being beaten within an inch of his life because you don't know what the bad guy looks like."

There was silence and Lucy immediately felt horrible for what she just said. It wasn't Nathaniel's fault, he was obviously exasperated by not knowing all the answers and Lucy wasn't making it any better, she was making it worse. She started to open her mouth to apologize but Nathaniel cut her off.

"I will go check on Dr. Hannon," he said quietly and before she could protest, he disappeared.

Lucy flopped back on the pillows and sighed.

She had fallen asleep by the time Nathaniel returned and woke the next morning with the nurse prodding her to eat a tray of what looked like drywall paste and 'get some energy back'. Nathaniel was sitting at the window still looking at the sky. As the nurse left, Lucy put the lid back on the plate and pushed the tray away.

"You know," Lucy said softly, "you can keep looking out there but it is not going to tell you why your new human girlfriend is a little bit nuts."

He turned and smiled at her and Lucy's heart melted.

"Dr. Hannon got out of surgery and is sleeping well. He should recover quickly and have minimal scaring. AND She's not a little bit nuts," Nathaniel jested while walking toward her, "she's full on insane," he said with a grin as he leaned forward and kissed her full on the lips.

"I'm sorry I was a jerk last night," Lucy started but Nathaniel cut her off.

"Nothing to be sorry about." He said, "I agree you need answers and I am very frustrated that I cannot give them to you but all I can say is that my instincts will know a Demon when I see one."

Lucy sighed, "You think so?"

He shrugged lightly, "We are mortal enemies after all." He sighed.

Lucy shuddered.

Lucy was released that day and after a visit to a sleeping Dr. Hannon and a worn, haggard, grateful Brian, Lucy took a cab back home with Nathaniel in tow. She had been excused from classes that week but had every intention of going tomorrow. School was calming to Lucy, not stressful. But for now, she took a long hot shower, cleaned the many "GET WELL" cards off her door and crawled into bed. She slept for sixteen hours. Nathaniel sat on the roof and waited.

Dr. Hannon was released from the hospital a week later and

told Lucy he hoped to be back at work soon. As Brian put it, "He was shaken but not stirred and wouldn't let anyone stop him from living his life." His lack of worry over the incident might have had something to do with the fact that he couldn't remember anything. Dr. Hannon found it to be frustrating that he, an expert on the human mind, had amnesia. Lucy felt it was a blessing.

Lucy tried to go back to her normal routine but it was impossible. Nathaniel hovered everywhere and insisted on sleeping on the roof where he could keep a better look out. Lucy was tense and nervous and lived her life in a constant state of worry. Time did pass though, and before she knew it, it was two weeks before finals. She buckled down and began to study non-stop in an effort to maintain her perfect GPA.

Contrary to what they originally thought, Nathaniel proved to be an excellent study partner. He was a fast reader, an excellent researcher and a fabulous editor. They worked casually in Lucy's dorm room so they could speak freely and Lucy loved spending time with him. She could get a great deal of work done and have Nathaniel close to her.

Lucy aced all her exams giving her one less thing to worry about. As she left her last test, she was was elated but clearly not every student felt as confident about his or her performance and she received many sour looks. Her first two semesters of college were done and she had achieved perfect scores. Despite the recent trauma, Lucy was thrilled. Nathaniel had promised to meet her in the lobby of the building and she scanned the room excitedly looking for him. She spotted him standing beside a large cement pillar in the corner. He was so gorgeous and he still took her breath away. She reached the pillar and stopped short feeling the now familiar disappointment that she couldn't throw herself into his arms in public. She wished now that they had met at her dorm room for some privacy.

Nathaniel reached out his hand and led Lucy behind the pillar. There was a small nook back there and Lucy realized that they couldn't be seen by anyone. Without a word, Nathaniel grabbed her face and kissed her deeply. Lucy felt her legs turn to water and she grabbed the front of his shirt for support. His mouth moved hungrily over hers and she responded greedily, wanting him, needing and craving him more and more. Nathaniel ran his hands roughly down Lucy's neck and back. She moaned softly. He forced himself against her pushing her into the wall. She pulled tighter on his shirt pulling him as close to her body as she could. After several minutes Nathaniel pulled back and rested his head on the wall over Lucy's shoulder breathing heavily. Lucy leaned back into the wall gasping for air because the room was spinning.

"I," he said panting, "have been wanting to do that for two weeks. I didn't want to distract you from studying." He smiled at her. "Congratulations my wonderful Lucy, you are done."

She looked up at him, still dizzy. "After that kiss I most certainly am done." She started to laugh and he joined her. He wrapped his arms around her waist and sighed.

"So now what?" he asked smiling down at her.

"Now," Lucy bit her lip thinking. "Now we go back to my room and do more of that." Nathaniel threw his head back and laughed.

"Hmmm, tempting but I believe you said that you need a new bag for your trip home tomorrow. The stores close in an hour." Lucy was going home to visit her mother Sandra for the short break she had between semesters and she had been harassing Nathaniel to join her.

"You mean OUR trip tomorrow and yes, I do need a new bag. But after shopping, more kissing."

"I'm still thinking about it and yes, more kissing later," he said kissing her lightly on the lips.

They caught the bus into town. Lucy was an expert at not moving her lips while talking and they chatted easily over the loud engine. Lucy bought a new carry on bag and they were walking back to the bus stop when it happened. They were walking nonchalantly down the street, Nathaniel was whistling softly when Lucy glanced across the road. Roman was standing directly across the street from them. He was staring at Lucy. She stopped and waved at him, "That's Roman, the guy I told you about. Anastasia is crazy about him." She said quietly to Nathaniel not moving her lips and being sure not to look at him.

Roman just stood there staring at her. Thinking that he most likely didn't recognize her, Lucy waved again. He looked irritated as he started to stride towards her. It was good that traffic was light because he didn't even look as he crossed the street; he just kept his eyes trained on Lucy. As he approached, Lucy saw that he wasn't just irritated, he was furious. Roman's hands were clenched into fists, his eyes were narrowed and his jaw tight. He also wasn't looking at Lucy. She was shocked that he seemed to be looking directly at Nathaniel with hate in his bright blue eyes. "Oh no," Nathaniel whispered, his voice full of dread. Lucy didn't know if Roman had ever had a near death experience that would allow him to see part of Nathaniel. That seemed the only explanation. Roman was only a few feet away when Nathaniel reached out and pulled Lucy behind him protectively.

Roman stopped a foot away, he was incensed, just barely holding in his fury and he wasn't focused on anything or anyone but Nathaniel. Lucy looked up and saw that Nathaniel was just as angry. She had never seen him angry. His brow furrowed and his eyes narrowed to slits, his breathing came sharp and quick.

Nathaniel's body was still relaxed though. They were almost the exact same height and build, one pale and blond, the other dark and tanned but Nathaniel's attitude gave the impression he had the upper hand.

"You don't belong here," Roman snarled in Nathaniel's face.

"That is none of your concern," Nathaniel said calmly. "Go about your," he paused, "business." Nathaniel clearly did not approve of whatever business Roman was in. Lucy assumed he wasn't just an engineering student.

"Wait a minute here," she said trying to sound authoritative as she looked at Roman. "You can see him?"

Roman's eyes went wide and his head snapped to stare at her. Lucy was frightened; he looked dangerous right now. "You can see him?" he demanded. Lucy nodded dumbly. Roman shook his head in confusion. "I knew it had something to do with her," he muttered almost to himself.

Nathaniel changed the topic not wanting the attention on Lucy. "Name?" he demanded of Roman.

Roman looked slowly at Nathaniel, gave a half smile, "Roman." Nathaniel snorted in response like he didn't believe him. "Name?" Roman countered.

"Nathaniel," he replied.

Roman laughed out loud, "Gift of God. How fitting!" His face sobered and he became angry again, "You don't belong here Nathaniel Gift of God. You will go."

"It is difficult to explain," Nathaniel replied. "And none of your concern."

Roman looked around them. People were starting to pay attention. He motioned towards a small diner two doors down. He turned sharply and began walking towards it. "Follow," he spat back over his shoulder at them. Nathaniel followed, pulling Lucy behind him.

"What's going on?" Lucy asked not bothering to hide her lip movement. "How do you know him?"

Nathaniel scoffed as he held the door of the diner open for her, "I don't know him."

"Well then?" Lucy asked quickly. The diner was almost empty and Roman was sitting in a back corner booth glaring at them.

Nathaniel put his hands on her shoulders and whispered in her ear,

"That, my Lucy, is a Demon."

Lucy sat at the table staring down at the soda in front of her. No one had spoken since they had sat down. Lucy was waiting. She had no idea what was going on and she thought it was best that she keep her mouth shut, for now anyway. She was terrified. Roman sat in the middle of his booth seat so it would appear he was talking to Lucy but he ignored her.

"What are you doing here?" he was still very angry but sounded more in control, like he had gotten over the original shock.

"I don't know," Nathaniel said. Lucy assumed he saw no benefit to lying.

Roman snorted, "I doubt that."

Nathaniel shrugged. "Believe what you want."

Roman leaned forward and pointed at Nathaniel, "You have to go back now!"

Nathaniel's back stiffened, "I don't have to do anything you tell me to Demon."

Roman's eye brows shot up in surprise, "Oh no? You don't think so?" Nathaniel shook his head slowly from side to side while never taking his eyes off Roman.

Lucy was getting irritated. "Look, I need some answers here…"

Roman interrupted her. "Little girl, the adults are talking. Please be quiet." He turned back to Nathaniel and missed the hateful stare Lucy threw in his direction. "You are breaking rules here pal, rules that are older than time itself. Your Guild stays up there," he pointed to the ceiling, "or things go awry. How long have you been here?"

"Since the Spring Equinox," Nathaniel answered.

Roman threw his hands up in exasperation. "That explains it," he leaned forward again, "your presence here is affecting this area. MY area."

"How?" Lucy asked.

Roman didn't even acknowledge her. He sat back and rolled his eyes in frustration. "It hasn't even rained since you've been here and yet everything is green and pretty isn't it? You have thrown everything out of whack. The seasons changed too early! People are in fine moods aren't they?" Roman pointed angrily at Nathaniel again, "You being here is affecting my job and that won't do my friend, that won't do at all. Whatever your purpose is here, get it done and get out. This is my turf. You have to follow the rules like we follow the rules."

"I don't know my purpose here," Nathaniel replied clearly.

Roman paused in shock as he took this in, "You REALLY don't know why they sent you? Who's running things these days? They just can't send you around without instructions! What kind of outfit is this anyway? They send an Angel down and don't tell him WHY?" He shook his head. "Whatever, I don't care, go back."

"I can't," Nathaniel replied plainly.

"Why not?" Roman shot back.

Nathaniel sighed, "I don't know why I am here or how I got

here or how I get back. I don't know why they sent me but I can only assume that I am here for a purpose. I have to figure out what that is."

"So they know you are here. You didn't sneak off?" Roman asked warily.

"Of course they know I'm here. They know everything," Nathaniel said as if that was obvious.

"And no one has come for you?" Roman was still suspicious, looking for deception.

"No," Nathaniel said casually, "but I'm sure they are watching."

"Don't threaten me," Roman snarled. Nathaniel shrugged. "Your Guild is overstepping the boundaries with this little stunt," he gestured to Nathaniel, "and I assure you my Guild is not happy about it. If you want to start making threats remember that we could cause serious problems if we decided to break the rules."

"Ok seriously," Lucy cut in, "what rules?"

Roman sighed and rolled his eyes to look at her, "You again," he said with irritation. Then he changed his tone so it sounded like he was speaking to a small child, "You see little girl; I am sure your little buddy here told you all about the delicate balance that the world runs upon. I," he touched his chest with reverence, "have the vital job of keeping this balance. The two Guilds struck a deal, long ago. His Guild must stay up on their high horses and we stay down here in the trenches. Each side must do their job to maintain the equilibrium. Your little guardian here is throwing that equilibrium off. His sheer presence here on street level is pushing things decidedly in their favor and that just isn't fair."

"And what exactly is your job?" Lucy asked not sure if she wanted to hear the answer.

Roman gave her a dazzling smile, "How would you recognize a good day if you didn't have a bad day to compare it to?"

"You make bad things happen?" she whispered. Lucy felt like she might be sick.

Roman sat back and opened his arms. "I provide a service to the human race," he said with his voice full of sugar. "I'm not a bad guy really, I have to do my job. I have no choice; somebody's got to do it. If I didn't, all of humanity would come crashing to a halt. Remember of course that it is free will. I can only provide the options, no more. And Angel boy being here affects everything." He sneered, "People are making different choices, they are less likely to lean my way and more likely to lean their way. The weather changes don't help either, When the weather is lovely, everyone is happy and content and again, less likely to follow my side of things. He has tipped the scales in his favor, and it is being noticed. Guys like me make the world go round little girl."

"What a hero," Lucy sneered at him. Then a thought struck her and she gritted her teeth. "It was YOU that attacked Dr. Hannon!" she snarled at him, barely able to contain her anger. "You could have killed him! You, you monster!"

Roman looked at her seriously for a moment. "No," he said quietly, "no, that wasn't me. That is not my... style. That was Bael, my Guild Prime." When both of them gave him blank stares he sighed with exasperation and explained. "I am the Demon charged with the tasks of this area of the Guild. My Guild Prime is a higher order of Demon charged with making sure that I do my job correctly. Bael suspected that something was up a long time ago. So did I," he added hastily, "so it seems that he was trying to flush the Angel out; causing trouble near the girl so that the Angel would come to her rescue."

"The rats!" Lucy exclaimed and Nathaniel looked at her with

confusion. She shook her head.

"Ah, Bael does enjoy using rats," Roman replied, "they are not my choice but he is a very old Demon and has his own...shall we say...methods?"

"So he's like your boss then?" Lucy surmised and Roman didn't reply, "Your performance hasn't been up to par lately. Bael has been all over you since Nathaniel got here trying to find out what the trouble is."

Roman stared at her for a minute but didn't react to Lucy's theory deciding instead on his own line of questioning.

"Now what is your role in all of this my little peanut? I'm sure you have figured out that you are very unique indeed. I knew you had something to do with it. I sought you out. He wasn't with you at any of the parties but I could see him all over you. It was disgusting. I figured that I was dealing with a minor touchdown but here you are, walking down the street with him." He shook his head slightly in amazement. "What an extraordinary thing you are my little girl. You looked so pretty the night we met. It's a shame that we couldn't..." he reached out to touch her hand. Lucy snapped it back off the table and Nathaniel shot out and grabbed Roman's wrist.

"Don't touch her," he growled. "She belongs to me!" Roman pulled his arm away as if it was on fire and glared at them. Then the truth dawned on him. He sat back in the booth and grinned with glee.

"Oh!" he exclaimed. "So that's how it is! This... this is tremendous!" He looked up at the ceiling and addressed the Heavens, "An Angel, in love with a mortal? Classic! Really! How are you going to get him out of this one?" He looked at Lucy mockery in his eyes, "Do you honestly think that you measure up my little girl? Really? Do you know what the girls look like where he comes from?

You are pretty girl, down right hot some days but compared to Angel chicks, you got nothing. Girl I gotta tell ya, he is going to drop you like a stone." Lucy looked down feeling tears sting the corner of her eyes.

Nathaniel reached over and placed his hand on hers, "Ignore him," he said quietly. Lucy nodded. She felt his warmth radiate up her arm and into her heart. She closed her eyes. Roman didn't hear them; he was still on his tirade.

"This is too good! This is too rich! Bael is going to have a field day with this one! This is fantastic!" Finally, he sat back and sighed as if tired now.

Nathaniel leaned forward, "Look, I have no interest in interfering with your," he paused and rolled his eyes, "work. But I seem to be stuck here. I have not done anything untoward in violation of the agreements made between the Guilds." Lucy thought this sounded like he was talking about political peace treaties rather than the complex vying battle between Heaven and Hell. "You may go about your business. I promise not to interfere."

Rage filled Roman's face. Lucy was getting dizzy with his rapid mood shifts. "What you are not understanding is that you don't have to do anything to screw things up," Roman almost yelled. "You're here and I don't like having to bust my ass so you can slum it with your little pet human girl here. You need to figure this out and quickly. Don't make me force your hand. As I said, Bael knows you are here and trust me, he would not take the time I have to discuss it with you. You have seen what he is capable of." he finished with his teeth clenched.

"I'll do my best," Nathaniel said stiffly.

"Good, you do that," Roman smiled again and spoke softly. "Because we mustn't forget what happened to the last guy your boss sent down here." He paused for effect, "and that was his very…

own… son."

"Enough Demon!" Nathaniel roared while slamming his fist on the table.

"Stay away from Anastasia," Lucy added quietly.

Roman laughed. "Oh no, little girl, I have no intention of staying away from her. I like her."

"I swear if you so much as…" she snarled at him.

Roman laughed again, "You'll do what?" he challenged. "Sic your little Angel here on me?" He leaned back opening his arms wide, "Well here I am pal, destroy me, go ahead, I dare you." Nathaniel didn't move. He glared at Roman. "I didn't think so," Roman continued, "you see pet, he won't lay a hand on me because he knows that would start a very ugly war, one that he's not too sure his side would win."

"Oh we would win," Nathaniel said quietly, his voice full of confidence.

Roman only snorted. "And I have no intentions of hurting Anastasia. She's lovely and fun and as I said, I am, deep down, a nice guy." He stood up, threw a ten-dollar bill on the table and looked at them. "My kind is not known for their patience Angel." Nathaniel and Lucy stood. Roman turned away from them and scanned the room. Several feet away, a waitress was carrying a full tray of food. She moved carefully making sure to keep the tray in line. Roman looked back at Nathaniel with a challenge in his eyes. He raised his hand and quickly pointed his finger at the waitress. The tray immediately began to tip forward. A panicked look crossed waitresses face as she struggled to keep the tray upright. The outcome seemed inevitable as the tray eased slowly forward and the plates began to shift and slide. The waitress gave a cry of horror. Roman looked back at them, victorious and mocking.

Nathaniel lifted up his hand and opened his palm toward

the waitress for a second. The tray slowly tilted backwards, the plates shifted back and the waitress straightened up under her now totally secure tray. "Nice save," a customer said appreciatively.

"Thanks," the waitress replied smiling with relief.

Roman looked at Nathaniel with mock disappointment. He raised one finger and wagged it back and forth tsking at Nathaniel, "No no no. Don't go doing things like that Angel. You promised," he chided.

"Don't toy with me Demon," Nathaniel replied with an authority Lucy had never heard from him before. Roman laughed and sauntered out of the diner. He walked like a man who didn't have a care in the world.

Lucy turned to Nathaniel amazed, "I don't mean to make light of this situation but I had no idea you could do that. That was cool," she said with appreciation.

Nathaniel half smiled and shrugged. "I shouldn't have done it. He was baiting me. It was immature."

Lucy flopped back in the booth. "Now what?" she asked.

Nathaniel sat beside her. "Now you pack," he said calmly, "we have to get out of here."

Back at Lucy's room she was finding it difficult to get anything done. Nathaniel of course had just wished for a bag and it was packed and ready sitting by the door. Their flight left at ten the next morning and Lucy thought it might take her until then to decide what to bring. The problem was that she couldn't focus on the task at hand. Lucy threw two shirts on the floor in frustration and sat beside Nathaniel on the couch who turned to her and waited. He knew of course that Lucy had questions, who wouldn't? She indeed had a lot of questions about their confrontation with Roman but one moment in particular stayed with her above the others and had to be dealt with first.

Lucy decided not to choose her words carefully. "Was Roman right?" she asked. "Are you embarrassed to be with me?"

Nathaniel rolled his eyes. "Lucy, Roman is a Demon and most of what comes out of his mouth is a lie. I want to be with you and trust me if people could see me I would be screaming from the roof tops that I am the luckiest man in the world that Lucy Bower is in love with me. When I said to Roman that you belonged to me Lucy, I wasn't being flippant. I believe that you do belong to me, you are mine." He grabbed her face and kissed her deeply and all of Lucy's doubts left her sifting away like sand in a sieve. Nathaniel lifted his head and looked her in the eye, his intense gaze piercing into her. "Roman was trying to make you feel insecure, that's what he does. He finds the most core emotions in someone and twists them so they serve his purpose."

"That's awful," Lucy replied.

"That's a Demon Lucy. That is who he is," Nathaniel replied with a sigh. "And a young one at that. I don't know how dangerous he is but with all the pressure he is obviously getting from that Bael, he might be pushed to do something foolish. He could become very dangerous indeed if he fears his way of life is being threatened."

"What am I going to do about Anastasia?" Lucy asked in worry.

"There isn't much you can do I'm afraid. She wouldn't believe you if you told her the truth. Anastasia doesn't seem the type to blindly follow orders if you told her to stay away from him. She would want more information."

"You're right," Lucy conceded. "But what if he hurts her? As you said, he could be dangerous." She imagined Dr. Hannon's face and shuddered.

"Roman isn't all bad Lucy, you yourself have seen him

charming and funny," he said.

"But, I've also seen him be horrible," Lucy thought of the sinister grin on Roman's face when he caused that tray to tip and she shuddered.

"He still has a soul Lucy and it is screaming at his behavior. He is in a constant battle with himself. This is increased by the fact that he is a young Demon, he hasn't lost all his humanity yet. He hasn't forgotten what's right. Did you notice how quickly his mood changed?" Lucy nodded remembering the erratic behavior. "That is the behavior of a deeply torn person. My presence also makes it worse. I am the opposite of him and a Heavenly presence only reminds him of all his mistakes."

"What would he have had to do to become a Demon?" Lucy asked.

"I have no idea," Nathaniel shook his head. "He was a very bad person when he lived on this Earth and he will pay for those mistakes until the end of time."

"How does his job actually work? I understand the Angel side of things but I am having a hard time imagining the opposite." Lucy pressed trying to comprehend.

"For example," he said picking up her hand and tracing her fingers with this own absentmindedly. "A man drops his wallet outside of a convenience store, he doesn't see it drop and keeps walking. There is a teenage boy standing nearby. Roman makes him look at the wallet."

"And then he waits to see what decision the boy will make."

"Exactly, Demons, like Angels can only give options and it's up to the person to make the choice. He can take the wallet and spend the money or he can call the man and give him his wallet back. It's up to him. But, like the other side of it, evil breeds evil. The kid that steals the wallet may then steal something else or learn to pick pocket. Each Guild has to work diligently to maintain the balance."

"Why do you use the term Guilds?" Lucy asked.

"What we do is a craft, an art if you will, and I know the Angels who perform this line of work take a lot of pride in what they do. It is a great honor to be a Guardian. I can only assume that it is the same for Demons." Nathaniel replied, "I didn't anticipate my presence here would change anything for the resident Demon but obviously, people are choosing to do the right thing more often making Roman's craft harder. It also doesn't help that he has a higher Demon putting pressure on him. It makes things very dangerous indeed."

Lucy thought for a moment. "But did God kind of shoot himself in the foot here?" she asked.

Nathaniel laughed a little. "What do you mean?"

"I mean, he could just make all the bad guys go away. He could make it so that everyone always does the right thing and no one is ever bad."

"God tried that Lucy, have you ever heard of a little place called the Garden of Eden?" he said with a smile. "It doesn't work that way. We have to have free will so we can make mistakes and grow and learn. What kind of life would we have if we couldn't make decisions for ourselves? Could you be happy if your entire life was planned for you? You would never make mistakes but you would never become a better person. Wouldn't that feel like a prison to you?"

"Yes," Lucy admitted, "it would."

"And that's not ok with God. If we only did the right thing all the time we would be just as bad as Roman who does the wrong thing all the time. God loves us too much to hinder us in any way."

"Ok," Lucy said nodding. "I get it, he's necessary."

"Sadly, yes."

"Will you have to fight him?" Lucy asked nervously.

"I hope not," Nathaniel replied sighing.

"Are you afraid of him?" Lucy wondered hoping he would be honest with her.

"Not half as afraid as he is of me," Nathaniel said smirking.

"Would you win?"

"Of course I would," Nathaniel said as if this was obvious. "But I don't want to fight them. I think if we go to Kansas, it will give Roman and Bael a little break from me. When we get back, I will lay low and try to figure out what to do. No more wandering around town. I'm sure I will come up with something."

Lucy noticed that he didn't sound totally sure of anything.

Chapter Nine
Travel

"Close your eyes I'll be on my way."
~John Denver

Upon check in the next morning, Lucy had requested a seat in the back and a row to herself. Since the plane wasn't full, she and Nathaniel sat comfortably, quietly talking under the roar of the engines and out of sight from the other passengers. The flight attendant dropped off their drinks not questioning why Lucy wanted two of everything. Within a few moments, both Lucy and Nathaniel felt the tension that had held them so tightly wound release slightly. They both sighed in unison.

Lucy sat back and smiled at Nathaniel, "I'm glad you came."

"So am I," he smiled back. "I don't know if I could have survived almost a week without you. I am so attached to you Lucy it's a little scary at times. I crave you when you are not around."

"I feel the same way," Lucy said with relief. "Do you think it's normal?"

"A girl with a photographic memory and a boy who is an

Angel from Heaven and you ask me if we are normal? I don't think so," he said with a grin.

"Good point," Lucy nodded. "So about the Angel thing."

"Yes?" he smirked suspecting more questions from an ever-curious Lucy.

"How powerful are you?" Lucy asked. "That thing yesterday with the tray was awesome, I didn't know you could do that."

"I can do that," he said as if this was sufficient.

"Can you move bigger things?" Lucy asked enthralled.

"Not people, I'm not allowed to move people," he said casually. "But I can move bigger things."

"Like a car?"

"Yes," again he was relaxed about it.

"Like this plane?"

"Yes, if I wanted to," he said looking uncomfortable with all the attention on him.

"Stop being so calm about this!" Lucy demanded. "You can move stuff with your mind!"

"No I can't," he corrected. "I move things with my hand."

"Big difference," Lucy rolled her eyes. "Why didn't you tell me you could do that?"

"Because I don't need to move things," he said. "I can get up and get stuff."

"What else can you do?" she asked excitedly.

"Nothing, that's it," he said curtly.

"Liar," Lucy laughed. "You have to tell me everything."

Nathaniel laughed, "Fine. Well, I can move stuff if I need to and I am really funny and smart..." Lucy raised her eyebrows in warning. He sighed and relented, "Well you know about the flowers right?"

"Yes, so are your powers mostly nature based then?"

"Yes, those are the things I can control. I can make those things pop out of no where but I can't make money appear, that's why I have to wish for that stuff."

"So Heaven gives you man made stuff for moving around but you can do stuff with nature anytime you want," Lucy concluded.

"Right, exactly."

"Show me."

"Nope," he said. "No way."

"Then show me one thing, just one thing."

"If I do will you drop it?" he asked smiling.

"Probably not but it would certainly shut me up for a while," she said grinning.

He sighed and looked at her, "the things I do for you Lucy…." He lifted up his hand and it was in a tight fist. He slowly opened his hand and Lucy gasped. Sitting in the middle of his palm was a perfect, tiny tornado spinning and swerving on his hand. He smiled at her reaction and closed his fist again making it disappear. Lucy stared at him for a moment stunned.

"Can you make a full sized one?" she asked with awe.

"I can," he said plainly.

"Can Roman?" she asked fearfully.

"He most likely has power to but doesn't need to," he said reassuring her.

"Then who causes the natural disasters and all that?"

He shook his head, "that's something else entirely, not Demons or Angels."

Lucy looked at him and grinned, "You are wonderful."

"It's no big deal," he said shrugging.

"Do it again," Lucy said sounding like a toddler. Nathaniel laughed and raised his fist again, when he opened it, there was a rainbow hovering on his palm. Lucy grinned.

Suddenly the plane dropped slightly. Everyone gave a small cry of surprize, followed quickly by a twitter of laughter. The flight attendants moved slowly but with urgency to each end of the plane. The seat belt sign came on. Lucy focused on putting on her own seatbelt and it wasn't until she was all secured in that she realized that Nathaniel wasn't sitting beside her anymore. He was standing a few feet away in the aisle of the plane, his hands were flexed tightly and his jaw was strained and he was looking at the ceiling of the aircraft.

The plane dropped again, farther, harder and with far less control. There was another cry this time from the passengers but this time without any giggles. An overhead bin opened and a few items trickled to the ground. No one moved to pick them up. Lucy noted that Nathaniel barely moved. The cabin was silent, somewhere further up in the plane, a baby started crying. This was quickly becoming a situation of worry. The plane dropped again, and swept to the side sharply. The cries turned into screams and Nathaniel vanished.

Lucy cried out but no one noticed because at this point everyone was screaming. Where could he have gone? Was he in the flight deck trying to see what was going on? Was he hanging onto the outside of the plane? Lucy craned her neck to try to see out the window but all she saw was blue sky. The plane was jerking violently now, dropping and bucking severely. This wasn't normal turbulence and Lucy could only hang on to her seat and brace against the fierce movement.

Against her will, her brain provided her with every image of a plane crash she had ever seen. She grunted as she tried to ignore the pictures flying through her consciousness. The passengers started panicking, yelling out and crying openly, someone was saying the rosary. It was clear to everyone, that nothing could take this kind of abuse for long. It was only a matter of time.

The turbulence stopped as quickly as it had started and the cabin went silent. It felt too good to be true. The captain's tense voice came over the speakers. "Folks, we seem to have passed through a deep turbulence area. I apologise that we didn't give you any warning on that. We have had no reports on bumps in this area."

"Bumps?" Someone said out loud. "More like craters."

"Please notify the flight attendants of any injuries. It will be a hopefully smooth next hour to Wichita."

Lucy leaned out to the window again. Where was Nathaniel? Panic surged through her as she pictured Dr. Hannon's mangled face.

"Nathaniel?" she whispered. "Please come."

Nothing.

She scanned the cabin searching for him but there was no sign of him. He could be anywhere on the planet. Or he could be dead. Lucy stifled a sob as she sat helplessly waiting. It seemed like hours. She snapped at the Flight Attendant when she came through to check on everyone. Suddenly, someone grabbed her arm. Lucy yelped in terror as she whipped around to look at her assailant. Relief swept through her as Nathaniel's dark face was within inches of her own. Not caring that no one could see him and she looked like a lunatic, Lucy threw her arms around his neck and kissed him hard. He kissed her back and wove his hands through her hair.

She sat back and sighed with relief. "Where have you been?"

Nathaniel shook his head, "I went up to the flight deck to make sure the pilots stayed safe."

"That wasn't normal turbulence was it?"

Nathaniel laughed ruefully, "No, no it wasn't."

"Did you see anything?" Lucy swallowed, "Was it Bael?"

"I didn't see him, but that wasn't natural." He looked out the window.

"Are you sure?" Lucy hoped, "Maybe it was just turbulence."

"Lucy," Nathaniel said calmly, "I don't want you to freak out but it was nothing common. The captain called in a possible SOS as a result of a foreign bogey."

Lucy's memory scanned the terminology and she gasped when she realized that this is the wording used for UFOs. The pilots thought that something was after them as well and it was something they could not identify. She shuddered.

"Now what?" she almost whimpered. She had never felt so vulnerable in her whole life. They were trapped on this plane and at the mercy of a Demon.

"Pray?" Nathaniel offered and wrapped his arms around her.

They arrived at the airport on time and the passengers could not wait to get off that plane. Lucy's hands were stiff from gripping onto the armrests the whole way. Lucy and Nathaniel left the secured area carrying their bags. As they descended the escalators, Lucy scanned the waiting crowd for her Mom.

"There she is," Nathaniel pointed out a well-dressed brunette standing in the crowd.

"How did you know?" Lucy muttered.

"She's beautiful," he replied. Lucy smiled at the compliment and waved at her Mom who waved back excitedly.

Sandra Bower stood five foot four inches tall with chestnut brown hair styled in a sweeping bouffant that looked like Jackie O hair but still modern and smart. She was shapely and wore a purple suit under a beige dress coat. Lucy ran into her mother's open arms and clutched her tightly.

"Oh my Lucy, my Lucy, you're home baby," Sandra's voice

was full of emotion as she held her daughter tight.

Lucy felt her throat constrict as she choked out, "I missed you Mom."

Sandra gave Lucy another squeeze and let her go. Holding her at arms length she looked Lucy over, "Let me look at you," she sniffed. "Oh you look gorgeous. Was it hot on the plane? You're flushed honey." Lucy had no intention of telling her mother about the trouble on the plane. She couldn't tell her much of anything that had happened to her lately. Sandra was a pretty cool mom but she was still a mom and her worrying would become tiresome.

"Yes," Lucy mumbled awkwardly, "It was ....um…hot on the plane." Behind her Nathaniel chuckled. Lucy had to stop herself from introducing the two of them.

As if he could read her mind, Nathaniel leaned forward respectfully and said, "It's a pleasure to finally meet you Mrs. Bower, Lucy has told me so much about you." Lucy grinned, that would have to do.

"Come on," Sandra linked her arm through Lucy's and started heading for the large glass doors, "lets get out of here, I need some lunch and we have so much to talk about."

Sandra talked the entire time in the car on the way out of town. Lucy was pleased to hear her mother sounding so happy. She was concerned about Sandra in September when she left for Mulbridge. It had been only six months after her father's death and although the two had been divorced for five years Lucy's mom had been devastated by her father's death. It was good to see that her mother had bounced back.

Sandra Bower was the best realtor in Stonecreek and gave Lucy a detailed description of every deal she had made in the last six months since Lucy had been home. She told her every bit of gossip she could think of. Lucy's mom knew who was pregnant, getting married, getting a divorce or having an affair because all of these things needed a new home. If a husband was leaving his wife, Sandra Bower was the first to know because he'd always call for a confidential appraisal on the house.

She still had not run out of information when they sat down at the restaurant for lunch and prattled on about extended family and long lost friends.

"Are you hungry honey?" Sandra asked looking over the menu. Lucy nodded eagerly.

"This honey is starving, get extra Lucy," Nathaniel replied beside her. Lucy stifled a laugh as she ordered an appetizer, salad and the biggest plate of pasta she could see on the menu. Lucy's mom was so busy talking that she didn't even notice that the majority of Lucy's meal literally disappeared. When they were done, her mother looked at Lucy in shock.

"Lucy, you were hungry," she exclaimed. "I have never seen you eat that much. Aren't they feeding you there?"

Lucy laughed, "I haven't eaten all day Mom."

"Well, you should be eating regular meals," her mother chided. "Boys like a girl with a little meat on their bones."

Nathaniel laughed.

"Speaking of boys, are there any contenders honey?" she asked propping her elbows on the table. Lucy was about to lie and say that there were no prospects in her life but then she thought better of it. There was no reason to not tell her mother some of the truth. Lucy had never gotten to gush about Nathaniel like other girls did. There was no way her mom would ever find out the truth, she lived far enough away that Lucy was immune from normal parental inquiries. If she worded it right, she could gush about Nathaniel and still protect the truth.

"Well, there is one boy," she said already starting to blush at the prospect of discussing Nathaniel out loud.

"Do tell," her mother leaned forward intrigued.

"Lucy," Nathaniel said in a warning tone but Lucy ignored him.

"His name is Nathaniel, and mom he is absolutely gorgeous!" Lucy beamed.

Nathaniel sat back in his chair and rolled his eyes, "Oh no, Lucy please don't make me sit here and listen to this."

Lucy grinned and kept going, "He's tall, dark and handsome. He is the most gorgeous guy I have ever seen!"

"That's enough," Nathaniel said starting to blush.

Lucy couldn't stop now even if she wanted to. "And his eyes mom. Oh his eyes are unbelievable! They are this crystal grey color I have never seen before and they change shades. He looks like a movie star!" Beside her, Nathaniel groaned. "And he's so funny and so smart and kind and he's just the best guy I have ever met. I am just crazy about him."

"Oh my goodness Lucy," Sandra exclaimed, "he sounds wonderful! How long have you two been seeing each other?" Now sadly, Lucy had to lie because she couldn't have her mother asking for pictures of him or calling Dr. Hannon about him.

"Well, that's the thing mom," she said sadly, "we aren't seeing each other." Her mother's face fell. "It's like," she stopped for dramatic effect, "It's like I'm invisible to him!"

"Oh for the love of…," Nathaniel exploded beside her.

"Lucy," her mother was irritated, "you are beautiful girl. You are wonderful. This guy doesn't know what he's missing."

"This is painful," Nathaniel moaned.

"You have to make him see you. Ask him out for Pete's sake! It's the twenty first century! Assert yourself! And if he says no, well, he's an idiot and not worth your time!"

"Ok," Lucy said deciding to shut this down before Nathaniel started throwing things. "I will, thanks mom."

Sandra patted Lucy's hand and looked at her watch, "Oh yikes, we have to get going." She stood up and started pulling on her coat.

Lucy stood too, "Do you have plans?" they moved to the door and walked out to the street.

"Um yeah, I kind of do," Sandra answered unlocking the car doors. Nathaniel appeared into the back seat as Lucy got into the front. Sandra slid into the drivers seat.

"So where are you going?" Lucy asked.

"Well, um," her mom started the car and pulled out into the street, "um well um ....I have a date," she finished finally.

"Oh," Lucy didn't know what to say to that. Honestly, she had never even thought of that as an option.

"I'm sorry," Sandra said apologetically, "it's your first night home and if you want me to cancel, I certainly will but this was the only night that worked for him and well...um... honey are you ok with this?" Lucy realized that her mom had been nervous to tell her about the date. Lucy's heart went out to her, no wonder she had been so chatty this whole time. She was avoiding this topic.

"Mom," Lucy reached out and touched her leg; "you and Dad have been divorced for like five years."

"Well, I know that honey but I loved your father, even after the divorce. It wasn't like we hated each other; we just disagreed on some things." Lucy knew her Mom had moved past her father's death but now she realized that she hadn't quite gotten over it. Her heart broke a little. Lucy had lost her father but Sandra had lost the love of her life. "I still on some level," her mother continued softly, "feel like I am cheating on him. I just don't know how he would feel about this. Do you think he minds I'm dating?"

Lucy knew the answer but for confirmation looked into the backseat where Nathaniel was confidently shaking his head slowly side to side. "Mom, Dad wouldn't mind at all. He would want you to be happy."

Sandra breathed a sigh of relief, "And you honey, do you mind?"

"Not at all Mom, have fun," Lucy said just as confident in her answer.

Her mother smiled, "Thank you Lucy."

"So…." Lucy sang out, "where did you meet him?"

"Well to be honest, I met him on a dating website," her mother admitted.

"Oh man!" Lucy groaned.

"Now don't be like that," Sandra defended. "Miles seems very nice and our profiles match quite well."

"Ok fine," Lucy relented. "But can I meet him and check him out?"

"Sure! But honey, you have no veto power," Sandra grinned as she pulled into the driveway. "Your old mom is pretty lonely these days. I swear the Devil himself could walk in the door and if he was willing to buy me dinner I'd still go out with him." Nathaniel burst into laughter from the back seat. Lucy started to giggle. "It's true!" her mother started laughing, "I think the Devil might be a better date than most of the men in this town!"

"Oh I hope not!" Nathaniel yelled at the ceiling laughing. Lucy got out of the car doubled over with laughter. Her Mom was up at the front door using her key to unlock it. Lucy closed the back door and paused, grinning at Nathaniel.

He grinned back and kissed her forehead, "What are you doing to me Lucy?" he mumbled in her hair.

"Loving you," she muttered under her breath.

They turned and headed towards the door. Lucy's childhood home was a typical middle class three-bedroom two-story house. It was white with black trim and a bright red door. As Lucy walked in she hadn't realized how much she had missed it. The cozy den was on the right, the family room with the most comfortable couch in the world was on the right and at the back of the house was Sandra's blue and white kitchen with the kitchen nook that had glass doors that led to the backyard. Lucy loved it all. It felt a little foreign after all her time spent in her tiny dorm room at Mulbridge but it was still her home. She paused and took a deep breath, she was home and she was happy.

"Welcome home baby," her mom said lovingly and gave her a hug.

Lucy hugged her back tightly, "Thanks Mom, I love you."

"Love you too my little Click," Sandra looked at her watch again. "I've got to go get ready, Miles will be here in an hour." She paused and looked at Lucy, "Are you sure this is alright with you?"

"It's more than alright," Lucy assured her. "I think it's great. Plus it will give me a chance to take a long soaking bath. I have been dying for a bath for months."

"Oh honey I'm sorry," her mother said. "I'm redoing the main bathroom, the tub is gone. They were supposed to have it done by now but you know contractors!"

"No way!" Lucy groaned. "Mom, other than seeing you, that is all I was looking forward to."

"I am so sorry honey!" Sandra started to bolt up the stairs like a girl getting ready for the prom. "Tomorrow will make up for it, it's all about us. I've got spa time, shopping, lunch, the works!"

"Sounds great!" Lucy yelled up the stairs. "A bath sounds good too!"

"Get over it!" her mother joked back yelling down the stairs.

Lucy heard her mother's door close.

"Click?" Nathaniel asked over her shoulder. Lucy smiled and walked towards the kitchen, motioning for him to follow. She poured a glass of water, took a sip and slid it across the counter for him to finish. Nathaniel sat on the stool at the counter and drained the water.

Lucy lowered her voice even though she could hear her mother's shower running, "When they first discovered my photographic memory, I was only two years old so my vocabulary was still really limited. My Mom came up with the idea of asking me to take a picture of something to get me to remember it. I used to look at whatever it was, say 'click' like a camera and they knew I had it." She shrugged. "The nickname stuck and still to this day, once in a while I'll say 'click' out of habit when I want to remember something and lock it in."

"But do you have to lock it in?" Nathaniel asked. "Or does your brain just remember everything?"

"Now it locks everything in but I used to have to ask it to. I do sometimes say the word just as a confirmation to myself that I've locked it in. If it's something I really want to remember or if it's important."

Nathaniel nodded, lifted his hand, extended his index finger and beckoned her towards him. Lucy leaned over and kissed him, loving every second, when they parted Lucy whispered, "Click."

Nathaniel grinned; "So I look like a movie star huh?" he sat back amused.

"Well, you know," Lucy said lightly. "I had to build it up for my mom. I couldn't tell her you were all homely now could I?" Nathaniel laughed taking the joke with ease and kissed her again. "Wanna see my room?" Lucy asked in her best junior high voice.

"Only if there is a minimum of three spelling bee trophies up there," Nathaniel replied seriously.

"Shut up," she laughed. "There are six."

"I'm in!"

Lucy could hear the Rolling Stones pounding from her mother's room as they walked down the hall past her room. Lucy rolled her eyes, it was like she was a teenager again. At least they wouldn't have to worry about whispering.

Lucy's room was exactly as she had left it. Her double bed was neat and tidy with it's flowered bedspread and the books she left behind when she left for college were stacking the shelves. There were three extra shelves that held pictures and trophies and other memorabilia. Her desk was almost bare with a few pictures and a stationary set.

Lucy went through her room and showed him her trophies and pictures and all the tiny details of a girls room. Throughout, he was fascinated. He asked questions and handled her things with care. While Lucy was reenacting her last debate and the trophy she won, the doorbell rang.

They froze, looked at each other with glee and in unison said, "He's here!" Lucy giggled as she dropped the trophy on the bed and bolted for the door. She ran down the stairs, two at a time and almost slammed into the front door. Lucy paused briefly to catch her breath, gave Nathaniel a meaningful look and whipped open the door. She didn't know what to expect but Lucy did not expect this.

Miles could not look less like her father. He was tall and well built with a deep south Florida tan that in Kansas could only come artificially. His black hair was slicked back and his deep blue eyes twinkled with the knowledge that he was a forty-something eligible bachelor. He wore a silver suit that was actually shiny, a black shirt and salmon pink tie. His shoes were so glossy that they reflected the spring light. Lucy stopped.

"Well at least he made an effort," Nathaniel humored beside her. "Say hello Lucy, you're gawking."

Lucy composed herself, "Hi! You must be Miles!" she said over enthusiastically as she stuck out her hand. "I'm Lucy, Sandra's daughter."

Miles smiled a thousand dollar bleached smile and replied in a voice only a TV show audience could love, "Hello Lucy, I've heard so much about you." His handshake was strong but the waft of cologne that accompanied it was dizzying. Lucy moved aside so he could come in and to avoid the onslaught of Drakkar.

"Mom! You have a visitor!" Lucy yelled up the stairs. It was clear her mother had heard the doorbell and was waiting for her big entrance. She stepped out of her room and descended the stairs in a way that would make Scarlet O'Hara proud.

Sandra looked gorgeous in her silk navy blue dress. Her hair was styled to perfection and she looked nowhere near her forty-five years. Miles apparently thought the same thing because he had a stunned, dumbfounded look on his face. Lucy felt proud, *that's my mom,* she thought to herself.

"Miles," Lucy's mother exclaimed. "It's so nice to see you in person." She glided over to him and gave him a light hug.

"And you Sandra. Might I say that your profile picture does not do you justice? That dress is stunning."

Sandra laughed, "Oh really? Well thank you." The two of them stared at each other for a moment. Lucy backed up awkwardly to the stairs and Nathaniel followed.

"We should go," Miles finally broke the silence. "We have reservations."

"Of course!" Sandra exclaimed. She walked over to Lucy and hugged her. "Don't wait up," she whispered in Lucy's ear. "He's gorgeous!"

Lucy stopped herself from gagging, "Have fun Mom." Sandra turned and walked towards the door. Miles held her coat out for her and as she pulled it on, Nathaniel whispered in Lucy's ear,

"Most certainly not the Dark Lord but definitely a car salesman." Lucy bit her lip to prevent herself from laughing. With a smile from her mom and a wink from Miles, they went out the door and closed it. Lucy looked at Nathaniel and he shrugged, "she looks happy Lucy."

"I have to agree," Lucy said with a sigh. Nathaniel reached down and wrapped his arms around her. Lucy wiggled back into his chest.

"Now what?" he asked.

"I think we should eat, watch a movie and sleep."

"This is why we are together, we think the same way," he said resting his chin on the top of her head.

The next morning, Lucy slept until ten. She hadn't slept that late in months. She rolled over and reached for Nathaniel but found the other side of the bed empty. Lucy had woken up with Nathaniel beside her almost every morning since they met. Panic struck her as she sat straight up in bed. Was he gone? Had they taken him back so soon? Why? She looked around the room whispering, "Not yet, please not yet." Lucy looked back at the bed and relief swept through her. A single daisy sat on Nathaniel's pillow beside a note:

Have fun with your Mom today.

I have a few things to do. I'll be back tonight.

Call me if you need me.

Always yours,

N

Lucy sighed. A whole day without Nathaniel sounded horrible. They hadn't been apart for more than a few hours since they met. Lucy tucked the note and flower under her pillow as Sandra popped her head in the room.

"Oh good," her mom said. "You're up. We've got massages in an hour then manicures, pedicures and after lunch we have some serious shopping to do." She grinned excitedly and left the room.

"I'm up. I'm up," Lucy said crawling out of bed and starting to dress. She had to admit that the agenda for the day did sound good even if Nathaniel couldn't be there. She doubted he had anything to do but just didn't want to spend the day doing girl stuff. What boy would really? She smiled thinking of him and headed downstairs to begin a fun filled day with her mom.

It was a great day. Sandra gave Lucy the rundown on her date with Miles and he did sound very nice. Lucy told her mom all about school, her friends and work, filling her in on every detail. Sandra loved every second of it. They seemed to talk all day long and someone was always saying something. Sandra bought Lucy so many clothes that they had to buy a second suitcase for her to carry it all to Mulbridge. They made a simple spaghetti dinner and ate in front of the TV while watching their favorite movie 'Breakfast at Tiffany's'.

It was ten o'clock when they decided to go to bed. Lucy was exhausted. Sandra had a full day of work the next day so Lucy would be on her own until dinner. Mother and daughter hugged at the top of the stairs.

"That was a great day mom, thanks," Lucy said.

"Thank you for coming honey," Sandra replied. "Now have a good sleep, I won't wake you before I go."

Lucy walked into the bathroom and gave the crater that was supposed to hold the bathtub a dirty look. She would love a bath right now. She began brushing her teeth and immediately her thoughts went to Nathaniel. She would call him the second she was in her room. Urgency gripped her as she thought of him being only seconds away. Lucy began to crave him as she washed her face and pulled on her pajamas. She had missed him today, badly and now she needed him.

She hurried back to her room ready to call his name the moment her door closed but she stopped herself. Nathaniel was waiting for her on her bed. His long legs were stretched out and crossed at the ankles and he looked like he always did, completely at home. His dazzling eyes lit up when he saw Lucy and he tossed the book he was reading aside to throw his arms open for her. Nathaniel smiled his 'for Lucy only' smile and her heart skipped several beats.

Lucy ran and jumped on him landing in a sitting position on his stomach. She laid her hands on his chest and leaned forward kissing him with every bit of love she could find for him. He responded fervently, twining his fingers in her hair and pulling her closer to him, pressing his lips into hers.

"I missed you," he said almost growling against her mouth.

"Show me," Lucy whispered back. Nathaniel responded by lifting her easily, flipping her sideways and rolling on top of her. Lucy's heart started to race as he kissed her mouth and down her neck. He snaked his arms under her and clutched her tightly. Lucy ran her hands through his thick black hair and wrapped her legs around his waist pulling him closer to her. Nathaniel slowed his kisses and lifted his head. Lucy groaned in protest and started kissing his neck.

"This is dangerous with your mom next door," he warned.

"I don't care," Lucy whispered into his neck. "I want more than just kissing, don't you?"

"Oh yes," he gave a small laugh. "I want much more," he gently pulled himself out of her grasp, "but not tonight." Lucy grabbed a pillow and hit him square across the side of the face with it.

"What was that for?" he asked incredulously.

"For being so damn good all the time!" Lucy pouted. Nathaniel smiled and flopped down beside her on the bed. She rolled on her side to face him and reached up to run his hands through her hair.

"How was your day?" he asked.

Lucy smiled, "it was great. How was yours?"

"Good," he replied smiling.

"What did you do?" Lucy asked.

Nathaniel shrugged. "Nothing much."

"Come on, tell me," Lucy begged.

"I promise to show you one day," he replied earnestly.

"That's what you say about everything! I'm being cheated here. Don't you trust me?" she asked with a little pain in her voice.

He rested his hand on her cheek and looked down at her, "Lucy I trust you completely and I promise to show you everything."

"When?"

"Soon," he replied with confidence.

"Tomorrow?" she negotiated.

"No, but soon," she could hear the smile in his voice.

"Fine, but be put on notice that I am pissed off until then," she said with petulance.

"Duly noted," he kissed her head and she could feel him smelling her hair. "Good night my Lucy."

"Good night my Angel." The lights went out.

They had the whole next day to themselves and Lucy was

going to show Nathaniel around. They walked out of Lucy's house and turned right.

"Ok," Nathaniel said, eager for his tour, "what's first?"

"Neighborhood, high school and then the town," Lucy listed off. They walked a bit down Lucy's street and she saw Mrs. Turner was in her yard. Mrs. Turner had been widowed since before Lucy was born and was the queen of the neighborhood. She knew everyone and every detail about everyone's lives. She was a sweet old lady that always had a kind word for anyone passing by and baking for newcomers. Mrs. Turner had come to her father's funeral and made over a hundred sandwiches for the reception at their home. "Hi Mrs. Turner!" Lucy called and walked to the edge of her yard.

"Well, little Lucy Bower," the elderly lady exclaimed putting down her hand rake and standing up brushing dirt off her apron as she went. "How are you dear? How is school?"

"School is good, I have a four-point GPA," Lucy replied smiling.

"That is wonderful! Good girl! Your Mom's been just fine without you sweet heart. I've been keeping an eye on her."

"Well thank you Mrs. Turner, I appreciate that," Lucy smiled. "Well, I had better get going. You have a good day."

"You too darling!" Mrs. Turner sang as she waved Lucy on.

Lucy took about three steps before she heard a very different voice from behind her. It was a deep husky raspy voice, "How long are you planning on staying Angel?" Lucy turned to realize that the voice was coming from Mrs. Turner and she was talking directly to Nathaniel. Her eyes were narrowed into slits and one side of her mouth was turned up in a snarl. It was such a change from the moment before that Lucy blinked several times to make sure it wasn't an illusion.

"Not long Demon," Nathaniel answered calmly. "Not long."

Mrs. Turner glared at him. "Don't you cause any trouble while you're here. Understand?"

"Absolutely," Nathaniel said in the same calm voice.

"Humph, dammed well better understand" Mrs. Turner mumbled as she turned her back on them and went back to her weeding.

"Walk Lucy," Nathaniel ordered in a whisper. "She doesn't know you can see me."

They walked several blocks in silence before they reached a park Lucy used to play at. Lucy sat down on a bench.

"Mrs. Turner is a Demon?" she asked in shock.

"Yup," Nathaniel replied sitting beside her, "a very, very old Demon, that lady might have known Egyptian Kings."

"Seriously?" Lucy asked. "But she is the sweetest thing in the world!"

"I told you Lucy, they aren't bad to the core. I'm sure she likes you very much."

"Why did she talk to you with me right there if she doesn't know I can see you?" Lucy asked playing the scene out in her mind again.

"Well, Roman did that too. When Demons and Angels talk to each other, I don't think humans can't usually see or hear us. You are the exception. Mrs. Turner thinks I'm just following you around and you are completely unaware of that. It's good she thinks that."

"That was super creepy," Lucy said shuddering.

"Don't worry, she won't bother us. She has this place in her back pocket; I bet she doesn't even have to leave her house to do her job. An Angel like me couldn't have as strong an effect here as I do at Mulbridge where Roman is a much younger Demon and isn't as astute at his job." His tone changed from light to serious as he continued, "But a word of warning Lucy, she is incredibly powerful so don't ever and I mean ever irritate that woman in any way shape or form."

"Ok...I'll do my best," she said shaking her head still in shock that the kindly old neighborhood lady was an ancient Demon.

"Try not to worry Lucy," he said putting his arm around her. "Nothing can hurt you when I'm around. I would never allow that."

Lucy took a deep breath, comforted by his words. "Should we go back and hide in the house or can we keep going?"

"We can go on, I won't let some Demon ruin my day with you," he said lightly. "I don't think we should ever walk past her house again though."

"Ok," Lucy smiled back. "On we go with the tour."

Lucy's high school was only a few blocks away and when they arrived, school was still in session. Lucy checked in with the office and said hello to the principal and administrators before showing Nathaniel around. She showed him where her classes had been and they perused the trophy case that showed Lucy's name more often than not. They went out the back door to cut through the field as a short cut to town. The whole backfield of the school was lined with lilac bushes.

"In the summer, these are all in bloom. It's really pretty," Lucy explained. "It's kind of sad that I won't see it this year."

They crossed the field and arrived at the pathway on the other side.

"Can we stop for a moment please?" Nathaniel asked. Lucy stopped and looked at him. He glanced around as if making sure no one was watching before he said in a sneaky voice, "Wanna see what I can do?" Without waiting for a response, he reached out and ran his hand down the branches of the closest lilac bush. It immediately began to tremble in reaction to his touch. "Come on," he whispered to it, "I know it's a little early but can you do it for Lucy please?" The entire bush began to shake violently until finally it seemed to explode as every single inch of it burst into beautiful purple blooms.

Lucy watched in awe as each of the bushes in turn quivered and exploded in color all around the field until the entire square was awake and covered in blooms. She breathed in deeply as her nose was hit with the heady scent of lilacs. Nathaniel turned to her grinning. "There, now you won't miss anything."

"It's beautiful," Lucy managed to choke out. "Thank you."

Nathaniel shrugged, "anything for you Lucy." He turned to the bush, "Thank you, it's wonderful," he whispered to it. The lilac shook lightly in response. He took Lucy's hand and pulled her gently away from the field, she could barely take her eyes off the gorgeous sight.

They walked down Stonecreek Main Street passing the antique stores, hardware store and boutiques. Lucy gave tidbits of information under her breath about each place, the owners and any memories she had of each location. They stopped at a street corner to wait for a light and Nathaniel pointed to a store across the street. "What's that place?" he asked. It had a neon sign in the window that read:

'Lady Soral – Know your future, find your angel.'

Lucy looked at Nathaniel doubtfully. "Seriously?" she muttered.

"Well, it's worth a shot," he elbowed her lightly. "Come on, let's give it a try."

Lucy rolled her eyes as they crossed the street and walked

up to the small grungy door. "Nathaniel," Lucy said patiently, "this lady is probably a crackpot. She's a scammer."

"How do you know?" he asked hopefully. "Maybe she has some answers."

Lucy sighed and pushed open the door. There was a jingling as the bell announced their arrival. The front part of the store was small and dark with statues and knickknacks lining the dusty narrow shelves. A tiny wrinkled woman dressed in a flowing dress emerged from behind a beaded curtain at the back of the store. Her hair was blue washed and built up in a beehive, she had about fifteen necklaces on; some were beaded, others were medallions and one Lucy was pretty sure was just a piece of string. Every one of her bony fingers held a ring, each gaudier than the one beside it. The woman smiled a mouthful of yellow teeth, "Welcome, I am Lady Soral. What can I do for you?" her voice was intense.

"I," Lucy stammered, "I wondered how much a reading is?"

"Twenty dollars," Lady Soral replied. "I can take you in right now, I've had a cancellation."

Yeah right. Lucy thought. "Um, ok," she said. Lady Soral reached out one skeletal hand, palm up. Lucy was confused, was she supposed to shake her hand or give her a high five?

"We should take care of money matters first dear," Lady Soral explained graciously. "Then both of you can come in the back for your reading."

"Both of us?" Lucy asked suspiciously. "I'm alone."

"You and your Angel dear," Lady Soral said politely.

"Pay the lady," Nathaniel urged quickly into Lucy's ear. Lucy couldn't pull her money out fast enough and Lady Soral turned and led them through the beaded curtain to an even darker back room. Lucy looked back at Nathaniel with her eyebrows raised in surprise. Nathaniel had the same look on his face. Maybe this woman did have some answers for them. The room held nothing but a table covered in a silk tablecloth and three chairs. Lady Soral sat down and motioned for Lucy to take the one across from her.

"Your Angel may sit in the third chair," she said to Lucy. Nathaniel almost jumped into the chair he was so excited to be included. Lady Soral reached across the table and took Lucy's hands in her own. She took several deep breaths, closed her eyes and wiggled a bit in her chair to settle in. Lucy waited silently. Finally, she opened her eyes and stared at Lucy intently, "Angels are all around us dear." Lucy didn't reply - this was obviously her standard opening. "People are assigned an Angel who moves through their life at their side."

"Wrong," Nathaniel blurted out.

"If you ignore your Angel, they will punish you and make bad things happen to you."

"Wrong!" Nathaniel sounded agitated.

"Angels are jealous of us and want to be alive again so we have to deal with them gently."

"So very incorrect," Nathaniel contested.

"It is only by coming to see me that you can understand what your Angel wants from you to keep them happy," Lady Soral got her plug in.

"What?" Nathaniel almost yelled beside her. Lucy bit her lip to stop from laughing.

"If your Angel is happy, wonderful things will happen to you, you will become more successful in life; make more money, find love and get all the material goods you desire."

"NO!" Nathaniel did yell this time and Lucy had to sit placidly, pretending he didn't exist.

"I see your Angel dear," she paused for dramatic effect. Lucy leaned forward, she felt Nathaniel do the same. "Your Angel's name is," another pause, "Ingrid."

"Ingrid?" Lucy and Nathaniel said in unison.

"Yes Ingrid," Lady Soral explained. "She is an old cranky woman, bent over with arthritis."

"ARGH!!!" Nathaniel yelled and threw his hands up in the air. "What is she talking about? Can you imagine a Heaven with arthritis? Who can be cranky in Heaven? Seriously! This is ridiculous!" Lucy pressed her lips together to stop from laughing out loud at this bizarre scene before her.

"Do you want to know what your Angel's instructions are for you?" Lady Soral asked smiling.

"No!" Nathaniel shot at her.

"Yes please," Lucy said as evenly as she could.

"Ingrid wants you to study more dear. You have a terrible memory, as you well know, and you need to buckle down with the books dear to improve your grades. If you do that, Ingrid will send you a boyfriend."

There was a pause, "You were right," Nathaniel said in a monotone voice beside her, "she's a crackpot. Let's get out of here." He stood up to leave but stopped, thinking better of it and instead, he turned back to the table and leaned over it to address Lady Soral. He was not even a foot in front of her face. She stared placidly at Lucy. "How do you sleep at night?" Nathaniel yelled at Lady Soral. "How dare you take people's money and lie to them! What is wrong with you? You know none of this is true! You are making this up as you go! You ought to be ashamed of yourself! The real Angels are watching lady and this does not bode well for you in the long run!" He waved his hands in front of Lady Soral's blank face, "HELLO! HELLO! Angel right in front of you! HELLO!" Lucy put her face in her hands and started to laugh. Lady Soral was saying something but Lucy couldn't hear her over Nathaniel's raging. Lucy finally stood up and knocked the chair over trying to leave. Nathaniel was blocking her way while he berated an ignorant Lady Soral.

"Um thank you," Lucy said pushing on Nathaniel to get him to move. "Come on, Ingrid lets go." She looked over and saw Lady Soral's approving smile.

"You are in trouble Lady! I know people!" Nathaniel hollered over his shoulder. "Ever heard of a little thing called Karma? It's a THING! A real THING!" He stalked out of the store and stood fuming on the street. Lucy followed him out, let the door close behind her, sat down on the step and started to laugh. Tears poured from her eyes as she laughed so hard her stomach hurt.

"How can you be laughing?" Nathaniel demanded. "That woman is a thief! A charlatan! We should call the police! Do you have any idea how wrong she is? No wonder everyone has all these misconceptions about Angels it's because of people like THAT!" he pointed angrily at the door. "She just makes stuff up. How dare she?" Lucy laughed even harder, gripping her stomach. Nathaniel finally ran out of gas and sat down beside her. "What?" he asked.

Lucy took a deep lungful of air to try and compose her self. Finally she could speak, "Nathaniel, you didn't see yourself in there! That was the funniest thing I have ever seen. You freaking out and screaming at her and she can't even see you? It was hilarious."

Nathaniel thought about it and started to laugh too, "The Ingrid thing is pretty funny too." They started laughing anew but their laughter was cut off by a deafening screech from the street. Lucy looked up and saw a car stopped in the middle of the road. A dog lay in front of the car and a little boy knelt beside the dog. Lucy sprinted over and landed on her knees beside the boy. The golden retriever on the ground was broken and bloodied, barely breathing. It was clear he wasn't going to last long. A few people had stopped to look but no one came forward. The boy was alone. The driver got out of his car horrified at what he had done, "It came out of no where I couldn't stop in time! Ah dammit kid, I am so sorry. I'll call for help." He pulled out his phone and turned his back to make the call.

Lucy wrapped her arms around the little boy who was howling in anguish, "Buster! Buster! No No No Buster Don't Die!" Lucy squeezed the boy tightly as she began to cry too. She rocked him back and forth.

"Shh shh," Lucy managed to comfort him through her tears. The boy wailed and sobbed for his best friend. Buster let out a soft whine and the boy screamed outright shaking with grief. Nathaniel was crouched on the ground in front of them looking saddened. Lucy looked at him beseechingly with tears blurring her vision.

"Fix it," she begged. She didn't bother to cover her voice. No one could hear her over the boy's wails not even the boy. Nathaniel looked at her, his eyes full of regret, and shook his head slowly side to side. "I know you can fix this!" she said through clenched teeth. "Look at him! Fix it!" Nathaniel shook his head again. "You can only do parlor tricks huh?" Lucy shot at him in anger. "You can't do anything that really matters can you?" Nathaniel didn't look hurt or upset at her words; he just shook his head again.

In front of them, Buster took one last shuddering breath and laid still. The boy screamed and Lucy had to hold him back from leaping on the dog. He wailed and kicked but she held him tight sobbing with him. Suddenly, there was movement in the crowd and a man ran forward, "Tommy? Tommy?"

"Daddy!" the boy wailed, "Buster! Daddy! Buster!" Tommy's father took him gently from Lucy's arms.

"I know pal, I'm so sorry," he said starting to cry at his son's pain. "It will be alright." He held Tommy tightly and stood up. Tommy started to kick and fight again to get back to Buster. He kicked and scratched and punched at his Dad trying to escape. The father held tight, taking the assault and refusing to put him down. Tommy fought harder, hysterical now. "No no no no no!" he screamed red faced. Nathaniel stood and slowly walked over to father and son.

He reached over and laid his hand on the back of Tommy's head, cupping his skull gently. Tommy relaxed immediately. His face returned to a normal color, he stopped fighting and his limbs went limp. He flopped over his father's shoulder, fast asleep. Nathaniel backed away. The police showed up. Tommy's father spoke to them and gave them instructions. Lucy stood up and stumbled back to the sidewalk. A woman in the crowd reached out and touched her arm.

"Good job honey," she said. Lucy just nodded and walked, defeated, for home. When they got to Lucy's house, she walked in and flopped on the couch in the family room. She pulled her legs up and hugged her knees. Nathaniel sat beside her and waited. It only took a moment for Lucy to explode.

"It's just a stupid dog!" she yelled. "It's just a dog! It doesn't affect the delicate balance of the universe! It was a little boy's dog and you let it die when you could change it! Why? What difference does it make if that dog lives or dies?"

"All the difference Lucy," Nathaniel said evenly. "If I changed it today, it would change everything."

"Like what?" Lucy threw her hands up. "Like little Tommy doesn't cry himself to sleep for the next month? Or if he wasn't traumatized today? Man, that would suck Nathaniel, it's good you kept that going!" she said sarcastically. "Too bad that kid isn't going to grow up to believe in Angels or miracles!"

Nathaniel ignored her tone, "And what about the next time something bad happens to Tommy? Something bigger? What about the day his Grandfather dies or his brother gets into an accident and lands in the ICU? What then Lucy? What will Tommy do then? Will he sit back and wait for a miracle because he thinks bad things don't happen to him? Or will he be able to handle it because when he was eight, his dog Buster was hit by a car and he lived through the pain and became a stronger person?" He paused and added softly, "Which way is better for Tommy in the long run Lucy?"

She sat back and took a deep breath. "You're right." She shook her head, "but it just seems so cruel."

"I know it does," he said with understanding. "But at a farm on the outskirts of town, a litter of puppies is being born to make other little boys happy. That's how it works."

"Did a Demon make that happen?" Lucy asked imagining Mrs. Turner showing up at Tommy's house with some cookies to make him feel better. She shuddered.

"No," Nathaniel replied, "that was just chance. The man decided to leave his house at a certain moment and decided to take a certain route and Tommy decided to cross the street at a certain moment and their paths crossed."

Lucy sighed and sat back, Nathaniel wrapped his arms around her. "I'm sorry I said those mean things to you. I was angry, I didn't mean them," she said.

"I know you didn't," he smiled at her. "One of your best qualities is your compassion for other people. You are a very good person."

"Not as good as you," Lucy said.

"Why do you say that?" he asked puzzled.

Lucy smiled, "Because if I was the Angel, I would have saved that dog in a heart beat." She thought for a moment and added, "And made it so he could talk." Nathaniel threw his head back and laughed. He kissed her softly on the neck.

Chapter Ten
Lies

"The cruelest lies are often told in silence."
~Robert Louis Stevenson

The phone rang. Lucy jumped up to get it. It was her mom.

"I am so sorry honey but I just got a call for an offer on the Anderson place," she explained. "I have to go and this could take hours."

"That's ok mom," Lucy replied. "No big deal."

"But you're there all alone. Why don't you call some girls from high school? I'm sure they would love to catch up." Sandra sounded riddled with guilt.

"I might mom," Lucy replied having no intentions of doing so but wanting to pacify her mother's guilt. "Good idea."

"Oh good, well I'm glad you won't be all alone tonight. I love you," Sandra answered.

"Love you too mom. Good luck with the deal!" She hung up the phone and turned to Nathaniel, "It's just you and me tonight, Mom has to work."

"That's too bad. You wanted to spend time with her."

"It's ok," Lucy said shrugging. "We have a dinner date for tomorrow before we leave on Wednesday and now I get to spend the evening with my favorite person."

Nathaniel eyed her suspiciously, "That's me right?"

Lucy laughed, "Yes, that's you." Her stomach growled, "I'm starving, let's eat something."

"Can I cook?" Nathaniel asked.

Lucy looked at him in shock, "You can cook?"

He rolled his eyes, "I'm an Angel Lucy, not an idiot."

"Then lead the way," Lucy smiled as he walked past her to the kitchen.

Lucy was thrilled to discover that Nathaniel was an excellent cook. He made a Salmon Wellington that Lucy devoured. When they finished eating, Nathaniel stood up to clear the plates and Lucy followed him into the kitchen. He stood at the sink washing and Lucy leaned against the doorway watching him. She marveled at how integral he had become to her. Nathaniel wasn't an option anymore. She honestly couldn't understand how she could have considered herself happy before she met him. She walked up behind him and wrapped her arms around his waist tucking her cheek into his shoulder blades. "You're wonderful," she murmured into his back.

Nathaniel put his wet hand on hers and replied quietly, "I'm just trying to keep up with you."

After the dishes were done, they retired to the den where they sat on the floor and looked through photo albums.

"This is when I swam for the first time," Lucy said pointing to one picture. Because Lucy's memory was so exact, she could give as much detail as Nathaniel wanted on each picture.

"Is that your dad?" he asked pointing to a bearded man in

the pool with a five year old Lucy.

"Yup," Lucy smiled, "that's him. He shaved the beard shortly after this picture because I complained it was too scratchy. He didn't want to though; he thought he looked younger with it."

"He was a nice dad," Nathaniel observed.

"He was," Lucy sighed. "I miss him." Nathaniel didn't reply but reached over and put his hand on hers. The familiar heat pressed into her hand and up her arm. "Is he in Heaven?" Lucy asked.

Nathaniel smiled, "Heaven is a very big place Lucy. I'm sure he's there. A guy who shaves his beard at the whim of his five year old daughter makes it to Heaven." Lucy nodded feeling a lump form in the throat. "But I promise," Nathaniel continued. "That when I get back, I'll find him and your dad and I are going to spend some quality time together."

Lucy's face fell further and tears stung at her eyes, "<u>When</u> you get back," she repeated. Remembering the past loss of her father coupled with the future loss of Nathaniel was not a good combination. She took a deep shaky breath, "So you have to go back?"

"Yes," Nathaniel said quietly, "Roman was right about that. I do eventually have to leave. I don't know how that is going to come about but it will come about. My presence is having an affect that won't be tolerated for long."

"No," Lucy said plainly. She took another deep breath and found some resolve. She looked Nathaniel in the eye, "No," she said again with more confidence. "That's not acceptable."

"But Lucy…" Nathaniel started but she cut him off.

"No," she repeated. "You said I have free will?" she said angrily as fear gripped her insides. "Fine. This is my decision. I choose you, forever, for the rest of my life. I choose you, no other, no one else. You say I can pick my own path in life? This is the path I pick. I choose you. This is cruel what they are doing. They can't choose my path for me."

"Lucy please listen," he pleaded, "I don't know why I was sent here but I know that it wasn't out of cruelty. I have to go back Lucy."

"We'll run away," she pleaded with him. "We will go and live in the middle of no where, just the two of us. I don't care. I don't need anyone but you."

"Lucy," he said sadly. "That isn't true. You need friends and family in your life. I can't live your life <u>with</u> you I, I can only watch you live your life and that isn't fair for you."

"I don't care," she replied. "I don't care that no one can see you but me. I don't care about the Demons or that you are screwing the world up. I don't even care if you want to go back. I need you. This isn't fair!"

"I know it isn't fair but we will be together again one day. After you have lived a long and happy life Lucy, we will be together again and it will be for forever. I will be waiting for you," he swallowed, "I promise."

A thought dawned on Lucy and she lifted her head and looked at the Angel with new resolve. "Who says I am going to live a long life?" she asked thoughtfully. "I don't have to live the rest of my life without you."

"Lucy, you are in perfect health, you..." he stopped in shock as he comprehended what she was proposing. "Lucy, listen to me."

"The moment they take you, I could just follow right along..." she trailed off thinking. "It's so simple, why didn't I think of it before?"

"Lucy!" he yelled at her. Nathaniel turned her around so she was facing him and gripped her arms in his muscular hands, "Lucy!

Listen to me!" he shook her shoulders. "That is not an option. Do you understand me? Stop thinking about that right now!" he commanded. "You don't understand Lucy! People who throw away their life do not go to the same place that I'm from! We would not be together if you took your own life!" he yelled desperately. "Do you understand me? There is nothing more damaging to a human soul. Nothing! Promise me Lucy." She stood in shock. Nathaniel had never raised his voice to her. "Promise me!" he yelled again.

"I promise," she finally said quietly. He relaxed his grip and exhaled. "But what else can I do?" she begged.

"I'm here now Lucy, can we just be grateful for the time we are given? Can we try to forget that it isn't for forever? I am so happy when we are together and I hate to see you miserable because of me."

"I'm not miserable because of you," Lucy explained. "I am miserable at the thought of losing you. I..." she struggled. "I require you now. You are a part of my existence. You are like oxygen and the thought of giving you up is the equivalent of drowning. I understand it is a very strong reaction but I can't explain it."

"You don't need to Lucy," he stroked her cheek. "Don't you know that I feel the same way? It will be just as painful for me when I go."

"Sure!" she said. "But you get to go to Heaven and I'm stuck here alone. Not to mention, I have a Demon as a neighbor and a Demon as my best friend's boyfriend, oh yeah and his boss is a Guild Prime Demon too. Not fun."

"I wish it were different Lucy," he said quietly. He hugged her and she relaxed in his embrace.

"Will you know when they are coming for you?" Lucy asked tucking her head under his jaw.

"Yes," he said with a slight nod. "I will."

"Good," Lucy replied while wiping her eyes, "a warning would be nice."

Nathaniel nodded in agreement. He stood up and stretched. He looked over the books lining the shelves. "You've read all these I take it?" he asked casually trying to change the subject. He reached down and offered his hand to Lucy and gently helped her up.

Lucy nodded, "These were my fathers; they were the first books I ever read."

"What was the very first?" he asked.

Lucy gestured to the second shelf. "The first book I ever read on my own was 'Alice in Wonderland,' well 'Alice through the looking glass.'"

Nathaniel pulled it from the shelf. "Favorite part?" he asked.

Lucy quoted,

"'When I use a word', Humpty Dumpty said, 'It means exactly what I choose it to mean.' 'The question is,' said Alice, 'if words can mean different things.' 'The questions is,' said Humpty Dumpty, 'who is to be master.'"

"Interesting choice," Nathaniel said flipping through the book. "Why is that your favorite?"

"Well," Lucy began but she stopped short as a piece of paper fell out of the book and floated to the ground. They both looked at it. "Is that from you?" Lucy asked smiling at Nathaniel.

"Not at all," he said surprised.

"Hmm," her brow furrowed. "I haven't opened that book for twelve years." She reached down and picked up the paper. It was folded in half.

For My Lucy

It read in plain block letters. "That's my father's writing," she said dragging her thumb slowly across the printing. Nathaniel replaced the book and stood looking expectantly at her. She opened the note but inside was just a date.

June 21, 1992

Nathaniel looked over her shoulder as Lucy flipped the paper over. "That's it," she said with disappointment.

"What does it mean?" Nathaniel asked.

Lucy shook her head, "I have no idea." She thought back, "My birth date is September 9 1990 so I would have been just under two." She shrugged, "I bet there was something he was meaning to show me; an interesting article maybe."

"It looks pretty official for a casual reminder," Nathaniel observed.

"My dad was a pretty official guy," she replied. She shrugged, tucked the note in her pocket and reached around him. "What was it you were saying about us cherishing every moment we have together?"

"Mmm right," he said looking into her eyes. The deep stone color of them cut through her and Lucy felt all her worries leave. "Carpe Diem," he murmured as he leaned down to kiss her.

The next day was their last day in Kansas. Their flight left early the next morning and Lucy would spend a long weekend preparing for the new semester to start on Monday. Sadly, Lucy's mom had to work again but she gave Lucy some money to shop for some new school supplies. They would meet at four for dinner. Lucy and Nathaniel slept in again - she hadn't realized how sleep deprived she was. Over their late breakfast Nathaniel asked what Lucy was up to for the day.

"I have to buy school supplies," she replied. "I'll get my textbooks at school on Friday. I might pop by the library and look up that date my Dad left for me. You?"

Nathaniel smiled, "Stuff." Lucy rolled her eyes. He stood up, cleared the cereal bowls, loaded the dishwasher and started it. He walked back and kissed her on the neck, "Have a good day. Call me if you need me." He kissed her again and walked out the door. Lucy smiled. Even if this was all temporary, Lucy would take and love every minute of it.

School shopping took Lucy a few hours. Lucy got all the boring stuff, pens, notepads and binders. There were also a few reference manuals she wanted to read but they didn't have them in town. Lucy decided to look up the publisher to make sure the materials were available at the Mulbridge bookstore and if not, order them online. She headed to the Stonecreek public library.

The library was alive with activity. There were several groups of children and their mothers milling about. Adults perused the shelves and there were many high school students taking up the tables with final studies. Lucy looked to the busy circulation desk and saw Mrs. Jensen, the head librarian waving to her. Lucy waved back.

"How's school going Lucy?" Mrs. Jensen called over the heads of people in line.

"Good!" Lucy called back. "Just home for a visit. I dropped by to look something up!" Mrs. Jensen nodded and smiled as she moved on to the next person in line. Lucy found an empty computer; looked up the manuals she needed and found that they were available at her school bookstore. She would get them on Friday when she got her textbooks. Lucy looked at her watch and saw that she still had a half an hour before she had to meet her mom. She reached into her pocket and pulled out her father's note. She figured she might as well look it up while she was there.

Lucy stood and headed to the microfiche room. It was empty. As the door closed behind her, the noise from the library died away and she was surrounded by silence. Lucy didn't need help finding the microfiche she was looking for. The article could have been in any newspaper but Lucy thought she should start small. She pulled the box for the Stonecreek Gazette June 1992 and rifled through it for the 21. She pulled it out, walked over to the machine, loaded the film and turned on the lamp. The first few pages were the inserts. Lucy turned the dial flipping through the coupons and car ads. She got to the first page of the paper and froze.

Lucy read the article quickly and then reread it to fully comprehend its contents. Her breath stopped and tears and anger created a red haze over her vision. She reached up and put her hand gently on the screen, closed her eyes and lowered her head. She could hear the patter as her tears ran down her cheeks and hit the desk.

"Nathaniel, I need you. Please come," she barely whispered hoping that was enough because she had no capability for moderation right now and it was either whisper or scream. Ten seconds passed and she felt him behind her. He was out of breath.

"Lucy? Lucy?" he spun her chair and knelt in front of her. He grabbed her face, "what is it?"

"They lied to me," was all she could manage to say as more tears flowed.

"Who lied to you?" he asked angrily. "Are you hurt?" he asked while scanning her body for injuries. Lucy shook her head and pointed at the screen. Nathaniel followed her finger and looked. The front-page picture was of Lucy as a toddler laying in a hospital bed smiling. Her mother and father stood beside the bed grinning at Lucy from ear to ear. The entire bed was full of stuffed animals.

She's a Miracle!
Little Lucy Bower could not be luckier. Her parents and hospital

staff are touting her a miracle after she came back to life. Yesterday afternoon was a peaceful time at the Stonecreek public pool. Richard Bower, Lucy's father, was taking Lucy swimming for the first time. The horror began when Bower turned his back for a second and heard a splash. His twenty one month old toddler had fallen in the deep end of the pool. Bower and lifeguards reacted quickly but little Lucy sunk to the bottom rapidly. Bower himself pulled his daughter's lifeless body from the pool and lifeguards began CPR. Paramedics arrived in three minutes and continued life saving procedures during the seven-minute drive to Stonecreek hospital. Doctors worked tirelessly for another twenty minutes on the little girl, frantic to bring her back. It had been thirty minutes since Lucy had fallen in the pool and the medical staff had done everything they could with Lucy not responding in any way. Her death was called at 1:27pm June 20 1992. Lucy's parents were distraught and Sandra Bower, Lucy's mother, threw herself at the child's body screaming, "Lucy come back!"

Miraculously, and despite the fact that all life saving measures had been stopped for a full five minutes, the little girl opened her eyes and took a deep breath. The doctors helped revive her. They were stunned, "In my thirty years as a physician," Chief of Staff Dr. Marcotte was quoted as saying, "I have never seen anything like it. I have no scientific explanation for these events. All I can tell you is that little girl wanted to live."

And indeed she does. Lucy is almost fully recovered and continuously asks to get up to play. She is bright and happy and has no recollection of the event. "She doesn't even remember going to the pool," Richard Bower said. "We are just so thankful for the dedication and hard work of all the medical staff and life guards who saved our daughter's life." The family thanks the community for their outpouring of support and the many gifts sent to Lucy's bedside. Lucy's medical bills have been covered from the family's insurance and they ask that all donations go directly to Stonecreek Hospital so they can continue to save lives.

Nathaniel looked at Lucy, stunned. "This must be a great shock for you. I am so sorry," he said hugging her tightly. Lucy had stopped crying. She wasn't sad anymore, she was angry. She sat silently; stiff and pale faced. She reached over to the microfiche machine and hit print. As if she were in a trance, Lucy stood, walked over to the printer, removed the page and walked to the door. "Where are you going?" Nathaniel asked concerned.

Lucy paused, turned slightly and in a monotone voice said, "I am late to meet my mother for dinner." She walked out the door.

Nathaniel leapt after her. "Lucy, listen to me. You can't go in there and freak out ok? Your mother owes you an explanation but you won't get anything from her if you scream and yell at her to get those answers." He continued the monologue down the street on the short walk to the restaurant. "I don't know why they didn't tell you. But they love you and if they kept this from you it was because they thought it was the right thing. Lucy!"

She stopped outside the door of the restaurant. Lucy turned to him and said, "I have no intentions of screaming at her but if I don't get a remarkably good answer for this deception, I will never speak to my mother again."

Sandra Bower was sitting at a table in the middle of the restaurant. She beamed when she saw Lucy and waved with excitement. Lucy walked up to the table and stood staring at her mother, rage piercing through her.

"Lucy? Honey what's wrong?" Mrs. Bower was worried. Lucy did not reply but sat down and put the article in the middle of the table. Sandra looked and immediately recognized it and her face filled with horror. "Where did you get this?" she asked stunned. Again, Lucy did not answer but pulled her father's note from her pocket and tossed it on top of the article. Sandra sighed, "Your father," she said as if this was expected. "Lucy," she began pleadingly. Lucy held up one finger and her mother fell silent.

"First," Lucy was surprised at how calm she was. Nathaniel was starting to rub off on her. "You will apologize for lying to me my entire life. Then you will answer my questions. You owe me that." Sandra nodded dumbly and began to cry.

"Oh Lucy, I am so very sorry for not telling you. If there was anything in my life that I would change, it would be that."

"Why didn't you tell me?" Lucy asked baffled.

"Oh honey!" Sandra said exasperated. "I don't even know anymore! At first you were too young, you didn't remember it and we didn't see the point. But then as you got older, I didn't see the point," she said emphasizing the 'I'. "Your father wanted to tell you," her mother said. "When you were five, he came home from a business trip and said that he had thought about it and you should know. That was the first night we fought over it."

"The first?" Lucy asked.

Sandra looked at her squarely, "Yes Lucy, your father and I fought every night over it until he left. For a decade we fought about it." She sighed sadly. "But I dug in my heels, I was so stubborn, I couldn't see why you needed to know."

"So I would know the truth about my life?" Lucy raised her voice. Nathaniel tightened his grip. But Sandra Bower wasn't fighting about this anymore.

"That's exactly what he said," she said sounding tired and defeated. Lucy's anger softened slightly. "You are so much like him Lucy, it is painful at times. I should have told you." She looked at Lucy with tears in her eyes. "Don't you see that I've suffered for that decision? I lost my husband because of my stubborn behavior. I lost the only man I ever loved because I was an idiot. You can't say anything to me that I haven't said to myself." She looked at her daughter with tears pouring down her face, "I paid my price Lucy! I lost my heart. I can't lose you too. Please forgive me."

Lucy's anger melted away as she thought of losing Nathaniel and how much pain that would cause. Her mother had done what she thought was best. Sandra loved her daughter; she loved her enough to call her back from the dead. Lucy reached her hand out and laid it on Sandra's. "I understand mom, I forgive you."

"You do?" her mother asked hopefully.

"I do." Lucy reached up with her other hand and touched Nathaniel's hand resting on her shoulder. "I understand more than you know."

"Thank you sweetheart," her mother squeezed her hand and let go to use the napkin to wipe her tears. Lucy did the same. The server, sensing that whatever had happened was over now, approached the table warily. They ordered from her hastily and sat half smiling at each other. The table beside them left so Nathaniel sat down.

"I still have some more questions if that's ok," Lucy said.

"Of course honey, whatever you need to know," Sandra encouraged.

"Well," Lucy thought about it, "how did it happen? The article wasn't clear on the details."

Sandra took a deep breath and a sip of her wine, "We don't know really. Your father took you to the pool to swim for the fist time. He had your hand and was more than five feet from the edge when he let go to put the towels down. He turned back and you were already in the pool."

Lucy was confused. "So I ran and jumped?"

Sandra nodded. "You must have, which was strange because you were generally nervous of water."

"Could I have been," Lucy gulped at the horror of it, "pushed?"

"We certainly considered that but everyone at the pool was questioned. It was fairly busy and no one saw anything."

"That's good," said Lucy relieved. "Then what?"

"Then your dad jumped in after you and so did several other people but your father was a strong swimmer. He said you were already unconscious by the time he got to you. He said at night when he closed his eyes, he was always haunted by the image of you drifting lifeless to the bottom of the pool." Lucy shuddered. "I agree," her mother replied. "I'm very glad I didn't see that."

"When did you get there?"

"I beat the ambulance to the hospital." Sandra looked up at the ceiling trying to remember every detail. She knew that would be important to Lucy. "They ran you in. I didn't get to see you because they kept us out of the room. Then finally, the doctor came out, we saw his face and we knew." Sandra looked down at the table and was silent for a moment. She didn't look up as she continued, "I hope Lucy, that nothing like that ever happens to you. I would not wish that kind of pain on anyone. It was like my very soul shattered into a million pieces, never to be repaired. I lost it, I snapped. I don't even remember what your father was doing. All I remember is that someone was screaming and then realizing that it was me. I don't remember knocking over a nurse to get to you but they told me that later. I do remember what happened when I got to the bed. There you were, your skin grey and waxy there was no breath in you and certainly no life. Your entire existence flashed before me. I saw everything in perfect sequential order; the pregnancy test, the first time you kicked, your birth, your first smile, the day you rolled over, walked and spoke. I couldn't take it. I screamed in your face for you to come back to me. I could feel them pulling me away but I swung and kicked at them wildly fighting to get you back. And then," she finally looked up at Lucy, her eyes full of remembrance, "you opened your eyes. I was so stunned. You tried to take a breath but they had tubes down your throat. Someone, I don't know who, reached over and pulled them out and you coughed, and looked around the room smiling." She shook her head in disbelief, "I went from total despair to total joy in a matter of seconds. It was unbelievable, everyone started screaming and running around. I tell you Lucy, I have thanked God every single day for that moment."

Lucy's mouth fell open. "You have never mentioned God to me before."

"Oh I know honey," Sandra replied shrugging, "but that doesn't mean I don't believe in it. I don't talk to God for any other reason than to thank him for you," she paused, "well, that's not true. Once I did ask him for a facelift but that didn't work."

"She doesn't need one," Nathaniel said.

"You don't need one mom," Lucy said for him.

"Thank you," Sandra said laughing.

Lucy thought for a moment, "Did I say anything when I woke up?" Their food arrived and Lucy dug in starving. She glanced sideways at Nathaniel who shook his head. He wasn't hungry, which was good because Lucy thought she for once could finish a meal.

"Yes, you did," Sandra replied picking up her sandwich. "You said 'Lucy go back.'" Sandra swallowed and smiled, "So I knew that you had heard me. It was a big moment."

"So that picture of Dad and I swimming when I was five?" Lucy prompted.

Sandra nodded finishing her bite and taking a sip of wine. "That wasn't your first time swimming. That was the first time I let you get back in the pool after the accident."

"Does Dr. Hannon know?" Lucy asked.

Sandra nodded, "I swore him to secrecy. Don't be angry with

him Lucy," she warned.

"I'm not," Lucy replied. "But did he want to tell me?"

"Yes, but he didn't want anyone else to know," Sandra replied.

"Why not?" Lucy asked confused.

Sandra put down her sandwich and wiped her hands on her napkin. "He was concerned, and I agree, that other people might try it."

"Try what?"

"Drowning and coming back to life to get your abilities," her mother replied like this was obvious.

It hit Lucy like a brick to the face. Up until this moment, it hadn't even occurred to her that the drowning had anything to do with her photographic memory. Now it hit home. That's why her mother didn't want her to know. She wanted Lucy to think that it was a natural ability. She pushed her plate away immediately nauseous at the thought. Nathaniel jumped up and assumed his position behind her. Her parents had told her that her memory started to manifest itself shortly after she turned two; right after the accident.

"I'm a fraud," she said staring at nothing. "I wasn't born with this and I'm not gifted. I'm a scientific freak show."

Sandra leaned across the table. "Lucy no!" she exclaimed. "That isn't true. We don't know if you developed your memory as a result of the accident. That's why Dr. Hannon didn't want anyone to know. There are crazies out there honey that would literally die for your gift. You could have had your memory before. We don't know and why does it matter?" She reached for Lucy's hand and Lucy gave it but let it lie limp.

"Did I dream before the accident?" Lucy asked blankly.

"Lucy," her mother pleaded, "you were a baby! How were

we to guess before you could..." Lucy cut her off by slamming her hand on the table. Sandra flinched. "Yes," she said in a small voice, "you did"

Lucy sat back and nodded. This was the confirmation. Before the accident, she was totally normal and after, she wasn't. "My memory is nothing more than the byproduct of a disaster." She jumped up from the table with such force that she caught Nathaniel off guard. He reached for her again but she dodged him and ran.

Lucy ran and ran and ran. She ran through the streets, through parking lots, through fields and right out past the borders of the town and kept running. She was in a wheat field when she finally stopped, exhausted. She sat down in the wheat and cried.

"I don't want my memory if I wasn't born with it," she said to no one. "I have lived a total and complete lie of a life. I have no right to be proud of myself, I am nothing but an accident, a mistake. I have no gifts, no talent. Anyone could be me...if only they were willing to die for it. Pathetic. Sad Lucy, very sad."

Lucy heard Nathaniel approaching and sighed in relief. She needed him more than ever right now. She looked up eager for his warm embrace and his words of comfort but froze suspended in terror. It wasn't Nathaniel coming for her.

Chapter Eleven
Epiphanies

"There's a world of difference between truth and facts
Facts can obscure the truth."
~Maya Angelou

Roman walked slowly up to her. He wore a tight black t-shirt and a pair of jeans. How could something so horrible look so much like a Greek God? Lucy's heart stopped beating. She was gripped with terror and could not force herself to move or scream or fight. He sat down affably in the wheat beside her. Lucy stiffened at his closeness and looked down, trying not to make eye contact. Roman didn't seem to sense her discomfort as he reached over and casually plucked off a stalk of wheat and twiddled it in his finger. Lucy swallowed and forced herself to breathe.

"Bad day?" he asked as though they were old friends. His voice was like butter.

"Go to Hell," she managed to say through clenched teeth. She decided not to ask about the plane incident. There was no reason for him to know that they had been frightened. The fact that he wasn't bragging about it made Lucy think that it wasn't him and someone else. Who though? Bael? Mrs. Turner? Lucy was suddenly surrounded by Demons. She didn't like it.

Roman threw his head back and laughed, "Oh, you are funny Lucy. Good one."

"I won't be alone for long," she warned him. "You don't want to be here."

"Oh you are wrong there," he said with mock disappointment, "he's not coming I'm afraid."

Panic ripped through Lucy as she glared at him. "Why?" she demanded, "what happened?"

Roman laughed again. "Oh we are attached aren't we?" he said and touched the wheat stalk to Lucy's nose. She flinched. "It's sweet really. No, no, your cherub isn't gone for good. Not yet anyway," he added with a sly smile. "Don't worry, he's standing in the middle of town frantic and livid right now."

"Why?" Lucy asked.

Roman sighed like she was an idiot, "Because once you run away from an Angel or tell them to leave, they can't come back until you call them silly. Didn't he tell you anything?"

Lucy instantly opened her mouth, "Na…" was all she got out before Roman leapt on her and clamped his hand over her mouth. Lucy struggled against him. He was incredibly strong and she knew she would be bruised tomorrow.

If she made it to tomorrow.

She bucked and fought against him but it was like fighting against a brick wall. Roman just held her tight. "No no no peanut, not yet," he said patiently like he was talking to an unruly child. "Calm down Lucy. Don't make me shut your mouth permanently," he warned in her ear. She screamed under his hand. "I don't know if your Angel has shown you all of our capabilities but I assure you that you do not wish to irritate me little girl." She stopped struggling - he wasn't bluffing. She thought of Dr. Hannon's face, she didn't know if Roman was capable of the same monstrosities that Bael was but she didn't want to take the chance. She sat quietly in her circle of fear. Roman slowly removed his hand, "Good girl." He leaned back and sat beside her again. "Now don't worry, I have no intentions of hurting you and you can call him the moment I am gone. I just want us to have a chance to discuss a few things alone."

"Like what?" Lucy whispered. The terror had gripped her and she sat spell bound and alert.

"I can help you Lucy," he said kindly. "I can fix all of this." Lucy noticed that he wasn't mentioning Bael; most likely trying to play the nice guy.

"What do you mean?" she asked.

"You are a fraud," he said. Lucy scowled at him. "That is unfair. Don't you see?" he pointed at the sky. "They did this to you." He pointed to himself, "Not us." Lucy shook her head not understanding what Heaven or Hell had to do with any of this. "You see sweetie," Roman continued patiently, his voice smooth, "they make all the decisions. They gave you this curse and made them all lie to you about it. Your Angel is wrong. It's a big puppet show up there. They gave you all the heartache you are feeling right now and they are sitting back watching you for the results. You are nothing but a petri dish to them."

"Na…" Lucy started but Roman raised a finger in warning, "he…" she corrected, "would never lie to me."

"That is true Lucy," Roman nodded. "But he doesn't even know the truth. They have lied to him too." Lucy looked doubtful as he continued, "Why do you think my boss is where he is? Because he figured it out and so they kicked him out. He didn't want to lie anymore." Lucy assumed that he was talking about Lucifer now and not Bael. She didn't know what to believe. She shook her head to clear it. "I know," he said with sympathy, "it's a lot to take in but all you need to know is that I have the power to fix it."

"How?" Lucy couldn't imagine anyone being able to fix it.

"I'll take it all away," he said simply and the wheat stalk in his hand disappeared. "Poof," he held up his hands like a magician, "all gone."

"Take what away?" Lucy was suddenly intrigued.

"What ever you want Lucy. Where I come from, you call the shots, not some mystical being in the clouds. I can take away your photographic memory so you are a regular girl. I can take away the drowning and I can put you right where you should be as if none of their meddling had ever happened."

"I wouldn't be me," Lucy countered.

"Of course you would!" he replied with conviction. "You will still have lived the same life but with out all the lies."

"What do you want in return?" she asked suspiciously.

Roman laughed, "Oh, you are a smart one aren't you?"

"What?" Lucy pressed. She didn't know if she would risk her soul for a life of normalcy.

"Well, I don't want your soul if that's what you're thinking. Your soul is useless to me," he smiled and shrugged. "I ask only a small thing. I ask only that you send him back."

"I can't do that," she replied. "I don't have the power to do that."

"Lucy," he snickered at her ignorance. "Don't you understand that you are the one keeping him here? If he came here because of you so it stands to reason that you would be the one who can send him back. If you were to wish him back to the clouds?" he snapped his fingers. "He would be gone."

"But I don't want him gone," Lucy said blankly. That was the last thing she could handle right now.

Roman was frustrated, "Honey, they are coming for him eventually. Not even the puppet masters can allow this to continue for much longer. It's inevitable. You would only be shortening his visit and in exchange, you have a totally normal life."

"I..." Lucy was confused; she couldn't think straight, "I don't know... I love him."

"Ah but – here's the rub. He hasn't told you he loves you has he?" Roman asked quietly. She turned and met his eyes. Roman was really very handsome; tall, blond, blue eyed and he seemed so very sincere.

"Well," Lucy replied. Nathaniel had not spoken those three words and it had not gone unnoticed. Until this moment it hadn't really bothered her. He had showed it in so many ways.

"And why do you think that is?" Roman asked with sweetness and kindness, "Because he doesn't Lucy." Lucy felt the wind pick up and the sound of a coyote howling far away. Was he right? Was that possible? "Lucy," Roman continued patiently, "Angels are singular creatures, they have only one thing on their mind and that is Heaven. He doesn't love you as much as he loves Heaven. He can't wait to get back to be honest. Who wouldn't? It's Heaven after all. He is staying here for you. It would be better for him if you let him go. He would be happier."

The wind howled again and whipped the wheat stalks at Lucy's face. She was so confused. She had to admit that Roman made some sense. How could Nathaniel be as happy here as he was in Heaven? Here he was invisible, living his life beside her and having no life of his own. In Heaven, which he himself could not describe because of how wonderful it was, he had a life. Still, if he wanted to go back, why hadn't he told Lucy that? She was so confused

"I can bring back your father Lucy," Roman whispered in her ear.

That was the trump card.

"What?" Lucy stared at him.

"I can make it so the car accident that killed him never happened. Couple that with you never drowning and they would have never gotten divorced. Your father would be alive, your parents together and you would be one happy family." He leaned in even closer, she could feel his breath on her ear, "Think about it Lucy. The guy you can have for a short while or your father, your family…forever?"

Lucy couldn't help but think about that idea. She saw her father's face in her head, his smiling happy face. Oh to have that back, to have her parents together. Her mother would be so happy, they all would be. She would be normal, not a freakish accident. Then she saw Nathaniel's face in her minds eye. He was glowing and gorgeous and laughing.

"Now don't be selfish Lucy," Roman whispered the warning as if he could read her mind. "Think of all the joy you would bring to your mother and your father. Loving someone doesn't make them good for you."

The wind kept howling making it difficult for Lucy to think. She furrowed her brow and tried to focus. She pulled one memory from her thoughts and reviewed it like a movie in her head. It was her favorite memory of her father, the day he gave her 'Alice in Wonderland.' He had handed Lucy the book, open to her favorite quote – the one she had started to discuss with Nathaniel just the night before. She remembered asking what the words meant.

"It's about the truth Lucy," Richard Bower had explained in his careful voice. "Lies are the twisting of words and ideas, making them mean something different. Your job in this world my Lucy, is always to find the truth, as painful as the truth is sometimes to identify. You must quest to always see what is true, even if it is twisted through a looking glass. You are master of your life, what you do with your gift is up to you. You must find the truth and own it in your heart and only then can you be master of your destiny."

The five-year-old Lucy had not fully understood this explanation but the eighteen-year-old Lucy did. Her father was trying to tell her that when she found out about the origins of her abilities, she would still be her own master. Lucy had worked at her memory; she had fostered it and fed it. She didn't have to do that. She could have sat on her butt for the last sixteen years and played video games and memorized the McDonalds menu rather than literature or history. She had decided her fate, no one else. Lucy was exactly who her father had wanted her to be. She was exactly who she should be and Nathaniel was a part of who she was. Her parent's divorce and her father's death, as painful as those truths were, were a part of who Lucy was today. She listened to her father's words and looked into her heart. Nathaniel stood there, all alone, waiting for her with open arms. Lucy knew she was being lied to.

"I've decided," she said with a nod.

"Excellent," Roman perked up, "now we'll hash out the details later. But first."

Lucy smiled at Roman, her best, most wonderful smile. He smiled back warmly at her. "I've decided," she said grinning, "who is to be master." Roman kept smiling and shook his head slightly in confusion. "Nathaniel! I need you!" she yelled.

Roman's eyes narrowed in hate for a second before he suddenly hunched forward as if punched in the stomach. He was quickly pushed back by an invisible hand and flew back cutting a swath ten feet long through the wheat. Lucy looked up and there stood her Angel. Her savior. He glowed in the dying light and took his eyes off Roman for a split second to smile for her.

"You can't get rid of me Angel!" Roman screamed. He was on his feet now. "I will haunt her until the day she dies! If she won't be cajoled into sending you back then she will be forced to!"

He raised his hand and pointed at Lucy. She flinched, expecting pain. Instead, she screamed in panic as the wheat around her lit on fire, encircling her in flames. The wheat caught quickly, she could hear the crackle as each stalk ignited. Massive waves of heat pushed at her from all sides. Lucy spun around, frantically looking for an escape but there was none. She gasped as the smoke filled her lungs instantly cutting off her oxygen. In desperation, she dropped to her knees sucking in air.

"Do not move Lucy," Nathaniel said calmly. Lucy squinted through the flames to see Nathaniel raise his hand to the sky. She heard a hissing sound and felt tiny droplets of rain touching the back of her neck. Within seconds she was sitting in a torrential downpour as the rain easily extinguished the flames and left nothing but a blackened, smoldering ring around her. She looked up to see that Nathaniel and Roman had stayed dry.

"Go Demon! You have your answer and now you will leave her," Nathaniel commanded in a voice Lucy had never heard from him before. He wasn't just angry. He was irate and powerful and he knew it.

"I will keep pushing until the end of time!" Roman raged. He was wild with fury. "Do not get comfortable Angel, you are not staying!"

"I said go Demon!" Nathaniel commanded again.

"We will find a way Angel," Roman yelled while starting to stalk away backwards. "My kind always does!" He vanished into thin air.

Lucy ran into Nathaniel's arms. He grabbed her fiercely, wrapping his arms tightly around her. He pulled back and clutched at her face, "Lucy Bower, don't you ever run away from me again! Ever!" He hugged her tightly again breathing rapidly.

"I'm sorry," she said into his chest. "I didn't know."

"I didn't tell you. I should have, I'm sorry," he said kissing her head. Nathaniel looked back at the spot where Roman had been a moment before. His eyes narrowed again in fury, "Lucy it took everything I had not to rip him to shreds. I don't think I have ever been so angry."

He looked her over and shook his head in disgust, "Your face is starting to bruise. Hold still." He gently placed his hand over her mouth in the same manner that Roman had. The difference in the two touches was astounding. Nathaniel's hand felt just as strong as Romans but his touch was soft. Lucy felt warmth spread across her skin under his hand. It intensified to an almost searing heat before he took his hand away and examined her again. "There, all gone," he said nodding. "Now we have to get you home, but I can't bring you back in this condition."

Lucy looked down at herself, her clothes were soaked through and her hair hung wet and limp on her head. There were huge streaks of black soot on her chest and legs. She grimaced at herself. Nathaniel smiled, "You are beautiful Lucy." She felt a light breeze and suddenly her mass of tangled red hair and clothes were dry and clean. Nathaniel looked back at the field. The wheat was scorched in a circle and trampled and broken all around. Nathaniel raised one hand and aimed it at the field. Immediately, the stalks began to shiver and shake violently. The stalks slowly healed from the ground up. The black soot disappeared and the stalks pulled themselves upright. Within seconds, the field looked perfect again.

They walked back home in silence. Their conversation

would have to wait until they were alone. For now, Lucy had to
deal with her Mother. When they walked in the door, Sandra leapt
off the couch and sprinted to Lucy. She had the phone in her hand.

"I was so worried honey! Thank God you are alright!"
Sandra yelled while clutching on to Lucy.

"I'm sorry I scared you Mom. I just needed to think," Lucy
sighed into her mother's shoulder.

Sandra realized she still had the phone in her hand. "She's
here!" she yelled into the handset. She paused as she listened, "No,
she's ok," pause. "I will," pause, "Thanks, ok, bye." She hung up and
looked at Lucy, "Dr. Hannon," she explained. "I thought you might
have tried to call him." Lucy sighed again thinking about how she
would have to deal with that later too. For now though, Lucy
realized that she was totally exhausted. The events of the day and
the shock of the last crisis had left her spent of all emotional and
physical energy. "Honey listen," Sandra began but Lucy cut her off.

"Mom, I'm fine, I'm ok. I'm not mad or depressed or sad,"
Lucy explained pressing her forehead against her mothers. "I am
totally fine. I'm just really, really tired and I have to sleep. I don't
leave until tomorrow afternoon, we'll talk over breakfast ok?"

"Ok," Sandra whispered, relief flooding her voice. "I love
you."

"Love you too," Lucy answered. "But I would love you more
if I could take a bath."

Sandra smiled, "Sorry babe."

"Night mom and thanks for loving me so much."

"That's an easy thing to do baby," Sandra replied kissing
Lucy on the forehead.

Lucy trudged up the stairs and when she got to her room
she didn't turn on the light or change out of her clothes. She just
kicked off her shoes, pulled off her jeans and crawled under the

covers. She felt Nathaniel slip in gently beside her and wrap his arms around her. Lucy fell into a deep, deep sleep.

When she woke up, it was still the middle of the night. Lucy could see the moon sitting high and bright through her window. She rolled over and looked at Nathaniel, he was awake and smiling at her. She smiled back.

"Do you want to talk about it?" he asked.

Lucy nodded. "I was terrified," she admitted.

"I know," he said apologetically. "I'm sorry I didn't tell you about running away. It never occurred to me that you would ever run away from me."

"I wasn't running away from you," she explained. "I was just running. I thought you would follow. I thought he was you at first when I heard him coming."

"I know," he said.

"Then he sat down beside me and said..."

"I know what he said," Nathaniel said softly.

"You know?" Lucy asked shocked. "How?"

"I heard the whole thing," he said ruefully. "It was..." he paused, searching for the words, "painful. I was trapped, not being able to get to you, knowing you were in danger and incapable of helping."

"How did you hear us?" she asked.

"Roman made sure I did," he said seething at the name. "He was so positive he could get you. He was confident he could strike that deal and he wanted me to witness every horrid second of it. To torture me."

"Oh," Lucy said. So that meant that he had heard Roman talking about how Nathaniel had never told Lucy he loved her. She wondered what he thought about that portion of the conversation but didn't want to ask outright for fear of sounding desperate and clingy. "What did you think about it?" she asked generally.

Nathaniel thought for a moment. "I wonder how you came to your final decision?" he asked.

"I did the right thing didn't I?" Lucy asked concerned.

"Oh yes," he nodded emphatically, "yes you did. But what made the decision for you?"

Lucy thought about it. "Well, to be honest," she said carefully, not wanting to insult him, "it was tempting."

"I'm sure it was, that's the nature of a deal with the Devil," he replied.

"I was sitting there and I thought about my father and now nice it would be to have him back. I thought about the day he explained that quote from 'Alice in Wonderland' to me and how important honesty was to him. I realized the lengths he went to so I could learn the truth. He sacrificed his family and the love of his life in an effort for me to see the truth. I suddenly knew that he would not want me to take that deal. I knew that I was being lied to, that Roman was tricking me. The wind kept howling and it was difficult to think straight. But then I thought about you and how you have never lied to me. That's what ultimately made the decision for me. You."

"That wasn't the wind howling Lucy," he said looking at her. "That was me."

"Really?" her eyes went wide.

He nodded, "I was half mad listening to him lie to you. I'm glad you saw the looking glass for what it was - a pack of deception."

Lucy recalled the power of the wind in the field and thought that Nathaniel must care for her very much indeed. But was Roman right? Did he love her?

"So everything he said was a lie?" she prodded.

"Most of it, yes," he replied.

"So he couldn't bring back my father or take my photographic memory away?"

"Oh no, he most certainly has the power to do that," Nathaniel answered with conviction. "But it wouldn't be your father Lucy. It would be a soulless creature pretending to be Richard Bower. It would not be him. The free soul is the only thing that Hell cannot control or reproduce. It is the essence of a person. How you behave in your life determines where your soul will go when you die. Once a soul has chosen a path, it cannot be altered. Your father's soul is in Heaven and there is no way Roman could get to him."

"And if I had made the deal?" Lucy asked warily, already knowing the answer.

"The Devil collects souls like some collect knickknacks. Once you allow the Devil to alter your life, Heaven cannot take you," he explained.

Lucy shuddered, grateful that she had made the decision she had. "You said that he only lied about most things?" she prompted. "What did he tell the truth about?" Lucy looked down, waiting for the blow, for him to say that he didn't love her.

"That you are the factor keeping me here," he said plainly.

Lucy flinched, that was almost the same thing. "Oh," she swallowed. "I see. Well, I'll just send you back so you can be happy then," she said quietly. Lucy felt a chasm of pain begin to open up inside her. "I wouldn't want you to stay here on my account, suffering," she whispered.

Nathaniel reached over and lifted her face gently to look at him. "You will do nothing of the sort," he said softly. "Roman was right about you having to power to send me away but he was wrong about me."

Lucy felt a ray of hope, "Really?"

"Do you think he knows me?" Nathaniel asked. "Do you think he has any idea what I want? Lucy if you sent me back, I would be devastated. I don't think I can be happy without you, even in Heaven."

Was that the same thing as saying he loved her? No, but it was close and as with so many other things with Nathaniel, Lucy had to take what she could get. Nathaniel leaned in and kissed her, oblivious to her inner thoughts and wishes. The kiss had so much passion that Lucy felt like she had turned to water. She lay back on the pillow and pulled him down on top of her, feeling his weight pressing down upon her. Nathaniel lifted his head breathing heavily. Lucy gave him a sneaky smile.

"What's that smile?" he asked with a grin.

"You kicked his ass," Lucy said smiling.

Nathaniel laughed, "I was angry. He is very lucky he survived that encounter."

"Are Angels allowed to tear Demon's to shreds?" Lucy asked.

"Angels usually don't have to," he looked at her lovingly. "But when it comes to you Lucy, I'll do anything to keep you safe."

"Will he come at me again?"

"Oh yes," Nathaniel said ruefully. "It is evident that neither he nor Bael will stop until you make me go away."

"I won't do it," Lucy said with conviction. Nathaniel just nodded and smiled at her. She thought for a moment. "You looked so hot," she said breaking the quiet.

"What?" Nathaniel said like Lucy was crazy.

"When you were all mad and doing your magical Angel stuff, standing there, all glowing and defending me," Lucy explained grinning. "You looked really hot."

Nathaniel threw his head back and laughed. "Lucy," he said shaking his head, "you were in a ring of flames. You were in very serious danger, not to mention the fact that thirty seconds before that you were tempted to sell your soul to the Devil and all you can think of was what I looked like?"

"Don't get me wrong, I was terrified. But my memory allows me to look back on it with perfect clarity and you looked so gorgeous." He laughed for a moment before kissing her again.

"So speaking of your memory," he said while breaking off the kiss, "how do you feel now about it's origins?"

Lucy sighed and flopped her head back on the pillow. "I'm ok with it now. It just sucks that it all started as an accident. A fluke, no gifts, no chosen one, just…" she shrugged, "a mistake."

Nathaniel pushed him self up and sat beside her. Lucy pulled up the covers instinctively, not for modesty but because she so missed his warmth. He held out both his hands, each held a single wheat stalk. Lucy shook her head. How did he do that?

"This wheat stalk," he shook his right hand slightly, "was a result of natural germination. This one," he shook the left, "is the result of planting. Can you tell them apart?"

Lucy shook her head. "How do you know where the wheat stalks come from?"

"Well," he said nonchalantly, "I just know these things. Anyway," he continued, "the natural one started as a tiny dried out seed that fell off its main stalk. It blew haplessly in the wind for a while, flopping and flipping around until it caught on a tiny pebble. There it stayed, waiting for the rain to start its roots and begin its life. It was a total fluke. After that, the seed had to fight for its existence. As far as the other one is concerned, a farmer came along and planted it purposefully in the soil for it to grow. He watered it and sprayed it with pesticides to keep the bugs off. It was created on purpose. The seed had to put in very little effort towards its own success" He paused to smile at her and Lucy smiled back. "They have two completely opposite beginnings and yet they can't be told apart. But," he raised a finger, "which one will make a superior product?"

He closed his hands into fists and when he opened them, each had a small amount of flour in it. Even with only the moon as her source of light, Lucy could tell the difference. The man made wheat made a flour that was grayish and grainy but the natural one was soft, powdery and white as snow.

"Oh," Lucy said in awe.

"Yup," Nathaniel closed his hands again and the flour disappeared. "Lucy, the best things in this world are the result of accidents. And you are no different. Your photographic memory was not of anyone's doing and it required you to fight to make it the true gift it is. That is what is so wonderful about it."

"Thank you," she said smiling at him.

"Anything for you," he said laying back down beside her. Lucy yawned. "Still tired?" he asked. She nodded. He turned on his side and wrapped his arms around her. Lucy snuggled against his chest. Nathaniel kissed her forehead. "Sleep my miracle," he whispered in her hair. She did.

The next day went smoothly. Lucy and Sandra had a long breakfast and talked everything over. Lucy described her epiphanies in the field omitting huge amounts of detail of course. Sandra of course was relieved that her mistakes of the past did not develop any resentment in her daughter. Lucy was sad to leave her mom because she wouldn't see her again until Thanksgiving. Lucy worried less about her mom this time. With Sandra dating and her work going well Lucy was confident that she would be ok. The mother and daughter hugged tightly at the airport, neither wanting to let go. Lucy finally did and boarded the plane with Nathaniel leading the way.

The return flight was not as eventful as the outbound and Lucy rejoiced at the moments of peace. Sadly, the flight was almost full and Lucy could not get an empty seat beside her. Nathaniel sat several rows back in an empty aisle seat and when Lucy walked back under the guise of going to the bathroom she found him fast asleep. She realized that yesterday had been exhausting for him too and she suspected that he hadn't slept the night before. Lucy knew now that he had stayed awake all night making sure she was safe. Her heart warmed at the thought and she fought the urge to bend over to kiss him on her way by.

They took a cab back to the University, using part of the huge wad of cash Sandra had pressed into Lucy's hand at the gate. Lucy had protested at first but now she was thankful because the bus would be a nightmare with Lucy's extra bags from the shopping sprees in Kansas. Lucy was happy to get back to her little dorm room. It felt like an anchor of reality after the surreal trip. While unpacking she called Dr. Hannon and left a message telling him that she was fine and that she would come to his office on Monday to talk over lunch.

She was cramming the last of her new clothes into her already jammed closet when Nathaniel asked, "Are we going to the bookstore to get your books for Monday?"

Lucy shoved the closet door closed and it groaned in protest. "Naw," she said. "Let's do it tomorrow."

"Let's go tonight," he countered. "Then you have a three day weekend to relax before classes start. The bookstore is open until nine."

"I guess," Lucy said thinking that three days off would be nice, "but you don't have to come with me."

"Yes I do," Nathaniel said standing up. "Roman wasn't bluffing, he'll try to get to you again and I can't have you alone."

Lucy nodded ruefully. "Alright," she grabbed her wallet and book list, "let's get it over with."

They walked out of the dorm and saw that Nathaniel was right. Roman was sitting on a park bench twenty yards away. He was sitting casually but when he saw them his eyes narrowed and he sat forward.

"Ignore him," Nathaniel said. They walked quickly through the quad to the student's union building.

"Is he going to do something?" Lucy asked nervously.

"No," Nathaniel said shaking his head. "Roman has the disadvantage of being visible to humans. He has no interest in causing trouble. The last thing he needs is someone to call the police." He looked back over his shoulder, "No, he'll wait to get you alone somewhere."

Lucy shuddered, "That sounds bad."

"Don't worry," he assured her. "You are stuck with me for every spare moment of the day."

"That sounds better," Lucy said as they walked into the bookstore.

Shopping at night was a good idea. The bookstore was mostly empty and Lucy didn't have to stand in an hour-long line like she would have to the next day. Half an hour later they walked out with Lucy carrying two huge bags of books. Once they got into the quad Nathaniel motioned to the bags.

"No one is looking," he said, "hand the bags over, they are heavy."

"No," said Lucy pulling the bags away, "he's still there and I want your hands free." Nathaniel looked up and sighed seeing Roman hadn't moved. They walked through the quad and to Lucy's dorm doors not making eye contact with the Demon.

"Hey Lucy, I just talked to my new girl," Roman yelled from the bench, "we have a date for tomorrow night. I'm really pumped!"

Rage shot through Lucy and she started to turn ready to yell something very unladylike at him. Nathaniel whipped the door open and all but threw Lucy inside and ushered her to the stairs.

"That...that..." Lucy fumed through clenched teeth struggling to find the perfect expletive to describe the monster outside.

"Demon?" Nathaniel offered.

"Exactly, thank you," Lucy said scowling.

When they got to her room, Lucy dropped the bags and ran for the window hoping to yell something down at Roman.

"He's gone," she said searching the quad. She turned back and looked beseechingly at Nathaniel, "How can I keep him away from Anastasia?"

"You can't Lucy," Nathaniel said sadly. "She has to make her own choices."

"What if he hurts her?" Lucy pleaded. "How would I ever live with myself?"

"Demon's aren't all bad Lucy," he said. "Most lead relatively normal lives. Think about Mrs. Turner, she's a nice lady when she doesn't have to work. She has lived in your neighborhood for how long now? Decades? And no one knows a thing." He sat down on the couch and Lucy plopped down beside him. "I have made Roman very angry so his most basic evil tendencies are being pushed to the forefront. My connection with Heaven is like sandpaper to him. That, mixed with the pressure he is feeling from Bael, and we have a dangerous combination on our hands. There is little chance that Anastasia could ever make him that angry."

"You don't know Anastasia," Lucy replied. She took a deep

breath, "I guess I will have to sit back and hope for the best."

"Yes," Nathaniel said agreeing, "and in the meantime, you should get some sleep."

Although Nathaniel looked as flawless as ever, Lucy was sure he must be tired. "Are you going to stay awake all night watching over me?"

"If I said yes," he replied with a smile, "would you be angry with me?"

"Yes."

Nathaniel stood and stared at her silently apparently deciding to say nothing than lie. Lucy glared at him until he spoke.

"Lucy, I can't risk him or Bael getting a hold of you," he replied factually.

Lucy sighed. "Fine," she threw her hands up. "I'm sleeping, you do what you want." She shook her head at his stubbornness, grabbed her shower bag and pajamas and headed to the bathroom. When she returned, Nathaniel had pulled out the bed, changed into pajamas and had stretched out on the bed with the intent of reading. The only problem was that he was totally asleep. Lucy smiled at him her heart filling again with love for him. He was trying just as hard as she was to keep them together.

Lucy walked over to the bed and climbed in gently so as not to disturb him. She snuggled under the covers only then realizing that she had left the light on. She wished Nathaniel was awake so he could turn it off from bed.

"I need the light off," she whispered to no one. Maybe it would work, you never know. Nothing happened. She sighed. "Fine," she whispered, "Nathaniel needs the light off." Nothing happened. It seemed like the bulb shone brighter, mocking her. "Aww come on!" she whispered, "please?"

"Lucy," Nathaniel said in a deadpan voice beside her,

"Heaven doesn't appreciate laziness." Lucy reached back and slapped his leg in response. He laughed. "You're keeping me hostage from Heaven and here you are making demands upon them? Seriously?"

She slapped his leg again and laughed. "Shut off the light Nathaniel."

"Now you're talking." The light went out.

Chapter Twelve
Road Trip

"It is not down in any map; true places never are."
~Herman Melville

Lucy woke up the next morning to bright sunshine streaming through her window. She looked at her clock it was 10 a.m. *Now that's how you start a relaxing weekend.* She thought to herself. Lucy looked up and Nathaniel was standing in front of her holding two coffees and a bag. He was grinning from ear to ear. He looked extra handsome today in a pair of cargo kakis and a deep grey/green shirt that almost did his eyes justice.

"Morning," Lucy said hoarsely. "You look awfully spry for someone who didn't sleep." He sat down on the edge of the bed and handed her a coffee. As Lucy sat up to take it he pulled a bagel out of the bag and put it in her other hand.

"Can you tell me please, from your extensive fantastic memory, what I said the first night we met?" he asked smiling.

Lucy blinked. She was not fully awake. "Huh?" she said groggily. She took a sip of her coffee hoping it would help. "Which part?" she said drinking more coffee. It was lukewarm. "This coffee isn't hot," she said. "How long were you standing there waiting for me to wake up?"

Nathaniel shook his head, "Like forty five minutes," he said quickly dismissing the interjection. He was like a kid on Christmas; he was practically bouncing off the walls. "Come on, Lucy, think." He looked at her like he was asking the million-dollar question. "What was the last thing I said to you that night?"

"Um," Lucy took a bite of her bagel and more coffee willing her groggy mind to function. She saw him standing in the dorm lobby. "You touched the door handle, I asked 'where are you going now?' you stopped, turned towards me, smiled and said, 'That Lucy, I don't know.'" She nodded at Nathaniel as if that settled the matter and took another bite of her bagel.

"Was that the last thing I said?" Nathaniel said confused.

"Yup," Lucy said with her mouth full.

He shook his head impatiently. "Ok, before that then," he pressed.

The coffee was doing its job and Lucy's mind was at full capacity. "You said, 'goodnight Lucy,'" she replied.

Nathaniel rolled his eyes, "I am glad your memory is so good because apparently mine sucks. Before that."

Lucy rewound her images and remembered the first time he touched her face. She could almost feel those first warm tingles spreading up to her hairline. They were so familiar now but to remember the first time was wonderful. *I should review these memories more often.* She thought to herself. It all came back to her in perfect clarity and she felt goose bumps break out on her arms all again just recalling the details. She closed her eyes and smiled.

"Lucy! Focus!" Nathaniel's urgent voice cut through her reverie.

She opened her eyes. "Ok...ok...um," Lucy rewound a second more and nodded, "I asked, 'Where do you live?" and you said, 'I promise to show you one day.'" She looked at him expectantly and immediately knew she got the right answer.

His face lit up as he said, "Guess what today is?"

"Someday?" Lucy asked hopefully.

"Yup," he said with excitement, "eat your bagel and get dressed, it's a long way."

Lucy was confused and questions flooded her mind, "Wait a minute," she stammered. "Where? What? How are we getting there?"

Nathaniel looked at her, "Lucy do you trust me?"

"Yes," Lucy replied without hesitation, "completely."

"Good," he smiled. "Then trust me. We are going away for the weekend. I have some things I have to show you. Will you come with me?"

"Of course!" she yelled excited now too. She would find out more about the man she loved. "I have to pack though."

"Done," he said pointing to two bags on the floor.

"You had this all planned didn't you?" she asked him. "That's why you wanted me to buy my books yesterday."

Nathaniel smiled smugly. "Yup," he grinned. "Now let's go! I'll wait outside." He grabbed the bags and walked out the door. Lucy stood for a moment, excited and expectant. She got dressed and neatened her room. She grabbed a novel and a textbook out of her bag of new books. If they were going to be on a bus for a while she might as well get started on her reading.

Nathaniel was waiting in the hallway. They went downstairs and out the door. Lucy looked suspiciously around for Roman.

"He's not here," Nathaniel said in reply.

Lucy nodded, pleased that the trip wouldn't start off on a sour note. She looked up at him, "Where to?" She felt like she was on a treasure hunt.

"You drive," he said handing her a set of car keys. Lucy stared at the keys in her hand and looked back at Nathaniel. He jerked his head in the direction of the road and parked directly in front of the dorm was a black jeep. Lucy smiled. Nathaniel shrugged, "We need a car for the weekend, let's go." Lucy ran down the stairs and opened the trunk for Nathaniel to load the bags. She closed it and walked to the passenger side. There were a few students about so she pretended to look in the door pocket for something as Nathaniel slipped in. Lucy closed the door and got in the drivers side.

"Can I ask how far the drive is?" she asked while adjusting the mirrors and pulling on her seatbelt.

"I've never driven it," Nathaniel replied thoughtfully, "but I would think around three or four hours."

"Ok," said Lucy while starting the engine, "let's go!"

Nathaniel gave her directions that led them to the highway and within twenty minutes, they were on the open road. Nathaniel had his window half open and he sat smiling in the passenger seat. His dark curls blowing about his head. They listened to the radio and talked for a bit. After a while they fell into a nice silence and Lucy saw Nathaniel starting to fall asleep. She turned down the music to let him catch up on his rest and she let her mind wander.

Nathaniel was so excited about this trip. Lucy could understand that he would be excited about finally being able to share something of himself but he seemed more pumped than she had ever seen him. Then a thought struck her, as she glanced over at his gorgeous face. He was a college-aged boy after all. It was not surprising that he would be excited about a weekend away with his girlfriend. Was this <u>the</u> weekend? Lucy had dated in high school but she had never gone all the way. Not that the high school boys hadn't put in a solid effort, they had, Lucy just wanted to save it for someone she really loved. And here he was, the love of her life.

Lucy was both nervous and excited about this idea. She was nervous because she had never done it before and she had no idea if she was any good at it. Lucy was also nervous because Nathaniel was an Angel and he had to have pretty high expectations. Did they have sex in Heaven? How could she compare to that? Lucy was excited because this was something that she wanted. There was no one else she would feel more comfortable with. She loved Nathaniel with every fiber of her being and she wanted to share this with him. Lucy wanted to give him everything she could before he left so he would know how much she loved him. Lucy was mostly excited because judging from Nathaniel's kisses; this was going to be good.

"Slow down," Nathaniel instructed cutting into her thoughts. "The turn is coming up soon." Lucy turned onto a smaller single lane highway where they passed acreages and small farms. He directed her again and she turned onto a smaller road. This continued for another hour with Nathaniel directing Lucy onto less and less distinct roadways. She had been tracking their journey with the map of the state in her head and found that they were directly in the middle of nowhere. There was a small mountain range nearby but no towns or civilization for a hundred miles.

They were on a gravel road in a dense wooded area when Lucy said, "It must be nice to have a connection with Heaven and get everything you need handed to you," Lucy said jealously. "Why is it so far away?"

"You'll see," he replied. "Trust me."

He had her turn onto what was once a logging road and the jeep started to bump and kick with the uneven terrain.

Conversation was impossible. They drove for another thirty minutes until the road stopped. There was dense wood surrounding them. Lucy stepped out of the jeep and looked at Nathaniel skeptically. She was not anticipating a camp out.

"We will walk from here, it's not far," he said getting out and retrieving their bags. Lucy was pleased she had worn her sneakers and not sandals on this trip. She wondered if they should lock the jeep and then laughed at her self. There was no one around who could take it and it wasn't theirs anyway. She followed Nathaniel's enthusiastic gait into the woods.

"So," she asked walking behind him. The bush was too dense for them to walk side by side. "Why haven't I been here before?" She was struggling through the brush where Nathaniel walked with his normal casual gait. Lucy was once more amazed at his strength and grace.

"You'll see," he said again. "Trust me." They walked for a short while until Nathaniel suddenly stopped. "We're here," he said grinning. "Thank you for coming, I hope you like it."

We're where? Lucy thought. She could see nothing but more trees and dense bush. Then Nathaniel moved aside and Lucy gasped in surprise. Two huge trees stood about six feet apart with their branches curving and connecting above. In between them was a cobblestone path. It looked like a doorway to a secret garden. Nathaniel put the bags down and reached for her hand. They walked through the doorway.

On the other side was a huge circular clearing filled with bright white daisies. Lucy looked up and saw a house. Not just any house. One of the most beautiful houses Lucy had ever seen. It wasn't large but it was constructed of huge stones and pine beams. It had an A frame roof with a large square window on the second floor. There was a wrap around deck made of the same natural pine. There were two large windows on either side of the huge pine door. The entire house was covered in thick ivy. It twisted in and out of the pine beams and around the deck. The ivy covered the roof climbing and twisting all around.

"It's perfect," Lucy said breathlessly. Nathaniel smiled and pulled her forward. They walked up the three deck steps to the door and Nathaniel opened it because there was no lock. They walked in and again Lucy gasped. Where the outside of the house looked like it had been there for a hundred years, the inside looked brand new. They were standing in a large open room with huge brown leather couches, a square coffee table and a massive fireplace made of the same large stones as the outside. It was so big that Lucy was sure she could walk right into it if she wanted to. The entire back wall of the house was made of windows that looked out into the dense forest and the mountains beyond. The kitchen was modern and stylish with a copper hood fan, granite counter tops and shiny stainless steel appliances. There were French doors off the kitchen to the deck.

"Wow," was all Lucy could manage. Nathaniel directed her to the wooden spiral staircase and left to retrieve the bags. The loft was the bedroom. It looked over the main floor and had the huge front window over the bed. The bed was huge and constructed of rough pine beams. The bed linens were light blue and brown. Lucy opened a small door to the side that led to a good-sized bathroom with white tiles, a large standup shower, toilet and sink. The towels on the rack were in the same pale blue and brown from the bedroom.

Looking up at the ceiling Lucy saw that the ivy had invaded the house. The entire ceiling was covered in twisted dark green leaves. It was beautiful and so perfect for Nathaniel. He climbed the stairs and dropped the bags on the floor.

"Good?" he said looking at her for approval.

Lucy leapt into his arms and kissed him. "Great," she said kissing him again. "I can't believe you wished for all this and Heaven just gave it to you."

"No," Nathaniel corrected smiling, "Heaven gave me a small one room house. I built this one."

"What?" Lucy said, "You built this?"

"Yes Lucy," he said looking at her. "I built it for you."

She thought her heart might just explode with love and gratitude. "Thank you," she said her voice cracking with emotion. "But... how...?"

"Well," he looked around, "The building materials I got from the woods obviously and Heaven did provide me with the necessary tools and materials that were man made. They gave me the furnishings and household items obviously. But I made the bed."

She took a moment to stare at the king sized bed. Lucy and Nathaniel had slept beside each other many times but with Lucy's new theories about the purpose of the trip, the bed took on a new significance. She smiled thinking of what was to come. She wasn't nervous – she couldn't wait.

"This is what you have been doing everyday?" she asked. No one had ever shown so much dedication to her in all her life.

"I wanted you to have a house Lucy," he said looking into her eyes. "I have no history or memories to share with you. This is how I can show you who I really am. I am a man who would build a house for you."

"I love you," Lucy said.

"I'm glad you like it," was all he said back. Lucy would take it. The house was enough...for now. "Can I show you around outside a little? If you want to take a nap or shower or anything..."

Lucy shook her head. "I want to see everything," she replied.

"Ok, let's go," he took her by the hand and led her down the stairs. Lucy took a look at the bed and the walls around and tried to imagine all the effort that he put into this for her. She smiled to herself at how lucky she was. "I'll just take you around the meadow. We'll go farther tomorrow. It will be dark soon"

Lucy followed him out the front door and Nathaniel closed it behind her. She took one step down the deck stairs and froze in panic. Lucy only had one defense mechanism - her memory. It kicked in and brought up every nature book and wildlife documentary she had ever seen. She had the creature classified immediately, *Ursus arctos horribilis carnivora*- not that this would do them any good at all. Of course if you were going to die, it was always preferable to know exactly what was going to kill you. Despite all the information, Lucy could only say one simple, powerful word.

"Bear," she whispered.

Not five feet away, standing on all fours was a massive grizzly bear. Its brown fur glistened in the sun and it stood there regarding Lucy with interest. *We are going to die,* Lucy thought, *right here and now.* Nathaniel was stronger than the average man but Lucy wasn't sure if he was a match for a full grown grizzly. She started to lift one foot to slowly back up into the house when she felt Nathaniel's hands on her shoulders.

"Don't move Lucy. Don't say a word," he whispered in her ear. Lucy froze and wondered if he had a gun stashed somewhere. Nathaniel certainly didn't seem like a gun guy. She watched in shock as he stepped around her carefully but without fear. He descended the stairs and walked towards the massive animal. It was like he was committing suicide and Lucy had to bite her tongue to stop herself from screaming at him to stop. Nathaniel continued towards the bear and stopped a foot away. Lucy winced not knowing if she could watch him be torn limb from limb. The bear seemed to pay little attention to Nathaniel. It craned its neck slowly around him to keep its eyes on Lucy. Nathaniel reached out and again Lucy had to stop her self from screaming in horror.

He laid his hand gently on the bear's neck which was almost level with his own. "Don't be afraid," he said softly to it. Lucy was in awe of his bravery or his stupidity – she didn't know which. The bear only snuffed lightly while keeping its eyes trained on Lucy. "That's my Lucy," Nathaniel said smiling. Amazingly, the bear reacted by almost breathing a sigh of relief and sitting back on its haunches like a dog. Nathaniel smiled and buried his fingers in its fur. "I told you I would bring her one day." Lucy was stunned. This was too bizarre. Was Nathaniel really having a chat with a wild grizzly bear right now? He would never cease to amaze her.

Nathaniel turned slightly, "Come here Lucy," he said calmly like they were at a cocktail party. "There is someone I would like you to meet."

Lucy shook her head slowly, every human instinct screaming in protest. "It will eat me," she whispered. The bear snuffed again and Lucy thought it sounded quite a bit like laughing.

Nathaniel smiled, "No she won't, I promise."

Lucy swallowed, "Does she understand us?" The bear seemed to take offense to that and huffed.

"Yes," Nathaniel said. "Perfectly, now come here. Trust me."

Lucy, showing her biggest display of trust to date, slowly walked down the last two steps. She shuffled towards Nathaniel's out reached hand and clasped it like a lifeline. Fear bubbled through her and she could taste it in the back of her throat. She swallowed again.

"Lucy," Nathaniel said politely, "this is Mother."

"Hello Mother," Lucy said awkwardly. "It's um, nice to meet you." Nathaniel took her hand and laid it beside his on the bear's neck. Lucy was surprised that the fur was soft. Her hand disappeared in the thick coat and Lucy smiled warily.

"Mother?" Lucy whispered at Nathaniel.

He shrugged. "It felt wrong to give her a name like a pet and it felt wrong to call her 'bear'. She seems to like it," he replied. The bear almost nodded in agreement. "I met her my first night here," he explained. "We were fast friends. I've told her all about you because really, whom else can I tell? I think at times she tired of it." He rubbed her fur affectionately. Mother huffed a little and Nathaniel laughed.

"Can you understand her?" Lucy asked.

"Well, she can't talk if that's what you mean," he replied. "But anyone can understand her if they try."

Lucy looked at Mother's face. It was far more expressive than she would have thought. Her eyes were a deep brown and had flecks of gold in them. The fur around her eyes and muzzle were a lighter tawny color and her brow was heavy but communicative.

"You're beautiful," Lucy said quietly. Mother huffed again, her eyes brightened and she all but smiled. Lucy laughed.

"How are the babies?" Nathaniel asked. Mother motioned her head towards the forest. He looked at Lucy with his eyes glowing, "Do you want to meet the cubs?"

"Yes!" Lucy answered immediately, the magic of the moment melting her fears.

"Alright then," he took a step back from Mother, "lead the way."

Mother stood on all fours and started lumbering for the trees and trudged ahead of them into the dense bush. Nathaniel and Lucy followed. Lucy shook her head at the wonderful surrealism of this moment. She was grateful that she would never ever forget it. They walked through the bush, the ground climbed under them.

"So I'm guessing that animals can see you?" Lucy asked.

"Not domesticated ones," Nathaniel answered over his shoulder. "Cats and dogs are as oblivious to me as their owners but wild animals can see me."

"Had Mother even seen a human before you?" Lucy asked thinking of the dense vegetation and lack of trails.

"Yes," he called. "I think it was a hunter because she was very wary of me at first." Mother stopped ahead of them looking back. Was that impatience on her face? "We're coming, we're coming," Nathaniel called to her. Mother practically rolled her eyes. Lucy felt slightly embarrassed knowing she was the one holding up the caravan. When Nathaniel and Mother made this trek on their own they were no doubt much faster. She picked up her pace.

"I don't think she likes me," Lucy whispered to Nathaniel's back.

He glanced back at her, "Oh she likes you because I like you." He smiled, "If she didn't like you Lucy, you would be dead." Lucy shuddered at the thought and made a mental note not to aggravate the bear in any way. Nathaniel saw her face and laughed, "I'm kidding Lucy. I would never let her hurt you."

"You can stop a grizzly bear?" Lucy shot back doubtfully.

"Yes Lucy," he said with confidence, "I can stop a grizzly bear." He smiled again and kept walking.

Ahead, Mother had stopped again but it seemed that they had reached their destination. There was a small clearing in the bush and the afternoon sun shone brightly down. In the corner of the meadow was a hill with a hole in it. Mother headed there and Lucy thought the hole looked far too small for the bear's hulking mass but Mother slipped in easily.

Nathaniel stopped at the edge of the clearing and turned to Lucy, "You don't want to go in there," he explained. "It's cramped and it doesn't smell very nice." Lucy nodded. There was movement at the mouth of the den. Out of the darkness came three little bear cubs, followed by Mother who was shuffling them along with her nose. The three tumbled out of the den blinking in the bright light. Nathaniel sat on the ground and Lucy followed suit.

"Hey pals," Nathaniel said grinning and all three cubs broke into a sprint towards him. They hit him at the same time and Nathaniel leaned back laughing. Lucy grinned. He grabbed each bear in turn and introduced him or her to Lucy as the others clamored over his legs wrestling. "This one," he said holding up the darkest cub, "is Daughter. She's fast and clever." He put Daughter down and picked up the next one, "This one," Nathaniel said of the lightest cub, "is Brother One. He's the soft one and a little timid." He put Brother One down and almost grunted with the effort of lifting the biggest cub, "And this one is Brother Two. He is rough and tumble, a real trouble maker." Lucy grinned at the trio and looked at Mother who had lain down in the grass a few feet away.

"They're wonderful," Lucy said to the bear. Mother recognized the compliment and seemed to nod her head in thanks. Suddenly, Sister noticed Lucy's presence and leapt at her chest. "Oh," Lucy said surprised, "hello." Sister batted at Lucy's shirt and rolled over her legs. Lucy tumbled the cub around gently with her hands laughing. She looked at Nathaniel as he rolled around on the ground with the two boys and she felt another surge of overwhelming love for him. He grinned back at her, a piece of grass stuck in his hair. "Thank you," Lucy said softly to him. It sounded like a weak explanation of her gratitude so she added, "I love you." Nathaniel only grinned at her as Brother Two jumped on his back and he tumbled forward. Lucy laughed.

The afternoon light had faded when the cubs ran out of steam and started to rest. Sister was cuddled upon Lucy's lap, barely awake, the two brothers sat lazily on either side of Nathaniel and Mother dozed lightly in the grass. Suddenly, Mother lifted her head up and she sniffed the air. She gave a barking growl and the three cubs jumped up in response and headed for the den obediently. Nathaniel and Lucy stood up. Mother sat up and then with agility beyond what Lucy could expect from such a large creature, gracefully raised herself up on her hind legs still sniffing the air. On her hind legs she had to be at least ten feet tall.

"What's wrong?" whispered Lucy. Mother came back down on all fours with a thump and huffed at Lucy and Nathaniel aiming her nose in the direction they had come.

"We have to go now," Nathaniel said quickly. He took Lucy's hand and pulled her towards the trees.

"Thank you," Lucy said to Mother. The bear huffed at her with urgency again directing her to the trees. Lucy and Nathaniel left quickly and hurried down the slope.

"What did I do?" Lucy asked when they reached the front yard of the house.

"Nothing, I told you she likes you," he said pausing in the daisies. "There is food nearby, she needs to hunt."

"Oh," Lucy said relieved she hadn't insulted anyone.

"I know I don't want to see her take down a moose and I don't think you do either."

"No, not really," Lucy said and hurried into the house.

"You go up and take a shower," Nathaniel offered as they walked in, "I'll make dinner."

"Sounds good to me!" Lucy replied loving this whole scenario and headed up the stairs. Nathaniel had packed her well. Lucy took a long hot shower and changed into a pair of tight sweat pants and a tank top. When she came back down, Nathaniel was putting their plates on the table. He looked up at her but quickly looked back down. Lucy sat at the table eagerly – she was starving and the chicken in mushroom sauce looked delicious. Nathaniel sat down and they dug in and ate in silence for a while.

"This is great," Lucy said finally.

"Thanks," Nathaniel replied sincerely, "I made it up."

"No," Lucy said putting down her knife and fork, "this is great. Everything is great." She reached out and took his hand, "I love it all, thank you."

"I'm glad you like it," he said quickly. Then he suddenly released her hand and looked back down at his plate and kept eating.

"I love it," Lucy said to the top of his head. She waited for a response and didn't get one. "I love you," Lucy said. Nathaniel only nodded with his face still looking down.

Lucy was confused and suddenly very frustrated. Nathaniel was being so terse. She looked down and pushed her plate away. How many times was she going to throw herself out there like this? What was Nathaniel waiting for? He was sending so many mixed signals. Why would he build her a house and yet not tell her that he loved her? Did he regret it now? Roman's words came back to her, 'he doesn't love you,'. Was that possible? Why would he do all this for her if he didn't love her? Or did he know it was time for him to leave? Was this their last meal together? Did he build a house as a remembrance of himself? Lucy was torn.

"You all done?" Nathaniel asked oblivious to her inner turmoil. Lucy nodded. He grabbed her plate and walked to the sink. He did the dishes in record time and whistled the whole time. Lucy sat there, staring at his back. What was wrong with her? How could she not be enough for him? What more could she do? He walked quickly past her, not looking at her and headed to the living room. He knelt in front of the fireplace and lit a fire quickly.

Lucy followed him. For the first time she felt awkward in his presence. She curled up on the couch and tried to dismiss the tense feeling in the air.

"So what now?" Lucy asked trying to sound casual. She so desperately wanted to make whatever this was better.

"Now," Nathaniel said standing up and brushing off his hands, "I have to go out and you are going to relax here."

"What?" Lucy said shocked, "I thought you had to stay with me."

He shook his head. Lucy noticed that he was still not making eye contact with her. "Not here. Here, you are safe. No Demon could find you here."

"Oh," said Lucy trying not to cry. The mood in the room was tangible; it was desperation – Lucy's desperation to keep Nathaniel there and Nathaniel's obvious desperation to escape. "I thought we could...um... spend some time together," she said lamely.

"Lucy, we've been together almost every second for days," he said while pulling on his shoes. "You'll get sick of me."

"Never," Lucy said while looking down at her lap. She heard him pull on his jacket.

"If anything happens, and I don't think it will, just call me," he said with no emotion. Lucy nodded and didn't look up. "If for some reason, you can't say my name, just scream. Mother is close and she will come."

Lucy nodded again, tears stinging so close to the surface. *Just go*, she thought, *just go so I can cry.* He walked over quickly and kissed the top of her head.

"I'll be late, don't wait up," he said while walking back to the door. Lucy swallowed a sob and didn't even nod this time. *Just go*, *please just go. I don't want you to see me cry this time.* "See ya," he said lightly as he opened the door. She could hear the urgency in his movements. *He can't wait to get away from you.*

Lucy heard Nathaniel open the door and pause for a second. Then he left, closing the door softly behind him. She didn't care that he was most likely still on the porch when she put her head in her hands and sobbed. She wondered why Nathaniel had told her he wanted to stay with her. Why didn't he ask her to send him back if he didn't want to be with her? Why did he act like he loved her but never do anything about it? Was he sick of her? If he wanted to go back, maybe this trip was a way to let her down easy - here's a house, now I have to go because I really don't love you as much as I love Heaven. If he wanted to go, then Lucy would send him, it was that simple. It would put her in a mental institution but she wouldn't hold him hostage if he didn't love her.

Lucy took a deep breath and started to calm her sobs. She decided to wait for Nathaniel to come back to force this discussion. If she was going to be shattered, it was going to be on her terms. She wiped her eyes and sniffed. It was really very uncomplicated, she would wait for him, she would let him out of whatever contract they had here, he would leave and she would die inside. It was a daunting task but Lucy needed to get it over with because she couldn't live in this limbo forever. She was in her own little purgatory and it had to end – one-way or the other. Lucy nodded to herself and stared blankly at the wall for what seemed like an hour.

Finally Lucy picked up one of her schoolbooks, opened it to the first page and began to read. She had to pass the time or she would be insane by the time Nathaniel returned. Two hundred pages later, he still wasn't back. Lucy sighed and stretched. She was getting sleepy – the fresh air and warm fire having an effect on her. Her eyes started to droop, she willed them back open determined to confront Nathaniel - they closed again.

A short while later, Lucy did not wake as Nathaniel lifted her gently off the couch and up to bed. He tucked her in, watched her sleep for a moment and went back down to the living room. He lay down on the couch and sighed.

Chapter Thirteen
Heat

"Heat is the process of energy transfer from one body or system to another due to thermal contact."
~Wikipedia

Lucy was livid. She could not believe that she allowed herself to fall asleep the night before. She wished she had forced herself to stay awake last night and forced a confrontation with Nathaniel. Lucy stared up at the ivy covered ceiling and listened to the sounds of the house. She could hear Nathaniel downstairs in the kitchen. She got up and dressed, dreading the day. The only logical reason for Nathaniel's behaviour the night before was that he didn't want to be with her anymore. A heavy weight sat in her stomach as she descended the stairs.

"Morning!" Nathaniel called happily.

"Morning," Lucy replied with misery. He walked over and kissed her lightly on the cheek and walked back to the stove to plate up bacon and eggs. Lucy stood for a moment. She bit her bottom lip trying to savor what she realized could be their last moments together. Nathaniel set the plates on the table and pulled a chair out for Lucy. She sat and he sat beside her, grabbed his fork and dug in. Lucy didn't move. After three bites he noticed and looked at her.

"Lucy, is something wrong?" he asked with concern in his face.

"I…" she stammered. She didn't think she could say it. Lucy considered running for the door and then he couldn't follow her. She dismissed the idea when she realized that she needed to hear this from Nathaniel himself. She would replay it in her mind and remember every excruciating detail. Even though she knew that would be torture, it was oddly comforting. "I wanted to talk to you about something," she said quietly, suppressing her desire to howl with grief.

Nathaniel looked her in the eye, "Lucy, I just need one more day to show you some things. It's going to be a wonderful day, one that I have been waiting for since the day I met you. Can you trust me for just one more day and everything will be explained. If you want to have this conversation tomorrow, we can but please just give me today."

Lucy took a deep breath. She had no choice but to trust him. He was worth it. She sighed and nodded.

"Good, eat up, we have a long hike ahead of us."

"A hike?" she asked, "I thought I was supposed to be relaxing."

"Oh, we'll get to that," he said eating. "But it's a ways to get there. I'll carry you if you'll let me. It's important."

"Well it sounds fun!" Lucy replied feigning enthusiasm. Nathaniel smiled slyly at her - she wasn't fooling him.

Lucy hated hiking. She never understood the point of it. Why would you wish this upon yourself? Her back ached, her legs burned and the blisters on her feet were excruciating. Nathaniel had bought her a pair of hiking boots for the trip but they were brand new and Lucy wondered if they were constructed with tacks on the inside. They had been hiking for two hours and Lucy was almost ready to stomp her foot like a toddler and refuse to go one step further. Nathaniel had slowed the pace to a crawl and had offered to carry her a hundred times. Lucy had declined, being too stubborn to accept the help. At this point though, Lucy thought her legs might fall off if she walked three more steps. Finally, she swallowed her pride and opened her mouth to beg to be carried.

"I can't believe you've lasted this long Lucy," Nathaniel said with admiration in his voice. "It's not much farther now." Lucy snapped her mouth shut. Another half an hour passed and Lucy was about to start begging again when Nathaniel stopped and turned back to her. He didn't look flushed or tired in the least. "I'm going to climb this ledge and then pull you up," he instructed.

Climbing? Lucy thought to herself, *Are you kidding me?* He boosted himself up easily on the six-foot rock face. Lucy found a foothold and boosted herself up. Her legs began shaking with the effort. She looked up to Nathaniel's smiling face and reached for his outstretched hands. He pulled her up effortlessly.

"We're here, thank you for doing that," he said smiling at her. Once again, they seemed to be in just denser bush. Lucy was filthy, exhausted and irritated. *This better be good,* she thought to herself ruefully. He reached out for her hand. Lucy took it and he led her through one last bit of foliage. Lucy gasped. "Worth the hike?" Nathaniel whispered in her ear. Lucy could only manage to nod dumbly.

They were in a huge flat clearing. All around was soft ankle length grass dotted here and there with wildflowers. Trees circled one third of the field, another third was a huge wall of granite rock face and the last third was completely open to the mountains around. Lucy gazed out over the cliff to the breathtaking view of forest and sky that went on forever. In the middle of the meadow was an oval natural spring that cut down into the rock. It was filled with steaming hot water and sat still and calm in the afternoon sun.

"I finally found you a bathtub," Nathaniel said grinning.

Lucy turned and clutched him tightly. "Oh it's the most beautiful place I have ever seen. Thank you," she said into his chest. Nathaniel grinned down at her. "Can we go in there?" Lucy asked.

He nodded and pointed to a cluster of trees a few feet away, "You will find your bathing suit and a towel over there." Lucy smiled and darted for the trees giggling with excitement. Her two-piece bathing suit lay over a branch beside a towel. She didn't even wonder where it came from; Nathaniel's magic was slowly becoming commonplace to her. She changed quickly, draping her dirty, sweaty clothes over the same branch. She grabbed the white fluffy towel and headed back to the clearing.

Nathaniel was already in the spring waiting for her. He stood in the middle, the water reaching him just below his perfectly formed stomach. Lucy had never seen him with his shirt off before and her heart skipped a beat. His tanned skin was flawless over a muscular chest and stomach. Lucy headed to the edge and sat down dipping her feet in. The water was perfectly warm and the aches in her toes from the hike rapidly melted away. Nathaniel waded over to her and placed his hands on her knees. Lucy felt butterflies fill her stomach as he ran his hands up her thighs, over her hips and to her waist.

"There is a ledge on this side that you can sit on," he explained. Lucy let him lift and ease her into the water and place her gently onto the ledge. She felt the water rising up her body and its heat melted away every ache and pain. Lucy tilted her head back in the water and sighed softly.

"Oh, wow," she said with her eyes closed.

"Pretty great hey?" he said moving beside her and sitting down.

"Mmmm hmmm," was all Lucy could manage, "thank you."

"Anything for you Lucy," he replied and tilted his own head back and closed his eyes. They sat in peace for a long time. Lucy wasn't sleepy; she was just totally and incredibly relaxed. Her whole body felt malleable and warm. "Hungry?" Nathaniel finally said beside her.

"I could eat," Lucy said without moving.

"The picnic is over there," he replied sitting up and swimming over to the other side of the pool. Lucy followed him and saw a huge blanket with six huge pillows arranged around a massive picnic basket. It hadn't been there before. Lucy looked at him.

"You are amazing Nathaniel," she said in awe as he lifted her out of the spring. He gave her a slightly embarrassed shrug and climbed out of the pool. Lucy dried herself off with her towel. She was a little chilly but she certainly didn't want to put her dirty hiking clothes back on. She walked over and picked Nathaniel's t-shirt up off a branch. It was fresh and clean and didn't hold a clue that it had gone through a grueling two-hour hike. She pulled it over her head. It was soft and warm on her skin and its heady sweet scent encompassed her. Lucy paused and impulsively reached under the shirt, untied her bikini top and tossed it playfully aside. Nathaniel watched her, an amused look on his face.

"I don't want to get your shirt wet," Lucy said with a shrug. Nathaniel looked her slowly up and down with approval in his face but he said nothing. They sat down on the blanket and Nathaniel opened the basket and began pulling out a feast of epic proportions. He dished out cold roast chicken, potatoes, buns and veggies. Lucy ate like a champ and after filling herself to capacity, laid lazily back on the pillows. She stared at Nathaniel through half closed eyes – he glowed in the afternoon sun, his ebony hair glinting in the light. He lay back beside her and looked up at the sky.

"I gotta tell ya," Lucy said, "I am not looking forward to the hike back."

Nathaniel smiled, and didn't turn his head to say, "I'll carry you."

"You are going to have to pal, because I am too relaxed to walk. Thank you for this, it's wonderful."

"I'll carry you," he replied.

"You'll regret saying that an hour into the hike."

He laughed. They fell silent. Lucy was totally tranquil and content. Suddenly, Nathaniel rolled over and grabbed Lucy behind the neck. She gasped at the unexpected movement. He stared intensely into her eyes and Lucy's breathing sped up as she lost herself in his cavernous gaze.

"I heard what Roman said," he spoke carefully.

"Which part?" Lucy whispered although she already knew.

"About me not loving you," he replied. Lucy just stared and held her breath. "It isn't true Lucy." She exhaled deeply and waited. He tightened his grip on her neck, "I love you Lucy Bower. I love you more than anyone has ever loved you. I love you more than anyone has ever loved anything, ever. I love you so much that sometimes I am quite sure that it would kill me if you left me. I love your mind and your smile and your laughter. I love your anger and your sadness and your stubbornness. I love your face, your body and your soul. I feel like I have loved you since before I met you, long before I think. I love you." He stopped, breathing heavily and gazed at her. Lucy lifted one hand and laid it on his face. A single tear formed in her eye and rolled slowly down her face and across his fingers.

"Why did you wait so long to say it?" she asked barely over a whisper.

"Because before you know you love me, you have to see this." Without warning, he sprang to his feet. Lucy sat up shocked and watched as he smiled a beautiful smile at her, turned and sprinted headlong towards the edge of the cliff. Lucy screamed in terror and leapt to her feet starting to run after him but he was far too fast. Without a pause or a look back he jumped off the cliff face to the open chasm below and disappeared. Lucy screamed again and froze in place allowing the shock of the last ten seconds to encompass her. Shock ripped through her making her muscles shake and her blood run cold.

"Nathaniel!" she shrieked knowing it was useless. He couldn't hear her.

"I'm right here," came his voice from the other side of the cliff. Relief swept through Lucy and then confusion as she questioned how this was possible. Slowly, Nathaniel came into view, floating up from the other side of the cliff. Lucy took a step back when she realized how he was floating. Nathaniel hovered over the edge supported by a set of massive wings.

Chapter Fourteen
Pieces of Heaven

"The 'Kingdom of Heaven' is a condition of the heart - no
something that comes 'upon the earth' or 'after death.'"
~Friedrich Nietzsche

Nathaniel stepped casually onto the ground and took a tentative step towards Lucy. She stood and took him all in. Nathaniel had always been beautiful but now he was breathtaking. His handsome face and perfect skin radiated light. The wings arched up above his shoulders and tapered into a heart shape along the sides of his body with the tips barely brushing the ground. Nathaniel spread them out slowly, stretching them to their fullest. Lucy judged them to be at least twelve feet tip to tip. She walked slowly forward, and was surprised that Nathaniel seemed anxious. Lucy reached him and carefully reached out and laid her hand on his bare chest as if confirming he was real. He placed his hand on top of hers.

"Is this," he asked tentatively, "ok?" Lucy gazed at him amazed that he could be nervous about showing this to her. He looked like he was expecting her to run in fear.

Lucy laughed a little. "Ok?" she asked astounded, "this is amazing."

"Lucy," Nathaniel said looking into her eyes, "It's a little freakish."

She smiled and shook her head. "Not at all," she said earnestly, "you have never looked more dazzling." Nathaniel looked relieved. "Can I," she paused, "see them?" she asked. He turned a quarter turn in response. She stepped behind him. The wings attached five inches apart between Nathaniel's shoulder blades and were obviously powerful. They were thick and covered in thousands of perfectly formed white feathers. Lucy ran her fingers gently along the ridge and down the side. "Can you feel that?" she asked. He nodded and flapped them lightly in response. Lucy jumped back and laughed as a gust of air blew her hair back.

Lucy walked back in front of him. "So is this why we had to come all the way up here?" she asked amused.

Nathaniel shrugged, "It was more the bath but it's not like I could have spread these out in your dorm room now could I?" Lucy smiled. He would have cracked through a wall. "But now you have seen me Lucy," he said, "all of me and now and only now can you decide if you love me." Nathaniel turned and held her hands to his chest, "Because you can only truly love someone if you've seen their true form."

"Now that I have seen you," Lucy said, "in your true form," she paused," although I am not happy with how you showed me. I could have lived without the jump." Nathaniel only grinned in response. "I love you more than I did five minutes ago," she said choking on emotion, "there is no man in this world or the next that I could ever love more than I love you Nathaniel. I love you and no other until the end of time."

The emotion on his face was tangible. He pulled Lucy forward and kissed her with such power that Lucy's legs failed her and Nathaniel was holding her up – his lips the only anchor. Nathaniel wordlessly picked her up and cradled her in his arms. "I told you I would carry you home Lucy," he said smiling at her. Lucy wrapped her arms around his neck and allowed her body to sink into his. She felt a burst of wind as he beat his great wings and they lifted off the ground. Immediately they were airborne. Lucy wasn't frightened; in fact, she had never felt so safe.

They rose a mile in the air and Lucy looked about her. The view was stunning and she gazed about taking in the mountains and forest and the sky in all their glory. Nathaniel beat his wings again and they took off with a speed that would rival a 737. The flight would have been a short one but Nathaniel took Lucy on a tour. They flew past an eagle's nest tucked high in the trees and paused to see the fledging eaglets blind and chirping at the sun. He flew low over a wolf family, cuddled up and sleeping like lap dogs in the moss. He flew over a huge glistening lake and Lucy reached out and ran her hand through the water as the trout jumped for her fingers. Lucy laughed.

"Let's go home," Lucy whispered in his ear. Nathaniel picked up speed and flew straight for the house. He ignored the door and instead headed straight for the second story window that opened by itself upon their arrival. He laid Lucy gently on the bed and his wings disappeared from sight. Lucy did not care to ask where they went. It wasn't important right now. Nathaniel lay beside her and kissed her, running his hand up her back, under the t-shirt and clasping the back of her neck.

Lucy reached her arms around him and traced his bare back with her fingertips. Nathaniel responded by kissing her harder, seeking more and more of her as he pressed her body closer to his.

"So beautiful," he reveled. Lucy grabbed his neck and pulled him towards her. He kissed her mouth, her face and her neck before pulling up to gaze at her.

"Are we going to?" Lucy trailed off at the end of her question not because she was embarrassed or uncomfortable but because all words seemed trivial now.

"No," he said plainly.

"Oh," Lucy replied feeling the disappointment sting her pride.

"Lucy," he said reading her face. "Do you not realize how much I want you?" Lucy shook her head confused. "Why do you think I had to leave last night?" he asked not waiting for an answer. "It wasn't because I was angry or bored with you. It was because if I stayed for one more second I wouldn't have been able to control myself." Lucy thought back to his attitude the night before and tried to reconcile it with one of passion but simply couldn't do it. She shook her head again. "When you came downstairs from your shower," he explained, "in those sweatpants and a tank top with your hair all wet from the shower, it was all I could do to stop myself from throwing you across the table and taking you right there. Don't you realize my love, how beautiful you are?"

"Then why don't we…" Lucy started.

"That's my point," he said brushing the hair back from her face, "I want to more than I've ever wanted anything. It's just that I can't."

"Oh," said Lucy – now not wanting to bruise his ego, "you can't."

Nathaniel laughed a little. "No," he explained, "I am quite capable; it's just that I am not allowed to." He paused. "You see, as you know there are rules that Heavenly souls have to abide by. There are some that I have been bending but this one cannot be violated in any way. Immortal Heavenly Creatures cannot have sex with mortals. It simply isn't allowed." Lucy was about to protest and tell him that this wasn't fair. What would they do if he broke the rule anyway? "But," he continued, "I would like to try something else."

"If you are going to tell me that playing Monopoly is just as fun, I won't believe you," Lucy said with a smirk.

He laughed, "No Monopoly but I would like to give myself to you in a different way. Do you trust me?"

"Yes," Lucy said without hesitation. Nathaniel leaned down and kissed her, Lucy kissed him back with passion, excited for what ever was about to happen next.

"Don't be afraid," he whispered against her mouth.

"I'm not," she whispered back, "I trust you." He ran his hand around her body and laid it softly on her stomach under the t-shirt. Lucy's heart skipped a beat. He slowly and gently began to run his hand up her abdomen. He looked away slightly and squinted his wide eyes in concentration. "Are you looking for something?" Lucy whispered

"Your soul," he said quietly. Lucy's heart began to race at a breakneck speed as his hand continued upward and came to rest in between her ribs. "I love you Lucy. You are mine." he whispered as he looked deeply into her eyes and smiled at her. Before Lucy could reply, it began and she was unable to speak.

It started as a warmth deep inside her chest like she had just swallowed hot coffee too fast. It was intense though and formed itself into a ball of heat. It warmed more and began to pulse. Slowly, it grew, taking up more and more space inside her. Lucy looked at Nathaniel and he was shining with his skin giving off a radiant white light. His eyes were intense and Lucy got the impression that this was taking some effort but he was smiling his deep devoted smile. The pulsing heat inside Lucy grew more powerful and pushed against her body as if trying to find escape. Lucy sucked in air willing it to stay for this was the most glorious feeling she had ever experienced.

"Are you ready?" Nathaniel whispered.

"There's more?" Lucy asked amazed.

"This is just your soul Lucy," he said smiling, "you haven't even felt mine yet." He pushed his hand into her and she felt an electric shock run from his hand directly into her. Red heat seared into her and the ball of warmth grabbed it, wrapped around it and the two exploded out of Lucy and Nathaniel with such force that she had to arch her back to support it's power. The bed began to shake beneath them as Lucy felt every nerve in her body alight with sensation. The light spilled out through Lucy's arms and legs and neck. She lifted one hand and saw that there were beams of light spilling from her fingertips. She looked at the ceiling where the ivy was shaking as light danced across it.

Lucy's mind emptied of every thought, every memory and filled only with light, love and complete happiness. Nathaniel was the only thing holding her to this Earth. He was her beginning, her end and everything in between. There was nothing but Nathaniel and his devotion to her – nothing at all. Lucy knew that she would die or kill for his love and feel no regret for it. There was nothing else that mattered. She closed her eyes and allowed the light to consume her.

Slowly, she felt the pressure from Nathaniel's hand ease up and the light began to fade. Lucy felt it retreat one inch at a time back along her appendages to her torso and further until it was a pulsing small light once more until she couldn't feel it anymore. Nathaniel laid her gently back on the bed. He pulled the covers up over her and brushed a hair back off her forehead.

"That's what's it is like where I come from," he whispered to her. Lucy was speechless for the first time in her life. She had been given a piece of Heaven. Nathaniel wrapped his arms around her and they both fell into a deep uncompromising sleep. A few moments' later, snowflakes fell from the ceiling onto their entwined bodies.

Lucy woke up when it was still dark outside. The moon cast its glow across the bed and she gazed at Nathaniel's peaceful sleeping face. She knew looking at him what she had known all along but was now deeply, soulfully sure – she would never let him go. Lucy could never be without him. "I love you," she whispered. Before today those words held such meaning, such significance for her but now they seemed trivial and weak. She looked up at the ivy covered ceiling and like every other day since she met him whispered, "Thank you from the bottom of my heart for sending him to me and please understand that you can never have him back." She rolled back onto her side. In his sleep, Nathaniel reached around her pulling her against him and she fell back asleep.

When she awoke again, Nathaniel was gone. On his pillow was another gift and a note. It wasn't a flower this time. Nathaniel had left her one singular, huge, crisp white feather.

I'll be back
I Love You
N

He must have gone to say goodbye to Mother and the cubs. Lucy picked up the feather and twirled it in her fingers. It was beautiful, like everything that had anything to do with Nathaniel. She sighed with happiness and walked to the bathroom. Lucy took a long shower, dressed, made the bed and packed their bags. A few minutes later, the front door opened and Nathaniel came in. Lucy realized that she had missed him terribly. She ran down the stairs, across the living room and into his waiting arms. She kissed him hard on the lips.

"Remind me to go out more often if that's the reception I get," he said grinning. Lucy laughed and kissed him again.

"You don't get to leave me, ever," she said smiling.

"Sadly though," he replied. "We do have to leave here."

"Can't we just stay here forever?" Lucy asked pouting.

"No, you have school tomorrow," he answered.

"Ok fine," Lucy replied. "Are we driving or flying?" she asked with a grin. Nathaniel laughed.

"I'll fly us back to the jeep but I am not flying all the way back to the University."

"Is it tiring?" she asked.

"No but it would not be comfortable for you for long distances." he replied

Lucy hugged him. "Oh Nathaniel, I had the most amazing time. Can we come back here?"

"Of course, I built it for you." He opened the front door as Lucy pulled on her shoes and took one last look around sighing. She really didn't want to go.

Chapter Fifteen
Soul Mates

"Whatever our souls are made of, his and mine are the same."
~Emily Brontë

Nathaniel flew them and the bags easily back to the jeep. They piled in and Lucy turned the car around and headed back down the bumpy logging road. Lucy thought of how much this weekend had changed her. When she had taken this drive forty-eight hours ago she was hoping for a romantic weekend with her boyfriend. Now, everything felt different. She knew Nathaniel so much better. No other connection she would ever have with anyone in her life would ever be this strong. When they reached the highway Lucy started asking questions.

"How did you do that?" she asked not having to explain what she meant.

"I wouldn't have been able to do that with anyone else but you Lucy," he answered.

"Why?"

"Because we are soul mates Lucy," he said smiling. "Only

two souls that belong together can connect like that."

"Is that what they do in Heaven?"

"Yes," he nodded. "But I've never done it before."

"Why not?"

"Obviously, because my soul mate was down here."

"Oh," Lucy smiled. "How do you know that this connection was different then?"

"I was surprised that your soul reached out for mine as though they knew each other. It was a far more intense reaction than I thought possible."

"Then why did you wait until now to do it?" Lucy asked. "I mean I think we have both known from the first night that our connection was unreasonably close."

"Well for one," he replied. "I needed to let you see my wings first and for two, we couldn't do that in your dorm room."

"Why?" Lucy asked curious.

"Lucy," he smiled. "Didn't you feel the bed shaking?"

"Yes," she replied. "But to be honest, I thought that was just me. I also thought I saw the leaves on the ceiling shaking." She tried to think back but for once her memory was hazy.

"That wasn't the leaves Lucy," he replied grinning. "That was the roof."

"What?" said Lucy stunned and laughing. "We made the roof shake?"

Nathaniel grinned wider. "We made the whole house shake. There were cracks in the foundation this morning and several dishes broke in the kitchen," he said. "If we had tried that in your dorm room we would have reduced that old building to shambles."

"You built that house to withstand that kind of force didn't you?"

"I certainly did," he said nodding.

"So your wings," Lucy asked. "Is that where you go when you're away from me?"

"Usually yes," he nodded. "They need to be stretched every few days."

"And where are they right now?" she asked. He twisted in response and pulled up the back of his shirt. Keeping her eyes on the road, Lucy reached out and felt two faint ridges running between his shoulder blades. They were noticeable to Lucy but no one else would think anything of them.

"The day you called me in the library in Stonecreek, I was flying. I barely got my shirt back on before I walked in the room."

"You were out of breath," Lucy remembered.

"I was in a hurry to get to you," he said.

"Ok," she said shortly, "have I seen everything you can do? Am I aware of all your powers now?"

"What else could there be?" he asked laughing.

"Pal," Lucy raised her eyebrows, "I thought the invisibility was enough of a power. You can't walk on water or anything can you?"

"Only one guy could do that Lucy," Nathaniel grinned at her. "Nope, you've seen it all." They fell silent for a minute. "I owe you an apology Lucy, for the way I acted the other night. I am so sorry I made you cry."

"It's alright as long as you were trying to prevent yourself from breaking a Heavenly rule," Lucy said. She hadn't even thought about it since. "Where did you go anyway?"

"No where," he said frankly. "I sat on the roof and listened to you cry, hating myself."

"Don't worry about it, really," Lucy squeezed his hand and felt the familiar tingling sensation. She was starting to realize it wasn't just Nathaniel's effect on her but it was their effect together.

There was another pause and they drove in comfortable silence for a while.

"You aren't leaving," Lucy said plainly. This was now a fact, not a question or a wish. Nathaniel was not going anywhere.

"Lucy," he said softly. "I think we should discuss this." Lucy started to protest but he cut her off. "Now hear me out. I have to think of what is best for you. Is this what's best for you? I'm invisible, you can't marry me, you can't have children with me, there are so many things you deserve in life that I can not give you. I can't even get a job! I can't live without you but I worry that you will be giving up so much to be with me." Lucy reacted immediately by violently pulling the jeep over and skidding to a stop. She threw it in park and turned to face Nathaniel. Lucy saw him wince at her furious face.

"Listen to me very carefully Nathaniel," she said quickly and clearly, "because we are only going to have this conversation this one and only time. I don't want anyone else, I won't have anyone else and I don't deserve any less than you. I don't care that you are invisible, I never have and I never will. I don't want children if I can't have them with you." She pointed at him. "You are good for me, you are all there is for me, I will live everyday of my life with you and that is final. Do I make myself clear?" She was yelling now so Nathaniel just nodded. "Good," she said as the matter was now settled. "You are not going anywhere."

"Ok," he replied cautiously. "I guess we are not going to discuss this. I'm not going back."

Lucy put the car in drive, checked her mirror, signaled and pulled out onto the highway and picked up speed. She was completely calm now. She changed lanes muttering, "can't get a job like that flipping matters." She laughed to herself.

"Lucy," Nathaniel said grinning at her, "I love you but you

scare me a little sometimes."

She laughed again. "Don't piss me off like that again pal," she said grinning. Nathaniel chuckled and shook his head. "So how do we keep you here?" Lucy was in soldier mode now. They would solve this problem and get this done.

"Well," Nathaniel replied. "I have been asking, well to be honest, I've been begging, for some guidance but I am getting nothing back."

"Hmm," Lucy said thoughtfully, "do you think they're listening?"

"They're always listening."

"So what's the problem?"

"Well, I've figured a few things out and for me to stay, I would have to change a little."

"Why?" she asked changing lanes to pass a camper.

"It's the Heavenly part of me that is affecting my surroundings. I am still technically an Angel of Heaven. That's the part that is angering Roman and Bael so much. I do offset the balance and I would have to sever my connection with Heaven to stop having that effect. I leave traces of Heaven everywhere I go and that can't continue."

"So if you sever your connection with Heaven, you will still be an Angel, just one tied to the ground and not the sky?" Lucy concluded.

"Right."

"So how do we cut the cord?"

"I don't know."

"Would a Demon know?" she asked.

"I doubt it and even if they did know they wouldn't tell me. But," he added hopefully, "I have a plan. I'm going to do some research while you are in class. Somewhere, there must be an answer."

"I thought you couldn't leave me alone?" Lucy asked. She realized that she might be addicted to him. The thought wasn't that upsetting.

"I think you will be safe in class," he replied. "I'll make short trips and come back."

"Ok," Lucy said. She took a deep breath. That would have to be the plan for now. They had no other options. "You are not leaving me."

"I am not leaving you," he said and took her hand again, "ever."

They got back to the dorm in early afternoon. Lucy parked the jeep on the street, made sure no one she knew was around and hopped out of it quickly. They walked up the steps and when she glanced back, the jeep was gone. She sighed; it would be so nice to have a vehicle full time. Nathaniel sensed her disappointment.

"I know it's sad but we really don't need a car now do we?" he said.

"It would still be nice," Lucy mumbled. They spent the rest of the day getting Lucy ready for classes to start the next morning. She had a slightly lighter load but still wanted to be prepared. Lucy read ahead in several of her texts and organized her supplies. It was after dinner when a knock came at the door. Lucy froze in fear. Was it Roman or Bael? Would they bother to knock? She looked at Nathaniel expectantly. He shrugged and stood beside her as she unlocked and opened the door. Anastasia burst into the room like wildfire.

"What's with the locked door? I thought you were getting back Thursday from Kansas? How was it? Did you have fun?" she plopped herself down on the couch and grinned at Lucy. "And

OMG do I have news for you." Lucy heard Nathaniel sigh beside her. Listening to girl gossip was not his idea of a fun evening.

"I'm going to go hang out on the roof," he whispered in Lucy's ear. She nodded lightly as she walked towards the couch. He was gone before she sat down.

"Ok," she smiled at Anastasia. "I locked my door because I felt like it. I stayed later at my Mom's. Yes, I had fun. Mom is dating, it's a little weird but good for her and I found out I died when I was a baby and came back to life which might or might not have something to do with my memory but I don't really care."

"You died?" Anastasia asked incredulously. "How? Details!"

Lucy ran through the whole scenario omitting Nathaniel and (of course) Romans involvement. Anastasia was amazed. "Are you ok with this?" she asked.

"Yes," Lucy smiled, "actually, I am. I mean I figured that it doesn't matter where my photographic memory comes from, it only matters what I do with it,"

"Very healthy," Anastasia nodded sharply. "I'm proud of you."

"Thanks," Lucy grinned. "So you have news?"

Anastasia perked up remembering. "Yes, yes I do," she grinned. "I'm in love." Lucy's heart sank. *No, no, no,* she thought, *please don't let it be.* "With Roman," Anastasia finished.

Lucy closed her eyes and swallowed hard. "Are you sure?" she asked softly fighting the urge to shake her friend.

"Of course I'm sure!" Anastasia beamed. "He's wonderful Luc seriously!"

"Really?" Lucy had to tread carefully. "Because he kind of came across as a little self involved to me."

"No!" Anastasia protested. "Not at all! Oh Lucy, he's so nice and funny and genuine and I think he might be in love with me too."

"Really?" Lucy replied.

"Yes!" Anastasia almost yelled. "He kept acting on Saturday like he wanted to tell me something but kept changing his mind. And when he kissed me Lucy…"

"You kissed him?" Lucy yelled at her not being able to hide the disgust in her voice. Anastasia was taken aback and Lucy could see the hurt in her eyes. "Well," Lucy calmed her voice, "you just met him after all."

"Lucy it was just a good night kiss, it's not like we…"

"Tell me you didn't sleep with him!" Lucy almost yelled in panic.

"What kind of girl do you think I am?" Anastasia looked confused. "Aren't you happy for me?" Lucy sighed. It was so difficult for her to reconcile the wheeling dealing cruel hearted Demon she knew with this wonderful guy Anastasia was describing. Lucy couldn't let her friend walk into this fire.

"Anastasia, I have something to tell you," she said impulsively, ready to spill everything. A loud thump came from the ceiling making the light fixture shake. Nathaniel had sent down a warning shot.

"What was that?" Anastasia said staring at the ceiling.

"It was a very large, very annoying bird," Lucy said angrily. She sighed again. Nathaniel was right of course. Anastasia would never believe Lucy. She stared at her friend's face. Anastasia looked how Lucy felt, radiantly in love and suddenly, Lucy could not take that away from her.

"I am very happy for you. I love you and if Roman is what makes you happy, then I am happy," she said with a smile.

"Oh thanks babe," Anastasia said while hugging Lucy. "Don't worry, you'll find a guy soon enough and we will double date. It will be so much fun!"

Lucy held back a laugh. "That would be..." *horrid?* "great," she said. Anastasia gushed about Roman for another forty minutes and Lucy endured it smiling and nodding. She left as suddenly as she arrived.

"I have to get my stuff ready to teach tomorrow," she explained moving to the door. There weren't any dance classes during the summer semester so Anastasia was teaching dance camp programs all day. Parents had signed up their daughters to dance all day with performance majors to keep them out of trouble.

"You better make them call you Miss. Rooke," Lucy said grinning.

"Oh you bet it will," Anastasia replied laughing. "I need a stick!" They both giggled at the image of casual fun Anastasia with a dance instructor's stick. "Lunch tomorrow?"

"Can't," Lucy replied. "I'm meeting Dr. Hannon."

"Ok, then dinner."

"It's a date," Lucy smiled.

"Don't forget about the Summer Solstice Party, June 20th," Anastasia said looking Lucy directly in the eye.

Lucy tapped her temple. "Got it," she said. Lucy suspected that the only reason Anastasia took the summer camp job was to stay on campus to attend the party. It was notoriously one of the biggest parties of the year. They hugged again and Anastasia flew out the door.

Lucy grabbed her pajamas and bathroom bag and headed for the bathroom. When she returned, Nathaniel was sitting in bed in his pajamas. She crawled gratefully into his arms.

"I know, I know," she mumbled ruefully. "I did the right thing not telling her. But that was excruciating."

"Roman makes her happy Lucy," he replied.

"But she doesn't know him," Lucy pleaded.

"Some people are married for thirty years and don't really know their spouse. Anastasia is happy, that's all that matters for now." He kissed her head as it lay on his shoulder.

"I just wish that I could tell her all about you. I share everything with her," Lucy said sadly.

"Well," he said with a smile, "you always have me. Go on Lucy, tell me how great I am."

Lucy laughed, "Well, where do I begin?"

"No, no, no," he said sitting up. "I was kidding. "

Lucy ignored him and used her best adolescent girl voice, "Well, like I have totally found my soul mate!" Nathaniel laughed out loud and she continued as if talking to a thirteen year old. "And OMG is he ever awesome. He's like totally this like Angel and he like flies and like can do stuff and like when he kisses me I get all these like warm tingles and like...." Nathaniel stopped her mouth with a kiss. Lucy wrapped her arms around him. After a moment, he lifted his head.

"Anastasia said OMG too," he said. "What does that mean?"

Lucy giggled at the irony of it all. "It means 'Oh my God' and Anastasia wants to double date. How awkward would that be?" Nathaniel threw his head back and laughed. He looked down at her.

"I love you Lucy, you make me laugh," he said grinning at her. He kissed her and Lucy's mind drained of the worries of the day. A few moments later, the lights turned off.

Chapter Sixteen
Research

"What you don't know would make a great book."
~Sydney Smith

The next morning they left for class early. Lucy had three classes, then a two-hour lunch and two more classes after. Each day would be the same for the summer semester. Roman was sitting in the quad again. He said nothing and they said nothing but Lucy trembled at his icy glare. He wasn't there at lunch when Lucy and Nathaniel made their way to Dr. Hannon's office. He was finally back at work after the attack.

"This must be boring for you," Lucy whispered to Nathaniel in the stairwell. "Following me around like this."

"Not at all," he replied earnestly, "I love spending time with you." She smiled and knocked on Dr. Hannon's door.

"Come in Lucy!" he called from within.

"I have sushi!" Lucy said pushing the door open and leaving it open for Nathaniel to sneak in behind her. Dr. Hannon looked casual in a pair of kakis and a golf shirt. His face had healed very well and his handsome features were starting to come back.

"How are you Lucy?" he said cocking his head to one side and looking at her like she was a lost puppy.

Lucy laughed. "I'm fine doc," she said hugging him, it was so like him to worry about HER when he was the one who was actually injured.

"Let me make something clear," he replied, "I feel fine, I look gorgeous and I DON'T want to talk about the violent incident unless you want to talk about it. Ok?" He raised his eyebrows looking for acknowledgement and Lucy nodded with a grin. Relief washed over his face. "Are you angry with me? About the whole drowning thing?" he asked warily. "For not telling you?"

"Not at all," Lucy replied. "It wasn't your place to tell me."

"Well," he shrugged, "I should have been more stern with your Mother. I could have convinced her to tell you."

Lucy put the plastic sushi boxes on the coffee table and sat down shrugging out of her coat.

"Have you met my mother? Do you honestly think you could have changed her mind?"

Dr. Hannon laughed. "Good point." He sat at the other end of the couch. "But I still feel like I could have done more. You must have been so shocked." Lucy nodded while popping a California roll in her mouth. Nathaniel sat on the floor against the wall eating from his own box. Lucy glanced over at him and he winked at her. She smiled. "Your mom didn't go into details," Dr. Hannon said. "How did you find out?"

So Lucy gave the same version of the story she had given Anastasia. Dr. Hannon listened with interest.

"Do you really think it's wrong that we tell people about the source of my photographic memory?" Lucy asked him when she was done with the story.

"Lucy, I've looked into this," he said. "People who have near death experiences have the same brain function as before the incident. Some claim of course that they can now see the future or see the dead but none of that has ever been proven or validated scientifically. None of them have ever claimed heightened brain function. In fact, most have decreased function as a result of whatever trauma caused their deaths in the first place. I know the physicality of your brain better than anyone and if your memory is the result of a drowning, I can see no evidence of that."

"Hmm," said Lucy. "So I could have been born with this."

"Absolutely," he confirmed, "in fact that is far more likely. All I have ever studied is your brain function. I have never discussed or examined where it came from because frankly, that isn't relevant."

"Makes sense," Lucy and Nathaniel said in unison. She flashed him a quick smile.

"Your mind is extraordinary in its performance but there is nothing all that different physically from me or anyone else. Therefore as a scientist I am limited to focusing on its abilities not its origins."

"True," Lucy said. "But did my father think that my memory had something to do with the accident? Is that why he wanted me to know so badly?"

"No," Dr. Hannon shook his head. "Your father didn't question your abilities. He was sure you were born with them. He wanted you to know because he felt you had a right to know."

"He was right," Lucy said bluntly.

"And I agree," Dr. Hannon conceded. "But your mother was adamant and we both knew she was only doing what she thought was best."

"When I had my little well, freak out in March." Lucy

started. "You asked me if I had come up with any new memories. Is the drowning what you were thinking of?"

"Yes," Dr. Hannon nodded. "I forgot I asked you that. I was wondering if your brain had spat out a memory of the accident and you were reacting to it."

"That explains it. Thanks Doc. I feel even better about it now," Lucy said smiling.

"Good," he smiled back. He got up and poured them some coffees. "Can we talk about our Polish visitors?"

"Yes," Lucy said and rewound her mind to their last conversation, "the sleep guy right. Is that still a go? You feel up to it?"

"I told you I don't want to talk about it. I wouldn't suggest it if I didn't think I was ready." Dr. Hannon sat back down. "This scientist is bringing half his faculty with him – at his own expense I might add. It's turning into a big thing. Are you ok with that?"

"How many people are going to watch me sleep?" Lucy asked nervously.

"Just a select few. I made sure of that. All of them are coming to the conference on the 21st of June," Dr. Hannon explained. "Dr. Gorski will be sending a team of four on the 19th. We'll do the tests that night and the rest of the group shows up on the 20th." Lucy stored all the information. Dr. Hannon looked directly at her while giving her the instructions knowing that she needed the visual clues for it to lock.

"Sounds good to me but I can't do anything on the 20th," she replied.

"That's fine," Dr. Hannon said. "We will be doing boring scholar wine and cheese stuff in the afternoon, Brian is going to hate me for it." Lucy grinned. "But just out of curiosity, what's on the 20th?"

"The summer solstice party," Lucy said with a smile. "It's supposed to be a good one."

Dr. Hannon laughed, "Well, we can't have you miss the party now can we?"

"No way Doc, not for all the polish sausage in the world."

"Well, be sure to get some sleep after the party because you are going to have to be on for the next day."

"Deal," Lucy said saluting to make her point.

They chatted for a bit longer about her classes and plans for the summer. Lucy looked at her watch and got up to leave. Dr. Hannon hugged her and told her he'd be in touch with final details for the conference. She hugged him back tightly grateful for his friendship and left the room slowly allowing Nathaniel to slip out before her.

They reached the English building where Lucy's next two classes were. Nathaniel walked her in the first classroom and sat beside her.

"Your next class is right next door," he said. "I'm going to run an errand but I'll be back before the end of Dramatic Literature." Lucy was nervous. Other students surrounded her so she couldn't even whisper. Frustrated that they couldn't have a proper conversation in public, she opened her notebook and wrote.

Are you sure?

Nathaniel glanced at the paper. "Yes," he assured her. "He won't come near you with so many people around you."

Where are you going?

"I need to do some research and I hate to say it but your library is woefully lacking in the kind of information I need."

I love you – come back to me

"I love you too, I will always come for you." He slipped out of the row and disappeared. Lucy was immediately anxious without Nathaniel beside her. The class passed slowly. Every time a student came in late, coughed or dropped something, Lucy jumped. When 2:00 rolled around she quickly collected her things and stayed in the crowd. As it turned out, most people from her Middle English class were in her Dramatic Literature class so she moved in the middle of a throng of students to the next classroom.

Lucy felt calmer now. Nathaniel would be back in less than an hour. She focused on the class and kept notes. 3:00 crept up on her and before she knew it the professor was casually dismissing them and the students started to pack up and leave. Nathaniel still wasn't back. Lucy started to worry. What had happened to him? There wasn't a class after hers so within moments the classroom was empty and Lucy was totally alone. Panic flooded through her. Would Roman or Bael be able to tell if Nathaniel wasn't with her? She had a feeling they could.

She stood up, collected her things and headed for the door. Lucy would have to find another crowded area. She decided to head to the Students Union Building where the largest population of students would be. She might even find Anastasia there, which would certainly curb any violence from Roman. Lucy hurried out of the empty classroom into an even emptier hall. She and Nathaniel hadn't been able to have a private conversation all day. Why now did she find herself totally isolated? She paused in the hallway not sure which door to go out. The door to the right was a faster route to the Student's Union Building but it was less used than the path that let out the left doors.

Indecision gripped her. This could be a life or death choice. She whimpered a little at the severity of this moment. Nathaniel was not coming for her – that could mean that they had somehow incapacitated him, which Lucy had to admit, sounded impossible. She was on her own, possibly forever and a Demon was most likely coming to kill her.

"Nathaniel," she pleaded to the empty hallway. "Where are you?"

The lights went out.

Lucy stood frozen in fear. The only light was from each of the glass doors at either end of the hallway.

A figure appeared silhouetted in the far end of the hall. Lucy braced herself to bolt left but then a familiar voice cut through the air.

"Hey is everyone ok in here?" Lucy paused and wished her memory included auditory cues. Either way, the voice fostered a feeling of comfort for Lucy. Her instincts told her that there was no danger here. The figure approached and finally Lucy recognized the shape and vague facial features of Cliff, the maintenance man who had come to her rescue in the laundry room. Lucy's tension eased further.

"It's me," she called out in the dark, "Lucy Bower from 4B in the dorms. The lights have gone out." She laughed lightly, "It appears that I am afraid of the dark."

Cliff came closer, "Ah Lucy," he said in a fatherly voice, "we are all a little afraid of the dark." He approached in the casual gait of a man who has little worries. Lucy smiled as he came closer. "We should be afraid." Lucy paused, something wasn't right. Cliff came closer and even in the dark Lucy could see his features coming into focus. "You especially Lucy, should be very very afraid." His eyes were totally black inside.

"Let me introduce myself," he said with a smile.

"Bael," Lucy whispered.

"Clever girl."

She turned and sprinted for the far door. She made it ten feet when a wall of fire alighted in front of her. Lucy spun quickly into the stairwell, dropped her book bag and flew as fast as she could up the stairs. She knew that it couldn't be fast enough. She knew how fast Nathaniel could move, Bael must move at least that quick. She sobbed a little in panic as she reached the landing and paused. He wasn't coming after her. Lucy took a sharp breath and swallowed her terror. No one else was here. If she was going to live, she was going to have to save herself and she couldn't do that when she was petrified. She forced her breathing to slow and calmed her mind.

If Lucy could make it to the roof, she could certainly garner some attention from the quad. She had no idea if she could make it to the roof. She thought of the animal that had sniffed her in Dr. Hannons office but supressed it. If he was in human form than that is what she was dealing with.

"He's just human," Lucy whispered to herself and she started creeping up the stairs whether it was right or not was irrelevant. It made her feel calmer, and that's what she needed right now. "He is a human being and can be beat," she breathed. She made it to the second floor landing but aimed for the service door to the right. This opened to a smaller stairway and Lucy climbed it up to another door. Gently, quietly, she reached up and turned the heavy silver handle on the metal door. She winced as it made the faintest creak. Lucy opened the door only far enough to squeeze her body out. She exhaled as the sun shone down on her face, she had made it out onto the roof.

Bael stood directly in front of her with his arms crossed against his chest. He was no longer wearing the uniform of a maintenance man but a very expensive suit. His hair was slicked back and Lucy realized that he was much younger than she had originally thought. Gone was the dowdy maintenance man and in front of her was a dashingly handsome blond but black eyed Demon.

"Tsk tsk tsk little child," he cooed while picking a piece of lint off his jacket, "do you honestly think you could get away from me?" Lucy stopped but forced herself to not become hysterical. "Roman has done a piss poor job around here." The Guild Prime drawled, "you and that Angel have been running amok and I simply won't have it. I have no interest in offering you any deals. You will now die and then so will your Angel and I will be on the golf course within a half an hour. Roman has handled this whole thing horribly but I am here to rectify the situation." His temper flared and his black eyes darkened further. Lucy stayed calm even though her heart was pounding in terror and while Bael talked on, she glanced at the structure of the roof.

She was in the middle of the flat graveled surface, and it was a good 20 feet to the edge. They would have to get closer if Lucy wanted to be seen. Between the door and the edge of the roof and scattered all about her were huge metal boxes of varying sizes. Some were roof top air conditioning units, others were for things like the elevator shafts. Lucy decided that if she was going to die, than this guy was going to come with her. If she could get to the other side of one of those boxes and scream loud enough, her murder would be seen from the quad. Therefore, her death would not be in vain. "I have no idea how they do things where your boyfriend comes from, but in my Guild, we don't tolerate this kind of complete disrespect!" He was yelling now. "Roman will suffer for this kind of epic failure and you and the winged cherub will die!"

While Bael was mid-sentence, Lucy bolted for the farthest box. She heard Bael lunge after her. She started to scream but realized that he had frozen her voice in her throat. It was like a horror film, Lucy was running for her life and could not scream for help. But she could still run. She quickly changed course and dashed right, diving behind another air unit. By luck, this one had a fire safety box next to it. Without thinking, Lucy smashed the glass and grabbed the crash axe inside. She heard the smallest crunch of gravel to her right and on instinct, she swung.

She heard a light choking sound and looking right, she saw the axe imbedded into the throat of Bael. Lucy screamed and let go of the handle but it stayed at its mark. Bael stood stunned as blood poured rapidly out of his neck in a wave. His black eyes cleared to a bright human blue and they trained themselves on Lucy. She stepped back, having no idea what he was still capable of even being so incapacitated. The Demon didn't go for her though; he just stood there as blood poured out of his body over the suit and down to his once shiny shoes. He grinned and looked down at himself. He shook his head at Lucy and his expression turned dark.

"You will pay for this," he growled. Lucy jumped as the Demon burst into flames and vanished.

Lucy collapsed to the roof and leaned back against the air return breathing heavily. Tears poured from her eyes. Relief and fear and regret coursed through her. Another crunch of gravel brought her focus forward again. Nathaniel's face surfaced in front of her. He didn't speak but simply gathered her in his arms. She leaned into him and sobbed.

"What have you done?" an all too familiar voice floated over them. Lucy's shoulders tensed again, Roman had come, presumably to finish what Bael had started. Lucy didn't have any energy left to fight; she didn't even raise her head to look at him. Nathaniel however, did have some fight left in him, quite a lot of it actually. He leapt up to face Roman, fists and jaw clenched.

Roman just stood regarding both of them and the empty spot where Bael had been. "What have you done?" he said again and then he smiled. Lucy stared at him incredulously. How evil could something be? He looked at both of them like they were missing the punch line of a joke. "Do you not know?" he said to Nathaniel who shook his head. Roman rolled his eyes, "When the Guild Prime dies, the Demon who witnesses it becomes the new Guild Prime."

Lucy swallowed the bile that had risen in her throat, "You are happy," she forced out, "that you got a promotion?"

Before he could answer, a crow suddenly landed on the air unit beside them. It was huge and regarded them all with a cold eye.

"I have to go," Roman said while not taking his eye off the crow. Then he rounded on Nathaniel, "But make no mistake Angel. You might have managed to kill Bael but you will not get so lucky with me. Your clock is still ticking." He leaned in and pointed at Nathaniel's chest, but he looked at Lucy. "Send him back or you both die."

Nathaniel moved himself into his line of vision, "Stay away from her or you will die too Roman!" he raged.

"I will destroy her," Roman spat out pointing at Lucy. "I will annihilate her soul! I will make her a shell of a creature! She will beg me for mercy! She will pray for a death from your God!" The crow squawked at him as if to hurry him along. "Last chance Angel, go or her soul pays the price."

With that, he and the crow vanished.

"Come Lucy," Nathaniel said while gently guiding her away. She was shaking as they walked quickly and quietly back to the dorm. When she got into her room, Lucy trudged over to the window. She sighed and let her shoulders slump as she rested her forehead against the cool glass. Nathaniel wrapped his arms around her, always comforting, always calming.

"I'm so sorry I wasn't there," he said, his voice choking in his throat. "I lost track of time, please forgive me."

"It's fine," Lucy said. "You should be able to be three minutes late without a Demon trying to kill me." She looked out the window to the quad. Students walked around happily living their lives. They threw Frisbees and laughed and gossiped. She was one of them not a few short months ago. Lucy had been completely oblivious to the delicate balance of good and evil in the universe. She had never even considered that there were Angels or Demons in the world because it didn't really matter to her at the time. Now though, that was all she dealt with. "I killed a man Nathaniel," she started to sob, "two months ago I was worried about what shoes I could wear with my new bag and today, I KILLED A MAN!" She screamed.

"He was NOT a man Lucy," Nathaniel said into her hair. He gripped her tighter, "Bael died a very long time ago, he isn't human and he's not a person. You had to defend yourself. You have done nothing wrong. You can't kill something that isn't alive."

Lucy knew he was right but that didn't make it any easier. She just kept seeing all that blood over and over again. She shuddered. Nathaniel just held her as she released all the pain and the terror and the exhaustion. "I'm tired of fighting Hell, I'm tired of fighting Heaven, I'm tired of lying to my friends and family Nathaniel," she sobbed into the window leaving breath marks on the glass. "I just don't understand why everyone wants us to be apart?" She lifted her head and turned to face him, "Why is it that neither the bad guys nor the good guys want us to be happy?"

Nathaniel's face was full of concern in his reflection in the glass. "Lucy my beloved, I think this has very little to do with you and me. The Demons want me gone, your involvement is merely a bargaining tool and they," he pointed to the ceiling, "want us to be happy but they know as well as we do that this can only be temporary. I am so sorry you have to deal with all of this," he paused. "Not to bring it up again but..."

Lucy's head snapped up and she jabbed a finger into his chest. "Don't you dare!" she warned. "You leaving is not an option." Nathaniel just smiled and shook his head. "Where is Bael now?" Lucy whispered.

"Back in Hell," Nathaniel whispered back, "I assume. Lucy," he clarified again, "he isn't dead, just one of his many human forms is dead."

"And where is Roman?" she asked.

"In Hell as well," Nathaniel answered, "that's what the crow was there for."

"Could you understand the crow?"

He nodded, "It came to call him back. He isn't in trouble though, you were right, he is getting a promotion. On the bright side, we should be fairly safe while he is gone. It should give me some time to find some answers."

She sighed and let him lead her to the couch. She rested her head on Nathaniel's chest. He played with her hair, waiting for the next question. Lucy always had another question. She noticed for the first time that Nathaniel had brought a bag with him. It was a brown leather satchel. "What's that?" she asked nodding toward the bag.

"Oh this," he said leaning over and picking it up, "is why I was late." He opened it and pulled out five books all in varying sizes -some no bigger than a pamphlet and one as large as a foot across. This largest one drew the most attention – it looked like it weighed a hundred pounds because it was bound in ornate gold. Lucy reached over and ran her hand gently over it. It was exquisite.

"Where did you get this?" she asked with wonder in her voice.

"The Vatican," Nathaniel replied casually like he had picked it up at the gas station.

Lucy stared at him, her mouth agape. "The Vatican?" she said, "like in Rome?"

Nathaniel nodded. "I thought about the best place to research Angels and found myself in the Vatican Library. Fascinating place."

"I would think so," Lucy said. She let out a whistle, "You stole books from the Vatican."

"Lucy I didn't steal them," he said clarifying. "I'm going to bring them back tomorrow. I just don't have time to read through them while you are in class. Don't forget who I am Lucy, I am quite sure the Pope would loan me the books if he knew I needed them."

Lucy's eyes brightened with realization. "The Pope!" she exclaimed. "He's the holiest person alive! Can he see you?"

"No," he replied his voice full of disappointment. "I thought of that too."

"So…" Lucy smiled ruefully, "how is His Holiness today?"

"He's good," Nathaniel said casually, smiling at the joke. "He has a bit of a cold."

"That's too bad," Lucy said in the same laid-back voice. Nathaniel nodded and smiled. He opened the book on his lap. It was in Latin and beautifully illustrated. Lucy gasped. "It's stunning."

"Isn't it?" Nathaniel said as he gently ran his hand over the text. "Hopefully it's not just a pretty face and it can be of some assistance."

Lucy was completely spent so she lay down with her head on Nathaniel's lap. Within seconds she was asleep. Nathaniel sighed and leaned his head back.

"What can I do?" he asked to the ceiling. Silence. He sighed and picked up the book.

A while later there was a knock at the door. Lucy roused

and looked at her watch. She stretched and looked up at Nathaniel. She smiled warily.

"Dinner time," she whispered. "Are you coming?"

"I'd better," he said while packing up his bag and pulling the strap over his shoulder. "Don't want to leave these lying around."

Lucy took a deep breath and opened the door to a beaming Anastasia. "So Miss. Rooke, I take it you had a good day?"

"Unbelievable!" Anastasia cried. "So great!" Lucy left the door wide open so Nathaniel could sneak out while she grabbed her keys.

"That's awesome! Were the kids good?"

"Oh they're great but I'll tell you all about it over dinner but the best thing happened when I got back. I just got back to my room and Roman had left this for me. He said he has to go away for a few days with his uncle or something but said that I was 'on his mind'. " She held up her arm to show a Tiffany charm bracelet. Lucy's eyes went wide.

"Wow," was all she could manage to say.

"I know!" Anastasia gushed. "And look! He already bought me a charm for it." Lucy looked closer for some reason she didn't want to touch it. Dangling from one of the links was a perfect, tiny pair of ballet shoes.

"That's a very thoughtful gift," Lucy said truthfully. Once again she was torn between the two people she knew as Roman – this kind, thoughtful boyfriend who gave Anastasia such joy and the hateful cruel Demon that was torturing her and Nathaniel. She shook her head with the contrast of it all.

"Tell me about your students," Lucy offered hoping to distract Anastasia from the topic. It worked. Throughout dinner, Anastasia described in detail each student and their capabilities. They talked about Lucy's day and once again she had to edit to the point of foolishness. Lucy told her about the conference, reassuring Anastasia that if wouldn't interfere with the Summer Solstice party. They were both returning to work on Friday and they gossiped about the server roster for the summer. Lucy and Anastasia had been promised the ever-coveted patio for the season and they were thrilled about it.

It felt good for Lucy to talk about regular college girl things. It was anchoring and calming. Despite the Angels and the Demons and the Papal Library books, Lucy was a ordinary girl and it was nice to remember that again. Saying goodbye on the stairwell, Lucy hugged her friend tightly. Although she could not share her whole life with Anastasia she still felt so very close to her. Anastasia hugged Lucy back and Lucy could hear the charm bracelet tinkle slightly on her shoulder – an ominous reminder that all was not well. Not normal. No matter how much Lucy tried to pretend.

"I love you Stasia," was all Lucy could think to say.

"Love you too loser."

They broke apart and Lucy and Nathaniel headed upstairs. When they got back to Lucy's room Nathaniel sat on the couch and Lucy sat next to him. They both sighed in unison.

"You did a good job of keeping the topic away from Roman," he said with approval.

"Thanks but it's getting tough to keep my mouth shut."

"It's a nice bracelet," he said.

"I guess," Lucy shrugged while curling up under his arm.

"I never know with you Lucy," he said thoughtfully. "Is that something you would want?"

Lucy sat up and looked at him. "You think I would want expensive gifts from a Demon?"

"I'm just trying to figure you out Lucy," he said plainly.

She put her hand on his cheek and looked into his eyes so he would know she was telling the truth. "I want rare precious flowers, visits with bear cubs and feathers."

Nathaniel smiled, "Well feathers are something that I have in abundance."

"Good, because I don't need anything but you."

Nathaniel tilted his head and kissed her softly. "I love you my beloved Lucy," he whispered.

"I love you my Angel." He kissed her again and Lucy felt her heart quicken in response. She wrapped herself around him and shivered as Nathaniel ran his hands up her back. His lips traveled down her jawbone and settled into the softest part of her neck. Lucy sighed softly and ran her fingertips through his dark locks and felt goose bumps emerge under his skin.

"It is becoming increasingly difficult to resist you," he murmured into her neck. His words and his warm breath on her skin caused a jolt to run through her. She had no respect for rules right now.

"Then don't resist," she whispered heavily. He responded quickly by reaching under her hip and pulling hard. Lucy gasped as she realized that she was suddenly lying down with Nathaniel's weight pressing down upon her. His kisses were powerful and wanting and Lucy responded with equal fervor. She ran her fingers lightly down his back feeling the light ridges where his wings should be. Nathaniel sighed with pleasure, grabbed her by the back of the neck and assaulted her with more kisses.

Lucy was starting to feel dizzy, she couldn't see straight and the room began to spin about her. Was today the day he would leave her? Tomorrow? When? Was this the last time she would kiss him? Feel him? Tell him she loved him? She wanted Nathaniel so badly and she could taste his want for her on his skin. She had felt his soul but now all she wanted was him – his physical beautiful, flawless body. Lucy pulled him tightly to her, desperate to keep him as close to her as she could.

Nathaniel reached up and hooked one finger under the strap of her tank top and flipped it down over her shoulder where it hung limply. He leaned down and kissed along her shoulder where her strap had been. Lucy tilted her head back and let out a gust of air. Nathaniel ran his kisses across her collarbone, flipped off the other strap and kissed where it had lain.

"Oh," Lucy breathed, not being able to form any other word. He chuckled softly and again his breath on her skin sent shivers across her. She silently cursed what felt like pounds of fabric between them and she reached down to pull off Nathaniel's shirt. He did not stop kissing her but reached down, entwined his fingers with hers and slowly but forcefully lifted her arm away from his body and over her head pining it there. He let his lips travel leisurely along her jaw line where he kissed her ear. Not giving in so easily, Lucy threaded her other hand between them and got a hold of her own shirt. Again, Nathaniel slowly took her hand in his and pined this one above her head too. Now Lucy was stuck with both hands over her head. She growled her displeasure audibly.

"Sorry love, rules are rules," he whispered into her ear. His hands were so large that it only took one to restrain both of Lucy's arms. His free hand traveled down her face and neck. Lucy's body tensed and she pulled against his restraining hand. "Shh," he said as he lightly kissed her ear.

"Give me back my hands," she said playfully. "I promise to be good."

"Oh I don't think so," he replied. She could feel him grinning. He slid his free hand under her and up her back and Lucy arched in response adoring the feeling of his hands on her.

"Are you sure it's an actual rule?" she asked trying to focus.

"I mean, is it written some where I could see it?" Nathaniel laughed quietly and let his lips travel to the other side of her neck. Lucy was fairly sure she might pass-out.

"You'll have to trust me," he mumbled between kisses.

"I do trust you," she said as her breath caught in her throat. She tried to free her hands again but Nathaniel held fast. "But you've been out of the loop for a while now and well… they could have changed the rules while you've been gone."

He chuckled again. "I doubt it," he whispered. "Now stop talking, I'm trying to get something done here." He moved up to her ear and kissed it tenderly.

"What is it that you are trying to do exactly other than drive me insane?" Lucy asked. Her speech was slurring slightly. He stopped, lifted his head and looked her in the eyes.

He was grinning. "Well now that's precisely what I am trying to do." Lucy laughed and growled at the same time and pulled against his hands again. He lowered his lips back down to her ear. "Now where was I?" he pondered. "Oh yes, right….about…here." Lucy's head began to swim again. She rolled her eyes and smiled. She would take what she could get.

Chapter Seventeen
Sleep

"Man should forget his anger before he lies down to sleep."
~Mohandas Gandhi

The next few weeks passed quickly for Lucy and Nathaniel. Too quickly. Lucy delved into her schoolwork with fervor. With Roman gone, they could both breathe easily. Nathaniel got more and more holy books from increasingly bizarre locations. One he pulled out of his bag and blew a skiff of sand off before opening. Lucy did not want to ask what fine Egyptian Pharaoh was missing a manuscript from his secret tomb. Nothing as of yet had been of any concrete help and Nathaniel grew frustrated. He poured diligently over page after page of text in languages Lucy didn't even recognize. She appreciated his dedication but deep down knew that it was most likely all for nothing.

Lucy returned to work two nights a week under the watchful eye of her Angel who was always in her section. He enjoyed listening in to customer conversations and giving Lucy useless tidbits of information. One guy thought she was hot but his grandmother felt that Lucy's skirt was far too short to be appropriate. Anastasia talked more of Roman and the wonderful places they would go when he got back from being with his 'Uncle'. Lucy at times had to physically bite her tongue to restrain herself. Dr. Hannon, fully recovered now, narrowed down the details of the conference making sure Lucy was well informed. The worst thing about that time was that Lucy and Nathaniel felt they were waiting for something. Waiting for anything is difficult but waiting for tragedy to strike was torture. Nathaniel described it as the 'calm before the storm'. Lucy felt this was a massive understatement and that 'calm before the horrific natural disaster' was better.

Lucy did not think past his possible departure. She could not subject herself to a deliberation of the future. With Nathaniel's disappearance would come Lucy's undoing. No contingency plans could be laid, no thoughts past the moment of her aloneness could be considered. She simply did not know what would become of her and did not dare seek further. Lucy's morning panic and prayers were becoming desperate. Every day that she opened her eyes to Nathaniel's beautiful face, she offered her thanks for being granted one more day and presented again her sincere apologies that Heaven could never have him back. He was hers. She hoped the depth of her commitment was turning heads.

On the afternoon of the 19th of June Lucy and Nathaniel had a late lunch/early dinner. Lucy had to be at the sleep clinic by 5:00 p.m. for the testing to begin. Dr. Hannon was sending a car for her in forty-five minutes.

"So you can just sleep with all those people watching you?" Nathaniel asked taking a bite of fries. They were once again eating in Lucy's room for privacy. The cafeteria staff were getting curious about her. Nathaniel overheard one lady wonder aloud if Lucy had an eating disorder. Lucy didn't mind; she needed to have as much alone time with Nathaniel as she could.

"Well, I'm in a room by myself. They will all be behind a two way mirror." Lucy shrugged. "I've done it a couple times, it's no big deal."

"And Dr. Hannon will be there the whole time?" Nathaniel asked.

"Yup," she finished her plate and sat back. That's another reason I feel ok with it. He watches everything and makes sure it's all up to his standard. The only thing I hate about these tests is the lack of coffee." Lucy wasn't allowed any stimulants past noon and without her afternoon coffee she was feeling punchy. "Are you going to stay with me?" she asked hopefully.

"Oh absolutely," Nathaniel replied with enthusiasm. "I want to see this."

"I just sleep Nathaniel, it will be boring."

"Not for me," he protested. "I love watching you sleep."

Lucy looked at her watch. "We should go wait for the car." Nathaniel nodded and stood reaching down for her hand. He pulled her up and wrapped his arms around her. Lucy held him tightly, feeling his warm security. She sighed. If only they could stay like this forever, right here, not moving. This was where Lucy was happiest. Nathaniel kissed her neck and let go of her to pick up her bag to head down. They waited only a few minutes before a navy town car pulled up. The driver got out and greeted Lucy, he had a coffee stain on his shirt - Lucy was envious. He opened the door for her and Lucy pretended to tie her shoelace so Nathaniel could get in the car. She got in after him. The driver started making conversation and asked why Lucy was going to a sleep clinic. She filled him in on the details.

"You don't dream?" he asked. His eyes were wide in the rearview mirror.

"No," Lucy said smiling.

"Man, that would suck!" he hit his palm on the steering wheel to emphasize his point.

"I wouldn't know."

"Yeah, I guess you can't miss something you've never had."

"Nope," Lucy replied hoping this was the end of the conversation. She would not be so lucky.

"Although I have had some whacked out dreams," he started. *Oh here we go.* Lucy thought. "There was one time that I ate a whole Tandoori Pizza and dreamt I was on this boat full of clowns..." Lucy nodded and listened assuming an air of interest through the rest of the ride. This was an inevitable side effect of telling people you don't have dreams - they think you need theirs. From what Lucy had heard of dreams, she wasn't missing anything. Nathaniel laughed through the whole thing. When they arrived, Lucy opened the door herself and let Nathaniel out. The driver turned back to her and yelled, "Sweet Dreams!"

"Good one!" Lucy said before slamming the door shut and rolling her eyes. She could hear his guffaws of laughter even as he pulled away.

Lucy didn't have to wait at the sleep clinic. They ushered her into a lounge area where the preliminary testing would take place. Dr. Hannon was there with three men. They looked like stereotypical grad students; beards and ratty tweed jackets.

"Lucy!" Dr. Hannon called. "Here she is!" He walked over and put his arm around her shoulders. "Gentlemen, this is Lucy Bower." The men nodded in her direction, Lucy nodded back and smiled. "Communication has been a bit of a challenge," Dr. Hannon whispered in her ear. The men were smiling but not with warmth. They seemed to be sizing her up and wondering if she was worth the long plane ride. One of the men stepped forward.

"I am George," he said with a heavy accent. "These are my associates; Christopher and Charles." Lucy shook his hand - he was sweating. "We are looking forward to seeing marvel of memory." Lucy just smiled and nodded.

"Excellent," Dr. Hannon said while rocking back on his heals. "If we could all take our seats?" Lucy sat in one of the four armchairs, ready and waiting. It appeared that George was the only one who spoke English for he asked all the questions and translated the answers to Christopher and Charles. He reviewed Lucy's history and the nature of her abilities even though he would have received her complete file. Most new doctors did that and Lucy never understood why. She answered each question slowly, giving George a chance to translate to Charles who was writing everything down.

To test her memory, George pulled out a huge deck of flash cards. He laid five out on the coffee table. They were symbols in black and white - a sun, a stick figure, a circle, a flower and a table.

"How long you need?" George asked pointing to the cards.

"To remember those?" Lucy asked slightly insulted. A five year old could remember that sequence.

George nodded. "We start small."

Lucy had no patience for starting small. She politely reached out her hand and took the entire deck of cards from George. There had to be at least a hundred flash cards because Lucy was having a difficult time even holding them all in one hand. Without explaining herself, she began to look through the cards one by one flipping them over on the table after she viewed them. No one said anything and Lucy didn't look around. Two minutes later she silently passed the stack back to George. He took them and stared at her.

"Glass, chair, car, lamp, egg, clock, house, tree, truck,

television, candle, fence, bird...." Lucy said listing the cards in order. George scrambled to catch up after he realized what she was doing. She listed each card in perfect order. "Sock, butter, letter, snowman," she said as George viewed the last cards. He stared at her then he turned towards his colleagues and uttered something quickly in Polish.

"Ahh," Christopher and Charles said in unison.

"Show off," Nathaniel and Dr. Hannon said together. Lucy shrugged in response.

"Amazing," George said with awe.

Lucy smiled. "Thank you," she replied sincerely.

It appeared that George had hoped this test would take much longer. He seemed to have little to do now. Lucy looked at Dr. Hannon with her eyebrows raised.

"Lucy can also remember other written languages," he offered. "Even ones she does not know." To demonstrate, he reached over and slowly pulled Charles' notebook from his hands. He passed it to Lucy. She took her time with the page of foreign letters. When she was ready, Dr. Hannon took the notebook from her, handed it back to Charles and gave Lucy a fresh notepad and pen. She got to work writing exactly what she had seen. When she was finished, Lucy handed the page to Charles who compared the two copies side by side. He looked at George, his face full of shock and said something. George took a sharp breath and sat back in his chair. He stared at Lucy and shook his head side to side in amazement. Lucy smiled but this was getting boring.

"Doctor," George addressed Dr. Hannon, "we think before now you...exaggerate girl's abilities but now we know you do not."

Dr. Hannon grinned with pride. "Lucy is extraordinary for sure."

"Yes," said George blankly. There was a pause as the Polish

students just gawked at Lucy. Lucy looked at Dr. Hannon awkwardly.

"Would you like to test more of Lucy's knowledge?" Dr. Hannon asked.

This snapped George out of his reverie. "What more does she know?"

"Oh," Dr. Hannon replied grinning, "Lucy knows most things." He turned to Lucy with his eyes twinkling. "Lucy, please list the countries of the world in alphabetical order and each capitol."

Lucy nodded sharply and began.

After two more hours of quiz time, a nurse led Lucy to a room. There was a regular twin bed surrounded by numerous monitors and equipment. She was asked to change and the nurse left the room. Nathaniel had waited outside so when the nurse came back he slipped in behind her. Lucy was sitting upright in the bed wearing a hospital gown. The nurse took Lucy's vitals and began hooking her up to the monitors. She explained each instrument as she attached it not knowing that Lucy didn't really care. Finally, Lucy was hooked up. She had wires protruding all along her hairline, two on her chest, four on her back and two on each index finger.

"Lay down Sweetie," the nurse instructed. "Gently now, don't disturb the wires." Lucy did so and once she was lying down with wires splayed about her at all angles she looked sideways at Nathaniel.

"You still look beautiful," he said with a grin.

Lucy smiled and shimmied her shoulders to make herself more comfortable. The nurse looked up at the large mirror in the wall and said clearly, "She's ready!"

Lucy heard Dr. Hannon's voice over the intercom. "Ok,

Lucy, you know the drill. Just sleep. We may wake you in the night."

"You stay there Doc," Lucy half confirmed and half ordered.

"I'm not going anywhere," he reassured her. "Good night." Lucy smiled at the camera imbedded in the ceiling above her head. Nathaniel stood up and smiled at her.

"Goodnight Lucy, I love you," he kissed her forehead and Lucy closed her eyes. She was exhausted from the rigorous testing and the lack of coffee and soon she fell into a deep, dreamless sleep.

Lucy felt herself being shaken gently awake. She opened her eyes. It was dark except from a small light beside her. The same nurse was there and holding a flashlight.

"Sweetie, I need you to drink this for me," she said as she pulled Lucy gently to a sitting position. As she sat up, Lucy could dimly see Nathaniel sitting in the chair still. He smiled at her. The nurse put a cup in Lucy's hand. "Drink honey." Lucy took the cup, raised it in the air as if giving a toast and called out,

"Doc?"

"Its fine Lucy," Dr. Hannon said over the intercom. "It's a glucose solution. I poured it myself." His voice was strained. He was tired. Lucy nodded and drained the sweet beverage, handed the empty cup to the nurse and lay back down. She was asleep within a minute. She woke up again but on her own. It was morning and as usual, Lucy had slept well.

She sat up and stretched while smiling at Nathaniel sitting in the chair. He looked fresh and awake, not like someone who had been sitting in a chair for twelve hours. A different nurse came in with a breakfast tray.

"Good Morning Dear," she said happily.

"Tell me there is coffee on that tray and you get to be my new best friend," Lucy said smiling.

"There is!" the nurse replied laughing. "Take your time to eat and get dressed. They want to do some more tests. You caused quite a stir with those foreign men."

"Really?" Lucy said while lifting the lid off her plate. She was saddened to see cold cereal – she had been hoping for something more substantial. The coffee made up for it though. "Why?"

"They've never seen anyone without dream waves," the nurse replied in a conspiratorial tone. "Well, to be honest, neither have we but they are quite in a tizzy about the whole thing." She began to tenderly pull the wires off of Lucy.

"Hmm," Lucy said taking a bite of toast. "What more tests do they want to do?"

"More memory things I think," the nurse replied. She looked over her shoulder and added in a whisper, "one of them wanted to give you something to increase your brain function but that handsome Doctor of yours would have none of it."

"Good," Lucy replied relieved.

"Finish your breakfast, get dressed and I'll be back to get you in a little bit. Change in the bathroom dear, I think one of them is still in the observation room." Lucy nodded because she was gulping her coffee. The nurse smiled, patted her leg and left. Lucy could not even mumble to Nathaniel if someone was watching her but he piped up.

"She doesn't know the half of it," he said standing up. "Good morning my beloved." He kissed her head and sat back down. Lucy half smiled as she kept her head over the plate. "I went over there a few times and Dr. Hannon spent most of the night arguing with them." Lucy raised her eyebrows quickly in response. "Yes," he continued, "they kept suggesting things like injecting you with stimulants while you slept to try to elicit a reaction. Dr. Hannon settled on the sugar solution but of course nothing happened. I think the Charles one would put your brain in a jar on his desk if he could. At one point they wondered aloud what effect electric shock therapy would have." Lucy raised her eyebrows again. "I thought the good doctor was going to punch his lights out." She smiled, not being able to imagine Dr. Hannon being violent at all. "I wish I could kiss you right now, you always look so beautiful in the morning." Lucy quietly scoffed as she hopped out of bed and headed to the bathroom. Looking at herself in the mirror, she was fairly sure that Nathaniel needed his eyes checked. Her hair was sticking up all around her face from the wires and she still had the glue residue in most spots along her temple and hairline. She washed most of it off, wet her hair to slick it back down and got dressed. When she came out, the nurse was changing the bed linens.

"They are waiting for you in the lounge dear. Do you need me to show you the way?" she asked.

"No, I can find it," Lucy replied.

"Good, good," the nurse said barely looking up. "Thank you for coming and take care of yourself."

Lucy and Nathaniel went to the same lounge. Dr. Hannon greeted her and the three students nodded stiffly at her. Lucy noticed that Charles was looking at her with a sense of awe. It was a little disconcerting. Nathaniel was right; he wanted Lucy's brain in a jar. They ran through some more tests. Lucy listed off the cards again without having to consult the deck and answered numerous more questions. After two hours, they were done. Everyone stood and Lucy shook each of their hands in turn. She had to awkwardly pull her arm back from Charles who didn't seem keen to let her go.

"Will we see you at party today?" George asked warmly.

"No," Dr. Hannon jumped in, "Lucy has other obligations. You will see her at the conference tomorrow." He was being protective and Lucy was grateful. She normally didn't like being handled but in this case, especially with Charles leering at her, she was appreciative. They said goodbyes again and Dr. Hannon led Lucy out of the building to his car. On the drive home, Dr. Hannon gave Lucy the inside scoop on the night.

"They were of course astounded at your memory, that was a given but once they saw your silent brain patterns, things changed." He shook his head. "They stopped seeing you as a person and saw you as a lab rat. It was unnerving. They couldn't comprehend why you go to school at all. Why didn't I have you traveling around like an academic sideshow to make money? They wanted to inject you with numerous drugs, some of which have been banned in the U.S. for years, to see what the effect would be. I spent most of the night arguing with them. I'm exhausted."

"I'm sorry Doc," Lucy said sympathetically. "You still have to go to that wine and cheese this afternoon. Why didn't you have me take the bus so you could go home for a bit to rest?"

"Oh that's kind of you but remember I still have to pick up Dr. Gorski at the airport in a couple hours and I left the flight information in my office. I have to go back to the University anyway. I am going to meet Brian at the event."

"Thank you for watching out for me Doc," Lucy said truly grateful for him.

"It's my job," he said smiling.

"No," Lucy said shaking her head. "It's not. They aren't the first scientists we have run into who think of me like a specimen and I am thankful that you go the extra mile to make them all see that I am a person."

"Well doll," he said reaching out and taking her hand. "I love you like a daughter." He laughed a little. "I thought I might have to hit that Charles character over the head with something. He sure took a shining to you." Lucy gave an involuntary shudder as they pulled up to her dorm. "Ah the young fun parties," Dr. Hannon said looking out his window at the quad. Preparations were well underway for the Summer Solstice party. A band was setting up on stage, lights were being strung and tables were being set up with BBQs.

"You could ditch the wine and cheese and come," Lucy offered with a smile.

"Too old Lucy, too old," he replied sadly. "But you have fun and don't stay up too late, the conference is at ten."

"I'll be there, thanks again Doc," Lucy said leaning over and hugging him.

"You made me proud again Lucy," he replied squeezing her tightly. She got out and let Nathaniel out of the back seat as she grabbed her bag. They climbed the stairs and as they approached Lucy's room, she started to laugh. Six individual post-it notes were stuck to Lucy's door. Written on them were the letters.

P A R T Y !

"Anastasia," she and Nathaniel said in unison laughing. Nathaniel leaned in and examined the notes closely.

"What is that written in?"

Lucy didn't have to look closer. "Lipstick," she answered grinning. "She's a dance major, what does she need a pen for?" She let them into her room still laughing quietly and closed the door. Lucy turned to see Nathaniel standing inches away from her. She looked up at him, he was not smiling but was gazing at her with an intense smoldering look.

"What?" she half whispered. She could feel his breath on her cheeks and his chest was lightly brushing up against her. Lucy breathed in his sweet smell.

"It is very difficult for me to be so close to you and not be able to touch you," he said softly. "It has been a very long night for me." Lucy realized that they had not had a moment alone for nineteen hours. That was the longest they had ever gone without touching each other. Lucy felt an immediate need to touch him. She laid her hands on his chest.

"Miss me?" she breathed as she grabbed his shirt and pulled him toward her. Nathaniel wrapped his arms around her and they both leaned back against the door. He tilted his head and kissed Lucy with such force that her legs failed her. Lucy's hands traveled over his shoulders, arms and through his thick black hair, trying to keep as much of her in contact with him.

There was the familiar desperation in both their kisses as they responded to each other with more and more urgency. Again the questions popped into Lucy's head. Was today the day? Was this the last kiss? Was this the last time she would hold him? Feel him? Kiss him? The last time she would feel his breath on her skin or smell his intoxicating smell? Nathaniel added so much to Lucy's existence that life void of his light and shine would be a pale, black and white comparison. She gripped him tighter, feeling her so familiar panic and desire cocktail of emotions.

Nathaniel paused and looked into her eyes. "You never cease to surprise me Lucy."

She smiled in response. "Stick around for more." He kissed her again, softly and tenderly this time. "I wish now that we didn't have to go to the party," she said sighing.

"It will be fun," he assured her.

"For you though?" she asked.

"It's still fun for me," he said shrugging. "I like your friends even if they can't see me."

"Good," Lucy said. "I should go and shower and get ready to go."

"All right," he sighed. "I guess I can let you go for a little while." He squeezed her tightly and kissed her again.

"Don't ever let go," she whispered against his lips. She stepped back and thought for a moment. "May I have a flower for my hair please?"

"What kind?" he asked raising a closed fist.

"I don't know," Lucy shrugged, "something pretty." Nathaniel thought for a moment and then opened his hand. Sitting in the middle of his palm was a white orchid. Lucy smiled and reached for it but Nathaniel closed his hand again. She looked at him confused.

"Wrong color," he explained and opened his hand again to reveal another orchid but purple.

"Perfect," she said picking it up. She kissed him lightly again and headed to the bathroom.

The bathroom was empty; most girls were already at the party. Lucy showered and dressed slowly, taking her time to look her best. She wore a tank top and a pair of Capri jeans. She dried and brushed her hair and put on a little makeup. She was humming to herself as she secured the flower in her hair with a bobby pin.

She didn't hear him.

She didn't see him coming.

She couldn't see him, no one could.

The Angel wasn't the only one who could be invisible.

She didn't know he had been waiting all morning for her.

He stood behind her for a moment as she regarded herself in the mirror. Slowly, carefully he reached out. She sensed something and began to look behind her but she was unconscious before she moved an inch.

Chapter Eighteen
Fallen

"There is no greater sorrow than to recall in misery
the time when we were happy."
~Dante

In Lucy's dorm room Nathaniel jumped up. Something had happened – something monstrous. Ignoring all rules of politeness, he sprinted down the hall and burst into the bathroom, "Lucy?" he called out. "Luc…." There it was. The purple orchid lay on the tile floor. It was withered and brown - something evil had touched it. "No!" Nathaniel raged as he sprinted for the window. He jumped though it destroying the glass and metal grate and part of the frame splintered around him. He felt his shirt rip to shreds in mid-air as his wings unfurled behind him. Furious, he began to search the little town. The Demon would not go far, not beyond his own area anyway. Fear and wild fury coursed through him. He stopped at the top of the church steeple, out of breath. He collapsed to one knee at the tallest point in town.

"Please," he begged at the clouds. "Tell me where she is."

There was silence. Of course there was. There was always silence. What had he done? "Tell me where she is!" He raged at the sky. Nathaniel knew that he and Lucy were soul mates the moment he saw her. He should have left her that first night. He should have waited – she would have come to him eventually. Instead, he went ahead, fell totally in love with Lucy and allowed her to fall in love with him. How selfish could he be?

Nathaniel knew he had ruined every chance Lucy had ever had for a normal life. If he got to stay, he would still be invisible and unable to give Lucy the life she deserved. If he left then it would destroy them both. The most responsible thing to do would have been to leave her on that sidewalk and go. But he couldn't have left her. The compulsion he had felt to be near her had been overwhelming. Because of that compulsion, now Lucy was in danger and he hated himself for that. If something happened to her he couldn't imagine what it would do to him.

He sat at the top of the church steeple and waited. He waited to hear her voice calling his name. No matter how far Lucy was, Nathaniel could hear her say his name as clear as the church bell he sat beside. Then once she said his name, her location would pinpoint itself and he would be there in a moment. He clenched and unclenched his fists as he sat and waited. He was getting angrier every second, angry at Heaven for not helping, angry with himself for putting Lucy in danger but most of all, Nathaniel was angry with Roman. Roman would pay for this. He looked again at the clouds, his eyes full of determination. "Forgive me Lord but I am going to kill that Demon today."

Lucy's eyes fluttered open. *Roman* she thought with hate. She was crouched on her knees on the dirt ground. It was still day but Lucy couldn't see around her because of her position. She tried to jump to her feet but the ground around her shook and thick leather straps erupted out of the soil. Acting seemingly of their own wills, the straps whipped about and fell over Lucy's calves, back and shoulders, securing her in the kneeling position with her face shoved in the dirt. Two more straps grew out of the Earth and wrapped tightly around each wrist. One more erupted and to Lucy's horror, wrapped around her neck. She froze in alarm.

She tilted her head and glanced upwards and around her. She was in a fenced yard - a junkyard to be exact. Piles of debris and wreckage lay about her and the afternoon sun beat down on her shoulders. Lucy didn't know how long she had been there but her throat was dry with thirst and her muscles were cramped. She had never been to this place before. She wasn't even sure if it was in town. She lifted her head and looked up. The strap around her neck loosened enough to give her a marginal amount of space and allow her to at least sit up on her heels.

There he was.

Roman sat perched on top of a pile of scrap metal. Lucy remembered that Nathaniel had told her she could only love him if she saw his true form. Now she knew pure hate as she saw Roman's true form for the first time. He was shirtless and barefoot wearing only a pair of dark blue jeans. His eyes were sunken and dark, the veins in his chest and arms were black as though filled with crude oil and out of his back emerged a pair of massive black bat-like wings – leathery and thick. They were for more than flying though and like bat wings they each had a huge black claw on the front tip that dug into the scrap metal and held tight, balancing him. Lucy whimpered in fear. He grinned at her unease and hopped leisurely down to the ground.

He walked slowly over to her. Lucy's breathing quickened and she tried to recoil pulling back from the straps to put distance between them. The straps held tight and she was trapped. Roman stopped inches from Lucy and crouched down in front of her.

"I apologize for our less than hygienic surroundings," he cooed softly to her. "I feel the lack of nature gives me a small advantage." His breath was hot on her face and Lucy recoiled in horror. Roman reached out and ran his finger down the side of her cheek. Pain seared in a line through her face and she winced and pulled away. "Call him," Roman whispered.

Lucy didn't have to be told twice. "Nathaniel, help me!" she yelled. The words weren't out of her mouth before she realized the mistake she had made. She saw the elation on Roman's face and she knew she had been tricked. Roman wanted her to call Nathaniel so he could kill them both. How could she be so stupid?

It would prove to be the biggest mistake of her life.

Roman grinned. "Thank you," he said triumphantly as he stood and walked ten feet away. He stopped and waited. His wings splayed out and the claws dug into the ground, ready for battle. Nathaniel appeared ten feet from Lucy and Roman each. His skin radiated heat and his eyes shone with an inner light. They created a triangle with Nathaniel at the peak and Roman and Lucy each at a bottom point. He looked at Lucy and fury filled his face. His jaw was tight and his fists clenched.

"Release her Demon or suffer my wrath!" he commanded. Nathaniel took one step towards Lucy with his arm raised. Lucy expected to feel the binds loosed and fall. Instead she felt the whip around her neck tighten considerably, cutting off her oxygen. She made a choking sound as she struggled with her arm binds to free her hands. Black spots swam through her vision as she began to lose consciousness.

"I will snap her neck Angel, step back!" Roman growled.

Through her fading vision, Lucy saw Nathaniel look at her with angst and reluctantly take a step back. Immediately the whip loosened. Fresh air burst into Lucy's lungs and she collapsed on the ground sucking it in gratefully. "Release her!" Nathaniel demanded again. "This has nothing to do with her. Deal with me!"

"Listen to me!" Roman yelled back angry and frustrated. "I will not hurt the creature if you hear me out!"

"No more deals Demon. She goes free or you die."

Roman put up his hands defensively. His wings released the ground and folded half behind his back.

"Don't you understand that I don't want to hurt her?" he asked in a slightly softer tone.

"You have a crappy way of showing it!" Lucy yelled. She felt the straps tighten in warning around her.

"I have orders little girl," Roman fired at her. "And where I come from, orders are obeyed or there are dire consequences! I have been named Guild Prime and with that came the responsibility of taking care of this business. It is something I intend to deal with."

Lucy did not respond. Roman looked back at Nathaniel and his mood softened further.

"Look pal, I really don't want to hurt anyone here. I just have an order that's all. My Lord isn't big on excuses so listen up." Nathaniel didn't acknowledge the request – they both knew he had no choice but to listen. "Here's the thing," Roman began calmly. "I'm sure you have figured out by now that you have to cut that ridiculous umbilical cord you have to the clouds in order to stay on Earth." He paused. His wings shuddered involuntarily waiting for confirmation. Nathaniel nodded while clenching his jaw. "Sadly, as smart as the two of you are, you haven't thought of the most obvious solution." Nathaniel and Lucy looked at each other – no they hadn't. "You switch to the other side." Roman finished plainly.

"No!" Lucy screamed trying to jump to her feet. The straps held fast and she bucked and struggled under them.

Nathaniel squared his shoulders and jutted out his jaw. "Never!"

"Now, now, now," Roman spoke like a teacher. "Hear me out." Lucy knelt on the ground waiting. "You don't have to do my job. That's why I'm here and might I say, I'm very good at what I do." Lucy rolled her eyes. "But you would be mortal, able to live a normal life - a life with lovely Lucy here. You can be seen and heard." He lowered his tone further, speaking with almost kindness. "You can have children with her, grow old together, have the life you two deserve because to be honest, not even I can deny the connection you have. Really it's extraordinary."

Nathaniel did not answer.

"They left you here my friend. Can't you see that?" Roman almost pleaded. "They abandoned you here, not being able to give Lucy the life she truly, truly deserves. Can't you see? They cast you down with no help, no guidance, nothing but your own wits. Who does that?"

Nathaniel looked at Lucy. His expression was unreadable. "Will I have to…"

"Meet my boss?" Roman offered. "Of course not. You stay here with your Lucy and love her how she deserves to be loved. You share her life rather than just be a witness to it. Can't you see my friend that this is the only way?"

Lucy's mind raced. Why the change in Roman's behavior? Why was he trying to help them? She rewound her memory over every confrontation that they had had with him. They were all focused on Lucy making Nathaniel leave, why now did he want him to stay? Then she thought back to the field in Kansas. When

Lucy had assumed that Roman wanted her soul in exchange for getting her father back, he had replied, 'your soul is useless to me'. Now Lucy understood his motivation. He had been after Nathaniel's soul all along.

"You must get some serious brownie points for convincing an Angel to sell his soul to the Devil huh Roman?" she yelled. He looked at her with hate. *Nailed it.* She thought.

Roman sighed. "Fine," he admitted. "You got me." He looked at Nathaniel. "My Lord is furious that you are here. He is angry that Bael did not rectify the situation and went and got himself killed. He wanted me to destroy both of you," he said with his voice full of false charity, "but I thought of a solution that would make everyone happy. You can stay with Lucy, I get a pat on the back and Lucy's gets you."

Nathaniel scoffed. "Of course you would benefit the most."

"I disagree!" Roman countered. "I am willing to live with you in my midst in exchange for Lucy's happiness. I'm thinking of her here. And so should you." Nathaniel didn't answer. He looked at Lucy and then at the sky. Roman seemed to know what he was thinking. "Hey, listen," he said kindly to Nathaniel, "Your God will get over it… he always does. This is the only way. He would never grant you this kind of gift Angel." He paused. "And deep down you know it too."

Nathaniel looked torn. He looked away and Lucy knew he was considering this option. She didn't know what to do. Was this what she wanted? She felt powerless. The only two things she had as weapons were her brain and her love for Nathaniel. If she combined the two, could she come up with the answer? If she used her mental search engine with her soul, would that tell her what to do? It was the only option she had. She looked down at the ground and focused her energy deep within her. How does one locate her own soul? She searched for that light that Nathaniel had found so easily inside her.

Slowly, she began to sense the ball of light she pulled at it, coaxing it out of hiding. It grew and pulsed and she engaged her mental search engine immediately. She asked her brain the most random question she had ever asked, hoping it would understand.

"What do I do?" she thought. She sent the question flying through her mind and felt her soul pulse and beat. Her mind flew into high gear powered not by nerves, synapses or blood but powered by her very own soul.

"What about when I die?" she heard Nathaniel ask. He sounded very far away. Roman responded something about crossing that bridge but Lucy wasn't listening. Her mind flew at breakneck speed, searching, pulsing with her love for Nathaniel. *What do I do? What do I do? What do I do?* The headache started immediately. The power of the search was almost too much for her brain to take. She felt her nose start to bleed and then her ears. Still she pushed and pushed knowing she was risking her life – she could have a brain aneurysm. Blood dripped from her face onto the ground beneath her creating a small river of blood and soil. Ashes to ashes, dust to dust – death might be preferable now. Lucy didn't have to dismiss any information. Her soul seemed to know what it was looking for and searched deeper and deeper into her memory for it. For the first time Lucy had no control over her own mind.

It finished.

Lucy's head snapped up. Her brain went silent and her soul retreated back to its spot deep within her. She had as much of an answer as she was going to get and her heart snapped with comprehension. Pain began to course through her but she stopped it and pushed it back. *Later* she thought. Her mind, well her soul, had come back with a random fact, one she had read at the age of ten. So random and yet when Lucy considered that her soul had delivered the answer, it was far more astute.

"The average lifespan of a North American female is 78 years"

Sixty years to go. Lucy thought. Could she? Could she survive sixty years without Nathaniel? No, no she couldn't. Well, she physically could – her organs would continue to function, her blood would pump and her lungs would fill and empty regularly. Inside though, Lucy would be dead. But it had to be done. Sixty years of Hell in exchange for an eternity with him. It was the only way to save his soul. He was considering giving his soul to Satan to be with her, she would not allow him to sacrifice so much. There were ways to shorten a lifespan without committing suicide. It had to be done. Sacrifices had to be made.

Lucy felt the chasm of pain begin to creak open in her chest and she forcefully closed it again. There would be years for that pain to dwell. She focused on the conversation in front of her. It appeared Roman was making progress.

"No!" Lucy yelled. They both stopped to look at her. It was apparent Roman had forgotten she was there. "No, Nathaniel." She said looking toward him but trying not to see his beautiful face and eyes. "You can't make that deal."

"Lucy," Nathaniel's voice was anxious. "You are covered in blood."

She shook her head to object to his comment. "You can't make that deal," she said again.

Roman rolled his eyes. "You stupid creature, I am trying to help you here."

Lucy ignored him. She looked at Nathaniel, the chasm fought with her trying to open and release anguish into her. She battled with it to keep it closed. *You will have sixty years to suffer – wait.*

"There is no other solution here Nathaniel," she looked away because he was beginning to register what she was doing and it horrified him.

"No Lucy!" Nathaniel almost yelled. "Please."

"What are you doing little girl?" Roman asked with a warning tone. The fact that he was unhappy with the direction she was going made it a fraction easier. She sucked in a mouthful of air, opened her eyes and looked directly at Nathaniel.

"I want you to go back to Heaven Nathaniel. I am sending you back."

His mouth opened slowly, his eyes dulled, his hands unclenched and hung listlessly at his thighs, his wings sunk several inches. "No," he whispered. Lucy could almost feel his pain. It hit her dead in the chest like a cannon ball. She could taste it in the air and feel his agony on her skin. She looked back at him with pleading in her eyes. He would have sixty years to try to understand. *What have I done?* She thought.

"No!" Roman screamed. His wings flapped nervously, he looked about him, his eyes black and bloodshot and pleading. "Don't you want him to stay?"

"No," Lucy said, "not if it means that he has to sell his soul to do it." She looked at Nathaniel and saw tears forming in his eyes, "I will see him again...one day" her voice cracked.

"I told him I could get you! I made promises! You don't make promises to the Dark Lord and then not fulfill them!" Roman screamed. "I will pay for your foolishness! Everything would have been fine if you had let him make the deal!" he raged at her.

Lucy winced at his words. Had she done the right thing? Would everything have been fine? Should she have let Nathaniel sacrifice his soul for her instead of her sacrificing her happiness for it? Only time would tell. She heard a noise and looked up. A huge black crow landed on the pile of scrap metal a few feet above Roman's head.

"Oh, no," he groaned putting his face in his hands. The black in his veins had faded to a light gray and he looked sickly and sad. "Look, I tried my best," he pleaded with the crow. "It's the female human's fault, blame her! Not me! She wouldn't listen to reason!" The crow stared at him impassively for a moment and then its black eyes narrowed in decision. It turned to Lucy then and let out a large, powerful squawk.

Terror ran through Lucy and she braced herself for pain. Instead, the ties binding her lifted off her skin and retreated back into the ground. She knelt on the dirt, too frightened to move. Lucy heard a flutter and then another. More crows arrived, silently, stealthfully until the piles of metal around Roman were bowing under the weight of hundreds of the massive black birds. Lucy looked to Nathaniel to see his reaction but he wasn't looking at the crows. He seemed totally unaware of their presence. He stared numbly at the ground, swaying slightly. Lucy's heart shattered.

"It's not my fault." Roman pleaded to the birds. "Tell Him I tried. Please. I don't have to be punished. We don't even have to tell Him. I'm begging you. Don't bring me back there. Please. I've worked so hard to be here." Lucy almost felt some sympathy for him. He was terrified at whatever horrors awaited him back in Hell. The head crow looked at Roman again and almost shook its head with disgust. The crow looked to Nathaniel and squawked again.

He nodded, looked at Lucy and said, "Time to leave."

"Angel!" Roman screamed, "I won't be gone for long! Know

that when I get back, you won't be here to protect her. Little girl will suffer for her mistakes here today!" The crow screamed at Roman and he flinched.

"I doubt that Demon," Nathaniel said looking over the crows. He walked quickly toward Lucy and didn't break his stride to scoop her up, beat his wings and lift them into the air. Lucy wrapped her arms around his neck and held on. Suddenly, every single crow began to scream, it was deafening even over the wind. Lucy craned her neck over Nathaniel's shoulder to look at what was happening but he lowered his arms, restricting her vision.

"Don't look," he ordered in a blank voice. Lucy heard Roman scream in terror and she tucked her head down into Nathaniel's chest as he put distance between them and the horrors of Hell beyond. Lucy could smell Nathaniel's skin and realized this was the last time she would touch him, smell him, feel him. She tightened her grip and a single tear dripped out of her eye and fell away into the wind.

"Where are we going?" she asked looking up at him. Nathaniel didn't look at her. He stared straight ahead with a face like a statue.

"The quad. I will return from where I fell."

"Are they coming?"

"Yes."

As they approached the University, Lucy took a minute to look at it. It might be the last time she would see it. She would certainly have to be hospitalized for a while after Nathaniel left. Would she be able to return? No, she doubted it. She would return to Kansas and hide in her mother's house. Her mother would get a nurse to care for her. When Lucy was strong enough, she would systematically try to kill herself by accident. That was the plan. Lucy would never see this University again. Ever.

The quad was packed with students enjoying the summer solstice party. Smoke poured from the numerous barbeques, the band thumped and people milled about dancing and having a great time. Again, Lucy thought, never again. It had still been worth it. She had sacrificed her mortal life for the soul of her true love. She had no other choice.

There was a bubble of empty space in the middle of the crowd, from experience; Lucy knew this could only be one thing. As they approached, she saw she was right. Where Nathaniel seemed to glow in his Angelic state, this one radiated. It was like the sun itself was standing on the grass. Lucy started to see his features more clearly. He wasn't as handsome as Nathaniel but he was still nice looking. He had light brown hair and was roughly middle age with small smile lines around the same familiar crystal grey eyes. He stood, his wings tucked behind his back, wearing nothing but a pair of loose fitting, white linen pants.

"Oh, I remember now…." Nathaniel said quietly to himself, "they said I would forget."

"Who is that?" Lucy whispered as they slowed.

"Gabriel," Nathaniel replied. He still stared straight ahead.

"But there is more than one Gabriel right?" Lucy asked warily. "He's not like the Virgin Mary Gabriel right? This is a different guy."

"No Lucy, there is only one Angel Gabriel."

"Oh," she didn't know what else to say.

"Don't be frightened of him, he is very kind." His tone was still blank and Lucy wasn't reassured. They landed several feet in front of Gabriel and Nathaniel put Lucy on her feet and pulled his hands back behind him. He couldn't touch her anymore. Lucy looked about them but people seemed oblivious to Lucy's presence as well. "They can't see any of us right now," Nathaniel said quietly.

They walked the few steps closer to the Arch Angel. Lucy's heart was aching and a pressure of sadness had settled upon her shoulders. She reminded herself to get used to both.

"Nathaniel my brother," Gabriel's voice was strong but smooth. "How are you?" he asked warmly.

"I am very sad Gabriel," Nathaniel replied.

"I know," Gabriel looked sad for him.

"I change my mind!" Lucy blurted out, "I change my mind! You can't have him back. He has to stay here with me! I can't be without him. I lied when I said I wanted him to go and now I take it back!"

Gabriel smiled at her.

"I didn't want him to sacrifice his soul for me. I would rather live for," she paused realizing the weight of her words, "sixty years without him and then have him for eternity then have him for sixty years and never again."

Nathaniel stared at her stunned. He shook his head slightly in disbelief before he said, "I love you."

"I know," Lucy replied as the chasm of pain inside her broke open again. She let it come. "And we will be together again, one day...when," the anguish overtook her and she choked on the rest of her words. Nathaniel grabbed her tightly and she sobbed against his bare chest. She felt his wings come forward and wrap around her. Sheltered there in feathers, Lucy realized that this was the last moment in her life she would feel totally safe. Nathaniel pulled his wings back and looked at her, she stared for the final time into those beautiful grey eyes. It felt like the first time again and she was lost in their depth. She turned and looked at Gabriel with anguish.

"How can you do this to us?" she sobbed at him. He looked at her with pity but nothing else. "How can you just drop him down here, let me fall in love with him and then take him away?"

"Lucy," Nathaniel cautioned. She ignored him not caring that she was yelling at the most powerful Angel in Heaven.

"What kind of system is this? You are torturing me! This is unfair and unjust. You ought to be ashamed of yourself! I just met him a few months ago!" she sobbed again.

"You didn't just meet him Lucy," Gabriel replied quietly.

Lucy stopped. "What?" she asked bleary eyed.

"You and Nathaniel met sixteen years ago today," he paused obviously thinking that this was a sufficient explanation. When Lucy still looked dumbfounded he continued. "You see, Nathaniel was the Angel that guided your soul into Heaven the day you drowned." Neither Lucy nor Nathaniel moved or spoke as they absorbed this information. "We knew immediately the strength of your connection. You were soul mates and we rejoiced."

"I was an infant," Lucy said.

Gabriel smiled at Lucy. "The soul knows no age Lucy. But I must make it clear that you weren't supposed to meet that day. You were not supposed to die. We don't know what twist of fate made you fall in the water all those years ago." He shook his head. "It is a mystery we have never solved."

"Why did I go back then?" Lucy asked.

"A mother's love is a very powerful force. We can only assume that you heard her and chose to go back. We think you might have been under the impression that Nathaniel would come with you. As your Mother told you, you said 'Lucy go back' once you realized what you had done. Nathaniel was devastated at his loss." He smiled lovingly at Nathaniel. "You only remember dreaming of Lucy that one time, but I assure you my friend that you dreamt of Lucy every single night for sixteen years." He sighed. "We didn't know what to do. Nathaniel could not be so unhappy; it pained us all to see him so. The unknown factor of course was you

Lucy. Because you didn't dream since the accident, we had no way of knowing if your soul remembered Nathaniel."

"So it was the drowning," Lucy was relieved to get a final answer.

"The drowning took away your ability to dream Lucy," Gabriel clarified. "But it did not give you your memory."

"Really?" Lucy asked hopefully.

"Really," he nodded. "You were born with your gift." He sighed again. "But Nathaniel could dream and each morning he would wake up sadder and sadder. We had no choice but to make an exception. We sent Nathaniel down with no memories of meeting you, just the one dream to see if his soul remembered yours." He laughed. "We had no idea how strong your bond truly was. As you know, you fell deeply in love with Nathaniel the first moment you met. But there is more to love than just attraction. Isn't there?" he said looking at Lucy. "Love involves sacrifice and that's what you were missing. Everyday you offered up a selfish prayer. One that only fed your needs." Nathaniel looked at Lucy with his eyebrows raised.

"I thanked them every morning for you but apologized that they could never have you back." She explained and Nathaniel shook his head in awe. "But I didn't know!" Lucy pleaded to Gabriel. He raised his hand and she stopped talking.

"Today though you finally realized the true nature of love. It is putting the other soul before your own. That was the choice we were waiting for. You exercised your free will to benefit the one you love even to your own detriment."

"So now you take him even though I did the right thing?" Lucy begged.

"The separation of soul mates is always painful but please remember that it is temporary." Lucy sobbed at the realization of his words. Nathaniel clutched her tighter. There was a large pause and Gabriel regarded the two of them. He smiled slowly. "Regardless of the temporary nature of your separation, I myself am not willing to be responsible for inflicting that kind of pain on anyone."

Lucy stopped and looked at him stunned. She wasn't sure if she had heard him right. She glanced up at Nathaniel who had the same disbelief in his face.

"Now the choice is set forth to you Nathaniel, brother, Angel of Heaven. Do you wish to sever your connection with us?"

Nathaniel did not hesitate. "Yes," he replied quickly before Gabriel could change his mind.

Gabriel smiled as if he already knew that answer. "Now, you will still be an Angel but a mortal one. You will age and die in your own time. You will keep most of your gifts and your wings of course however; you will have no more help from us. No more wishing for things. We will prepare a mortal existence for you but you are on your own from there to live how you see fit as you will no longer be bound by celestial law." He sobered and looked at Nathaniel. "I suggest you live a life we would be proud of young man."

"I intend to," Nathaniel said grinning. Lucy wasn't sure what was happening. Was this possible? Could this dream become a reality?

"What about Roman?" Lucy asked - ever full of questions and doubt.

"I would think that Roman will be back." Gabriel answered kindly. "My old friend Lucifer will punish him in his cruel way and return him to maintain the balance. Roman won't react to Nathaniel the same way because his ties to the Heavens will be cut. Roman may not want to co-exist with Nathaniel but really who knows? Maybe the two of them could become friends?" Nathaniel looked doubtful . "But Bael, will not be back. Not in your lifetime anyway."

Gabriel looked to Nathaniel. "Are you ready my Nathaniel?"

"Yes," Nathaniel said. Lucy stepped away from him and waited. Gabriel raised one hand, smiled at them both and quickly closed his palm into a fist. Nathaniel seemed to drop a few inches like he had gained ten pounds. His wings retreated away and a shirt materialized on his chest.

"How do you feel?" Lucy asked.

"Real," was all he said as he touched his hands to his chest. He looked at Gabriel. "How can I ever thank you enough?"

"Lucy has thanked us enough for the both of you," Gabriel replied smiling at Lucy. She thought her heart would burst with happiness. Tears of joy streamed down her cheeks. "I must go now," Gabriel said taking a step back from them. Suddenly he stopped, remembering something. "Oh yes, and one more thing." He addressed Nathaniel. "Five years from this day, Lucy will fall down a large flight of stairs."

"How did you?" Lucy started but he cut her off.

"I myself can not see the future but luckily I know someone who can," he replied smiling at the blue sky and then back at Nathaniel. "That friend suggests strongly that you be at the bottom of those stairs to catch her Nathaniel for although he sees it, he can not change it and the fall will surely kill her."

"I will be there," Nathaniel promised both to the Arch Angel and to Lucy.

Gabriel smiled. "I love you both very much. Goodbye."

They didn't say anything as he slowly faded from sight. Lucy looked up at Nathaniel.

They didn't speak at first - they didn't have to. Nathaniel picked Lucy up in his arms and swung her around before he put her back on her feet. He grabbed her face and kissed her. Lucy reached around his neck and kissed him with as much love as possible in Heaven or Earth.

"I love you Lucy."

"I love you Nathaniel."

"Lucy?" They looked up to see Anastasia staring at her in wonder. Nick, Paige, Simon, and Suzanne stood behind her staring with their mouths agape. She froze. Was Nathaniel still invisible? "Who's this?" Anastasia asked gesturing to Nathaniel. Relief washed over Lucy and she laughed a little as tears sprang to her eyes. Nathaniel composed himself first, stepped forward and offered his hand.

"I'm Nathaniel, I'm a new student here. It's nice to meet you."

Anastasia's eyes lit up. "Well Hi! It's nice to meet you!" Nathaniel shook hands with the rest of the gang. Anastasia darted to Lucy's side as Nathaniel laughed and talked with her friends. "He's gorgeous Lucy!" she hissed in Lucy's ear. "Are you guys....?"

"Yup," grinned Lucy. "He's mine."

"Nice," Anastasia replied not without a touch of envy. "At least one of us will have a boyfriend for the summer." Lucy looked at her with eyebrows raised in question. "Roman sent me a text," Anastasia explained sadly. "His parents are taking him to Europe for the rest of the summer."

She sounded so genuinely disappointed that Lucy replied earnestly, "That sucks."

"Oh well," Anastasia sighed and smiled, "what are ya gonna do? He'll be back in the fall. But seriously Lucy, where did you find this guy? Where is he from?"

And for the first time in three months, Lucy didn't have lie to her best friend. She turned, looked Anastasia in the eye and said, "He's from Heaven Stasia. He came from Heaven."

"I'll say!" Anastasia yelled and Lucy laughed. They walked back over to the group and she wrapped her arms tightly around Nathaniel's waist.

"Lucy!" Simon yelled over the band. "Nick and I are having an argument and you have to settle it!"

Lucy grinned and shook her head. "Give it to me, I know it all."

Epilogue

Lucy and Nathaniel had stayed late at the party celebrating their new life together. He walked her back to her dorm in the dark of night where they discovered a wallet, and a set of keys. The wallet held identification for Nathaniel Parish, a science student on a full scholarship at Mulbridge University, a driver's license, social insurance card and birth certificate. He was nineteen, his birth date was June 20 and he was born in Heaven Heights MA. The rest of the details he and Lucy would have to fill in as time went on.

There were keys for the men's dorm where they immediately went and found he had a private furnished dorm room on the top floor. The closet was stocked with clothes for every season and his books and lab materials for the fall semester lined the shelves. Lucy recognized another key and looked out the window to see the black jeep in a parking spot behind the dorm. The final key was a mystery to Lucy. It was Nathaniel who decided it was for the house.

Nathaniel still had his wings, he still had his powers of natural forces and move things and he still had more power and agility than the average man. He couldn't wish for things anymore but they both felt that the exchange was a fair one. He would have to turn off his own lights in order to be with Lucy and that felt more than just. Lucy had left his dorm room allowing everyone to see her go. She went back to her own room and waited. After the campus died down, she looked to her window and saw Nathaniel slipping in. She realized her window had no bars on it and had grown to accommodate an Angel. She thought that was a nice touch.

Now Lucy sat in the same place as she had a full season ago. She again was sitting on the stage for all to see. She again was not listening to Dr. Hannon's lecture. This time though, she wasn't bored. Nathaniel and Anastasia sat in the third row and Lucy had been watching them. They were fast friends and Lucy's heart rejoiced. Nathaniel leaned over and whispered something to Stasia who giggled under her breath. Lucy made a mental note to hear about the joke later. Nathaniel looked up at her and smiled his gorgeous smile and Lucy fell for him all over again.

He was hers forever and no one could take that away now.

She looked up at the sky and whispered,

"Thank you, Thank you. Thank God it's over."

The End

About the Author

Laurie Lyons wrote her first story at the age of 8 and hasn't really stopped since. She lives in Calgary Alberta, Canada with her husband Trevor and their two clever children. She loves writing, reading and spending time with her brilliant friends. "Feather" is the first of many novels from her.

You can find more information on Laurie and her future novels at www.featherthenovel.com and www.ringoffirebooks.com.

RING OF FIRE PUBLISHING

www.ringoffirebooks.com